To David

The Last Will of
Sven Andersen

Geoff Le Pard

With all my best

Geoff LePard

Acknowledgements

This book is the second in the Harry Spittle Saga, following the journey of Harold Spittle from hapless youth to hapless adult (the only difference being he becomes a little better at covering up the hapless bit). While in some ways his journey has mirrored my own, the characters depicted here are figments of my imagination and anyone who thinks they recognise themselves in this book should possibly consider counselling.
Several people have been involved in reaching this point and to each of you I owe a debt of gratitude. I just hope knowing that you are loved and cherished is sufficient.
If not, then form an orderly queue.

About the Author

Geoff (not Geoffrey, save for legal documents and to his Mother) Le Pard is a former lawyer, novelist, enthusiastic blogger (at www.geofflepard.com), someone who enjoys walking (especially with his dog) and lover of London. He has published a few books and a memoir, all of which can be found on Amazon.

Copyright

For more information about the author and upcoming books online,
please visit www.geofflepard.com

Thursday, 18th June 1981

Chapter One

In Which Harry Speaks to His Father and is None the Wiser

"Call for you, lover boy." Gloria, our receptionist loves her little jokes. "Sounds important too."

"Who—?" Before I can finish, Gloria puts the call through. I glance nervously at the door; Jean will be back in a moment and I just know this is a conversation I won't want to have in front of her. Bloody hell. I really hate that sodding telephone. I force myself to sit up straight and say, "Hello, Mr Spittle speaking."

"Harold? Is that you? It's me."

My shoulders collapse a little and my heart rate drops below 150. It should be a relief, but I'm just irritated. My bloody Father. Wouldn't you know it? "Dad, I'm at work."

"I know that, Harold. That's why I called you there."

"I mean… never mind." I'm not meant to take personal calls at work – which Gloria knows only too well, not that she cares. In fact, the only people who seem to mind are the two senior secretaries, Jean and Edith. Both are ancient, tight-permed and horn-rimmed. Each hates the other with a passion.

"I tried you at home last night, but the phone's not working."

It's been cut off. Again.

"Do you have a minute?"

No, I want to scream. "If you're quick. I'm in the middle of some very important drafting." I am officially pathetic. All I'm doing is waiting for my secretary to correct my inept dictation, not that Dad realises. He thinks I work for a prestigious London law firm with a posh address just off Oxford Street. I lean back in my chair and stare at the flaking plaster above my head; it's probably only saved from total collapse by the myriad network of cobwebs that stretch across its surface.

"Of course. Won't take a mo. There are a couple of things I wanted to ask."

I hear footsteps on the stairs: Jean, coming to take dictation. "I'm really busy—"

"Yes, well, I had a caller today. You won't guess who."

Jean appears in the doorway. It is clear she knows this is a personal call from the way she shuffles her bosoms with her tight-folded arms. Jean's principle feature, other than those much-manoeuvred bosoms, is her beaky nose – down which she stares at me. Few things annoy Jean more than personal phone calls, although her marmalade not setting properly runs close. She sighs audibly and withdraws, although I know she's listening outside.

Dad goes on, a sort of tremulous excitement creeping into his voice as he continues to tease "…someone from way back…"

Please hurry, I silently beg as I pretend to open a file on my desk.

"…Sven Andersen!"

"Sven?" That's got my attention. "What did he want?"

"To give us a present. A sort of sorry for the trouble his family caused us."

"That was four years ago."

"Five, actually – it was 1976. He said to send you his regards and he'll see you soon."

"Most unlikely. I haven't seen him in…" I pause, not sure if Dad knows I went to Sven's Father's funeral.

Jean coughs from the corridor; her cough is not something one ignores lightly.

"I need to go. What was the present?"

"A box of moths. Death's-head hawk moths. You know they all have skulls on their necks? Only moths to make a noise. Macabre, don't you think? I wonder how he knew I was interested in moths. Did you mention it to him?"

"Probably. I really have to go—"

"Just one more thing. I… it's your Mother…" He sounds very tired. He and Mum have only just got back together, and I don't think I can deal with any long-winded explanations or self-exculpations.

"Dad, please—"

"Yes, of course. I'll let you get on. Don't tell your Mother about Andersen, will you? Not just now. It's—"

Jean's head appears and I put the handset down, ending the call. I shouldn't have done it and I will feel guilty for the rest of the day, but I somehow manage a smile. "All set?"

As she settles in her chair, I wonder briefly about Sven and what he's doing now. The one thing I'm pretty certain about is that he won't be seeing me soon, as suggested by Dad. To say I irritated him would be a big understatement. I'm brought back to the present by the tapping of Jean's pencil on her notepad. "Yes. What shall we do first?"

***

My name is Harry Spittle and I'm an articled clerk at Clifford, Risely & Co., solicitors and commissioners for oaths. I'm into the last six months of my articles, at the end of which I will be admitted to the Roll as a Solicitor of the High Courts of England and Wales. If this sounds at all glamorous, be assured that the job isn't. Given I spend most of my time either being humiliated through my ignorance or traipsing around the City and West End of London delivering bits of paper or trying to get writs issued or documents stamped by time-serving jobsworths, it's closer to being indentured than trained.

Jean – Jean Sampson – looks at me with impatience. "Perhaps you'd like to approve those and let me know if you require further amendments." She is both my worst nightmare and my constant saviour. The partner I work for – Jeremy Panther – is on holiday, which is why Jean is working for me, although of course it's more the other way around. Today's task is to prepare for a meeting I am to have with Sir Penshaw Grimsdale, Bart, a very important client of the firm, on the subject of his Will.

Given what I've said about my ingrained incompetence, it might seem strange that I'm trusted with the work for such a personage as Sir Penshaw. In theory, another partner – Lucinda Plum-Wardle in this instance – is notionally looking after Jeremy's clients in his absence. In practice, no other partner will get involved in another's matters, unless things are absolutely desperate. Partly that's territorial; partly it reflects the confidence Jeremy and Lucinda have in his support team: viz. Jean.

Sir Penshaw wasn't due to visit while Jeremy was away, but he called out of the blue asking to have a 'simple amendment' made to his Will and could we meet to discuss? As if such things are ever simple. Lucinda, however, dismissed my worries, "Just take instructions Harry and then you and I can discuss what's needed."

At Jean's prompting I prepare a list of questions to ask Sir Penshaw. I can see them on the top of the heap of typing but even from a glance I can see that the only thing that hasn't changed is the heading. I know she'd like to sit in on the meeting, but that would be even worse than handling it on my own.

I pick up the pristine sheet of typing, pretending to read it.

"I made a few slight alterations. To help it flow. But please feel free to change anything."

As if I would. One of Jean's special skills is the ability to make it clear, non-verbally, that she cannot imagine how I'll be ready to qualify next Christmas by the expedient of tapping the rubber on the end of her pencil against her chin. Technically I will be 'qualified' as a solicitor, although Jean has made it plain she thinks 'qualified' should be given the same weight and meaning as would be used in the expression, 'he has been a qualified success.'

"It looks splendid. Thank you." Flattery, of course, is easily repelled by one such as Jean.

"You are sure? Today's meeting is very important, Mr Spittle." Jean has soft, spongy ankles in contrast to everything else, which is sparse and hard. She crosses and uncrosses them in an unusual show of anxiety.

How can I be a purveyor of legal advice if I haven't got the courage to challenge a secretary? I try to read the questions again, but the letters seem determined to wander about the page. I look up and force myself to make eye contact. "I think everything is covered."

She puts her pad down. "Have one more read through, Mr Spittle. I'll go and fetch your tea. Five minutes. And then we can run through his latest draft Will. Again." She stands and then turns back. "If you are happy with that?"

"Yes. Yes, thank you."

"There's an attendance note, too. Although I believe it relates to a private matter."

She knows more law than I have cells in my body. I move the questions and the draft Will to one side and pick up the yellow attendance note. The message is written in Gloria's looping handwriting – Gloria Eagle is our receptionist and a complete contrast to Jean, but in her own way just as terrifying.

Penny rang. She'll be at Gary's do tonight.

That's good news.

Penny Bloom is/was/might still be my girlfriend, but currently we are on something of a break over a stupid misunderstanding involving a mutual friend, Natalie Tupps, an understairs cupboard and an unfortunate handprint on Natalie's left breast. I maintained we were trying to change a fuse, but Penny wasn't in a credulous frame of mind and has been staying at Natalie's 'for a few days' ever since. However, if she's coming to Dobbin's leaving do tonight – that's Gary Dobbs, my best mate and one of Penny and my flatmates before this latest hiatus – then maybe I've been forgiven.

There's a PS. *Is Gary your dishy flatmate? Any chance I can come along? I'm free tonight.*

I'm about to call down and make some excuse – she and Penny don't get on and if I'm going to make it up with my girlfriend I don't need Gloria stirring things up – when Jean's head appears round the door, breaking my reverie. She looks anxious. "Sir Penshaw is here. He's early." She tuts and then smiles. "You'll be fine, Mr Spittle. Just remember the questions."

Chapter Two

In Which an Old Friend Appears and Tests that Friendship

Sir Penshaw Grimsdale is the heir to a considerable lump of Wiltshire and an equally considerable lump of estate duty from the death of his Father. The only reason Jeremy is his lawyer, given that Jeremy isn't yet 30 and is about as incompetent as me when it comes to the law, is because he was the protégé of Crispin Martindale, a venerable and long-established solicitor who'd acted for the Grimsdale family for eons. Mr Martindale had become a consultant to Clifford, Risely & Co. in his later years and took a shine to Jeremy; when he died, he bequeathed him his practice. This was something of a surprise, but since the fees generated by the Grimsdale affairs are significant, Jeremy was offered a partnership forthwith.

Naturally neither Jeremy nor Jean told me any of this. The source of all gossip is Gloria. She is what my Mother would call a 'modern woman,' meaning she dresses in a way of which my Mother would not approve. There's a lot of cleavage for a start. She's tall – taller than me in her heels – and teases me about Penny. Well, about most things in fact. I pretend to enjoy it, but I am terrified, just as I am with Jean and Edith, the other senior secretary. If these three combined forces they'd be able to run the office, give pretty effective legal advice and dispense with the likes of me, but fortunately for the rest of us they are happiest when getting one up on each other.

Jean ushers Sir Penshaw into my office. I stand and reach out my hand, hoping it's not too sweaty. I daren't look at Jean; any sign of worry on her part and all my faux-confidence will evaporate. "Good afternoon, Sir Penshaw."

"Harry, good to see you again. How are you dear boy? And do call me Pen."

I can sense by the way Jean's shoulders hunch that if I so much as frame my mouth in a way that suggests I'm not using his full title, she will decapitate me with one of her extra sharp HH pencils. In truth, I couldn't call him Pen as it's what I call Penny half the time and my life is confusing enough as it is.

Sir Penshaw turns back to her and puts a hand on her arm. I'm sure she blushes. "Jean, you know how I like it? And do bring another cup for Harry. He looks like he could do with a brew."

I can feel the colour begin to drain from my cheeks at the thought that Jean is being sent to fetch tea and I'm to be included, but to my surprise she leaves with a mix of exhilaration and anxiety wafting after her. Her body language screams that she is torn between obeying such an important client and the inherent danger of leaving him and me unattended. As the door closes he adds, "I suspect you'd better make it Sir Pen. Jean is a bit of a stickler, isn't she?"

He makes himself comfortable in the chair by my desk and folds his hands across the silver-topped cane he is holding. He can only be about 50 but has the mannerisms of someone 20 years older. According to 'Queer as Folk,' a diary piece in the *Evening Standard* paper, Sir Penshaw Grimsdale is 'compulsively playful.' *Private Eye* suggests he's 'inclined to bend the other way.' In the office, no one mentions his personal predilections.

"And how are you? Still keeping Jeremy afloat? When do you qualify? And your girlfriend? Penelope, isn't it – she's an actress? How is she?"

I'm smitten. I love him already. He remembers everything about me, although I'm sure I've not told him the half of it. He must see my confusion when he's asking about Penny. He laughs. "Trade secret, Harry. I asked Lucinda about you. I have a special job for your attention, you see."

And things were going so well. My throat has become oddly devoid of moisture. I nod in what I hope suggests I'm confident and ready for this new role.

"I want to trust you with something very important to me."

I manage a smile. Jean's questions are in front of me. To give me a moment's thinking time, I pick up the piece of paper and say, "Yes, sir. Er, Sir Pen. It might be easiest if I asked some questions and—"

To my surprise and not a little consternation, he holds up a hand like he's stopping traffic. "I don't think they will help. Please let me explain. And please take notes if you like."

I manage a swallow and pick up my pen, praying for Jean's return. Sir Pen isn't about to wait. "As you know, I'm nearly divorced…"

I nod. It has been Jeremy's biggest challenge, Grimsdale v Grimsdale. Lady Annabelle is the most unloved person in our office mainly because her lawyer, Arnold Trimmer, clearly has had Jeremy on the run and Jeremy tends to take his frustrations out on the rest of us. Without Jean, we all fear Sir Pen wouldn't have come away with a penny. After months of painful negotiations, the Nisi was granted a short while ago and the Absolute is due next week. "The Absolute is a formality, sir."

He waves me quiet. "I know, boy. It's done. Once she's not my wife, I'm free to do as I please." He has been staring into space for a while but abruptly turns to gaze at me. "This is rather unfair, but if you are going to draw up my Will I think you need to understand this." He coughs while I freeze.

My brain cannot begin to compute the idea that one so important, so worldly-wise as Sir Pen would entrust me with writing his Will. His expression suggests he is and then the truth dawns on me, with the same relief I used to feel when, aged five or six, I found Muffin, my stuffed goat, after he'd been kidnapped by our mangy cat. He knows Jean will write it. The goat, by the way, was a toy even if his scent after days being experimented on by the cat suggested he might have once been a living, breathing mammal.

He's still speaking. "I've lived a strange life, Harry. Kept up appearances for so long. So long." He smiles. "You see, in the next week my accountant tells me we will have agreed a settlement with the Inland Revenue on Father's estate. And on Wednesday, as you say, the Absolute will be granted. I'm free of debt and free of my darling wife." For a moment, it looks like he might grab me or froth at the mouth, so intense is his expression. "And the first thing I'm going to do? You have any idea?"

"No sir." I'm still thinking about Muffin, wondering what happened to him. After all, if Jean is to write the Will I don't really need to focus too hard on Sir Pen's anecdotery.

"I'm going to come out." He looks mightily relieved, while I do well not to imitate a goldfish who has just been told he's an orphan. "There, I said it. I will have to get used to the idea. I know as my legal representative you will keep this to yourself, but at last I will be able to admit what only those closest to me know. I'm queer, Harry." He waits, like he's testing the words out on his lips, checking to see if they'll scald. "I am a full-on homo."

The door opens and Jean enters, tray balanced on her hip. I've never been so delighted to help someone act as Mother. Sadly, the distraction only lasts a few minutes. When the tea is poured, Jean begins to drift towards the old redundant fireplace, but Sir Pen has other ideas. "That is splendid, Jean. Now, could you perhaps go and dig out my old Will? And those tenancies of the converted barns at Grimsdale Hall? While you do that, Harry and I can debate the merits of Alderman's outswinger." His smile could melt glaciers. Jean almost skips away.

When the door closes, he taps his briefcase and grins, making his craggy face shed years. "She'll have a job finding those. Jeremy gave them to me last time we met." He stands and moves to the mantelpiece, staring at the mirror above it. As I watch, he adjusts his tie and then tilts his head forward slightly. He's thinning on top and there are three strands of hair that he moves carefully across his pinkish pate with short stubby fingers that seem inept for the task.

"I am being terribly unfair on you young man, telling you that. Maybe a dozen people know about me for a fact. Lots of speculation yes, but as a fact? Very few." He shakes his head. "Jeremy knows. Trimmer tried to raise it as a reason to get more money, but Jean came up with a neat strategy and he backed off." He nods at the door. "She knew from a long way back of course. Woman's intuition and all that. Thing is," he's back at my side looking at my desk, "I'm giving an interview this weekend, telling the world as such. I... I have a partner, you see. A man friend. We will commit to each other after a ceremony... a sort of marriage if you will, not that that's legal or ever likely to be. Sean and I will simply declare our love. Sweet, don't you think?" Sir Pen closes his eyes and waltzes around the room. He's light on his feet. Abruptly he stops. "I need a Will for Saturday. Simple Johnny. It'll be £10,000 to each of my two boys – they have their trust funds after all – and the rest to Sean. Now the settlement with Annabelle is nearly complete, I want the rest of my affairs in apple-pie order. Can you do that?"

I manage a nod. It seems far too simple compared with the complicated document in front of me that Jean has so carefully typed. "He... Mr Sean...? Can I have his full name?"

"Sean Latterly. An actor, and a plumber when he's not treading the boards. He's been in that musical at the Haymarket. Third taut buttock kind of thing. God, sorry Harry, but it's a relief to be honest. You're a man of the world, I know that. Your generation is much more understanding than mine. I imagine you have a lot of homosexual friends."

Nope, not really. Just one in fact. But he's right that it doesn't faze me. That one friend is a chap called Amos who I met at the same hotel where I met Sven, Penny and Natalie. Why, on this particular day, does everything seem to be circling back to that point in my life? Amos is queer and a manic; he has always been a loyal friendly face, especially back when we worked together surrounded by some complete psychos. I've not seen him for a while and wonder where he is now. Last I heard he had a job at a club on Pall Mall. Maybe Penny knows.

"Right, now do you—?" Before Sir Pen can finish his next request, the phone rings. We both stare at it. The light on the side indicates it is Gloria in reception. "Do you want to answer that?"

"It's only the receptionist, sir."

"Better pick up, Harry. I left my driver on a double yellow and he may be wanting to let me know he's had to move."

It sounds unlikely, but I answer it. "Hello?"

"Harry, can you come down now? There's… there's a man here, Ben or whatever it was, says he must see you now. He's a… he…" There's a noise that clearly involves Gloria trying to stop someone doing something before she comes back on. "Harry, sorry, but he's on his way up to you now."

"Ben? Did you say Ben? I don't know any Bens."

Sir Pen raises an eyebrow at me as the door bursts open and in strides Sven Andersen. Unlike the last time I saw him, his hair is cut short and his face seems grubby. The foppish, matinee idol look he used to employ is long gone.

"Sven? What on Earth?" I stand abruptly, my chair skittering backwards.

To my complete amazement, he walks right up to me and holds my arms, gazing at me with a maniacal stare. "Harold Spittle. Never have I wanted to see anyone so pathetic more in my life."

Chapter Three

In Which Harry is Asked to Show Willing

I haven't seen Sven Andersen since his Father's funeral. Robin Andersen was a crook, and Sven hated him for it. After some scary events in the ridiculously hot summer of 1976, I was indirectly responsible for a lorry load of silage crushing Mr Andersen – those injuries eventually killed him – but Sven never mentioned my part and, as far as I knew, neither blamed nor thanked me. He treated me in much the same way both before and after that incident: namely, with utter disdain. We haven't spoken in ages, at least a year. Honestly, I never expected to see or hear from him again and yet first my Father says he's given him a present and he's going to look me up, and the next thing he's here. Like an unwelcome virus.

Sven sways like he's been caught by a strong gust of wind and glares at Sir Pen. He sounds drunk. "Who the fuck is this Harold? I need privacy."

Sir Pen's expression is one of bemusement. Briefly he looks affronted and then stands. "Of course. Here." He indicates the chair he has vacated. "Sit. Tea? Mr…?"

Sven narrows his eyes. "Andersen." He holds Sir Pen's gaze for a moment and I'm pretty sure Sir Pen wants to say something, but he shakes his head and turns away.

While Sven takes the chair, Gloria and Edith appear on the landing outside my room. "You okay, Harry? Do you need any help?" Gloria appears to have rolled up the sleeves of her blouse. I notice a red tattoo on her bicep that I've not seen before, but don't have much chance to register what it is. Edith pushes in.

"Mr Spittle, we do not allow your acquaintances to disturb our most important clients. Perhaps you would show him to the door and arrange to meet him outside your contracted hours."

It's pretty intimidating having Gloria and Edith on the same side, but Sven doesn't seem to appreciate that he has released Marylebone's answer to Scylla and Charybdis. Instead he takes the proffered cup and sips from it.

Sir Pen is masterful. "Ladies, you mean well but we have everything under control. While Harry sorts out his friend here, perhaps one of you would show me the way to the gentleman's cloakroom?"

On our own, Sven wipes his face on his sleeve. He's sweating profusely. The Sven I once knew was always immaculately turned out, albeit in a somewhat old-fashioned sort of way. Today he's wearing jeans and a woollen jacket that could be a collage of browns or just filthy.

His face looks strained and his hands shake, rattling the cup in the saucer. "You know what, Harry? When we first met, I thought you were the wettest, most feeble person I'd ever come across. You were, too." He shakes his head. "You were desperate to shag Penny and Natalie and couldn't see how stupid you looked." He snorts a laugh. "Always your own worst enemy."

I glance at the door. I need to get him out of the building, not discuss mutual friends or start reminiscing. "What do you want Sven?"

"Ever the generous host. I need a lawyer and you'll have to do."

"The gentleman who poured you tea is a very important client. Sir Penshaw Grimsdale. Please, can we do this later... whatever it is?"

"Grimsdale? Never heard of him and anyway I need a Will."

"A Will?"

"Christ, Harry. A last Will and Testament, okay? You're the fucking lawyer and—"

"Yes, I know what it is. Why do—?"

He widens his eyes. "I want to leave my affairs in order."

"You're 24, like me. No one makes a Will at 24."

"Yes, but you didn't inherit a criminal empire on your 22 birthday, did you? You have any idea what that's like? No, of course you bloody don't."

"I thought you weren't going to have anything to do with that sort of thing?"

"I wasn't. I haven't." He grimaces. "Not true. When he died, I thought about renouncing it all. Mother has gone away and, well, you remember my sister Marita? She's..." His face contorts again. "Doesn't matter. I'm rationalising the businesses, making good. Cashing in the chips, if you like. I'm nearly done and then Marita will do something good with what I've realised. She's the one with the imagination, the working moral compass. Currently everything is in my name and someone told me if I die then it doesn't all go to her and I want it to. So I need a Will. I thought of you. Is that so strange?"

Utterly perplexing. Beyond bizarre.

"It's simple, isn't it? Leaving everything to one person?"

"Yes. You'll need to appoint executors. She could be one, but it's good to have two."

He seems to have lost concentration because he shakes his head and looks at me with the saddest expression. "Did you know Natalie is divorcing Miles?"

I'm determined not to be distracted by his non sequiturs even if this one really demands that I ask a whole bundle of questions. "No. And I really need to get on. Divorced? You sure?"

"She hates him. Penny does too. He's not what you'd call 'loyal.'"

"Look, I'm not surprised and usually I'd love to gossip, but I really do have work to do. Can we meet up? Later?"

He smiles. "There's a lot you don't know, isn't there? Poor dumb Harry, always the last to see what's right in front of his face. Anyway, Miles is a nutter whose nasty little secret will one day emerge. She'll be well rid of him."

"Can we do this later? I really am busy."

Sir Pen followed by Edith returns. She says, "Have you finished, Mr Spittle?"

"I…"

Before I can explain, Sven stands. "I need a Will. Today. It's rather important."

Sir Pen says, "Goodness, how exciting. Are you up to that Harry?"

Edith is seething. "Sir Penshaw, you really don't need to be so generous."

"It's fine, Edith. This young man – Mr Andersen, is it? – looks rather anxious. I think Harry should focus on him first." Sir Pen looks gimlet-eyed at Sven who won't meet his gaze.

I can feel sweat seep into my shirt despite the fact my room is permanently cold. I say, "Thank you, Sir Penshaw. Yes, I think so."

"Well, if Edith can set me up with a phone and Philip's television, I'm sure I can kill a little time." He leaves for Mr Risely's room, followed by a far from gruntled Edith. Being senior partner, Philip Risely is allowed the luxury of a TV in his office.

"Bloody hell Sven, you've really dropped me in it. Let's get this over with. Everything to Marita?"

"Every penny."

"Executors?"

"Would you? And a colleague?"

"*Me?*"

18

"Who else? You can charge for the service if that's what worries you."

The man has inherited a gangster's thousands, if not millions, and he thinks I'm worried about a fee? "I'll put in a charging clause. I'll include Jeremy – he's my principal here – as the other executor." I pick up the internal phone and call Gloria to fetch Jean from the basement. The sooner I can get this is done and then focus on Sir Pen, the better.

***

I assume Jean will also give me a bollocking, but it seems that because Edith is so put out Jean can be magnanimous. "A short Will, then? Tell me the names and I'll have it drafted in a jiffy. Shall I give it to Mr Andersen to check while you deal with Sir Penshaw?"

Sven holds out a hand. "Thanks, Harry. Sorry to cause you trouble with that old boy. Grimsdale was it? I'm sure he'll understand."

His informality, like they're old friends, irritates me. "It's Sir Penshaw and yes, it's very fortunate he's in a good mood."

"Any reason he's so chirpy?" He manages a smile. "Never mind. It hardly matters, does it? And it's nice to be given priority over a Knight of the Realm." He turns to Jean. "Where shall I wait?"

"I'll pop you in an empty office Mr Andersen, next to reception. You can check the draft and Mr Spittle can make any corrections." She whispers what she plans to draft, which sounds fine to me, and then leads him to the door.

He's nearly outside when he stops and says, "About Penny. You need to sort her out, too. You've messed each other around for long enough and the rest of us are getting a bit tired of clearing up after you."

"Sorry?"

"Her living with Natalie isn't a good idea, okay? They wind each other up about you, you know. Don't get distracted."

"What do you mean?" But he's already gone, following Jean downstairs. I suppose he must have been talking to Natalie, because Penny hasn't mentioned seeing him in ages.

I stare at my desk, stirring the untouched papers like cold coffee, waiting for Sir Pen to return. It's at times like this when my mind wanders, in this case to Sven's dishevelled appearance – I guess he looks the way he does to fit in with the rough crowd he must have been associating with if he's been sorting out his Father's dodgy business affairs.

Sir Pen pops his head around the door. "All sorted?"

"Yes, I think so. Thank you for being so understanding just now."

He moves slowly across to the seat next to me. "I've had friends like your Mr Andersen, Harry. Sometimes you just have to do what they ask. Mind you, he didn't look very well, that young fella. Do you think you ought to encourage him to see a quack? Mine's just around the corner in Harley Street if you want me to arrange something?"

"Really, I'm sure he'll be fine. He's had a tough time recently sorting out his Father's estate."

Sir Pen leans forward and taps my knee. "Yes, well, they can be a trouble, family businesses. Needs your help, I expect. Couldn't have sorted out my Father's mess without this firm."

I manage a tight smile. "Shall we look at those tenancies you asked about?" I feel more at home with these, without Jean's support, than I do about his new Will. Happily he agrees. The queries are quite easy to deal with. Halfway through, Jean pops in and I make a pretence of reading what she's drafted for Sven.

"I'll give it to him now. Hopefully he'll not barge in again." She smiles at Sir Pen who half-bows his head.

He seems pleased when we finish. "You've been a great help, Harry. I wonder, are you free Saturday? It occurred to me you could bring the Will and we can sort it all out. I'd also be delighted if you could join us for a glass to celebrate my news. My parties tend to be on the boisterous side and given I can let my hair down this time so, well, pack your jimjams, that's all I'm saying. The Orangery at Syon House out in the West London backwoods. Duke of Northumberland is an old pal of mine. Anyway, seven for champers and, well, it'll finish when the rozzers have had too many complaints."

He stands and I offer my hand. I say, "It's a shame Jeremy and Dale aren't going to be around. They'd enjoy it."

He pulls a face. "You think? I always feel he has a pole up his arse and daren't move too quickly or he'll rupture his bowel and she looks like she's the one who put it there. I… good God, what was that?"

Someone has shouted something obscene and it feels like the front door has slammed so hard it has to have shattered the glass. We hurry to the window and look down on Bentinck Mews. We are just in time to see Sven being hustled into a black Mercedes by a beefy man in a black suit and dark glasses. He doesn't struggle but he clearly does not want to go. Another man, equally thickset, looks up at us.

"Who on Earth are those men?"

My blood has frozen, I am chilled to the marrow. The man staring up sees me, smiles and nods. I feel like something vital has slipped inside my head as I'm taken straight back to a meeting outside the hotel, where I first met Sven. That was terrifying and painful. This is just stomach churning. It's Stephen McNoble, a man who, among other things, stabbed me and tried to pull off my testicles. He looks away, towards where Sven is being pushed into the car and pulls open the passenger door. Why's that beady-eyed neckless gorilla here, and what's he doing with Sven?

I feel Sir Pen's hand on my shoulder. "I think you might want to sit down, Harry. Should we call the police, do you think?"

"I... I don't think that's what he'd want." Sven was always his own man. Somehow involving the police, bearing in mind what he's been doing with his Father's businesses, may not be the best course of action.

"Well, Harry, you do have some interesting friends."

Chapter Four

In Which Harry is Given Some Good Advice and Fails to Impress Penny

We watch the car do a three-point turn while I explain Sven is an old acquaintance with parent issues. Sir Pen seems a little disappointed I don't say any more, but he doesn't press the matter. He does ask if I'm sure about the police and he disappears briefly to fetch me a glass of water. Before long, I'm on my own as Philip Risely, our senior partner, arrives from his club and suggests that he and Sir Pen 'watch a couple of overs over tea.' A strange quiet fills the office.

After what seems like an age but is probably no more than 10 minutes Gloria sticks her head round my door. I'm half-expecting her to say the police have arrived and I'm wanted for questioning, but it is just to say Penny has called and is running late.

Gloria moves to the desk and hitches up her skirt so she can sit on the edge; there's a lot of leg in my field of vision. "Well, that was fun. Are all your friends so odd? You know he insisted on using Philip's room to wait for whatever it was Jean was doing for him? Edith was incandescent, but he just hustled her out and shut the door."

"Oh God? Really?"

"Then he dashes off while I'm powdering my nose. Jean says he was abducted."

"Probably a misunderstanding."

"Yes. Pen said as much. I think he was talking about him."

"Who was talking about who? Whom?"

"Your friend. Ben. When he was waiting, he used Philip's phone. I'm sure he mentioned his name. Pen's name, I mean."

"I'd better check with Jean, see if he left the draft Will. God, what an afternoon."

"Makes a change from having to listen to an Old Bag's Convention." She shifts and re-crosses her legs; why does she have to do that? "I just thought, since Penny is late, why don't we go together?"

I manage a nod. "Yes, okay."

"And Lucinda asked if you'd pop up if you have a minute, before you go." She slips off the desk and smooths down her skirt. "I'll let you play at being big and important and see you at 5.30."

Some 30 minutes later and I'm outside Lucinda's room, ready to knock when she flies out, nearly bowling me over. "Sorry. Must dash. Can it keep?" She is tall – 'willowy' I heard someone describe her – and, to me, gives the impression of being on the verge of tipping over to the left. Rarely is she devoid of a frown, even when she smiles.

"You wanted a word?"

"Oh yes. Why don't you take these and meet me by the car?"

Her car, a maroon Jaguar, is parked at the back of our building by the Mews garage. I'm struggling to hold the files when she appears and tosses her bulging briefcases – she has two – onto the back seat, before popping open the boot for me to relieve myself of my burden. "It's Agatha's summer play – she's some sort of amphibian. I just wanted to say Pen has said some nice things about you, though Edith was less than complimentary about your 'friend.'" She studies me briefly. "Is everything all right? I heard there was some sort of fracas."

"Yes, thanks. He wanted help with a Will." I add, although I'm not sure why. "He's had a hard time, but he'll be okay. He always is."

She smiles. "Well, Pen loved it. He told me, 'Most exciting thing since Mother set fire to her hair with curling tongs.'" She does a passable imitation of Sir Pen's BBC vowels. "He's very important to Jeremy, you know. You've done well."

"Er, Lucinda. He's invited me to a party at the weekend."

Up shoots a beautifully pencilled eyebrow. "Has he? And are you going?" Do I mention his confession? Before I can say, she adds, "It'll be fun, though, he knows how to throw a bash." She checks behind her, to see if anyone else is about. "A word to the wise. Take a friend." She looks straight at me. "A *girl* friend."

***

The Portcullis is the sort of wine bar that is springing up everywhere, full of suits and dark booths and which sells overpriced paint stripper as their house white. Penny loves them. On the way there, Gloria insists on hanging on to my arm, which makes me very self-conscious, even more so when I spot Penny approaching from the other direction. So much for being late. Gloria takes an age to let go before she and Penny exchange coolish hellos and Gloria heads for the ladies.

Penny somehow manages to kiss me on the mouth in the most passionless way possible and yet leave me with a massive erection. "Did you ask Gloria?"

I know she's teasing me by the way her eyebrow arches, but I'm still tongue-tied. She laughs and links arms. "Come on, we need to go and make a fuss of Gary and tell him I'm coming back. I bet he'll be delighted."

"You are? Coming back I mean?"

"Didn't Gloria say? If you two will have me?"

I bridle at this. "Of course we will."

She scans the room. "Better not speak for Gary. Although I guess if I promise to squeeze the toothpaste 'in the approved manner' he'll be fine."

She's right. He's a fusspot over his version of bathroom etiquette, which for one so personally lacking in basic hygiene is ironic.

She stops scanning and faces me. "I'm still pissed off, you know? With you. I'm using the sofa."

That's exactly what I feared. My seven-year-old whinger rises to the surface. "I didn't mean to touch her. It—"

"Later, okay?" She forces me to meet her gaze. "Tonight is about Gary."

I am wondering whether this presages a rapprochement or is the last throes before some sort of annulment when she moves away, saying, "Let's get a drink."

We're waiting by the bar, a couple of rows from the front. Dobbin is to our right, chatting to some people I don't recognise and he hasn't seen us. I've moved slightly in front of her, so I don't have to meet her gaze. "Has Natalie thrown you out?" I know I sound bitter but I can't help it. It takes a moment to realise she's not responded; when I turn she's watching Gloria snog a rather surprised looking Dobbin. I grab the drinks and leave her gawping as I head for a booth. I feel irritated and frustrated.

A few moments later she appears with Dobbin in tow. Glancing back towards the crowd, he says, "Christ that woman is a nutcase."

Penny sits next to me, picks up her drink and sips it. "She's a tart. Don't kid yourself that was about you."

Dobbin sits and nods. He's drinking water. I ask, "Why so abstemious?"

"My new boss is about somewhere. Why he's come here I don't know. I hope he goes soon or I'll have the shittiest leaving do ever."

Penny gives a belly laugh – I love her laugh. Nice jiggly things happen to her when she laughs. "Did you invite him?"

"Not really." When Dobbin is morose, he sounds suicidal. "He rang today about my start date and it, well, it slipped out."

"Slipped out?"

"He suggested I come to their weekly get-together in the pub. I told him there was this leaving do and sorry I couldn't make it and the next thing I know, he's called my secretary and got himself invited."

"You think he's checking up on you?"

Dobbin doesn't answer. Like me, he is watching Gloria who is talking to two men with slicked back hair and wide red braces. You can see in their eyes they can't quite believe Gloria is giving them her attention. His sigh plumbs new depths. "That's him. The one whose eyes just popped out and fell into her cleavage. Oh God, this is a disaster." He covers his face, leans forward and rests his head on the table, moaning softly.

Penny says, "I've told Gary I'll behave and he won't notice me. You're okay with that, aren't you?"

The moaning increases, which could mean anything.

She says, "He suggested I could use Tim's room" – Tim's our other flatmate – "if I didn't fancy the sofa."

Great, so they've already discussed the fact that I've not been forgiven. "Is he moving out?"

Dobbin looks up. "Nah, he's emptied his room but that's just to refresh his stock. Whips are big amongst the traders just now."

It astonishes all of us that someone as dull as Tim – a trainee actuary, or so he says – should run a sideline in 'corrective equipment' and adult magazines. Normally his room is locked shut and he's rarely there, but he pays his rent and bills on time. In a way he's the ideal person to share with. Dobbin has a spare key 'for emergencies.'

A woman with a Purdey cut and hunched shoulders weaves over to us and tells Dobbin he needs to circulate. He nods and lets himself be led away. Penny manages a smile. "Come on you misery, this is Gary's evening." She reaches over and kisses me properly. "We'll work this out, Harry. You'll see. So, what's your news?"

"Sven called in to see me in the office."

"Sven?"

I'm rather pleased at the incredulity in her voice. "The one and only pretentious pillock."

"What? Why?"

"I can't say. Client confidentiality."

She begins to rise to the bait. "Don't be… ha ha ha. He said he might instruct you."

It's my turn to gawp. "What? When?"

"I'm not at liberty to say." She's grinning, and I grin back. "Ages ago." She turns to watch the crowd by the bar. "I'll get us another." She's up and away quickly. When she returns she says, "He said he might want help selling something of his Dad's. Was that it?"

Before I can answer, Dobbin interrupts us. He now has a beer. "We're moving on to Gino's. You up for a bop?"

I glance at Penny who quickly shakes her head. "Nah, we'll finish up here. We can go home and catch the highlights that way."

To my surprise, Penny stands and hugs him. "Thanks Gary. For letting me back."

He looks at me, over her shoulder, a quizzical expression on his face. "I've missed you too, fat girl."

Penny is anything but fat these days. When I first knew her she had curves everywhere, but a pauper's diet and the need to fit the young actress image has seen her slim down, happily without losing the curves where they matter most – to me, at least.

Penny breaks away and says to me, "Highlights?"

"Test series started today."

Dobbin grimaces. "Don't bother; we did awfully."

When he's gone, we sit in silence for a minute before I say, "Sven told me Natalie and Miles are divorcing. Is that why you've moved out?"

She concentrates on her drink before saying, "It's a bit tense, I suppose. But divorce? Not sure about that."

"He said something about Miles having a nasty little secret."

"That man is just nasty." She frowns and turns to me. "He wasn't talking to you about Natalie divorcing, was he? I mean, professionally?"

"A divorce? No, why would he?" I hesitate before I add, "He wanted me to draw up a Will."

I'm rather pleased at her confused expression, but rather disappointed that she doesn't press for details. Indeed, the silence soon morphs into an awkward chasm. I fill it with, "It's funny, really. Just before he turned up – unannounced, I should add – my Dad called to say he, Sven that is, had popped round to give my parents a present.

Some crap about a gift to say sorry for the hassles his family have caused mine. You'll never guess what it was."

Penny looks about as likely to have a guess as Mrs Thatcher is to invite Len Murray for beer and sandwiches at Number 10.

"Moths." That makes her turn to me, an unblinking stare that mixes surprise with disgust. She hates moths. "Not just any old moths either, but death's-head hawk moths."

"That sounds utterly gross. Like some sort of voodoo nonsense."

"No, they're really fascinating. They have skulls on their necks and—"

"Christ Harry, spare me the details." To be fair, she does look ready to gag.

"They're the sort of thing Dad would love, if they came from anyone but him. The weird bit is he told Dad that he'd be seeing me soon, and bingo: 30 minutes later there he is in my office. It's like he planned it that way."

Penny is staring at me really intensely. "I bet he did. If there's one thing I know about Sven Andersen, it's that he always does what he does for a reason, even if you only find out what that reason is a lot later." She finishes her drink. "Come on, let's go. I need an early night."

It's as we are walking home that I remember Sir Pen's invite. "When Sven called, I was with this really important client of Jeremy's. I don't know why, but he invited me and a friend to this party at the weekend. He's a knight and gay and his boyfriend is an actor. Sir Pen said they'll be loads of acting types there. I wondered if you wanted to come with me. You know, make a few contacts?"

I knew the word 'actor' would be like catnip to a moggy.

"Who's his boyfriend?"

"Sean Latterly."

Her eyes positively light up.

"No? Really?!" She can barely suppress her excitement.

Whatever she was thinking about a moment before has now gone, replaced by the possible opportunities of meeting people in 'the business.'

I tell her that it's going to be a sort of flamboyant gay thing where they make vows and all sorts like a wedding only it isn't, obviously, which gets her even more interested as well as panicked about what to wear. She begins to jabber on about her own acting hopes; poor thing has worked so hard at this treading the boards lark and yet between the odd acting job – and most are very odd and require a lot of nudity it seems – she works in a bar in Soho getting propositioned hourly and groped even more frequently. 'The tips are good,' is all she says by way of justification for putting up with the hassle.

I'm only vaguely taking in her blathering when I register the tone of her voice has changed. "I think Sven and Natalie might have had an affair."

"What? Seriously?"

"Miles thinks so too. Not that he's an angel. That's why I left. In Miles' eyes, Sven's my friend, so somehow I'm to blame. Natalie asked me to go. She said she'd sort it out better if I wasn't around."

"Didn't she say anything? About her and Sven?"

Penny shakes her head. "I'm sorry. I should have said. It's not fair on you to think... to think there might be another reason for... well, you know." She swallows hard. "I'd understand if... if you want to take someone else."

She won't meet my gaze.

I say, "There's no one else. Honest. How could there be?"

She looks at me then, but I'm still not sure if she's pleased or pitying.

"Why does Miles think Sven's your friend? Didn't he meet you both at Sven's dad's funeral?"

She nods. "He and Sven are working together. I think – and I may be wrong – but I think Natalie has used meeting me as an excuse for meeting Sven, so Miles thinks I'm in on something. That's a bit of a guess on my part but it makes some sense. Miles is so suspicious. He's away a lot on business and that makes him worse. Bit rich really, given he never says what he's been up to on these trips. Mind you, they do give Natalie a break from his moaning."

God, how complicated do things get? "Why are they working together, then?"

"Miles' businesses, well, the one's in London were funded by Sven's Father. That's why he was at the funeral. And it tells you all you need to know about how dodgy they are. Apparently, everything was okay until recently when Sven told Miles he'd be withdrawing the support. It's all part of Sven's plans to wind up his Father's businesses, but that's when Miles' mood changed and he started with the accusations."

"How come you know all this? How often have you seen Sven? You never mentioned him to me. Not for months."

Her sigh mirrors Dobbin's c̄ earlier for its profundity. "You always disliked him, Harry. If I said we'd met, had a drink, you'd have pretended to understand but you'd have got the hump. Probably a bit jealous."

"No, I wouldn't." But she's right, and we both know it. "Have you also been seeing McNoble?"

I don't know why I ask her this really, even though Sven and McNoble are linked in my head because of what happened earlier.

The impact, however, is immediate. She stumbles and while I know the street lights aren't great I'd swear she goes pale.

"Stephen? Why do you say that? Did Sven mention him?"

I want to press, make her tell me why she reacted as she did, but instead I back off. "No reason. I mean, he knew Miles too, didn't he? I just wondered if they were all in something together."

She has regained her composure and says, "I really wouldn't know. Come on, we'd better hurry if you want to see your cricket." She pulls herself closer. "And then let's see what happens, okay?" God, I love her.

Friday, 19th June 1981

Chapter Five

In Which Dobbin Dies a Million Deaths and Harry Receives a Letter

My flat is on the fourth floor of a mansion block halfway between Battersea and Wandsworth. The area was mostly a neighbourhood of small industries, but a lot have now moved away and some new flats are beginning to appear. Even so the atmosphere is dominated by the nearby brewery and gasworks, especially when there is a strong westerly wind. Most weekday mornings when I'm cycling to work, I'm lucky if the sulphurous farty tang has gone from the back of my throat by the time I reach Hyde Park.

After I got the job at Clifford Risely I had no idea how I'd find anywhere to live. Good fortune shone for once in the guise of Dobbin whose previous flatmate left mysteriously – he never says why – leaving the small room available for me. Dobbin was delighted for about a week until Penny came to stay… and stay and stay. Tim didn't mind – he was living here fulltime then – but Dobbin moaned fit to burst.

That was a year and something ago. In that time Penny has moved out twice, once for a job in the West Midlands and once last Christmas because we'd split up again – a fairly regular occurrence if I'm honest. Dobbin tried to be the consoling best mate, but he did seem to whistle a lot more in her absences.

When we left the wine bar, I harboured hopes that things might be on an upswing. But by the time the cricket highlights finished, she was so fast asleep that waking her up wouldn't have achieved the desired result, just a return to the grief of earlier.

Instead I make my own entertainment this morning with a leisurely hand-shandy in the shower before getting dressed. I know Penny will still be asleep, so I check on Dobbin instead.

"You want tea?"

"Grggh." He's on the floor, foetus-like cuddling his wicker waste bin.

"That a yes?"

"Fuck off. And yes. Please."

"When do you start the new job?"

31

"Monday. And fuck off."

"Paracetamol?"

"God yes. Will you fuck off now?"

"Before or after tea and painkillers?"

He ignores my witty repartee and drags himself and the duvet onto the mattress. "Turn the fucking sun down, can't you?"

When I return and tip two tablets into his sweaty hand, he says, "Did you see the tall bloke in the dark grey pinstripe leave?"

I try to remember who he means. "There was a bloke with a thin moustache and red braces. Or the one with the tie pin…"

"Red braces, that's him. God, do you think he saw me drunk? He's my new boss."

"No idea. I was deep in conversation with Penny most of the time."

He frowns. "Is she on the sofa?"

"I'd better go. Er, what happened to Gloria?"

He pushes his face in his pillow.

"What did you do, Garfield Dobbs?"

A groan.

"Tell me. I have to work with her."

By way of a reply he points at the mirror over his fireplace. In red lipstick someone has scrawled, *Thanks, Big Boy!*

"Great. You shagged her?"

"I think so. Things are a bit blurry."

"Oh, that just perfect." I stare around the room. "She's not still here, is she?"

An even deeper groan. *Oh, just die you thoughtless sod.*

As I turn to go, he says, "Everything okay? With Pen?"

"Sir Penshaw?"

"What?"

"Oh, sorry. You mean Penny?"

"You got a boyfriend with a title or something?"

"No. And things are fine, thank you very much."

"Good. I'm sorry, you know? About Gloria."

"Yeah, sure. She's hard to resist."

"Have you…? With her?"

"Christ no, not that I haven't imagined it."

"Only she's a bit," he pats his bottom, "if you know what I mean?"

I have no clue and really really don't want to know. "What do you mean?"

"Shit, I'm dying. Were you there when I fell off the table? I think my new boss might have seen that, too."

"I'm sure he'll understand."

"You think? And mate, I'm glad Penny's back. You are back together? Right?" He closes his eyes and slumps back into the pillows. "I think I need to die for a bit. Now you really do need to fuck off."

As I'm leaving he says, "Did I say I might be sent to Hong Kong? Wouldn't that be great?"

If it meant moving, it would be a disaster. Instead I smile, not that he sees.

Because I've wasted time with Dobbin, I'm still wheeling my bike round to the front of the block when the postman appears. Back home our postman was called Sid Poseidon, a ponderous, ruddy faced bear of a man. Here our postman is Gavin O'Rierdon, also known as Vern for unexplained reasons, ferret-faced and trotting everywhere, lugging his huge sack and offering hash and speed on the side. If I have any spare cash, which isn't often, I buy a joint's worth of cannabis. It's mellow, but unlike the weed we had back home it barely has any impact.

"Hi Harry. You need anything?"

"Just the post, Vern. I'm broke again."

"One for you and six for Gary. Oh, and a parcel for Timothy. From Holland." He winks. "Is yours from your Dad? How is he? And your Mum? All working out, is it? How's the B&B? And your Aunt Petunia? Back with your uncle?"

Does he read my post? I have no idea how he knows so much about my family. I stuff the letter in my bag and hurry away. Behind me, he's waylaid the tenant from the flat on the ground floor and is asking about her financial problems. The man has to be a spy.

Chapter Six

In Which Harry is Briefly a Marketing Genius but Fails Where it Matters

Morning coffee is a ritual that Lucinda introduced some years ago before I joined the company. It involves all of us gathering in her room to discuss any issues. Recently it has focused on the need to source new business and her pleas have become something of a scratched record. I tend to sit in the corner and let the chitchat float over me.

Today she surprises me by singling me out. "First, well done to Harry for satisfying Sir Pen and I hope the satisfaction continues over the weekend."

Gloria smirks, but I ignore her, giving what I hope is a grateful smile.

"And for encouraging your friend to come in to do his Will. Jean told me it has you and Jeremy as executors and there is a charging clause. So well done."

"Thanks." I feel a bit sheepish since I have no idea how to contact Sven to find out if he's happy with the draft Will Jean gave him. Maybe Penny can help.

The conversation is meandering a bit and I let my mind wander to a recurring theme that has been bugging me recently: my long-overdue pay rise. Today I will definitely ask about it, given I've garnered so much praise. When I glance around to be sure everyone is delighted for me, I see Mr Risely scowling. Miserable sod wouldn't give me the time of day let alone a rise. Something slips inside my head, releasing any semblance of self-preservation as I hear myself filling a silence with, "I have a friend who may be getting a divorce…"

Mr Risely looks like he'd rather be anywhere but here, and Edith might easily become transparent if any more blood leaches out of her face. Lucinda is, however, all smiles. "That's great Harry. Who is it?"

"Natalie Tupps." Why did I say that? "I heard last night. Maybe she'll need some help."

Lucinda beams. "There, everyone. If Harry can bring in new business so can all of us."

No one makes eye contact; I think they all hate me.

***

Gloria follows me out of the room. "Bravo, lover boy. The look on Phil's face was priceless. He loathes you now."

"I think I might ask for a raise." I know Gloria is on my side. She's tried to get me to ask before.

"I heard them discussing it recently. They're mean shits if they've not offered you anything yet." She gives me a sly look. "How much are you going to ask for?"

"How much? I thought I'd ask for a raise and then they'd offer me something?"

She sighs over-dramatically. "Oh, poor innocent Harry. If you let them come up with a number, you'll end up with a couple of luncheon vouchers and a few coppers. You need to go in with an idea at least, ask for more and try to end up above your bottom line." She nods, mostly to herself. "Go on. What are you worth?"

"Well, I get 40. A week. I thought maybe… 45?"

She points up.

"You think 50?"

The finger goes higher.

"More than 50?"

"Harry, dear sweet Harry. I'm paid 55 and I'm not employed for my brains. Don't undersell yourself. Try—"

"Harry?" Lucinda slides up behind us. "A word please."

Gloria moves away. When I glance after her she's mouthing '60.' Lucinda meanwhile is heading for her room and I hurry to catch up. She oozes energy, if of the rather frazzled kind. Once we're inside, she closes the door. "Sit."

I perch by the small painted fireplace; this must once have been a children's bedroom given the twee tiles around the grate and the faded frieze above the picture rail.

"Well done about the work. I mean it. When you qualify we may be able to keep you on if this carries on."

I'm stunned. It never occurred to me that by Christmas when I qualify I might also be out of a job, even though I'm well aware my articles last for two years. Bloody hell.

"And if you need any help with your friend and her divorce – if you'd like me to meet her, well, let me know."

Gloria's '60' echoes in my head. It's now or never. "Lucinda, can we, erm, talk about my salary?"

"Of course. I did say we would discuss it."

'Oh. Good."

"We haven't had a chance yet, but if you have a figure in mind, do say?"

"Erm…" I focus on the word '60.' It seems to be a very big, difficult word.

She just sits and smiles.

It's an easy word to say, 60. Usually. I need to be brave, grasp the nettle. It'll be fine. So of course, I ask, "How was the play? Agatha was a frog, wasn't she?"

She sighs and steeples her fingers under her chin. "Toad. In Toad Hall. Well, loosely. She is naturally slimy, like her Father. I sometimes think she has scales. There was a lot of applause that neither the acting nor script deserved. Do you think I'm a bad Mother? I mean I sit there, surrounded by these gushing adulators, all the time thinking my daughter is utterly crap and wondering how I'm going to fake the praise that is clearly expected. They seem to manage their duplicity well enough." She sighs. "I shouldn't have had her really, that's the truth. I'm not maternal enough. You'll make a good Father, though."

"Me?"

"Oh yes. Don't you have a nephew?"

"Yes. George. My sister Dina had him a few year ago."

"I think you mentioned it. Did you say she missed university?"

"She's hoping to go this autumn. Newcastle."

"What will happen to her son?"

I have no idea and am rather embarrassed that it seems I should know. In truth, Dina just copes. It's what makes her a pain in the posterior and useful to have around when I'm having a crisis. Which is fairly often.

"I hope she doesn't compromise her career for a child. Some would shoot me for saying that, but we need more intelligent women in the workplace, not stuck at home." She pauses. "Your raise…?"

"Ah, yes."

"Shall I suggest a figure?"

"Erm… please do."

She looks disappointed. "By now you should be on at least £50 a week."

That's not great but it's a start.

36

"But given the current financial situation we are prepared to go to £47 and if there is a job for you after Christmas we can discuss then how we might increase it again. How does that sound?"

Grim. Mean. Inadequate. Shocking. Tight-fisted. I nod.

"Good. And of course if your friend instructs us, we can consider a bonus."

***

Back in my room, I look at the heap of things I need to do, but I'm feeling rebellious, so I pull out Dad's letter; if Jean appears I'll tell her to wait while I read it.

Dear Harry

I'm sorry we didn't finish our conversation yesterday.

That's it, make me feel guilty why don't you?

We thought you should know the details of your Great Aunt's estate.

This is Edna, 'Nanty' to one and all. She died last year. I miss her terribly. Mum's going to get everything. Well, that's what I heard Dad say once.

It turns out there isn't as much money as anyone thought.

Oh dear…

To cut a long story short, she changed her Will…

Oh dear oh dear.

…and your uncle and aunt…

Oh no… this is Mum's sister Petunia and her husband Norman.

…hoped to benefit…

Maybe Mum is going to benefit after all.

…but there's not likely to be enough for them. That means they will have to sell the garage…

I have to read that twice. Or 10 times. I had no idea the garage business was failing again. A few years back, when Norman proved to be financially incompetent – he had relied on Nanty to organise the garage's finances and when she had her first stroke he was all at sea – he and Nanty nearly went bankrupt, but Mum bailed them out with money left to her by Grandpa, to which she added money left to Dina and me – it wasn't much but it was ours and we've never seen any of it. Of course, I don't resent this.

…which, while not good for them, does mean your Mother will now get back the money she is owed…

What about me?!! ME!!

... and you and Dina will get your money too...

Yes, quite. When do I get my share?

...which is what I wanted to talk about. We have great plans for the B&B, which with this money we can implement. However, we think it makes sense – it would be a good investment after all – if we added yours and Dina's money to your Mother's...

No, NO. NO.

...and then we can really ensure the business takes off. Mr Lewis – you remember him? He's the lawyer – he says he'll draw up something simple and send it to you to sign. I didn't want this to come as a surprise. Dina is keen...

...traitor, quisling, duplicitous rotter...

...and Mr Lewis says if you have questions to call him. It's an exciting opportunity and one that will bring great returns in due course.

He can't. They wouldn't. I don't believe they'd think I'd agree. I won't sign, Goddamn it.

You'll be delighted to know that Mr and Mrs Ohja are fully behind the plan. Pritti will be working with your Mother on the food offering and I'll be doing the marketing with help from Ravi. Asoka will help me on the day-to-day running of the house.

I do not care what their stupid plans are. I WANT MY MONEY BACK. I'm living on Pot Noodles and cheese sandwiches with no cheese. Sod it. Just because Dina and the Ohjas support their plan doesn't mean I have to.

Ravi and Pritti are displaced Ugandan Asians who came to stay with us back in the mid-1970s. Ravi is now general manager at the hotel where I met Sven, Penny and Natalie – Hemingways – while Mrs Ohja – I find calling her 'Pritti' too difficult – is a super cook and has ensured the food at the B&B doesn't kill anyone. Mum is what that poseur of a TV chef - the one with the wet lips and leery stare - might describe as culinarily experimental and often she tests things to destruction, including whoever is eating her offerings. No one has yet died but lifespans have undoubtedly been compromised. The Ohjas, including Pritti's Father Asoka, who is a yogi and confidante to my Father, and their two children have been great friends and supporters of my parents. Even so they are the worst sort of shits if they are on their side in this extortion racket.

There's more redundant news about the family cat Rascal and other local people, but I barely register it because I'm seething so much. I need to talk to Dina about this, make her see sense. She can't have said yes, surely?

There's a separate sheet I nearly miss.

PS When I saw that Andersen boy, he mentioned working with Jepson's boy. I thought you should know. You don't want to mix with that crowd, but I'm sure you understand that. He said Jepson was 'away' which I took to mean he is enjoying Her Majesty's hospitality. Good riddance, I say. Please don't mention Andersen or the others to your Mother. She's a little fragile just now. Everyone sends their love and Rascal sends a special purr.

How can Dad generate so much turmoil in a simple letter? Hopefully he'll never find out about the Will. As for Jepson – a former lover of Mum's, who caused Dad a lot of pain and who at one time I thought was my real Father – and his son, who I know as Stephen McNoble (he kept his Mother's maiden name) I really hope I see no more of either of them. I do wonder why the elder Jepson is in prison though.

"Mr Spittle are you ready for me to take dictation?" Jean has stopped in the doorway, as if she is waiting to be asked in. Perhaps she is a vampire. I'm not sure I like the uncertainty that comes with her being nice.

"Of course. I really need to sort out some of my work first and then Jeremy's."

"I think…" I'm sure she is on the cusp of telling me Jeremy's work, as a partner, takes priority, but she stops herself and walks into the room. "Of course. Where shall we start? With your friend?" Jean holds her pencil over the lined pad and waits. I take a deep breath and…

The words pour out. I'm not sure if I should write to Natalie as she's not spoken to me about the divorce, but since everyone seems to expect me to secure this work, I swallow any reservations and dictate a short simple letter. After that there is one to the Bishop of Pontefract on Jeremy's behalf. All the guff that normally bogs me down – about how to address people who are titled or bishops or whatever; like when do you use 'sir,' or their surname and when not; when you refer to the letter of the '3rd inst' or '5th ultimo;' and then there is that awful 'yours faithfully, truly or sincerely' conundrum – none of it matters today and Jean doesn't bother to correct me. At the end of each stream of consciousness, I wait for the tap of her pencil to indicate she's ready for the next piece of dictation and off I go again.

It is only later in the afternoon when Jean produces the letters for me to sign that I have second thoughts about the one to Natalie. Should I just go round to her flat and talk to her about it? She lives down near the river in Wapping, some sort of barn-like thing that was once an avocado warehouse. What if Miles opens the letter and they aren't divorcing? I'll be part of the reinforcements in some concrete foundations. "Can I keep this one back? I need to think about it again." If Jean's disappointed in me, she doesn't show it.

Just then Edith's head appears round the door. "Mr Spittle, Mr Risely needs you to run an errand. If you're not too important now that you have your 'own' clients."

I can see Jean is about to defend me and I stand quickly. "Love to help. What's required?" There are times when a tactical withdrawal is best for all concerned.

***

A week ago, I spent an awkward hour with Mr Risely and a junior counsel called Jonathan Sponge. 'Junior' is an odd term for someone who almost certainly served in the Boer War. He has eyebrows that are a fire hazard every time he seeks to relight his pipe – which is very often. Mr Risely has a client – some sort of relative – whose farm is burdened with an ancient right and we went to see Mr Sponge in the hope that he would propose how certain unexpected charges might be avoided. On our way to his room in chambers – a room very reminiscent of a cupboard but with lots of heavy-looking books – Mr Risely told me to 'watch and learn.'

The conference as these things are called – you have a conference with a junior Counsel and a consultation with a senior Counsel or QC – went something like this.

Mr Sponge: "This is fascinating."

Mr Risely: "Oh God. Really?"

Mr Sponge, settling into an armchair, each movement covering everything with what could be dust but on closer inspection appears to be dandruff: "I've not seen something like this in…"

Mr Risely: "Weeks?" His voice is faint but with a trace of hope.

Mr Sponge: "Decades. I think rationing was still in place. There's the rather unhelpful…"

Mr Risely groans.

Mr Sponge: "…but leading authority of Jenkins v The Cable and Knit Lasso Company Limited 1934, 2 All England 712, at 840. That establishes that in cases of such a claim it is the burden of the testator in rem—"

Mr Risely: 'Can I have some water?'

I left then so I never actually found out what Mr Sponge said next. When I returned with the clerk and a beaker of lukewarm water, Mr Sponge was writing something on the front of the papers and Mr Risely appeared to have lost the use of his left eye, which was facing upwards and when he walked seemed only capable of making circles.

As we waited on Fleet Street Mr Risely said, "You know what that lesson was, Harold? What you were meant to learn today?"

"No sir."

"Good. Because I haven't a clue either."

Today I'm charged with collecting some drafting from Mr Sponge and taking it to the client, a Mr Nowell-Jardine, for him to sign something. That means a bus back to Fleet Street, and then on to the City where the client works. I've just alighted from a second bus and am hurrying, head down trying to avoid the increasing rain. I'm not really concentrating: if I'm not seething about Dad's proposed duplicity with my money, I'm fantasising about Natalie. It's a common daydream, with me going to see her to talk about her divorce and arriving just as she emerges from the shower. As I turn a blind corner, I come to an abrupt halt as I bounce off a huge hard lump that is blocking my path.

McNoble. Would you effing believe it? So many memories, all of them involving him inflicting pain on me, compete for my attention. I can't help wincing in his presence: it's as hardwired as breathing and expecting to always lose to the Germans on penalties.

"You are one lucky prick, aren't you Spittle?"

"Me?"

"No, your sister. Of course you."

I wait; waiting is better than speaking because he tends to hit me after I speak. There's definitely a causal link.

"Don't you want to know what I want?"

This is tricky. While speaking inexorably leads to pain, not answering his questions leads to a greater degree of discomfort. "Erm, okay. What do you want?"

"I want a word." He pulls me away from the pavement and through a doorway, up a set of stone steps, next to which is a board covered in the names of the barristers whose rooms are to be found in the building. It's dark and a little too quiet for this to be described as 'cosy.' 'Utterly terrifying' is probably nearer the mark.

"What's your home number?"

"My home...? Why?"

He leans in. This is the point at which something tells me he is about to squeeze/pinch/punch/poke me. I suck in breath, hoping I will emit a manly groan not a pre-pubescent squeal.

"Because calling you in your office isn't clever and I assume you're too busy to talk now."

"Too busy?" I say. Now, correct me if I'm wrong but this definitely feels like he's trying to be accommodating. This surely can't be good?

"Exactly." He checks left and right, ostensibly I assume to make sure no one is around. He's very close, but I try to see where his hands are because this is the point where I will most likely piss myself if I don't brace for impact.

He does this thing with his mouth, which in other humans might be considered a smile. "Everything sorted with Andersen?"

I'm beginning to shake, even though the afternoon is very muggy. "Sven?" To try to counter the shakes I swing my head to and fro.

"You can't say?"

That stops me, and I make eye contact. He looks genuinely uncertain.

"No. Thing is..." I force myself to say, "Client confidentiality," and instantly regret how that's going to come across.

"Your number?"

"The phone's been disconnected."

He leans back and laughs. A genuine 'that's funny' laugh, not a 'you'd better be joking' laugh. "That's the best you can do? You are a hopeless twat, Spittle. I'll find you and we will talk."

"I know." I'm beginning to feel rather desperate for a urinal or at least a very quiet corner. "Can I go, please?"

He begins to grab a lapel and then seems to reconsider and smooths it back in place. "Sven Andersen isn't the man you think he is, okay? He's neither clever nor does he know what he's got himself into. If you care about him, you need to watch out for him Harry."

He pats my cheek.

By the time I've uncurled from the instinctive foetus position into which I have automatically twisted assuming a violent assault is imminent, he's nowhere to be seen. I'm drained of energy and slump down onto the hard steps.

What was all that about? And what's with the 'Harry?' He's never used my real name, never treated me like anything other than a target. He sounds genuinely concerned about Sven, which isn't normal McNoble behaviour and hardly fits with the kidnap of the other day. McNoble only 'takes care' of someone in a Mafiosi sort of way. What on Earth gives and what does he mean about Sven? And what's so important that we need to talk? I need to quiz Penny more, that's for sure.

Saturday, 20th June 1981

Chapter Seven

In Which Harry Helps Dobbin but doesn't Help Himself

I hate my life. It's not quite seven on Saturday morning, the daylight is barely penetrating the mizzly clouds and I'm hanging about on a cobbled lane in East London outside the block where Natalie lives. I'm sure I must look suspicious and try hard not to be seen. The river is a building away and it stinks of fish and diesel and faecal matter.

I'm on a mission to save myself from, at best, humiliation and at worst… No, I don't want to think about the worst. It's too horrible.

Instead I replay yesterday afternoon and evening to see if it makes any more sense now than it did then. After I left McNoble I was ready for a quiet evening in. Penny was doing a shift at the bar where she works – on the one hand that would be annoying because I couldn't pick her brains about McNoble and Andersen to see if she had any ideas, but on the other a quiet night in alone was appealing after my ordeal with McNoble. Dobbin was meant to be out with someone from work so I should have had the place to myself.

But my life is never that easy. I had just popped into the office to collect my cycle clips before going home when I found a message from Jean.

Sorry, Mr Spittle. I pp'ed the letter to Ms Tupps and posted it before I remembered you wanted a second read. I trust that will not cause you any inconvenience?

Bollocks. If by any unholy misalignment of the stars Miles opened the letter instead of Natalie, he would be straight round to 'explain' the error of my ways and that would probably involve realignment of my bowel and lower intestine. Somehow I needed to get word to Natalie to intercept it, but she wasn't answering her work number and I daren't call her at home.

With my mind in turmoil, I didn't notice that Dobbin was at home rather than out drinking somewhere. When he asked if I fancied going to see this new punk band – the Twats – who had been strongly recommended to him by someone at work because the lead singer was 'something else,' I initially told him I couldn't but then I thought mindless screaming at 100 decibels must just be the answer to quieten my fizzing brain.

The venue is a smelly back room at a pub called The Drunken Monk off Lillie Road in north Fulham. It was rammed, the band were shite, but the lead singer was indeed something else. For starters, she could barely find a note let alone hit it and the crowd became a touch boisterous as she maimed a Richard Hell and the Voidoids punk classic 'Love Comes in Spurts' even if her accompanying dance routine was both unique and quite likely to corrupt public morals. When she launched into a cover of X-Ray Spec's 'Oh Bondage Up Yours' a riot was on the cards. To calm them down she announced, "I'm gonna pierce the other nipple now," and sure enough up went the slashed T-shirt, out came her boob and in went a safety pin that until a moment or two before had been through the bass guitarist's nose.

Someone fainted, someone else tossed a pint of beer over the Mohicaned man helping the person who'd fainted, and the anticipated riot rapidly became a reality. I was about to drag Dobbin for the exit when someone in the band – a lanky pasty-faced guy with a tattooed neck and pierced eyebrow – appeared at our side and pointed us towards a wobbly looking door at the back of the room. When I hesitated, he shouted in my ear, "You don't want to go that way," indicating the door with the exit sign. I was still unsure but as soon as he held the dodgy door open, Dobbin was through it so I had to follow. One moment it was raucous and the next a throbbing silence.

About 15 people, I recognised someone else from the band and the rest I supposed were their friends, looked at me warily, like I was part of the riot. When they realised I was the most reluctant rioter there, they turned back to their conversation and I went looking for Dobbin who had disappeared. Some bloke in an orange suede jacket and red-framed specs caught my eye; he had someone in an armlock while the lead singer, still without a top, was hitting him. No one else seemed to care.

The man in the armlock was Dobbin who looked at me pleadingly. I was about to go to his rescue when the woman clattered the bouncer with her fist and he let go, reeling away. Dobbin stood up, blinking, testing his elbow but he had barely straightened it once before the woman grabbed his neck and pulled him into such a ferocious snog it was more like unarmed combat.

I didn't know what to do so I just gawped. The guy who'd shown us the door appeared next to me. "Leave her to it, mate. She'll not thank you if you try to interrupt."

Neither will Dobbin, I thought and I watched him begin to kiss her back.

I hadn't time to decide whether to leave them to it and go and interrupt when the door burst open and mayhem returned. In seconds we all disgorged outside. Dobbin gave the singer his jacket and, then they were running and laughing as they disappeared into the distance. The last I heard was Dobbin shouting, "See you later, Spittoon."

My ears were ringing and frankly I wanted my bed, so I headed home. There, my mood soured when I found Penny curled up on the sofa. I tried to wake her to come to bed but she pointedly turned away, wrapping herself tightly in the sheet she had taken like a cocoon.

About an hour after I got in – it took me ages to get off to sleep and I'd guess I managed about five minutes – Dobbin accompanied by who I assumed was the singer crashed through the door and proceeded to have cacophonous sex. At some point tiredness overcame even their vocal cords and I drifted off.

My watch said it was just after 3:40 when Dobbin shook me awake. He was in a total panic. "Her tit exploded and she's dead!"

He'd taken something – pupils like pin pricks and he wasn't making sense – but she was in a right old state. His room was a mess and her right breast looked awful – it wasn't the one she'd pierced on stage, it was the other one and it seemed to have a nail through the nipple. I called an ambulance and, since Dobbin had passed out twice by the time it arrived, I agreed with the ambulance driver to go with them to St Tommy's.

"What's her name?" the nurse was brisk and efficient and unbelievably smiley for the stupid hour.

I looked at Dobbin who was struggling to sit on a chair. He could barely speak.

"She calls herself Vera Copula…"

The triage nurse looked at me, amazed. "What? You're joking?"

"That's what the flyer for her band said."

Dobbin kept asking for water. It was clear the nurse knew they'd both taken something. She looked at me. "And you are?"

"His flatmate. They met after her gig when there were some crowd problems and she came back to ours. She pierced herself on stage. The safety pin. I think the nail was done before the gig. I don't know when."

The nurse nodded. "It's badly infected. I imagine the other will be the same. Still, you've done her a favour by getting her here." She smiled at me again, despite the racket outside from the Friday night/Saturday morning drunks. "Good job someone stayed off the pills. Any idea what they took?"

"Nope, sorry. Gary doesn't normally indulge so I guess she gave it to him. What's going to happen?"

"Given her condition, I'd imagine we will admit her, put her on IV antibiotics to fight the infection and keep her under observation. Septicaemia is a worry. Any idea who she really is? I mean, that can't be her real name can it?"

"She's probably a law student. It's Latin for, erm, consummation of marriage." I'm amazed I remembered.

"Are you a lawyer?"

"Training to be."

"You know your stuff. Look…"

"Harry. Harry Spittle."

Up went an eyebrow. I waited for the snigger that didn't come. She said, "My Mum's a Spittle. Maybe we're related."

"We should get together and compare family trees."

She studied me for a moment. "I think I'd like that, Harry Spittle." She grabbed my hand and, in biro, quickly wrote a phone number and 'Jackie' under it. "Why don't you take your friend home before one of the boys in blue find him? If you call this number," she handed me a note, "in the morning you can find out how 'Vera' is doing."

Now, I'm back in the present and really not ready to face a reality that has all the makings of something painful and permanent, I'm shivering. The river is less than 100 feet away and the chill from it has seeped up through my shoes and is already mid-calf. I can see the biro scrawl from Jackie which is still there, challenging me to call her. I wonder what Penny would say is she saw it. I'd like to think it would make her jealous but she's most likely to laugh.

I jump as I hear a whistle and a cheery voice calling a name. A be-turbaned man on a pushbike has turned into the road and is talking to someone I can't see. He finishes whatever he's saying and heads towards me – it's the postie. He's still has to deliver to several buildings before he reaches this block and since all these converted warehouses are now flats, he'll be a while. Having nothing better to do I watch as he approaches the first block. He rings a bell and is let in. It's the same at the next block. Maybe, when he reaches here, I can follow him inside and lurk in the hall, out of the cold. It's the nearest I've managed to formulating a plan to retrieve the letter. In my fevered imaginings I wrestle the letter from the postman, but in practice I'm just hopeful of catching Natalie before any damage is done.

The postman is still two buildings away when the sound of shutters going up drags me back to Natalie's block. It's an underground garage. I just have time to step out of sight of the driver before Miles in his bright red Porsche purrs away.

The postie is on his way to this block. I jam my finger on Natalie's buzzer. She takes an age. "What?"

"It's Harry. Harry Spittle."

"Who? Harry? Oh fuck, come up if you must."

I'm buzzed in and politely hold open the door for the postie. "Anything for Flat Four?"

The postie looks at his selection and hands me two envelopes. I mumble my thanks and head upstairs while the postie heads for a bank of letterboxes on the far wall and begins pushing letters through the slots.

Natalie is waiting by the door. She is in a long white towelling robe with another around her hair, just like yesterday's fantasy. She has a very symmetrical face that rarely shows much animation; smiles and frowns are not often seen – 'unreadable' might be the best way to put it. "I was in the shower," she explains, rather unnecessarily.

I watch as she moves slowly across the massive hall-cum-sitting-room-cum-dinner thinking about my daydream. Am I gifted with foresight? Ha, as if! Her movements are languid and sexy, and I shake my head, telling myself to get a grip. She heads for the stainless-steel kitchen. "Coffee?" She shakes out her hair, masses of honey blonde tresses and fights with it for a few moments before controlling it in some sort of band thingy. I'm so engrossed I don't realise she's stopped and is staring at me. "When will you stop staring at my breasts? Christ." I begin to stumble over an apology, but she waves it away. "Forget it; I know you can't help it. Come on, cheer me up why don't you? To what do I owe the pleasure?"

Before I can say, she reaches across and picks up my wrist. "Who's Jackie?"

How did she see that? I feel ill; this will get back to Penny but not in the way I imagined it. I fumble through an explanation about Dobbin and Vera, but I don't sound convincing even to myself. By the time I end up, feebly, saying I took the number so I could call her for an update, she is laughing. "You're a saint and a crap liar. Some nurse wants your babies more like." She peers at the number again like she's memorising it. "And does Penny know?"

"I've not seen her since last night."

"Perhaps you should get rid before she sees it. I mean, if you want her back."

"Does she want me?"

"That's the six-million-dollar question, isn't it?" She strokes my arm. "Don't be too needy, that's all I'll say."

"I'm not. Am I?"

She shakes her head. "She's still fancies you, you know. Just try not to be too much of a prat."

"You could help if you told her it was an accident."

"Was it?"

"Of course. You know it was…"

She narrows her eyes. "Maybe I like the idea of her thinking it was deliberate."

I'm still processing what she means by that when she laughs. "You are sweet, you know? Come on, tell me why you're really here so bright and early. If it's to talk about you and Penny and your crappy love life, then excuse me but I've been through it with Penny too many times. Talk to her, not me." Taking her coffee, she levers herself onto a stool. She seems stiff, like she's pulled a muscle.

I hand her the letter I've rescued. "Read this and either tell me to shove it or what I can do to help."

***

Natalie is in bits. I'll be the first to admit I'm really rubbish around weeping women; it's not a good trait but ever since Dina used tears as a way to get me into trouble as a child it's grated on me. Natalie can barely speak but manages to hitch up her robe and show me a bruise on her thigh and then pulls down the robe to expose her right shoulder that has a mark like a carpet burn on it. I'm left to understand these are Miles' handiwork following an argument, but she doesn't say so exactly. I let her sob herself to a halt, awkwardly holding her as she presses her head against my chest.

"Is Sven involved? You know, with you? In this?"

She pulls away and hugs herself like she's protecting herself from me too. "Sven? Why do you say that?"

"Penny mentioned something about Miles being jealous of him?"

She shakes her head. "I can't say, Harry. I just can't." Her eyes are pools of tears and snot is dripping from her nose.

I look away, wondering what she can't say. While I try to work out what to say – I'm so out of my depth – she lights a cigarette. When did she start smoking? I say, "Could you go and stay somewhere? Just while you sort out what you want to do."

She shakes her head.

"You could maybe crash at mine. My flatmate is mostly away." The idea of her using Tim's porn-grotto right now is appalling; we'd have to swap rooms. "What about Sven's? Maybe I could take you there? If you know the address."

She grinds out the cigarette and drops the butt in the half-drunk coffee. "Fuck it, Harry. What is it about Sven? Why would I know where he lives?" She shakes out her hair, hiding her face. When she throws it back, she glares at me. Well, I think it's a glare but who knows? "Just go, Harry. Miles might be back any minute and I don't want you here when he arrives."

"Hasn't he gone to work?"

She doesn't answer.

"Those bruises. I don't like to leave you."

"You don't know what you're talking about. Look," she stands, tugging her robe tight. "This isn't about you, okay? It's sweet you care but it's no one's business but mine. Miles and I will sort things out." She hands me the letter. "If things change I have your number and you'll be the first person I call. Now go. And tell Penny I don't appreciate her talking to you – or anyone for that matter – about my confidential conversations."

"Penny didn't tell me about you and Miles."

"Really? Who else is going to give you all the gory details?" She looks fit to explode.

"Sven." As soon as I say his name, I wish I hadn't.

Her expression goes from annoyed to anaemic. She sits down hard. "When did he speak to you? What did he say?"

"Nothing. We had a brief chat and—"

"Sven doesn't do brief chats. Please tell me. I need to know."

She does sound desperate. My professional conscience tells me it's a matter of client confidentiality but some hardwired need to help Natalie overrides prudence. "He wanted me to make his Will."

"His Will?"

I nod.

"I suppose Marita benefits."

"I can't—"

"That bloody sister of his will get him killed, you know." She shakes her head.

"I'm sorry but I don't—"

She waves me quiet. "There's a bottle. In that cupboard." While she shakes out and lights a cigarette, I pull a rather expensive looking single malt from the cupboard. "Pour yourself and me one. Glasses there and ice in the freezer." She stares out of the window towards a local church, like she's looking for guidance.

I give her the glass and sit on a stool next to her.

She swallows a mouthful, grimacing at the burn. "What did he tell you?"

"Nothing. It's just a simple Will."

Her laugh is hollow. "Nothing about Sven is simple." Using a fingernail, she picks out a strand of tobacco from her front teeth. "When his Father died – you remember Robin Andersen?"

I nod. "How am I going to forget?"

She nods in turn. "That accident? I forgot. Sven said he wanted nothing to do with his Father's businesses. You remember that?"

"I think Penny told me. Sven and I weren't exactly close."

"No. Of course." She screws up her face. "But all that changed."

"So I'm hearing. When?" I'm still surprised at the idea of Sven running his Father's empire. He always said how much he hated his Dad.

"A while back. He realised that if he merely let it go there could be some awful unintended consequences and he wanted to minimise the violence that might follow. But mostly it was because of her. Marita. She wanted to use the money for good deeds. Christ, she has this saint-complex or something. We tried to tell him he was mad, but she insisted and Stephen said—"

"McNoble?" I say, barely hiding my disdain.

"Harry, grow up can't you? He's not the same as he was when we worked at Hemingways. Okay, once he was a bit of an arse but he's different now. He's really helped Sven. And me. For goodness sake I would have ended up with Stephen if Miles hadn't come along. Did you know I met Miles at Robin's funeral?"

I shake my head. I have no recollection of Tupps being at the funeral.

"He wasn't there long but he took my number. He can be a charmer. He did business with Robin. He and Sven…" She peters out. "They play poker at Miles' club, but, well, it's not easy."

"Club?"

"Does Penny tell you anything? Miles's gambling club? Hasn't she ever invited you?"

Penny and I have always maintained our separate interests and friendships mostly because if I tried to get her to come along on Saturdays to cricket matches our relationship would have withered on the vine years ago.

Natalie lights another cigarette but just holds it. "Marita wants to save everything except herself and her brother. If you ask me they both want to self-destruct." She goes back to staring at the church. "He used to say the reason so many people turned up at the funeral was to make sure Robin was dead. And there were those huge men who carried the coffin, they didn't have any necks. It was like watching a bad gangster movie." She ends her reminiscence with a smile. "Sven talked about you. Often. He liked you, you know."

"Oh bollocks. He thought I was a complete tit and always said as much."

"He said you were the one honourable person he knew, the one person you could trust to do the right thing come what may." She turns to look at me, the ash from her cigarette forming a long unstable curve that might fall at any moment. "He told me I should have snaffled you up when I had the chance. That used to rile Penny."

I cannot look at her.

I love Penny but equally she pisses me off with monotonous regularity. And I must admit to having had more fantasies about Natalie than is probably healthy.

Bloody Sven. Why does he have to say such things?

I'm in my own little world, arguing with Sven and trying to imagine McNoble as something other than everyone's worst nightmare when I realise Natalie has stood up and ground out her cigarette.

"You need to go, Harry. I'll be fine, really. It's all a misunderstanding. I'll tell Sven to stop rumour-mongering." She offers me her hands and eases me from the stool. We are inches apart as she holds my gaze. "How come we never got together Harry?"

I can't answer that.

She uses her hand to pull me to her and kisses me firmly on my cheek. Then quickly she eases me outside and closes the door without a backwards glance.

Chapter Eight

In Which Harry Learns a Lesson about Vegetables and Finds an Old Friend

Penny is making coffee when I arrive home. "Where have you been?"

"Over at Natalie's. I wanted to find out if I could help her."

"Help her? With what?"

"If she was divorcing."

Penny frowns and then shakes her head. "I suppose you have to do that, as a lawyer."

"Do what?"

"Try to get work. It seems a bit, you know, mercenary." She carries on quickly. "Sorry, that's not fair. I know you want to help. What happened last night? You weren't around when I got back."

I give her a potted version of the Twats and the hospital visit.

She smiles and winces alternately. "I guess we'd better see how Gary is. Do you want to take him some coffee?"

"Okay."

I take a cup and put it by his bed. The only response I get when I ask if he's okay is a grunt. "Shall I see if I can find out how she is?"

A double grunt.

"I'll see if Mr Jones is in, so I can use his phone. Get a progress report."

Mr Jones lives in the flat below ours. He's a thin man with a prominent brow and a line in knitted cardigans that suggests a bulk buy from C&A circa 1957 that will probably see him out. As I wait for him to answer, I check my hand and Jackie's number. I'm rubbing it off when the door opens. He's happy to lend me the phone and a pen so I can scribble her number on the card she gave me, like it's official. Of course I'll not call her.

When I return, Dobbin has Penny making toast and is in bed checking his face in a hand mirror. "Is my skin red? I feel like I'm on fire."

"You look like shit, but then you always do."

He shrugs off the blankets and turns over, tugging down his pyjamas. "My arse stings to all buggery. What's it look like?"

He tugs the cheeks apart revealing a very red-looking anus.

55

"Oh, choice. I'll leave you boys to it." Penny is right behind me, pulls a face and leaves the toast on the table.

"What can you see, Spittoon? It feels awful. Do you think she's shoved something up it?"

"Garfield Dobbs. You are my best mate and for you I will do a lot, but there is a limit and exploring the inner recesses of your rectum does not form any part of my understanding of the concept of 'friendship.'"

Dobbin is twisting, trying to see. "Fuck all help you are. Here, pass me that mirror."

I go to the window and stare out across the buildings towards the brewery. Over my shoulder I say to him, "The hospital says she has blood poisoning and they're keeping her in. She won't tell them who she is. Seems like she's frightened that her parents will find out.

"I'm sure she rogered me, you know. Fuck, isn't that a crime? You're the lawyer, you should know."

"You know what Dobbin? If there had been any cases of women anally raping men, I'm pretty bloody sure I'd remember hearing about them. And if you call me as a witness I'd have to say from all I heard last night that you were a very willing participant. She's really not well, you know. Much worse than your own little Ring of Fire. You should go and see her."

He stops his investigation and looks at me like I'm crazed. "Me? You're the fucking saint. You go if you want."

I shrug and come back to his bed to steal some toast.

He says, "Is Penny back for good then?"

"No idea. She slept on the sofa last night."

"At least she's here."

"Small mercies, eh?"

"Maybe when you go to see Vera she'll give me a bed bath."

"Yeah, I'm sure that'll help." I throw a crust at him and leave him to his renewed investigations.

***

Penny suggests she comes with me to visit Vera. Maybe she suspects something. She can't know about Jackie. I wonder for a moment if Natalie has somehow been telling tales about me.

I hate hospitals. Nanty, my Great Aunt, had kidney failure and to see her in one of those metal caged beds, a shadow of her former robust self, was gruesome. The smell was also awful.

Vera is in a side ward of six beds. Happily, we don't encounter Jackie and that relieves the tension that's building. The other beds are occupied by women between 70 and a million, all with wild hair, staring eyes and a scent reminiscent of bus shelters on Saturday nights. The contrast between Vera and the rest is enormous, what with her tinted spiky hair and pale smooth complexion. Without the heavy makeup and manic, druggy eyes she looks about 13. As we approach I realise I know her.

She confirms it. "Thought it was you last night. Can't be many Spittles around." She waits then adds, "Do you remember me?"

Penny looks from her to me and back. "You know each other?"

I nod. So does Vera. She says, "College of Law, Guildford, back in my boring middle-class phase. Brenda Silverman then, two rows in front of Harry. Sensible bob, black rimmed NHS glasses, tartan skirt at an appropriate length and..." She giggles and winces. "Fuck, my tits hurt."

"What happened to you, Bren? After college?"

"I saw the light in the Green Man in Shalford, January 1980. This punk band were doing a set and their lead passed out, having necked half a bottle of vodka and some biker's manhood. The lads asked if anyone could sing so I had a go. Didn't matter to them that I just made up the words."

It comes back to me in disjointed memories. She was, is, some judge's daughter and back in those interminable lectures she seemed as tense as a well-strung Stradivarius. Not that I've even seen a Strad, of course...

"How's your mate? Never did find out his name. Great shag mind."

I smile. "He's a bit sore... er..."

She nods. "Up the arse?"

"Yeah."

"Not surprised. He can't handle the pills, can he? He was coming in and out of it, so I improvised to keep him alert."

Penny sits on Brenda/Vera's bed. "Do tell," I encourage.

"It works, kiddo. If they're fading, and fuck me do you boys lose it quickly, you need to perk them up. My mate swears by MacLean's. Super white for perfect teeth is best she says. I improvised with a chilli I found in your fridge. Sharp as a pencil after that."

Penny goggles at me and back to Brenda/Vera. "You stuck a chilli up his arse?" she asks.

"It worked. He kept his end up for another hour. He probably shat it out first thing and doesn't even know what happened." She tries to sit up more and grimaces again. As she moves I notice the tube coming out of her wrist.

Penny says, "What's the story? They keeping you in?"

Brenda/Vera nods. "At least tonight. Your mate, Harry? What's his name? I should know it."

"Gary. Or Dobbin."

"Okay. Dobbin. Is that ironic 'cos he ain't hung like the proverbial, is he? Any chance I can stay at yours after I get out? My Mum'll kill me if she finds out what I did to my tits and if she comes here they'll tell her. I've managed to keep my real name out of it for now, but Mum'll be hiring a detective soon enough."

"But you're an adult. You can tell them not to say…"

She shakes her head. "You've not met Mum. Part of the Great and the Good and the Exceptionally Loud. There's no doctor or consultant who'd cope with her demanding to know what they've done to her precious bundle. Me. So do you think he'll let me stay?"

Penny grins. "Will he cope?"

I nod. "He'll be as happy as a sandboy. Just don't sodomise him with any more vegetables, spicy or otherwise. And keep him off the pills. He's too innocent, and anyway he starts a new job on Monday and I need him alive and employed to pay the rent."

As we leave Penny says, "Someone should tell her parents. She'll kill herself if she's left to her own devices."

"I'm more worried about Dobbin."

Chapter Nine

In Which Harry Goes Partying and has an Unexpected Success

"What's he like? This Lord Wotsit?" Penny has borrowed a jacket with large shoulder pads and looks like an American footballer. She is also wearing a short sparkly skirt and a black top that shows off lots and lots of cleavage. We've caught a train to Kew, then a bus and now we are walking towards Syon House. God, she is so sexy and seeing her in that skirt and top gives me a hard on. There's some sort of hedge to our left and I wonder if she'd let me…?

"Is he fun?" She looks across at me and smiles, then frowns. For some reason this makes me think about Vera and Dobbin and I wonder if Penny would ever think about sticking something up my arse to keep me 'keen.' Frankly that thought is so terrifying the random erection wilts in an instant. To my surprise she stops and puts her hands on her hips in a 'double teapot' gesture, which she uses when she's cross with me.

"The answer is no."

"No what?"

"I know you and what you're thinking, and no is the answer."

"You can't know…"

She smiles, reaches across and taps my bum. "Your anus is safe, boyo. Fear not." How does she do that?

We walk on in silence although at least she does link arms with me.

The magnificent entrance to Syon House is bedecked in fairy lights, and jugglers and fire-eaters are entertaining guests as they arrive. We appear to be the only two who have caught the tube, bus and then walked. As we stroll up the drive on a balmy evening Rollers and Bentleys and the odd Porsche cruise past. One is pillar-box red and for a moment I catch my breath fearing it's Miles and Natalie, but it contains a decrepit old boy who needs two sticks and the help of the pencil slim, six two bombshell who slithers out of the passenger seat. Penny nudges me. "You think she's his nurse?"

"In that dress? I think she's his death wish."

I have a momentary panic as we join the queue to the entrance as everyone is carrying a stiff white card with fancy black lettering. I have nothing.

"Sir? Madam?" The flunky looks down his elongated nose at us. "I…"

"Harry! Come here." Out of a crowd Sir Pen appears. He is wearing a beautifully tailored pinstriped jacket, MCC tie and a crisp white shirt. He does not appear to be wearing any trousers. He spots me looking. "A silly bet. For everyone I don't kiss within 10 minutes of their arriving I have to remove an item of clothing. It's a touch early to get my dingdong out so if you don't mind…?"

Penny smiles and moves forward allowing herself to be kissed on the lips. I stand bolt rigid wondering what's in store. He smiles. "Just a peck for now, eh Harry? We'll see how the party goes, shall we?"

His lips are moist and firmly planted on my cheek before he waves us towards some waiters carrying drinks and moves off.

"Sweet old boy."

"Sure."

"Your face is a picture. Can you believe the waiters?"

The waiters are all men and all are in a uniform of tight swimming trunks, stiff collar and black bowtie. They are all shaved and glistening with oil. Penny moves towards one carrying champagne flutes. "I'm glad I came, Harry. This is my sort of party."

It is going to be grim, but Penny is in her element so I force out a smile and some sound that I hope she interprets as enthusiasm. Not that I think she notices because she coos, waves and heads off towards a group who are all actors or 'in the business.' "I need to do some serious schmoozing," she says over her shoulder.

Alone, I drift towards a large indoor pond full of ridiculously fat goldfish and perch on the edge, determined that if I get drunk, I'll do it sitting to make sure I don't make a fool of myself too soon. Everyone is either very very old or very very beautiful and I'm feeling more and more out of place when a woman, who is obviously as uncomfortable as me, strides over.

"He tells me you're the only man who isn't a poof here. Talk to me." She holds out a gloved hand. "Isabella, his sister. Technically Lady Isabella but call me that and I'll push you in the pond. Izzy by preference. You his lawyer?"

Izzy is about my height but is what Mum would call 'generously curved.' She has a massive perm and startling blue-silver eyeshadow that suggests she models herself on a Top of the Pops dancer, which is in direct contrast with the rather severe business suit she is wearing. Her smile is warm and wide.

"Yes, I…" I want to explain I'm just the clerk, but she plonks herself next to me and says, "He made his Will, didn't he? Has he cut me out?"

"I can't say."

"Of course he fucking has. I would too if I was him. Mind you, he's mad. That boy of his will let him have his way for a few months then take him for what he can. You know I'm the only one who cares about him? In the family I mean. He thinks we didn't know he was bent but it's been bloody obvious since we were small. Silly lump. Still, when my ex was breaking my arms he… you don't believe me? Look." She pulls up a sleeve to reveal some horrid looking scars. "Enormous fucking scandal if it had come out and it would have killed Daddy; I couldn't say but Pen had him castrated or something and sent him to Morocco so that was all right." She studies me carefully. "I'm talking too much. You look too young to be his lawyer." She moves away slightly. "Have you met Sean yet?"

"No."

"Oh, you're in for a treat. I believe he will be singing later. Why are you here, exactly?"

"Sir Penshaw invited me."

She holds my gaze and then laughs, touching my arm. "Well done, young man. Pen bet me I couldn't find out what the Will says, and he wins. Here, hold this."

I take her glass and she reaches behind her, unzipping her skirt which slides to the floor revealing a silk slip that ends just above her plump knees. "Lesson one if you come to a Penshaw Grimsdale party. Wear lots of clothes." She waves at a waiter and hands him her dress, saying, "Are you a poof?"

The man looks surprised and shakes his head.

"How did you get in then? Still, I'm not complaining. I'll find you later." She turns to me. "If I were you, young man, I'd find your girlfriend. I know the guests are mostly men but there are a few women, and most of them are quite predatory. If you're not sure, try the room over there. They've installed this whirlpool thing and I wouldn't be surprised if she's been encouraged to jump in."

She leaves me, my mouth hanging open. Is she serious? I begin to head for the room she has pointed out when I recognise a man carrying a drinks' tray. It is Amos, one of the waiting staff when I was at Hemingways. He's going in the other direction and looking rather fraught. "Amos?"

That stops him. He turns and stares at me, clearly unaware who I am. Then the light dawns and he beams. "Harry Spittle! Well, wax my winky! Long-time no see." He glances around at a couple of stripped young men wandering away towards the lawns, arm in arm. "Didn't know this was your scene?"

"Sir Pen is a client of the law firm where I work. He asked me to come. You a guest?"

He pulls a face, a familiar expression of derision and disgust crossing his features. "God no, I'm just staff. Do you know they're using actors to serve, and they are all incompetent? In-fucking-competent. And they expect me to make everything go smoothly. The gents is like a tart's boudoir too." He closes his eyes as if in pain. "I wouldn't normally do this, but Gregory asked and, well, one does one's bit."

"And Gregory is who?"

Amos shivers and pouts. "Darling, he is divine. Stud material that one. Has this idea he will run his own catering company but right now he is trying to learn the ropes. They were short and I obliged." He leans in close, conspiratorially. "Hung like a breadfruit tree. A real mouthful." He winks lasciviously.

Amos always was outrageous, but he seems to have become even more so. "He's your, um, boyfriend?"

Amos sort of scoffs. "Soooo passé, sweetie. One doesn't have a boyfriend these days. That's for you straights and your boring monogamy. Speaking of which how is Penny? I saw her about six months ago. She said you two were still at it."

I force myself to laugh, but I know I'm blushing. Before I can answer, Amos catches sight of Sir Pen approaching. "Better be off, Harry. Speak later maybe?"

Sir Pen is all smiles. "Can we sort out the Will, Harry? I know I've rather tricked you by setting Izzy on you and you did do me those lovely instructions, but I'd be happier if you were there when it's signed. After, you can get as smashed as you like." He takes me by the elbow and eases me away from the noise in the opposite direction to the room Izzy mentioned. I can hear splashes and squeals fading as we walk along a corridor. What is going on back there?

As we are walking, he says, "Did you manage to sort out that young man's Will? Sven, wasn't it?"

"Yes, thanks." I wonder if he's happy with it. If we are going to get paid, he'll need to sign it.

"When I was his age, I think a Will was the last thing on my mind. He is obviously a cautious man."

"He has an unusual background."

"Really? Do tell. I just love gossip."

Suddenly I feel embarrassed. "I… I'm sorry but I probably shouldn't say."

"No, of course. Naughty of me to press."

"No, it's just… well, he is a client."

"Quite. Although I imagine he must be quite well heeled if he needs a Will?"

"Watch him, Harry." Lady Isabella appears behind us. She drapes an arm around me and looks at Sir Pen. "He will wheedle all sorts of secrets out of you if you let him. It's how he made his millions."

I watch them exchange an odd look.

She says, "Who were you talking about anyway?"

Sir Pen says quickly, "A friend of Harry's I met in his office. Sven something, wasn't it?"

I nod. "Andersen."

"That's it. Odd fellow. Didn't look well. I was just checking he was all right."

Lady Isabella folds her arms. "Uncharacteristically caring of you, Pen." She turns to me. "He sounds Swedish."

"I think his Father—"

Sir Pen interrupts. "Come on, Harry. Let's sort out the paperwork and then we can all have fun. See you later, my dear."

We go into a small office. Four men are waiting for us. Sir Pen goes up to a young man in a cream jacket and black trousers who looks like a cabaret singer and kisses him. "This is Sean, Harry. Sean, this is my lawyer."

"Hi." Sean holds out a hand. He has a nice smile and a rather confused look on his face. He's about my height. I suppose I assumed he'd be some hunky Adonis but he's just very ordinary. He turns to Sir Pen. "Don't do this Pen. You don't need to."

"I know that, but I want to."

"Everyone thinks I'm forcing you."

"Well, you're not."

"Izzy…"

"Izzy agrees with me. She pretends to mind but she wants what's best for me, and right now you are what's best for me."

I don't think anyone else can see his face as he says this, but I do and he's struggling not to cry.

"Right. Before we start, a little something to spice up the mood." Sir Pen waves and one of the other men appears at his side. In moments, a mirror is laid on the table and a rolled up twenty-pound note. Sir Pen snorts a line of the powder and offers the note to me.

"I… it's not…"

Sir Pen smiles. "That's fine. Like Sean, eh? Body is your temple, et cetera? This one," he indicates Sean who has his arms crossed and looks inscrutable, "won't even eat meat for God's sake." He hands the note to another man and says, "Now then Harry. What do we do about this Will?" The paperwork is laid out on the desk next to a rather grand-looking fountain pen.

I can feel everyone in the room look at me, like I'm important. I take them through the formalities, grateful Jean explained them to me. Sean watches, looking more and more miserable as first Sir Pen signs and then his two witnesses add their details. The fourth man, who has been leaning against the wall, steps forward. I see he is wearing a dog collar. No shirt, though. He and Sir Pen kiss. Does everyone here kiss?

"Do you want a line Cliff?"

Cliff shrugs and deftly hoovers up a small mound of coke. He moves to stand between Sir Pen and Sean. "This is meaningless in the eyes of the law," he looks at me, "and God for that matter," he glances up, "but, here, you are as good as married. May you be blessed with a long life and much joy, and may you honour and support each other through whatever trials and tribulations you face. Do you have the rings?"

I had thought there was going to be a big thing made of this 'wedding' but apparently there are only six of us.

One of the witnesses steps forward and hands a box to Cliff. "With these rings, you are joined forever until death do you part. Love each other and be loyal and true," he glares at Sean at that, not that anyone else seems to notice. "You can now kiss each other. Then I need a stiff drink."

After a lot of kissing which happily excludes me they produce a lovely scroll with a sweet message on it. Everyone signs it to 'witness the union.' Sir Pen says, "We will announce our marriage at 10 by the pool, but in the meantime keep Mum and have at it people." He looks at Sean and says, "I'm off to the tub. Don't see why the girls should have all the fun. You coming?"

"In a minute." He watches as Sir Pen and the other men head off. He takes my arm. "Come on. Pen says you like cricket and the highlights are on in five minutes."

Part of me wants to find out about Penny, but I'm convinced Izzy is just teasing me. I follow Sean to another side room where five or six men are sitting, smoking weed and waiting for the highlights to start.

I have a great time getting smoothly stoned – being a baronet clearly gives you access to some fabulous grass – while watching the Australians put England to the sword. Sean is knowledgeable and concentrates on the screen. I wonder briefly about if he's so body conscious why he sits amongst the rest of us smoking weed but the thought slips away as I watch Alderman's out-swinger, which is, as foreshadowed by Sir Pen the other day, a thing of devilish beauty. When the lights come up, Sean says, "I don't want his money, you know. If I can revoke the bloody Will, I will." Before I can respond he ups and leaves. Two men are snogging in one corner and in another a blond beanpole is quietly consoling a man who is blubbing rhythmically; I leave them all to it.

I check the whirlpool room, but there's no sign of Penny. Where the bloody hell has she gone now? I go for a wander, hoping I might spot her. Outside, the stately home of the Duke of Northumberland looks powerful and imposing. The fresh air clears my head a little but there are few people about, so I head back inside and follow the noise of squeals and shouts.

It's clear some sort of beauty parade is in progress. A line of stunning women is walking across the room towards a dark-haired woman with gimlet eyes and a Pinocchio nose. As I stare they all turn to face the conductress and pull their tops and swimsuits down or up as is necessary to expose their breasts. Everyone hoots and catcalls, and the women grin stupidly as they display themselves to the party goers. The dark-haired woman approaches the first and fondles her breasts. She proceeds to do the same to each woman. As she reaches Penny she appears to take a lot longer and is graced with a serious look from Pen before she moves on. I glance round but no one seems surprised or shocked. This is so far outside my comfort zone I feel sure it's obvious to everyone. Penny, however, seems to be enjoying herself along with all the others. I hope it's just good acting.

The judge takes a proffered microphone. "Ladies and gentlemen, fellow dykes and homos, I proudly declare that Fanny Newbury is Miss Pert Titties 1981!" She lets the winner take the stand and moves to the line of contestants, slipping next to Penny with whom she shares some huge joke based on the cartoon laughter they indulge in. Meanwhile Fanny shares her shapely breasts with us one more time to outrageous cheers of appreciation and then the crowd begins to drift away.

Finally, Penny sees me and comes over. "Damn, I thought I was in with a chance." She grins manically, part of which is patently chemically enhanced.

I say, "She took long enough checking yours."

Penny throws her head back in a crazy laugh. "Get you! You're not the only one who appreciates them, matey. Maggie is a hoot." She begins to tug at her hair, squeezing out some water. Her black top is soaked, and she's lost her skirt somewhere. It's clear, even in my befuddled state, that her face has the same flush that I've only noticed after we've had vigorous sex. Of course, I know I'm just being paranoid and it's probably just whatever she's taken, but still. "Who was that woman? Fondling you?"

"Maggie Cloud. She's a producer in the West End." She grabs me and kisses me unexpectedly. "Thank you for bringing me. I've met so many good contacts. I can see a future after this. Everyone has been so encouraging!"

I surprise myself by not caring. "So you've had fun?"

"Brilliant. And you?"

"Interesting. You want to go?" I look at the tub; it's a melee of thrashing bodies.

She follows my gaze. "Yes." She puts her arm found my waist. "Too much of a good thing. Can we slip away? I don't want to explain." She frowns. "Any idea where my skirt is?"

"Explain what?" But she's gone to find her clothes.

It takes us two hours to get back to the flat, walking and taking three buses, one of which goes in the wrong direction for miles and we snog and grope all the way. There's no sign of Dobbin, not that it would have mattered as she yanks my trousers down as soon as we get in. We make love there and then, up against the front door and again more slowly in the lounge, slipping off the sofa and ending up under the side table. After an hour's recuperation and two bowls of cereal we manage a third and fourth time in our bed. She suggests we take a shower then and we try to make cramped and slippery love but, it's something of a failure. In the end, we dry ourselves and go back to bed where she plays with my battered penis for a bit while my fingers and tongue bring her to several more orgasms. If I was counting she owes me about 17 blowjobs by now.

Eventually even she pushes my hand away. "Enough." She lifts and drops my floppy penis one final time. "Turn over. I could try some toothpaste."

"Shall we sleep on it?"

She nods and makes a spoon. I'm not quite asleep when my nob starts stirring again. I flip onto my back but she's fast asleep. It's quite a relief in truth.

Sunday, 21st June 1981

Chapter Ten

In Which Harry's Hopes Take a Knock and Then It Gets Worse

When I awake, Penny is already up. I lie in bed remembering last night. I can't help smiling, even though I dread to think what state my little fella is in. Penny's back and all is right with the world. I don't care about my job, my family, Sven, Natalie or anyone, only Penny. A little part of me wonders what she got up to in the pool at the party, but I push it away. Why does that matter? Not important. I'll ask. Sometime. It wouldn't be right now. No, today we'll make house, move some of her stuff in here – I look at my box of a room and wonder what I can do to create more space. Put up some shelves maybe? It's a shame we can't move into Tim's room. Maybe we can if all he wants is storage space.

Thinking about Penny makes me want her. Morning is definitely my time. I can hear her bashing about in the kitchen. I pull myself out of my stinking pit – maybe I'll wash the sheets, it must be the time for their six-monthly change – and stroll buck naked into the kitchen. "Morning. We're awake."

She's wearing one of my work shirts, standing by the sink. She's swigging water from a beaker. She doesn't look up at me as I wrap my arms around her, but I can feel her tense, ready to go again.

"We never christened here. You fancy a go?"

She turns and twists out of my grip, her eyes tight shut. "I need a bucket of tea. Can you go and grab some milk? Maybe bread would help too."

She looks pale and very, very interesting. Despite the punishing regime imposed on him less than eight hours ago, the little fella does his best to look perky. "Okay, although I've an alternative hangover cure if—"

"I need a shower." She pulls a mass of hair under her nose. "This smells like your spunk. Did you come in my hair at some point? Or I suppose that pool was full of all sorts. It could have been there." She rubs her temple, and then presses it hard between both hands. "Christ, what did I take? Fuck. My head feels like it's been vacuumed, and not very carefully." She manages a squint at me. "Please. Tea?"

I look at her curls. I'm pretty sure I sucked them last night. A lot. Geez, what have I ingested?

"Sure, Okay. Tea. Mind you, I could do with a shower, too. Maybe—"

She pushes past me. "Tea. Now."

In moments the bathroom door slams and the bolt is loudly slid into place.

Oh well, maybe after she's had some carbohydrates and caffeine she'll want to reconvene. I hope she doesn't talk about the pool. I want to know but then again, do I really?

I pull on some jeans and the one T-shirt that doesn't appear to have been used to wipe up. I need to do some laundry.

The shops are about 10 minutes' walk and I drift along the edge of the pavement in a dream, imagining what we might do later.

The nagging doubts borne of her reluctance to engage in any sort of renewed sexual activity or even some formless planning return as I reach the corner, but I'm good at the art of sunny-side up philosophising and increase my pace. The sooner I'm back, the sooner those doubts can be shown to be unfounded. I mean that pool, it was just harmless fun. Like the Best Breasts competition or whatever it was. If only she was a bit more of a morning person.

I let my mind contemplate the two of us, naked and sticky and greasy from bacon and ketchup, slipping and sliding together while we listen to Botham saving England on the radio. Or we could take the radio and a picnic to Battersea Park and risk an al fresco fuck behind the running track while cricket's colossus saves the day. Although the last time we tried it outdoors she moaned about the mozzie bites on her bum – God, they did love her bum. It looked like it had developed its own pox, not that I blamed the mozzies for their enthusiasm.

I have a serious erection by the time I reach Mr Patel's shop and it's beginning to rub awfully. I need to get the stuff and hurry back before some serious damage is done.

It's while I'm at the counter, waiting for him to encourage his ancient till into life, that I catch a headline in the paper… something about Botham. I pick it up and flick through the pages before suddenly losing the power to breathe.

"You all right, 'Arry? You sit, yes?" Mr Patel catches my elbow and guides me to a box of toffee crisps before I slide to the floor. "I get you water."

He disappears, leaving me gawping at the paper. It's a picture of Sven Andersen, at some social function in a black tie, under the headline.

TRAGEDY

My brain can't compute. The first paragraph says he's dead. Suddenly I can't be there. I drop the money for the paper and leave the rest as I hurry out of the shop to find somewhere to read the whole article.

Chapter Eleven

In Which Harry's Suspicions are Aroused and Dobbin Unexpectedly Gives Him Good Advice

I'm not sure how long I wander around. I know I try to sit a couple of times but as soon as anyone approaches I have to move on. Some bell in my brain reminds me I need milk, which I'm clutching when eventually I return home. What I can't understand is how no one else seems to care that Sven is dead. Don't they know? Haven't they heard? People are whistling, smiling and the day seems normal as I unlock the door to the block where the flat is. Mr Jones, who lives in the flat below ours, is cleaning his front door and offers me a cheery 'halloo,' which I ignore. I'm trying to think what to say to Penny. How do you break something like this? Why does it have to be me?

I'm not proud of myself when I realise Penny has gone and I feel nothing except huge relief. There's a note written in smudged pencil:

Maggie rang. I have a casting! See you later. We can talk then.

I can see she's written something else and rubbed it out. When I hold it to the light it's clear the last sentence was originally *we need to talk about last night*. Even optimistic little me knows she isn't planning on discussing the next shag.

Alone, I read and read the short article in the newspaper. It seems a jogger saw a body on the shore by Wandsworth Bridge where it was caught on something. If I crane out of Dobbin's bedroom window I can see that bridge. It's only about half a mile away. My head begins to fill with questions to which I have no answers. Why was he down this way? Does he live nearby? Or rather, did he? The idea he might have been looking for me or even following me crosses my mind but even as I think it, it becomes an absurd thought. Pictures of him being ushered into that car return, especially McNoble's blank expression as he looked up at me. Should I call the cops? Tell them what I saw? Tell them about his background, about what he was doing and about Miles? But what is there to tell? I don't know anything, only what others have told me. It's not me who should be speaking to them, it's Natalie and Penny and Marita. Anyway, what did I really witness at the office, and with McNoble? A man who is usually cool asking me to draw up a panicked Will before being whisked away by two heavies, including one I know to be a brute, in a Mercedes with blacked-out windows. Nothing suspicious there at all, Harry.

I desperately want to talk to Penny or Dina. They'd know what to do and then I kick myself at how pathetic that feels. I must stop relying on others. No, I'll wait for Dobbin. He'll have good advice. I go and switch on the TV to watch the test match that we will inevitably lose. It is a perfect setting for my mood.

***

"Keep schtum mate." Dobbin has bought a McDonald's vanilla milkshake. I don't know what he sees in them, personally. They're part Dulux magnolia emulsion, part glacier that gives you an ice headache and coats your teeth in slime that sensible brushing doesn't remove. They're so trendy, though, that even the ever-cynical Dobbin has bought into the hype. "It's not like he was a mate or anything. You speak to the pigs and they'll have you locked up," he clicks his fingers.

"Why? I made his Will; I don't benefit. All I'd be doing—"

"It means sticking your neck out unnecessarily. They'll give you a good beating mate. You've seen what they're like. Anyway, you decide, I'm off to collect Vera."

"So, she's staying?"

"Christ, you bet. Geez, is she voracious?"

"You know her real name is Brenda and she was a law student with me?"

"Look, fuck off will you? Why'd you want to spoil the illusion? Her name means 'sex with penetration' okay? She told me. And that's what I plan to do."

"You're a Latin scholar now, are you?"

"I'm off. If you do get arrested give someone else's name as a reference, okay? I intend on being very busy."

After he's gone, I hesitate for an hour and then go to the flat below to call the police. They're polite and take a message.

It's Sunday and whoever is in charge is busy, advising me to call back on Monday. Penny doesn't appear by nine and I'm exhausted. Anyway, the last thing I want now is either to have sex or even worse any sort of conversation where I have to tell her about Sven. Maybe if she comes back and wants to sleep with me I can pretend to have some awful illness – like throat cancer – and not be able to speak and then in the morning sneak off to work and she'll find out from someone else. As I turn off the light and crawl under the sheets – they are rank and crusty, and I should have washed them – I decide life officially sucks.

Monday, 22nd June 1981

Chapter Twelve

In Which Harry Tries to Hide at Work and Ends Up in Court

"Mr Spittle. Please concentrate."

"Sorry Jean. I had some bad news and—"

"Please." When Jean uses 'please' more than once in a five-minute spell, you know better than to ignore what it is she is trying to get you to do. She's in potty training mode and there's no point doing anything but follow her lead, which mostly means listening. "You are paid to work here, not seek counselling or whatever the modern expression is. That is what the lunch break is for. If we can sort out today's work and I can get on with the post then we can talk at one, if you like."

She smiles. Not exactly unkindly. More like my French teacher when I had a go at an instant translation once; he had said, 'perhaps you should have tried German' but not in an unsympathetic way.

In theory, life should be easier as she has made a major concession in our relationship, namely she has offered to take dictation for my work as well as Jeremy's. There is a mountain to get through with Jeremy away for another week. But exposing what I've been doing on the files I look after, without her beady eye having corrected me every step of the way, fills me full of trepidation. I just know she'll read the carbons and be disappointed and, right now, I don't need her sighs to add to my already depressed state.

When she offered to take my work this morning she said, "At least you won't have to use that 'thing.'" She means the Dictaphone and it's true, I find it nearly as intimidating as the telephone, especially when someone is listening to me dictate. Although having my work typed by Sandra – she types for everyone who isn't a partner – has its pluses as she never questions my burbles and mumbles or, more generally, why I'm here in the first place.

"Come on, Mr Spittle. You were saying…" She reads back the last paragraph. She smiles. "We'll soon knock this on the head."

Maybe the fact she uses 'we' to suggest we are some sort of team in which I might have a useful part to play frees me up, because when I open my mouth the words flow in something suggesting coherence. I know it will be corrected but that's because we are both part of this together. Even if the golden and crisp prose produced by Jean bears little resemblance to what I actually say, I gain the distinct impression she actually thinks, sometime, in the distant sunlit future I could actually become a solicitor.

I've just finished a letter when Lucinda calls, asking me to pop up. Jean graces me with a smile. "Let me know when you want to check your letters."

I begin to float up the stairs on a cloud of goodwill, before the memory that Sven is dead reappears from where I've tucked it away at the back of my mind. I still can't believe it's really true. I probably ought to do something about finding out if he signed the Will. Probably not if truth be told. I wonder if I should call Natalie to see if she has an address for him. Although if she doesn't know, do I really want to be the one to tell her?

There are 14 stairs between me and Lucinda and in the time it's taken me to climb them my mood has shifted from sunny intervals to imminent squalls.

Lucinda is talking to someone and sounds very happy. She waves me to a seat and then hangs up. "You made a good impression, young man."

"I did?"

"Quite stunning if what I'm hearing is anything to go by."

"Erm, sorry to be obtuse but who?"

"Pen and Sean. That was Izzy. Your girlfriend also entered into the spirit of things, I understand." Does she wink? "I'm not sure I'd let Humphrey get away with that but you're a different generation, aren't you?" Who on Earth is Humphrey? Is that her husband? I'm not sure she's ever mentioned his Christian name before. "Anyway, Izzy was so taken with your discretion she wants you to deal with her next venture. Seems like she's putting some money into a small business that must remain hush-hush. You okay with that? It would be big for us. We've looked after her domestic affairs but recently she's used several other lawyers for her business matters so if we can get more from her that would be a coup."

"Er, yes. Sure. Of course." Things are looking up.

"And Harry, be warned. She will come on to you. She did with Jeremy when he was a trainee. He… well, he didn't cope well. Not a first, but things seem alright now." She frowns, like she's not sure if she believes what she's saying. "Just be careful." Her smile sort of dismisses me. Then she has a second thought. "Oh, and Philip wants you to go to the Courts. Perhaps you can pop down and see Edith. She'll know what's needed."

Still the office dogsbody. Ah well, I'm not likely to get ideas above my station for a while yet.

As I turn to go she says, "By the way, did you friend instruct you over her divorce?"

I've forgotten about that. "Er, she's undecided if she wants to go ahead, but she says if she does we will get the work."

"Good man. I'm glad she's working on a reconciliation. She must be too young to give up so soon."

"It will be her second divorce. She married someone from uni at 20 in her last year and he left her to go to Australia six months later. I'm pretty sure she doesn't want a reconciliation with her current husband. He's… well, I think he may have… that is…"

Lucinda's face changes in an instant. "Is he violent?"

I can manage a nod, even if the words stick in my throat.

"You know the police don't take domestic violence seriously, don't you? Do you know the statistics for assaults in the home?"

A shake is also within my range of skills, as I try to avoid her beadiest of stares.

"Harry, look at me. Does she need help?"

"I… that is…"

"Here," she rummages in a drawer and pulls out a card. "This is a woman's shelter in Camden. She could try there if she needs to get away quickly."

I take the card and study the details. Just a phone number. I turn it over. Blank. "There's no address?"

Lucinda says with a sigh, "You only get the address if you call first; it is to stop husbands finding out where the women have gone."

I can't stop shuddering. This is the sort of thing you see on the TV. Not in real life.

"Please call her. Today."

***

Natalie is in a meeting so I leave my number. I feel a large dollop of relief that I know is wrong, but still how likely is it she is actually at risk? Because I'm essentially a coward, I head for the basement to find out what instructions Edith has. Being out of the office seems pretty attractive just now.

The secretaries' room is large but gloomy with three desks at which Jean, Edith and Sandra work. Sandra's desk and the floor around it are a mess while Jean and Edith vie to have the neatest space. Jean is just finishing something that she rips out of her typewriter as I enter. She looks at me quizzically as I hang back near the door.

As usual Sandra doesn't look up, her face hidden behind her straight hair that hangs over her work. I wonder, not for the first time, how she never catches it in the typewriter. I can see she has on the earphones and is stamping her foot, which means she is trying to hear what someone has dictated. Probably Mr Tobble, another consultant who rents a room upstairs and who pays to have Sandra type up his letters.

"I'm still typing the letters, Mr Spittle." Jean sounds irritated, like I'm trying to rush her.

"No, of course. It's Edith I need to see."

That generates a scowl from both women. To Edith I say, "Lucinda told me you had something that needed doing for Mr Risely? A trip to court?"

The scowl becomes a smirk. "Oh yes. I wasn't sure if you were still required to do menial tasks, but maybe your position isn't quite as lofty as some people suggest." This last comment is evidently aimed at Jean. I smile a thank you at her, but I'm favoured with a deeper scowl. Clearly coming here in person was a mistake. I should have rung, or better still asked Jean to collect whatever it is. Ah, the subtleties of office politics.

I catch Sandra peering at me. She looks away hurriedly. She has a largish nose, bushy eyebrows and the wettest snog I've ever experienced, like kissing a sponge. That snog happened during the office Christmas drinks when we were all pretty drunk. She was having her drinks topped up by Mr Risely and caught me on the way to the gents. I was surprised because I didn't know she'd even really noticed me much at that point. And I have to admit to having allowed myself a couple of small rather smutty fantasies as the evening progressed, but it all went pear-shaped when she collapsed waiting for a cab that Mr Risely had ordered for her. He made me take her to the nearest hospital – the Middlesex in Fitzrovia – because he had to get home and couldn't stay. I ended up waiting with her until her Father came and dragged her off. He never said thank you and no one spoke about it the next week when we got back to work. It was like she had no memory of it and I thought it best not to say anything in case she was embarrassed about the whole unfortunate event.

"Here you are, Mr Spittle. They are urgent." I glance at the accompanying note. Pretty straightforward in fact.

"Right-ho. I'll let you know when I'm back, Jean."

None of the women say a word. I'm officially dismissed by them all.

***

The High Courts of Justice are on the junction of Fleet Street and the Strand, just where the Aldwych ends. The bus I catch, a number 15, stops by the Waldorf Hotel and I jump off while the bus is slowing. The curved façade of the buildings along the Aldwych seems to me a thing of beauty today. I take several paces towards Kingsway and then stop. Penny is a few yards away, talking to a woman who is pretty obviously actually a man dressed as a woman. I'm about to wave when the realisation that I've not told her about Sven hits me and I spin around and hide in the shadow of an awning. In any event Penny is engrossed in her conversation and takes the man, the woman, whatever, she takes an arm and they enter the Aldwych theatre. The entrance is dark – on the billboard outside it says Nicholas Nickleby is just ending its run and a new Royal Shakespeare Company production is due to begin soon – As You Like It. Is Penny auditioning for this? That would be amazing.

To avoid her suddenly re-emerging and catching me I hurry off towards the Courts. They are busy, as ever. I queue to issue two writs for small debts and then seek to execute a default judgement – Mr Risely's clients want to send the bailiffs in. All this takes an hour – 50 minutes of queuing and 10 of form presentation and begging. Par for the course really.

On my way back outside, I pass through what's called the Bear Garden, an area adjacent to the Master's rooms where solicitors and barristers meet up before appearing before the Masters – the 'lowest form of judicial pond life' was how Jeremy described them when he showed me around for the first time. They make small adjustments to writs or award interest on unpaid debts and are unutterably appalling people. Waiting to appear is like counting down to your execution, only you live to be executed again and again.

This time, because I'm not attending before a Master I can stop and watch the world go by for a moment, enjoying the sensation that some other poor sod is about to be eviscerated. There they are, my fellow sufferers, young trainee barristers and other articled clerks who know bugger all and it shows. To one side, in a relaxed group and laughing easily, are the confident attendees, the knowledgeable brethren, the old boys (always men, always ancient) in their shabby raincoats whatever the weather, who are classed as outdoor clerks and who have been appearing in Masters' chambers for decades. The Masters know them from when they (the Masters) were trainee barristers and there's a camaraderie amongst the downtrodden; both Master and outdoor clerk know that we whippersnappers aspire to move beyond their level in our careers as they once did and, for the few hours that they can lord it over us, they intend to enjoy themselves. Basically, the whole place reeks of schadenfreude.

Today, sitting with his head in his hands is a former Law School colleague. I recognise his bald spot; his name escapes me.

His obvious distress can only mean one thing. I say to the prematurely thinning pate, "You okay? Been Rothered?" Master Rother is the worst of this evil bunch and he de-bowels articled clerks for fun.

"Fucker had me begging for the judgement. Order fucking 14 and he does that. Not opposed or anything. How are you, Harry?"

I'm sure he's called Chas or Brian but I hesitate for now. I say, "He made me whistle last time. My client was a musician who'd not been paid, and the sod said I had to whistle one of his tunes before he'd give me interest on the debt."

"Did you hear about Karen? You remember Karen Himcol?"

"Can't say I do."

"Do you remember me?"

"A hint."

"Think Welsh Cock."

"John Thomas."

"Thanks. I hoped you wouldn't guess. Karen was the one going out with the Geordie bloke with no front teeth. Blonde, bit chinless, had really long arms."

"Purple hat."

"I'd forgotten that. Yeah, anyway she has to go in front of Rother and she's wearing this black skirt that buttons up the front. Apparently, he spotted some leg and insisted on her showing him how much, in case she was inappropriately dressed for his court. He even got one of those creeps to measure her 'exposure.' Poor thing was mortified. Someone should complain."

"You?"

"Me? You're kidding? The way things are going I'll be joining the ranks of the creeps. There's no work for newly qualified solicitors and when I qualify in November my firm have said all they have is an outdoor clerk's job until something else comes up."

John has reminded me that I need to think about my career and what happens when I qualify. I say, "Do you know where Karen works? She was friendly with Brenda, wasn't she?"

"Bren? The punk? Yeah, they were chums. Why?"

"My mate is going out with Brenda."

"Bloody hell. Hope he's got a leather dick. She'll wear it out." He digs in his briefcase and pulls out an address book. "Karen Himcol. Oh, she's a star, isn't she? Middleton Priestly. You got a pen?"

I take her number. She was nice was Karen. It's a shame when you lose touch. As John writes out her details I glance at Jackie's number, which is still faintly visible on my hand. Penny never asked about it; I wonder if she noticed? Maybe that's what she wants the word about. When John has gone, I check I've still got the card with Jackie's name and number on it and push it safely into my wallet.

When I get back, Mr Risely and Lucinda are interviewing for the next articled clerk. Time seems to be galloping ahead and I need to make some decisions about my future.

Tuesday, 23rd June 1981

Chapter Thirteen

In Which Harry Upsets Penny and Natalie and is Told Off by Jean and Lucinda

In the office a police constable rings to ask about my call on Sunday night and Sven. I tell him the little I know. I haven't yet spoken to Natalie – she didn't return my call – and judge it best not to mention her and the link to Sven before I'm sure she knows the bad news. If the police turn up with Miles around asking questions, heaven knows what he might do. I am rather worried I haven't heard back from her.

I tried to tell Penny about Sven last night but I'm pretty sure it didn't register. She came back about 11:00 clearly very pissed. After relieving herself loudly and at length she stumbled into the sitting room and slammed the door – I'd said I'd make tea and was in the kitchen. After 10 minutes when she'd not appeared I took the mugs and pushed open the door. She was lying on her back on the floor fighting to take off her boots. Our exchange (you couldn't really call it a conversation) went like this:

Penny: "Fuck off. I need my bed."

Me: "You're drunk?"

Penny: "Yeah. Fuck. So what? Give me a hand, can't you?"

Me: "What else have you had?"

Penny: "Oh, fuck off. Grab my boot, will you?"

I put down the mugs.

Me: "Who were you with?"

Penny: "Just pull the boot."

I grab it and yank it off. She falls back, giggling.

Me: "I need to talk to you."

Penny: "Yeah? And I need to sleep. Grab the other."

Me: "No listen, this is important. I saw—"

Penny: "Really? That's a first. And what do you mean 'who were you with?'"

Me: "…you going into the theatre today."

Penny: "You spying on me?" She waves her other boot. "Grab it."

Me: "No, I…"

And that's where the exchange ended. Her boot had a lump of dog turd attached, which transferred to my fingers as soon as I took hold. Her reaction was to laugh and tell me to take the boot and stick it in the sink so she could wash it clean in the morning. By the time I came back having scrubbed my fingers clean, not that that removed the lingering stench, she'd crawled inside her sleeping bag and was clearly asleep although she snuffled like a pig rooting for truffles. When the heavy breathing abated, I stared at her still, calm face, beautiful in repose and hated her for, oh I don't know what. In my head I told her Sven was dead and that I strongly suspected either or both of McNoble and Tupps being involved. A sound like something between a grunt and a fart issued from the gap at the top of the sleeping bag followed by a belch.

That was last night. This morning she wouldn't wake up despite my shaking her. I leave a note – 'Call me.' I add my work number, even though she knows it. I don't know why I bother.

After speaking to the police, who merely note they may want a word at some unspecified later date, I try Natalie again. The secretary assures me she passed on yesterday's message and Natalie read it. "I'm sure she will call when she has a moment." I toy with telling her about Sven to pass it on but decide that would be too brutal. I'm still wondering what to do when Jean enters. She has on her hat and coat. I'm amazed and check my watch wondering if it is already one o'clock and she is off for lunch.

"Mr Spittle, you have been with us just over 18 months and in that time you have shown yourself to be a pleasant enough member of the firm. Yet in the last few days your mood has soured and you are not performing in the way I have come to expect. I hoped you would have been able to buck yourself up. but it seems not. Please, put on your coat and we will go somewhere private. For a word."

The Jameson Coffee House on Marylebone Lane is so old fashioned it must be in a Dickens' novel somewhere. The waitresses wear black uniforms with hats and pinnies made out of doilies. The one who takes our order almost curtsies to Jean.

Jean has taken off her coat but retains her hat, a multi-layered affair in purple felt. Slowly she removes her leather gloves, which with hat and coat suggest November, not a sticky June. "Harry," I assume she sees my surprise, "you don't mind 'Harry' out of the office, do you?"

"I'd be happy with it in the office."

She shakes her head. "No, that wouldn't do at all. I have a cousin. Younger than me, of course. Rather full of herself. She works for a City firm on Cheapside. She tells me that they have these things called 'Annual Appraisals.' Some American idea, no doubt. All whine and hot air, those Americans. During the War, they thought a pair of silk stockings and a packet of cigarettes and a girl was there for the asking." Her face breaks into a smile. "They were right, of course, but the presumption still grates." She lays down her gloves. "I doubt appraisals will reach Clifford, Risely & Co. in my time, of which I heartily applaud. However, for someone such as yourself, finding a way to discuss whatever it is that is worrying you will, I'm sure, free you up to," here she leans in close and says in a whisper that feels like she is shouting, "DO YOUR JOB PROPERLY."

I could almost cry. The coffee comes as do iced buns, and while she moves the cups and jugs around like chess pieces I tell her about Sven and Natalie and Miles and Stephen McNoble. I also tell her about my worries for Brenda/Vera and Dobbin, without mentioning the sex. I don't mention my biggest worry, which is that Penny is pushing me away. When I stop, she sips her coffee like she's gathering her thoughts.

"So, none of this is exactly work related?"

"No, not really. We did Sven's Will but that's all. If he signed it, we will need to deal with his estate as I'm an executor along with Jeremy. But I've no idea if he did."

"I recall. We can discuss what you need to do later. Good. You were right to tell the police what you did and to keep Natalie out of it. But you need to tell her what's going on. Can you go and see her without her husband seeing you? News like that has to be delivered face to face."

"I could go to her office. She's in advertising."

"If she's divorced once already and on the verge of divorcing again and only 24 I'd have guessed advertising or banking. What about this Brenda? She needs rest, clearly."

"I think someone should tell her parents, although she's reluctant for them to know."

"Does she want them to know? If she's your age then she has a right to decide who gets to find out, however keen her parents might be to keep an eye on her. If they are estranged that may be the last thing she wants. And isn't that something for your flatmate to help her with? You don't need to take on everyone's problems, Harry."

"Yes, I suppose, although Gary is tied up with a new job. I'll ask him what he thinks." I had plans to ask Karen if she knew Brenda's parents, but I shelve that for now.

"And I hear you are to act for the Lady Isabella on some hush-hush project?"

"Yes. Maybe we shouldn't discuss that here."

"Well done, Harry. The Lady Isabella is a good woman whose reputation is tarnished by a pusillanimous press. It will be good work but be careful."

"Lucinda mentioned something."

"Good. Forewarned is forearmed."

I'm beginning to wonder what might be in store. It sounds quite exciting in a scary sort of way.

***

Natalie's office is on Red Lion Square in Holborn, a modern construction of glass and metal. It looks like the architect wanted everyone to be able to see right through it. As I stand with my back to the Square I can see right up the skirts of the women who are standing in a huddle in a first-floor meeting room, eating sandwiches. Was that part of the design brief, I wonder?

The receptionist is the polar opposite of Gloria. She is sleek, sophisticated and glacial with a light tan, subtle makeup and flawless talons of the deepest red. She offers me a smile that could easily go one of two ways in the twitch of a muscle: full on delight at my arrival or sneering dismissal if I disappoint.

"I have an appointment with Natalie Tupps?"

"Tupps?"

"Pendant?" Of course, she's kept her maiden name.

"Of course. Who shall I say?"

"Harry Spittle. Her lawyer." Why did I add that? It allows the smile to maintain its neutral position and trigger an eyebrow raise, but I may have started some unnecessary gossip.

I wait for a few minutes, studying the artwork displayed around the reception. They have apparently employed untalented seven-year olds. Some community project, I suppose.

Natalie appears, looking every inch the powerful executive with shoulder pads as wide as the door. "Harry. I got your message. I was going to call but we're frantic with the scrubber."

"Scrubber?" I force away images of some sort of office strip-a-gram.

"Oh, it's technical."

I can't help glancing at the receptionist. Her smile crumbles off her lips and she scowls at Natalie. What have I missed?

"I'll be an hour, Wanda. Hold my calls please."

I can't believe her self-assurance. I ache for the day I can tell someone to 'hold my calls.' While I imagine myself in a suit that isn't as shiny as the marble floor we've just left behind and a shirt that is a uniform white, Natalie leads me to a pub on High Holborn. The pavement outside is jam-packed with men in short sleeves, sipping pints of lager and women in pencil tight skirts and pastel blouses that seem to be barely buttoned up. The average age has to be about 20. Natalie nods at a few people who raise their glasses back at her.

"Through here." We fight our way into the gloom. The pub is choking with smoke that creates crazy patterns in the sunlight filtering through the brown-stained windows. There's a small space at the far end of the bar near the toilet sign. Natalie stops, says something to a barman drying glasses and beckons me towards the door to the toilets. "There's a garden, courtyard really, out back. It's empty and Rog'll keep it that way."

We sit on two metal chairs and let the sun warm us while we wait for the drinks. When we have them – something with tomato juice for her, a pint for me – I say, "Impressive. What do you have to do to get the barman onside like that? And have the drinks delivered?"

"Miles part owns this place."

Ah well, yes, that would do it. We drink. Then she asks, "What is it, Harry? If you're pressing me about the divorce, then back off. Miles has been a sweetie since Saturday. He's taking me to Venice on the Orient Express. He's said we'll spend more time together. He'll cut the business trips too. He's really trying. If you have problems with Penny, then spill."

I hold up a hand. "I'm here if you need me about the divorce but it's entirely your call. A friend said you might want this."

She turns the card over. "What's this? It's just a number."

"It's a woman's refuge. Safety if things don't pan out."

She drops it in the ashtray she has pulled in front of her as she lights up. "Sweet thought but not necessary. And I don't appreciate you gossiping about me to your friends."

"I never mentioned any name. But, as I say, up to you. The other reason is Sven."

"He's gone AWOL. Hasn't returned my calls. I suppose…"

"He's dead, Natalie."

She goes pale under her makeup. "Dead? No, that's not right. He can't be."

"He was found by Wandsworth Bridge on Saturday night. I saw it in the Sunday papers."

"No that's not right."

"They had a picture of him."

"But did it say it was him?"

"Yes. It had his name."

Natalie's hands begin to shake and she drops her cigarette. I pick it up and give it back to her. She says, "Poor Marita. I assume she's been told? I wonder how she's coping."

"Are you in contact? I suppose I should call, to make sure."

"Why you?"

"I, er…" It can't matter now. "I told you he asked me to write his Will? If he signed it, I'm his executor." I wonder where it is.

"Christ Harry, what is it with you? Are you only interested in your bloody fees?"

"It's not that. I have a duty—"

"You're sick, you know that? You're beginning to sound like Miles, just interested in the money."

That shuts me up. Natalie finishes her cigarette and lights another from the stub. "For the record," she forces me to look at her, "I know what you're thinking. Miles was with me all day." Once she's finished her mini-speech she grinds the cigarette butt out.

I finish my pint. "No one is saying there's anything suspicious about his death." Like finding him under a bridge is normal, Harry. "I'm glad you and Miles are working things out. I'd better get on."

"You are sure it was Sven?"

"Yes."

"Does Penny know?"

I hesitate. "Yes. I told her last night."

"Poor thing. How was she?"

"Okay. Look, I must go."

She looks about to speak but then shakes her head. She puts the cigarette packet away with her gold lighter. The handbag has a logo on it I've seen on the telly. I guess it must be pricey. As we stand she takes my hand.

I say, "If you have Marita's number, can I have it? I should call her. About the Will."

She looks at me and shudders. "Sorry. Yes. I think I have it at home. I'll call you. She must be wretched." Natalie covers her mouth and screws up her eyes. "Christ, this can't be true."

I watch her face crumple, tears cutting a path through her makeup. I'm not sure if I should try to hold her. In the end I hop a bit closer and hold out my arms in case she wants to latch onto me. She leans in but lets her hands hang by her sides, not touching me. We stand like this for an age. I glance at the door to the pub. No one is bothering us.

Finally, she blows her nose and dabs at her eyes. "I must be a sight. I'd better go and repair the damage. You'd better go too." She pulls me into a hug and whispers in my ear, "Harry, I'm frightened. I…"

Abruptly she pulls away. She's looking over my shoulder; the barman is watching us. She says, "I'll call when I get back from Venice." She brushes her lips against my cheek and is gone. The barman is still there, unsmiling. Somehow I know this will get back to Miles.

I bend to collect my case from beside the table and notice the card from the woman's shelter is no longer in the ashtray.

Chapter Fourteen

In Which Penny Leaves Harry and Harry Helps Vera

Penny is watching TV with Brenda/Vera when I drag myself up the stairs and let myself in. Brenda/Vera looks pale and ill, but at least she smiles. Penny looks fabulous and ignores me.

"Hi. All okay?" I'm dripping with sweat from cycling in the sticky heat.

Brenda/Vera nods. "You've got great legs you know, Harry. Gary's are like knotted string. If you weren't spoken for I'd get you to wrap them around me." She coughs, which then takes a grip and makes her eyes water. "Shit, I wish I was well. I hate being ill."

Penny doesn't look away from the screen. "If you're thinking about me kiddo, then don't. He's all yours. Don't get excited mind."

I think both Brenda/Vera and I know from her tone that this might not be the joke it should be. Sod her. "Great. I'll be in the shower, happy to help either of you good ladies with any of your frustrations."

Five minutes later I'm naked in the bathroom trying to decide if Penny was joking when the door opens. For a mad moment, I assume it's Brenda/Vera and panic about what I'll do. My penis gives me a hint what it would like. Of course, it's Penny. She hovers by the door. After a moment's silence, I turn off the water and look round the curtain at her.

She stares at me moodily. "Sorry Harry. That was a stupid thing to say. I didn't get the part and it's a real bummer. It was just to play a fucking mushroom, too, and that's not even the lead vegetable."

"I saw you in the Aldwych yesterday, going into the theatre as I went past. I was off to the Courts. Would you be working there?"

"The Aldwych? I wish. No, off the Caledonian Road in one of those Victorian pubs. The audition was held where the director is currently working."

"Anything else in the pipeline?" I drop the curtain. "Come in if you like?"

She stays where she is. "A piece of experimental theatre in Clapham – I worked with the director before. I'm pretty sure I know what he wants."

"Yeah? What's his modus?"

"Last time I sat at the back of the stage in just a CND T-shirt, masturbating with the handle of a badminton racket while this bloke, John, stood with his back to the stage, naked, and ranted about the Tories."

"You actually masturbated?"

"Christ no. They wouldn't let it be performed. It's all simulated. John used to play with himself during the Saturday matinees. Talk about boring but it was good money." I peer round the edge; she's perched on the laundry basket, staring at the steamy mirror.

I wait, knowing if I turn on the shower she'll go. Eventually I say, "About last night."

"Yeah, thing is I don't think this will work if you keep checking up on me."

"Checking up?"

"Waiting up. It's like, oh I don't know."

"Do you remember what I said?"

She frowns. "Not really." Then smiles. "I've met some great people. That party was fantastic, you know."

"Really?"

She grins at me. "You enjoyed the afters, didn't you?"

It's my turn to frown. "Of course. But you went all funny and then disappeared."

"Don't be a clown. I thought about it and there's no harm in us having some fun, just I'm not sure, you know?"

"I'm a dumb male, okay? Big bold single syllable words please. Not sure about what?"

"Us. Look, we can talk about it later. I've just met some really great people, people who'll help with auditions and stuff. They sounded really interested. And it would be proper stuff, not this pseudo pornography bollocks."

"Like?"

"Well some twentieth-century classics – Coward, Rattigan, Pinter. Plus a Stoppard that is being written just now. Maggie was really confident he'd love me."

"She's the one with the tit fetish, isn't she?"

"That was a joke, okay? Maggie Cloud. Remember that name."

"Why not? I'm sure it'll really help my legal career."

"God, you are a selfish—"

I turn on the shower again and drown out her moaning. She can bugger off. I've just picked up the soap when her hand appears inside

92

the curtain and yanks it back. She reaches past me and turns the water off.

"Listen, will you?"

I turn and face her, hands on hips, hoping I don't get a stiffy and show myself to be officially pathetic. "I'm listening."

She sighs, knowing I'm being childish. Pointedly she keeps her gaze on my face. "I'd be away a bit. Rep. It's the best way to get experience and get known."

"Sure."

"So – us. You know. It might not be so easy."

"Is this what wasn't on the note you left me?"

"Sorry?" It's her turn to be confused.

"You'd rubbed out the bit about us needing to talk."

"You checked my note?"

"No. It was lying there surrounded by the little bits of rubber. I could hardly fail—"

"Shit Harry. Fuck. You are checking up on me. Did you follow me to the theatre as well?"

I turn the water back on, making her step back to avoid getting soaked. "I had to go to the Courts. It's my job. Don't you get it? I don't care if you have to go travelling. I love you for fuck's sake. I want an us."

There's what is called a pregnant pause as we both allow the words 'I love you' and all its connotations bounce off the walls, get caught in the water and slip swiftly down the plughole. After a long moment when the only noise is the cascading water she looks at my nob, shakes her head and leaves. Who needs words?

I finish my shower. I don't even manage a wank. Feeling guilty that I've still not said anything about Sven, I dry myself quickly but, when I emerge, she's already gone out. Brenda/Vera is back in Dobbin's room, still coughing. I knock and look around the door. She's lying on the bed, looking exhausted.

"You're not okay, are you? Are you taking medicine?"

"Fuck off, Harry."

"Where is it?" There's a pot by the bed. I fetch water and read the details. Two every two hours. "Come on."

"No. I don't believe in medicine."

"You what? You'll pop a pill to get blasted when you've no idea what's in it, but you won't take real medicine when it's prescribed?"

"It's just big companies trying to screw the real people."

"You're not with your punk friends now."

She tries to stand and falls back. Between wheezes she says, "Maybe I should be. They'd understand."

"Right. You'd inject something, would you, just to numb the pain? Tis a death wish, my lady."

She rolls over to stare at the wall.

"I know you're saying I wouldn't understand but try me."

She takes a while but rolls back. She also takes the pills and swallows them. "My parents expected me to be the first woman House of Lords judge. No pressure. I tried to tell them I didn't want to go into law. At least not their sort. Fighting prejudice and inequality, sure." She has to stop to ride out the next bout of coughing. "My step-Dad was disappointed I wouldn't go to the Bar; he organised articles with a city firm. It was the same day, after the interview, that I went to see the Twats. You know what happened at that firm? I met three partners, men, all my Father's age. They asked about boyfriends, my family plans. One even asked about my contraception. He made it into a joke but shit. Then, when they're seeing me out, the senior one, the one who was at school with darling step-Daddikins said they had four nice young men who they'd arrange for me to meet. It was like they were putting me out to stud. The only thing they didn't do," more coughs and this time there's also a globule of stringy green phlegm that lands an inch from my trousers, but she doesn't even seem to notice it, "was pat my arse on the way out."

"So what did you do?"

"I took the fucking job, didn't I?"

"But the hair? The piercings?"

She sighs. "I gave it a year. Then I left. Mummy knows but he thinks I'm still there. Or he did until a couple of weeks ago. He thinks I've been staying in this flat they own in the Barbican when actually I've been in a squat in Kilburn with the boys. Mummy knew I wasn't in the flat, but I've not told her where I was. Now I'll bet they're out to find me."

I don't really know how to respond to that. I say, "I think you should sleep. If you can."

She nods. "Those men, those partners, they think I'm a piece of meat, Harry. I'm not playing their games."

"Should I tell your Mum you're okay?"

94

She shakes her head. "She'll have to tell him. She's very loyal and not very strong. And I can't deal with his shit right now." A single tear slips down her face, which is violently wiped away.

"When did you last see your Mum?"

"A few weeks ago. After I moved out and into the squat. I spoke to her a week or so ago, let her know I was safe." She smiles. "The boys will be pleased I've left."

"Too crowded?"

She leers at me. "They can't handle my needs."

Something tells me that she's making it up. For the first time, I think she's actually very lonely.

"Dobbin's a good bloke, Bren."

"Vera, please. Brenda is so passé."

"Okay. Don't push him too hard, okay?"

She nods. "Fuck, this is luxury compared to the squat, even with Gary's pants everywhere. I'm not moving out in a hurry."

"And you're sure you don't want me to tell her you're okay?"

Brenda/Vera remains tight-lipped. After a minute or two of rattly breathing I get up. "There's a tin of soup, if you want some?" She nods. "Any idea where Dobbin is? Still at work?"

Another nod before she says, "He said there was a bonding session for the new trainee staff in a pub; he told me to expect him late, drunk and ready for it. I don't think I'll be."

"I imagine you've fought off bigger wankers than a drunk Garfield."

"Yeah. Mostly. But I don't want to let him down."

"He's a good bloke. I accept that the sex is particularly appealing to Mr Dobbs, but he'll want you well first. If you say back off, then he'll back off. I think you'll find he'll pretty much do what you want."

To my surprise, she frowns. "I'm not sure that's what I need right now."

Dobbin arrives at 10:00, drunk but not inarticulate. I tell him she doesn't need him pawing her.

"I know, mate. She asleep?"

"I think so."

"Is Penny sleeping on the sofa again?"

"God knows. She says she's off for some auditions or something. I suspect she may not come back."

"You told her about your new friend? The nurse? You shouldn't keep her in the dark."

"Thanks for the advice, but there's nothing to say."

"What about that friend who died? She knew him, didn't she?"

I manage a huge sigh. "I didn't manage to tell her that either. I did try." I can see he doesn't believe me. Sod it. "You need to get Vera to talk to her Mum. She'll be worried."

"Yeah, like I can force her. She's a grown up. She can decide who she tells." I can see he's feeling guilty though. What a pair we make.

"If you've got a number, I'll call her."

"Thanks, but let's leave it for now. You worry about Penny, okay?"

He's probably right. He's starting to sway a little, which isn't a good sign; it's his transition point and any moment he will lose both his memory and control of his limbs. "Go to bed and keep your hands to yourself."

He manages a smile. "Good night, granddad."

Friday, 26th June 1981

Chapter Fifteen

In Which Harry Receives a Surprise Gift and Nearly Dies

The week goes by fast. Between us Jean and I have everything under control. When Jeremy returns on Monday he will be amazed. Jean has even extended her offer to do my work so it continues after he comes back, but I say we should maybe wait and see what her workload is like first. She says that is the nicest thing any lawyer has said to her since she started at the firm in 1947. Meanwhile, Lady Isabella's assistant has set up for me to meet the people whose business she wants to invest in with her on Monday afternoon. "Details to follow. We can go for some supper after. The Ivy." I know sort of instinctively that Jean will not approve if I go for dinner, which means I won't tell her.

Natalie is in Venice. She sent me a letter at the office to say she had not been able to track down Marita and she is worried because she has been living with a maiden aunt but upped and left 10 days ago, leaving no explanation and no forwarding address. The aunt was horrified when she heard about Sven and rang off. Natalie tried to speak to her again, but the phone was permanently engaged. Natalie had also tried to find out what the funeral arrangements are. According to the police no one has claimed the body. "It's up to the executors, Harry. That's you, right?" My heart missed a beat at that. If Sven did sign the Will, that's me and Jeremy. I wonder if she's spoken to Penny. Her letter doesn't mention it and now she's away she won't be in contact. I'll have to do something and soon.

Brenda/Vera is much better, even if she does play with her boobs a lot. Apparently they itch. Dobbin says they haven't had sex since she arrived and he's wondering if she's stringing him along, but I'm pretty sure she's just a bit tender all round. Last night she began talking about calling her Mum. She said she didn't know how to tell her, and I mentioned Karen, wondering, as they had been friends, if she might help. She made it pretty clear what she thought about Karen. I still think she should call. Her Mum will be going nuts.

Dobbin's job sounds good. There's a real chance he could be sent to Hong Kong shortly. Two of the 10 trainees are sent in the first four weeks, but they have to prove their worth. Dobbin is even coming home with text books full of numbers. He hasn't looked at them but sleeps with them under his bed, hoping to absorb the detail by a process of osmosis or something.

I'm not avoiding the Penny issue; it's just I don't know what's going on. Since she walked out of the bathroom following my declaration of love, she's only been back to the flat once while I was out. I know she works in a pub in Soho but if I go there she'll only accuse me of being a creep or something. At least there's a large bag of her clothes behind the sofa, so she's technically still resident. I guess I'll just have to be patient.

I'm at my desk pondering this fact and wondering what it means when Gloria puts her head around my door. "You got a minute, big boy?"

"For you Gloria, of course."

"I thought you were spoken for?"

"Me too, but today I'm not so sure."

"How's that hunky flatmate Gary?"

"You remembered his name. Impressive. Today, he is spoken for."

She scratches her ear and perches on the edge of my desk, her gaze resting on Jeremy's empty chair. I look at her sweet face in profile and glance at her fantastic boobs, the way her legs enter her skirt like they want you to follow. It's utterly heartless, the way she does that. She says, "Seriously? He left me his new work number. He sounded pretty free to me."

"He's a fast mover, Gloria." There's something about her smile, something so bloody knowing that I add, "At his leaving do, did you, you know…?"

Her grin is even bigger. "Wouldn't you like to know?"

"Never mind." God, she is beyond annoying.

"Did he find my message?" She widens her eyes, and in a voice, as sultry and husky as a committed 50 a day Woodbine addict, says, "Big Boy?"

I bloody knew it; they shagged. I will kill Dobbin.

Her expression changes quickly as she crosses and uncrosses her legs. "It was just a one-nighter, Harry. He's a bit needy for me if I'm honest and he was so pissed nothing really happened." She stands and walks over to Jeremy's desk, straightening his blotter. "I have a bit of a confession. Last Friday I was meant to give you this." She lays a long white envelope on my blotter. "You know that friend who came in, demanding you sort out his Will? He told me that if he hadn't come back by end of business Friday to collect it, I was to give it to you. You didn't come back from your trip to Mr Nowell-Jardine, or if you did it was after I'd gone. And it slipped my mind until today."

I hold the letter up to the light. "I'm guessing it's his Will."

"Will you give it to him?"

"No, not me. Thing is, he died on Saturday." I rip open the top. "He made me his executor along with Jeremy, which means we will need to sort out the funeral. I…" I'm holding the single sheet of paper. On one side is the Will we discussed, typed by Jean. That has been struck through. On the other is a handwritten Will, following exactly the same format as the typed one. Sven has signed and Edith and Mr Risely have witnessed it. There is one crucial difference from the typed version. Harold Spittle is named by Sven Lars Andresen as his sole beneficiary.

"Are you all right, Mr Spittle?" Jean has entered with the typing. She takes the sheet from me and reads it. All I can think is that I would really rather like to crawl over to the fireplace and hide up the chimney.

"Gloria, please go and make Mr Spittle a strong sweet tea. Mr Spittle stay there – don't move."

I can't move anyway and am happy with her advice. The walls are slowly coming towards me; soon enough I'll be in a quiet dark place and happy. Right now, all this daylight and open space is too much. I fight the urge to slip under the desk. Gloria brings me the hot sweet tea and makes me sip it; it scalds my tongue, which brings me back to the present. Jean returns and says, "Mrs Plum-Wardle is coming down."

Lucinda appears and there is a hushed conversation about me and the Will. Lucinda pulls up a chair and faces me, while Jean sits in Jeremy's seat. I'm conscious that this must be important if she is prepared to violate the sanctity of her boss's throne.

"Harry, listen. Is this valid? So far as you know?"

"Yes. Jean typed the first one he asked for. He must have written his own in reception while I was with Sir Penshaw. I suppose those are proper witness signatures?"

"Edith assures me it was done properly. The young man was insistent although he covered the Will itself. Edith thought it very suspicious, but Philip approved it. Now, is it true he's dead?"

"Yes. He was found under Wandsworth Bridge on Saturday sometime. Quite near my flat. I've spoken to the police briefly."

"And where were you?"

I stare at her. "Me? When? Why?"

"Listen. I'm not thinking or suggesting anything. If it is suicide, then that is the end of the matter. Do you know?"

"I... no. I spoke to the police on Monday. I told them about the car."

"Car?"

"He left here in this car with two men. It looked sort of forced."

"What did the police say? When you spoke to them on Monday?"

"They said they'd come back to me if they needed to."

Lucinda lapses into a deep thought. Then she says, "Okay. Leave it for the weekend. Mr Andersen is going nowhere. They will keep the body until after the corner's verdict, I expect. Does he have next of kin?"

"His sister, Marita. I think his Mother is alive, but she lives abroad. They are... were estranged. There's an aunt. Oh, and his Father is dead."

"Are you in contact with any of them?"

"No. I... I heard this from a mutual friend. She is trying to find contact details for Marita."

"So as far as you know, no one is pressing for the body? For a cremation or burial or anything?"

"No. I don't think so."

"Fine. We will talk about this on Monday when Jeremy is back. If the police do call you should tell them all you know. About the Will, everything. As Jeremy's an executor too, he needs to be involved. Try not to think too hard about it, okay? Just have fun." She begins to leave. "And well done."

"Sorry?"

She leans across the desk and taps the bottom of the page. "The charging clause. We get our fees for all the work you do. And my guess is there will be a lot of work."

I feel ill.

Chapter Sixteen

In Which Harry Goes Out and has an Unexpected Encounter

When I get home, Dobbin and Brenda/Vera are in the kitchen. She's already on his lap; they giggle as I come in and my sense is they have just had or are about to have a romantic liaison. I suppose I'm just jealous.

"Hey Spittoon, you free tonight?"

I drink a pint of water, belch and shake my head.

"Vera's singing. The Twats are back. They're doing a gig in Tottenham. You coming? Bring Penny. It'll be amazing."

"I don't know." I fill the kettle. "Tea?"

"Yeah okay."

I say to Brenda/Vera, "You feeling okay, then?"

"Yeah. And Harry, you were right. I called my Mum."

"You did?" Brenda/Vera's cheeks are getting pinker. I can't see Dobbin's hands under the table. Dirty sod. "Good for you."

"Yeah. Christ Gary, stop for a minute. If you make me any wetter I'll stain the lino. Yeah, I told her I was playing again. She said she was proud of me. Be great if you could come. Sitting in bed, I wrote a new song. The boys will love it. Bet you will too."

"Don't you have to rehearse?"

She glances at Dobbin and they break down in giggles. Dobbin eventually says, "You heard them, Spittoon. Did it sound like they rehearse?"

She says, "Yeah. That's for those wankers who have a record deal; just part of the fucking patriarchal tyranny that tries to fill my fanny with their shit."

"Lovely image. I—"

The front door opens and closes, and Penny appears in the doorway. "Hi all. You're looking great, Vera." She barely glances my way.

"We were just asking Harry if you can come to my gig tonight. It'll be mental. I'm performing my new song."

"I… I'll have to pass. I'm… I'm going away for the weekend." She looks at me with that. "Meeting some people."

"Yeah?" Both Dobbin and Brenda/Vera look from me to Penny and back. "Somewhere special?"

"It's a house party in the Cotswolds. A few theatre people."

"Wow." Brenda/Vera is now staring at me. "Sounds posh."

"It's with Maggie and some friends, contacts of hers. Some really big people in the theatre will be there. Maybe."

"Really?" I say.

"Yes really." She sounds annoyed and I guess I do sound a bit sceptical. "Peter Hall. Jonathan Miller. Sean Latterly, maybe. He's Sir Penshaw's boyfriend. Harry and I met him at a party last weekend."

Brenda/Vera does this excited clapping thing that looks a bit like she's taking the mick to me, but Penny beams at her. "I might get some great intros this way. I'm just back to grab a bag and a few things. They are swinging by in about half an hour." All this is said at a rush.

The kettle has boiled. To keep from screaming I carefully warm the pot and open the drawer for a spoon. Three spoonfuls and one for the pot, as preached by Mum.

Brenda/Vera says, "Hey, that's a shame. Still sound great, doesn't it Harry?"

Before I can speak Penny says quickly. "Oh, Harry won't... I mean this is really just business. It would be great if he could come but it'll be really boring – loads of theatre gossip and little playlets – they perform for each other. Harry will be bored rigid! If he sees your set he can tell me all about it."

I'm still facing away from the others, looking at the wall behind the cupboards, holding the pot in one hand and the spoon in the other. This is so annoying; I don't trust myself to turn round and face them. Rather than put the pot down I use my hip to close the open drawer. It sticks, and I try again. And then harder. Fucking thing. I'm now determined to shut it and, taking out my frustration on it, I give it a real push and it flies back in place. As I'm still in my shorts from cycling, everything is rather loose and somehow I nip my left testicle as the drawer slams shuts. It's like being kicked by a rather angry tungsten-heeled mule.

Brenda/Vera is saying something like, "Are you okay?" I can feel their eyes on me. I can sense Penny's tension, wondering how I'll react, knowing I can't really scream like I want to with them there. In truth, I cannot breathe. My eyes are full of tears and my throat full of bile. Slowly, imperceptibly at first my knees give way and I sink to the floor. I manage to put the pot down on the way. Once I'm kneeling I lean my head on the kitchen unit and concentrate on my breathing while moaning deeply. I think I hear Penny say, "Oh for fuck's sake, grow a pair."

When after a few moments I look around, everyone has gone, embarrassed by my dramatic response to the news and totally unaware of my crushed testicle. Dobbins' bedroom door is shut, and the muffled noises suggest I was right about the sex. Part of Brenda/Vera's warm up.

I find Penny in the sitting room, checking the bag of her clothes. Before I can speak, she says, "That was childish. Don't you want me to get some real work or do you prefer me as a barmaid? Is that it? You have the proper job while I make do. Part of chivalrous Harry, who will look after me forever, lock me in my ivory tower and save me. Well, I want this. This is my chance and you aren't fucking it up for me."

"I want you to go."

"I haven't had a decent break since... What? You do?"

"Yeah. I've had a shit week and I'll be shit company. Go and have fun."

She stops, looking for a moment like her old self. She drops the bag and comes to me, putting her arms around my neck and kissing me. I don't respond. Not really. Much. "I need this."

"I know. And I need you, but those things may not fit together, yeah?"

She holds my gaze forever and nods. "Yeah. I—"

I put a finger on her lips. "Shush. My turn. I need to tell you about Sven."

"No wait. I think we may have to accept we aren't, you know, proper boyfriend and girlfriend."

"What's that even mean?"

She sighs. "We have fun. The sex is... it's good. No, great. But, well, you can't decide can you? If you want me or..."

"Is this about Natalie? Because that wasn't my fault."

She drops her gaze, then looks up. "No, it's not about her. It's about you. And me. We need to think. Really think." She reaches in and kisses me, holding me by the neck. "I fancy you rotten, okay? It's great when we fuck. But there's an awful lot of me wondering when you'll grow up."

"Me?"

She looks at her watch. "We can't do this now. Please?" Another kiss. "What about Sven?"

Clearly she doesn't know. Do I say now? It'll seem spiteful, and it'll ruin her weekend. Part of me says, why not after what she's just said, but the other part tells me this is the sort of thing she means about not being a grown up. It can't hurt to leave it, can it? And she has just kissed me, like, well, like we may still be a couple. Ish. Sometime. And she still likes the sex. Which is a plus. "It'll keep. You just have a great time and land the part you deserve."

She smiles and comes in for another kiss, rubbing against me. "Thanks." A car horn blasts from down below and she lets her head drop. She kisses me again. "Thanks Harry. Go and enjoy Vera getting her tits out, okay?"

"Oh right. Remember I've seen them explode with puss. I don't think they'll ever work as a stimulant, thanks."

"Take Gloria. She's game, isn't she?"

"You're not—"

She grabs my jaw in her hand, her eyes going dark. "Yes. I am. You need to see how much you care about me. Anyway, I may have to offer myself up for lesbian sex this weekend."

"Les…? What…?"

She picks up her bag and checks out of the window. "I must dash. Be good or be careful."

And she's gone.

Lesbian sex? Since when has she been a lesbian? Or even bisexual?

Moments later she's back. She dives behind the sofa and yanks out a bikini, dumping the top and keeping the bottoms. "There's a pool." She shrugs and is gone again.

When she's shut the front door, I go to the hall window and look down at the street below. A woman with a mass of hair, a mix of purples and gold is waving up at me. It's the woman from the farcical beauty pageant. Maggie, the boob squeezer. She's standing by a Triumph Stag with the roof down. When Penny emerges from the front door they kiss. Like Penny and I just kissed. Not like how friends kiss. Penny looks up and waves her bikini bottoms and climbs in. Maggie climbs in the driver's side and leans over and they kiss again. Bloody hell. She means it.

***

Four hours later with my balls still aching, partly from the kitchen crush and partly from the over-vigorous anger-wank I've had in the shower, Dobbin and I leave Brenda/Vera with her band, who already seem spaced out to me and head for the bar. The pub is full of Spurs supporters, chanting songs about their Jewishness and how Arsenal are all arse bandits. A boisterous bunch. "Will she be okay?" I ask. "Last time out the crowd nearly lynched the Twats."

"One of their own."

"What?"

"Haven't you twigged her surname?"

"Copula?"

"Her real name. Silverman. She's Jewish. They know apparently. Or so she says." He sups his pint. "Anyway, she has a trick or two up her sleeve. Or should I say shirt."

"Surely to Christ she's not stupid enough to mutilate her tits again?"

"Better. Much better. Watch and learn."

Dobbin leaves me to go for a piss and seems to have disappeared. I'm happy, positioned towards the back. My hair is too long for the boys here and I've been getting some odd looks. While I was polishing Percy in the shower, I thought about what Penny said. About Gloria, or other women. I'm pretty sure, in our occasional bust ups, she's gone off and had sex with other blokes but despite thinking about it, I remained loyal. Mostly because I'm pretty much a dick with women anyway. Which meant when we got back together there was always a whiff of, not exactly resentment, but something.

I keep an eye on the door. I called Jackie the nurse when I came out of the shower. The number she gave me is a nurses' home somewhere near the Elephant. The woman who answered promised to leave a message. She said 'Jacks' was knackered after a 12-hour shift but if she surfaced in time she'd mention the gig. She said, "You Colin?" When I said 'no' she sounded disappointed. I started to explain how we'd met but she rang off. I don't suppose she'll remember me and come to the gig, but it doesn't do any harm to have hope. It's a sort of test, to see if I can be attractive to another woman even if I don't want to exploit the opportunity.

In truth, I'll be glad if she doesn't come because I'm not sure what I'll do if she does. I'm certain – at least for about a minute – that Penny is off with Maggie and the chances are they will have weird sex. I mean Penny isn't a lesbian so it's going to be weird, isn't it? Some

106

sort of actor's thing? Or maybe they knew I was looking and did it for a joke. Sick fucking joke. I swallow a gulp of beer and choke. Maybe they've already had sex? I mean, Penny's been out a lot recently and sleeping on the sofa, so she could slip out or come back late. I check again. It would be good if Jackie did come, at least for my ego.

One benefit of this focus on me and Penny and how much of an us we still are is I haven't given much thought to Sven and his Will. I'm just wondering what being an executor really means when it's someone like Sven when the lights dip and the stage explodes with noise. The crowd go totally mental and the Twats appear. Brenda/Vera looks amazing. She's splashed red dye in her hair and it's dripped down her face and soaked into her T-shirt. Then I wonder if it's blood. She begins to screech into the mike and, whereas before the crowd booed and hated it, this lot love her. Having done a song that sounded like 'Fill me up you bastard' which might have been to do with buying petrol, although the gestures suggest otherwise, she leans forward and raises her hands; a sort of silence falls.

"Wotcha people." Her voice is thin and reedy and sounds amazing through the speakers. "I've been ill. Poor little me."

Huge muscled stevedores or whatever they are call back, "Ahhh" with their arms raised, tattoos rippling down their forearms like an approaching thunderstorm.

"But my boyfriend shagged me so hard and my fanny is so raw, it's like twat tartare." I doubt this culinary allusion has the anticipated resonance with this specific audience, whose idea of a fancy meal is to have meat with three veg, but the accompanying gestures make things pretty clear and more cheers ensue. The house goes mental again.

After that they just play and she screeches. It's giving me headache, so I head outside. Standing by the door, like she wants to come in but can't decide, is a woman of about 50 wearing a Burberry mac and paisley headscarf. Most of her face is hidden by huge dark glasses but as I squeeze past I see her profile. She's the spitting image of Brenda/Vera.

"Mrs Silverman?"

She stares, startled. "Do I know you?"

"No. Harry Spittle. Ve— Brenda is staying at my flat. She's… um… that is…"

"You're not Gary?"

"He's my flatmate."

She sighs. "Is she all right?"

"She's getting better. The tablets are working. Now that she's taking them."

"I meant in there. The audience sound… involved." She takes off her glasses to reveal worried eyes with dark bags underneath. "I've been very anxious about her. You said something about tablets?"

I look at her eyes. "Just some… anyway, she's going down a storm. Have you seen her on stage?"

"No, I… she wouldn't like it."

"She wouldn't know. She's not the voice of the century but she certainly has a presence."

It takes me a little more encouragement but eventually Zenda – she tells me her name much like a spy uses a special code – agrees. "You might look less conspicuous if you took off your coat and scarf."

She obliges. Her hair is tightly permed and has a blue hue.

"Brenda's hair is red tonight."

She ignores me, her eyes flitting here and there, taking in the mass of sweating bodies, men and women pogoing to the manic beat of the Twats. Brenda/Vera is standing in the middle of the stage apparently using the microphone as a dildo, the scraping noise as she rubs it against her torn tights sending feedback through the speakers. I'm beginning to wonder if I've made the right decision to encourage her Mum to watch.

The song ends, and Brenda/Vera turns to the lead guitarist. They exchange some sharp words before he shrugs, and she turns back to the crowd. "When I was in bed letting my tits get better," I've stopped looking at Zenda. This was a mistake. "I had an epiphany. I woke with this song fully formed in my head. Like fucking dope-head Coleridge."

I hope Zenda recognises the benefit of her daughter's private education because I'm sure Tottenham doesn't.

"See, it's the fascist fucking elite that have created the environment whereby you poor fucks are scrapping a living and have to come and listen to our shite as some sort of rebellion. So, this song is for all of you who are broke, on the dole or just fucked off with the State's oppressive machinery."

A few heads turn to their friends, bemused puzzlement creasing their brows, but I'm impressed; I never took Brenda for some sort of committed Socialist. I wonder what she'll make of Dobbin's super rich parents and their enormous house in Norfolk and boat at Cromer and summerhouse in the Dordogne. Mind you Zenda doesn't look short of a bob or two; I glance across. She's engrossed; captivated.

Brenda/Vera taps a beat on the mike stand and the Twats take it up. She nods along before launching into her call to revolution.

"Maggie Thatcher has no cunt, Maggie Thatcher has no cunt, Maggie Thatcher has no cunt. She's a fucking man."

I close my eyes. I cannot look at Zenda. I can hear the crowd pick up the lyrics (that appears to be the extent of them) and the song goes on for a good two minutes. When it finishes with a huge crescendo of roars I look at the stage. Brenda/Vera has dropped the mike and grabbed the hem of her T Shirt. With a yank, she rips the front in half to reveal her bare chest. Briefly I fear for her nipples, but I needn't. Someone has painted Maggie's head across her chest in the same blood red as her hair. They have managed to use her nipples as the pupils of Maggie's eyes, manically bloodshot, glaring out at us as they jiggle to the music.

I look towards Zenda expecting a mix of disgust and horror. Instead I see her Mum clapping above her head and then sticking two fingers in her mouth and letting off the most piercing whistle ever.

As the whistle cuts across the room, Brenda/Vera, whose arms are aloft, soaking up the adulation, stops and stares. Still topless she bends and picks up the mike from the floor. She points it towards Zenda and then bellows into it, "Hi Mum."

The crowd seem to envelope Zenda and propel her forwards. I move the other way towards the door. My brain is scrambled.

"Quite a show. Looks like she's better." It's Jackie. She is only about five three, which makes her stretch up to kiss me quickly on the mouth. "You want to stay or can we go somewhere for a pint and a pie? I'm famished."

It's after 11:00 and all the pubs will be shut. Or so I think. When I say this, she shakes her head. "Come on. There's a pub behind Bart's where the girls go after hours. It'll be a lock-in, but I'll sort it out.

The Frilly Pig is an awful looking place just off Aldersgate. It appears to be not just shut but ripe for demolition. Jackie doesn't try the front but goes down a side passage and begins to climb a wall. A less than friendly voice says, "Who's that?"

"Friend of CJs over from Tommy's. Bloke in tow."

"Right you are, love. Give us your hand."

One moment Jackie is standing on a box reaching over the wall, next she disappears with a scrape and a giggle. The same gruff voice says, "You coming or what?"

I follow on to the crate. It's easy to push onto the top of the wall and look down. Below is a small courtyard with Jackie pulling down her skirt and an old boy wearing a green knitted cardigan and dark cords watching her. He's holding a fag and grinning. I can see all this by the light that is spilling out the back door of the pub.

Inside it is rammed, mostly it seems with medical people, some still in uniform or white coats. The age range is wide, too, from kids who look about 12 but are all first-year medical students to a couple of old boys who Jackie says are the top oncologists in London. They are clearly all pissed.

"That singer was quite something. And her Mum. I can't imagine mine seeing me like that. God, I think she'd have a heart attack."

Jackie is incredibly easy to talk to. Or listen to as she chats away about the bastard doctors and the sweeties, the mad patients and the creeps. "You would not believe the number of men who think we are there to be groped. I blame Benny Hill, with those big breasted nurses chasing him everywhere. One old boy had in two drips and a drain and could barely lift his head, but he got a hand inside my uniform quick as you like."

Somehow we begin to talk about families. As I tell her about how Mum and Dad are back together in the family home I realise I haven't called them since I received Dad's letter. She asks about my sister Dina and again I feel guilty that I've not written. Last I heard, she was aiming to go to uni in Newcastle in September. "She's had a tough time. She's 21 and had a baby boy when she was 17. Screwed up her A levels – she got 10 Os, all As and Bs – she then went to a sixth form college and got three As. I think she plans on studying biology."

"What about her boy?"

"Yes, that's tough. She hated him at first. But the Father, Jim, is a good lad – car mechanic, a bit dim – he wants to be involved and his Mum has been amazing. Jim's Father left his Mother about the time they found out about the pregnancy. I think he's shacked up in Thailand. Dina lived with them while she went to college. I'm not sure how Jim will cope with Dina so far away if she takes George."

"Surely she can't?"

"I don't know. I'm certain, knowing Dina, that she'll have it all sorted."

"What did your parents think about being grandparents?"

"Mum was great when we found out Dina was pregnant," I shudder remembering how I had to get the pregnancy test checked, and how

Penny pretended it was hers, "and Dad… he never really said anything. They – Mum and Dad – were having some problems of their own at the time." I pause and look at Jackie. She has an easy smile and her face creases as I stare.

She taps my hand. "My round. Another?"

It must be my sixth pint spread over about six hours. I feel mellow rather than pissed. "Sure. I'll take a leak while you grab them."

The gents let you know their whereabouts long before you find the door. Why is it that medics prefer the most unsanitary of places to hang out? There's a man standing at the urinal when I push open the door. His back is vaguely familiar. As I approach I realise it's Stephen McNoble.

"Fuck. Spittle. Twice in a week? I am a lucky boy."

He stands by the sink, clearly with no intention on washing his hands, which from the state of the porcelain may well be a shrewd move, and says, "We should have that drink. Loads to catch up on."

"Really? Can't think what."

"Miles wonders why you're suddenly spending so much time with Natalie for instance. He's a possessive man."

"Am I?" Once upon a time I'd have been cowering in the corner with him in a small room alone but now, big though he is – and he is huge, having put on both muscle and a waist – I don't much care. Maybe it's the booze coursing through my system.

"Mate," that grates, "You want to think a bit. That bird is his trophy. If you start putting your fingers all over one of his trophies, it's like theft and he doesn't react kindly to that."

I shake off the last drips, regretting I haven't taken more care given the recent bruising. "Since when did you look out for my best interests?"

There's a standoff while I wait for him to move aside. I try to make the taps work without success. Behind me he says, "We need to talk. About Andersen. And his Will."

Moments later the door bangs shut. He's gone. There's no sign of him in the bar either. Jackie smiles at me. "You were saying about your parents?"

"What? Was I?"

"Are you okay?"

"Me? Yes, sure. Not much to tell. Pretty standard stuff. Mum had an affair with a crook who tried to cripple Dad. I thought the crook might be my real Father. According to a recent sighting Mum and Dad are back together. Yours?"

She's laughing. "Oh, much the same. If yours are back together that's good."

"Is it?"

"Are you always this miserable? You were full of the joys when you went into the toilets and you came out twitchy and with a face like a wet fart."

"I bumped into someone in there. He's... well, he gives me the creeps. Sorry, let's forget about him."

She shakes her head. "No. You have two minutes to get whatever off your chest and then we forget about that." She pulls one of those upside-down nurses' watches from her pocket and makes a show of looking at it. "...and go."

I manage a laugh. "Nothing in my life is great. I've got more problems than I know what to do with. At work they think I'm incompetent and I may not have a job at all soon. A friend, well sort of friend, has died and left me to look after his affairs. The police suspect me of having a part in his death, which may be suspicious. My girlfriend has left me for a lesbian. My family is the epitome of dysfunctional. My flatmate as you know has begun a relationship with a sex-mad sadist who sticks chillies up his anus. He—"

"Stop!" She grins. "Bloody hell Harry. There's so much there I want to ask about. Mostly the girlfriend."

"Not the chilli?"

"Later."

"You're not a lesbian, are you?"

"I've never tried. That said, I'm pretty happy with the status quo."

"Good."

"The chilli thing?"

"No. I mean, I'm not saying we'll get to that point but I'm not... what?"

She is weeping with laughter. "I was going to ask if you knew why."

"She said it prolongs his performance. Christ, she is so demanding I think he might well die. Does it?"

She shrugs and finishes her drink. "No idea. I'm pretty old fashioned where sex is concerned."

"Oh."

My face must give away my disappointment. She manages to combine a look of disapproval, similar to Mrs Johnson at primary school when I spilt red paint over the school hamster with a sort of sexy nurse tilt to her head that has come hither written right through it like Brighton rock. "This is barely a first date, Harry."

"Yes. No. It wasn't that."

She reaches out and takes my hand. "I meant I like sex to be straightforward. That's all."

"Right. Yes. So, another?"

"No, I think I'd like to go somewhere quieter."

Within no time she's dragged me from the pub to a quiet side street between Barts Hospital and Smithfield market. She seems to be very familiar with a loose hoarding covering a building that looks like it might actually be redeveloped. Once behind it, she pushes me against a wall and we kiss. That doesn't really do justice to the tongue Olympics that we indulge in. I manage to find a breast, even though I pretty instantly get cramp in my thumb because of the tightness of her upholstery. She whispers what sounds like 'take it off' but in the pitch dark and with the outer clothes that's beyond me. Instead my hand is, unexpectedly and gloriously eased under her skirt and inside her pants. Her moans and the way she very nearly severs my tongue in her excitement tells me all I need to know about her old-fashioned ideas on sex. The difficulty is that images of Penny keep coming back to me. I shake them away. She was the one who suggested I rummaged elsewhere after all.

"Your turn." I'm suddenly very aware that she's pulled my hand away and is opening my flies. There's a bit of struggle that is hardly a surprise as my penis has managed to convert the pints I had earlier into tungsten and then he's free. The cold air feels odd but then he's warm again and, well, it all happens a bit quickly.

She stands up and kisses me while still massaging my softening member in her free hand. "Sorry you can't come back to mine. Rules."

That's the perfect time when I should ask her to the flat. But between the moment she began to tug at my fly and now a tsunami of guilt has been building and overwhelms me. All I can think about is Penny, probably working hard at networking with all sorts of dull people (some of whom might be voracious predatory lesbians) while I'm accepting a blowjob from someone I barely know.

"I guess I'd better see you back then."

She lets my nob go and adjusts her skirt. "No. It's fine. I can get a bus." She takes my hand and we begin walking in silence, which she breaks with, "How long ago did you split up?"

I don't know what to say. I'm so bad at lying.

"It's just I sort of get the impression you'd now rather be somewhere else."

"No. I... look, that was fantastic. Really."

"I split up about nine months ago and work has been so manic I've not had a chance to, well, you know. Have sex. Maybe I misread things. Sorry."

I stop her and pull her to me. "You're right. My relationship is complicated, and it feels like it's broken but, well, sometimes... most of the time, I misread things too. That was brilliant and, well, I'd love it if... no, that's not right. Can we just maybe see? I know that sounds a bit pathetic."

She reaches up and kisses me. "That's the first proper orgasm I've had in ages so I'm not about to complain, even if you've given me thrush. But, no, I'm not going to make the mistake of putting effort into something if it doesn't have a decent prospect. So, make your mind up and then we can see. Okay?" A shaft of streetlight illuminates half her face giving her a somewhat manic stare. She laughs briefly. "Look at you! You're the one with the 'not tonight, Josephine' issue."

In the end she doesn't catch the bus and we walk all the way to the non-descript tower in Elephant and Castle where her residence is. We kiss a bit more and I offer her seconds, but she declines, which is a shame because I'm pretty sure I could manage a repeat.

After we say good night, I follow the river home. Soon I pause by the bridge where they found Sven, trying to imagine how he ended up there. It totally sours my mood and I'm craving my bed when I turn the last corner. Sitting on my doorstep, dozing on her rucksack, is my sister Dina. A small teddy bear hanging from the strap is pressed into her cheek making it look like she's being eaten.

I give her a shake. "Tea?"

She peers up at me and stretches. "You been out on the rut, H? What's her name?"

"Mind you own business. Come on. You can tell me to what I owe this pleasure."

Saturday, 27th June 1981

Chapter Seventeen

In Which Dina Sets Harry Up

I realised a while back that the fact Dina and Dobbin got on well would end badly for me. We are drinking tea at the kitchen table when Dobbin crawls out of his bedroom. He looks like the victim of a car crash what with red dye all over his torso, presumably transferred from Brenda/Vera. As soon as he sees Dina he perks up.

"What you doing here, sister? How's the boy? Greg? Geoff? No, George. Georgie Porgie, of course. And Jim. Good lad that one. Off to uni, I hear. What's the plan?"

Since Dina and I have been talking about Mum and Dad and the awful atmosphere at home we haven't moved on to her plans. "Yeah, great. George is good, thanks. With Mum just now but he's mostly been with Jim's Mum. I'm after an offer from Imperial. That's why I'm here, for a day of interviews and stuff to see if I can transfer my place at Newcastle; I'm trying Queen Mary's and King's too."

"You never said?" I pause, mug halfway to mouth.

"Thing is H, it's so far away and with George, I'm not sure I want to, you know..." she peters out.

Dobbin nods like he understands. "It'll be hard, with a kid and what-not and going to uni."

"He starts school this September and I'm hoping I can work it in. If I can get a place at a London uni then we, Jim, George and I can live here."

I put the mug down. Hard. "When you say 'here'?"

Dobbin pulls her into for a hug, "She means in this flat. Tim won't mind. It'll be great having you here."

Dina eyes me warily. "I'm not sure H is so keen..."

Dobbin waves vaguely at me. "Oh, he'll come round or he can move out. Vera and I were talking about having kids yesterday."

I goggle at him. "You were?"

He barely acknowledges my interruption. "We thought maybe four. She'll come off the pill just as soon as I know if I'm going to be based here or in Hong Kong."

"You're kidding me?"

Dina smiles. "That's fantastic. Er, who's Vera?"

"Me." Brenda/Vera wanders in, wearing a T-shirt that doesn't go as far as I would like. Dina doesn't seem to mind the sight of her pubes, but my tea is now very unappealing. She reaches up for a mug and I look away. When I look back she's on Dobbin's lap. He introduces Dina.

I leave them to it and go to shower and put on fresh clothes. They are still talking animatedly; I strip my bed and head for the 24-hour laundrette. When I get back, Dina is in Tim's bed reading and the baby-makers are together in the bathroom doing something gymnastic by the sound of it. I remake my bed with damp sheets and go to sleep.

***

Dina wakes me for lunch. We wander over the bridge towards Parson's Green and sit outside the Wandsworth Bridge Tavern. "Dobbin says Penny is moving out."

"Really? She's not said and frankly I don't understand how things are so it's perfectly possible."

"Who were you with last night? You never said."

"Nosey cow." Then, "A nurse I met. We snogged. What Dad would call heavy petting."

"She not fancy you?"

"Hard though it is to credit, she was the one who wanted more. I'm... I'm just being hopeful. And while it seems perfectly possible Penny is enjoying some sybaritic Sapphic sex, I'm not sure if that means I can indulge myself."

"You know what I think."

"Go on."

"If you want Penny to take you seriously you need to be serious about giving her up. Make her see what it is she might lose."

"Shag the nurse?"

"Yep."

"Nope, I'm not sure."

"Dobbin says she thinks you've already been naughty with Natalie."

"Actually, I think that was an excuse to wind me up. See, remember when she left last Christmas? I'm pretty sure she had a fling with that Aussie chap she worked with. It was all 'we need space' and 'we need to decide what we want' stuff. Then he loses his visa and

117

she's back in the flat and it's like nothing happened. Me, I just sulked. Like I always have when she walks away."

"I know. You love her, et cetera, et cetera."

"I actually told her in so many words."

"And that's what's precipitated this latest hiatus?"

"Yep."

We lapse into silence.

Then she asks, "Have you and Natalie ever done it?"

My mind flits back to a blurry memory of long ago to a swing in Sven's back garden in Hampshire when we may or may not have either had sex or she may have given me a blowjob. Bloody hell was I high that time. "Nope, never knowingly."

"The thing is everyone knows you want to. Penny especially. It makes you seem needy and a bit childish, all this puppy dog lusting from afar."

"Thanks for the vote of confidence."

"Changing the subject, Dobbin also said Sven Andersen's dead and you know something about it."

I sigh, my heart traveling to my boots. She's a know-all screw-bag who is always a step ahead of me but who has spectacularly tried to fuck up her own life more than I have mine. Slowly I tell her all that has happened since Sven appeared in my office.

"Geez H. You do have some fun. What are you going to do?"

"On Monday morning I am going to hand over to Jeremy-fucking-Panther and he can get the credit and I'll just sign whatever he puts in front of me."

"Yes, but what about the legacy?"

I have no answer. "Maybe there's nothing. I mean, if it was me there'd be nothing. A few albums and a tape machine and some worn-out clothes."

"He's the heir to his Dad's dodgy businesses. They must have been worth a bundle. Did he get that house near the old Roman fort?"

Sven's family lived about a mile from our house in the New Forest, not that I knew him until we worked together in Hemingways, the local hotel. "I think he said that went to his Mother when she divorced his Dad. She waited until he was bedridden and then got the hell out. There was that bungalow in the grounds Sven used, but I don't know much about that." I manage to shake away the speculation. "He told me, clear as anything, that he wanted it to go to his sister. They had plans to do good with it. Why leave it – whatever 'it' is – to me?"

118

"Did he leave a note, anything to explain himself?"

"Not that I know. I'll ask Gloria but I'm pretty sure she's given me everything."

She's frowning as she does when she knows there's more, something unsaid. "Something's missing. When did you say Natalie's back from Venice?"

"Tomorrow, but I'm not seeing her after what McNoble said about Miles."

"No. Sure. But between interviews there's nothing to stop me seeing her." She smiles, and it's good to see her smile. "We'll sort this out, H. You see if we don't. And if you become filthy rich, well, George has the best uncle in the world and that's good too."

It's only because of years of conditioning that we don't hug. One day we might, but not just yet.

"Okay, are you going to call this Nurse Jackie to see if she's free?"

"No. That's mental. I told you I want to wait until I've sorted this out for definite with Penny."

"I knew you'd say that. Dobbin told me about her anyway, last night while you were perving in the laundrette. I looked in your wallet. You are such a creature of habit. I phoned someone called Karen first – I didn't know the girl was called Jackie then – and Karen said you were an arse and she'd no more snog you than her horse."

"Tell me you didn't call Jackie."

She smiles her 'got you' smile. "When I went to the loo, about half an hour ago. Is that her?"

I turn. Jackie is strolling across Wandsworth Bridge Road in a flower print dress, floppy hat and cowboy boots, and I want sex with her now. Right on this table. From the way she looks at me, I'm guess she's thinking the same thing.

Dina stands. "Hi Jackie. Good to see you. My brother here doesn't know when he's well off. I'm away now to see a friend over in Hammersmith. Dobbin and Vera have promised to be out until six o'clock and Penny won't be back until late tomorrow night, if she comes at all; if I were you two I'd go back to the flat and make up for last night."

Dina give me a little wave, finishes her pineapple juice – she hates booze, limiting herself to the occasional spliff to show she's not perfect – and wanders off.

Jackie watches her go. "Is that really your sister?"

"Fairy godmother."

"I'm happy just to go for a walk, you know."

I look at Jackie, feeling packed tight with excitement. I want to say, 'Let's go and fuck' but instead I say, "Yes, okay."

We walk for what seems miles. The day feels like it holds all sorts of possibilities, none of which I'm about to enjoy. How can I feel so good and depressed?

Monday, 29th June 1981

Chapter Eighteen

In Which Harry Tells Penny and Everything Falls Apart

I have well and truly fucked up my life. Cycling to work this morning is the first time I've managed any sort of coherent analysis since the world officially disintegrated last night. My mature reflection leads me to conclude that (a) I hate my sister for calling Jackie, (b) I hate Dobbin for disapproving so obviously when he found me with Jackie in the flat, and (c) I hate Penny for first not seeming to care who Jackie is when Dobbin mentioned her on her return and then for dumping me in no uncertain terms.

What I can't really work out is why. Part of my failure to be even vaguely mature about the situation is because Jackie and I didn't do anything. We came back from our walk and were drinking tea when Dobbin and Brenda/Vera came in. He clearly thought the tea was some sort of post-coital rehydration. Jackie felt embarrassed and left, claiming she had to get ready for work and the atmosphere remained septic through the rest of the weekend. When Penny appeared on Sunday evening, Dobbin immediately asked her if she'd met 'my new friend.' What could I say? That nothing happened? No one would believe it, and anyway that would be ignoring the drunken fumble on the Friday, which wasn't my fault. Sort of. Christ, am I an idiot or what?

Penny wasn't really interested in anything. She'd been invited to another party and was flapping about getting ready. In the midst of her trying to choose what to wear and all that tosh, we had something approximating the following conversation. I was watching the TV and eating cereal when she came into the sitting room, doing something with her eyelashes.

"You were going to tell me something about Sven?"

"Was I?" It was only at that moment, some two hours or more after she got back, that I remembered I'd still not said anything. I just stared while she sighed.

"I need to go."

"Wait." I managed to stand and turn the TV off. We were about an arm's length apart.

"Well?" Penny did her best double teapot, clearly desperate to get going. I wanted to be sick. I needed to do this with sensitivity and tact.

"He's dead."

The silence wasn't helpful. I needed something to distract my brain from just blurting any old rubbish. "They found him under Wandsworth Bridge. The police won't say how he died. Sven I mean."

"Dead?"

I think she repeated 'dead' a few times, like she was trying out how it sounded in different tones of voice. But it could just be the word bounced around my head like a poltergeist possessed squash ball.

Finally, she got bored with 'dead' and tried, "Why didn't you tell me?" She seemed to prefer this in an angry tone of voice, with the last couple syllables accompanied by a jabbing finger and the word 'fuck' included for effect.

I didn't say anything. How could I? I felt like I was the shit I had clearly been. I mean, I know I could explain why, at the various times I had had the chance to say something I didn't, but right then there weren't any credible excuses. I saw her bunch her hand into a fist. I've never seen her throw a punch and she didn't this time but just seeing her do it – to see the potential for actual physical violence on her face, it spoke volumes for what I'd managed to do to our relationship.

"When did he die?"

I couldn't look at her anymore; she'd gone so pale I felt sure she would faint.

"A few days ago." *Just go,* I pleaded in my head.

"Why the fuck didn't you tell me?" Each word was sounded out like I was Portuguese and simple. And deaf.

"I wanted to. I was going to."

"You are an insensitive prick, aren't you? Here I am, off to a drinks party that might make or break my acting career and you dump this on me. Now."

"I'm insensitive? Me? Insensitive? I didn't tell you before because you were running off for a weekend of God knows what and—"

"Don't try to make this out to be my fault, you fucker. Just don't Harry. Shit, does Natalie know?"

"Yes, I told her."

Honestly, I thought her eyes might catch fire then. "Of course you did."

"What the fuck's that meant to mean?"

"It means… it means…"

123

"Yes, say it."

She looked fit to explode. "Fuck you. I hate you. I really fucking hate you. We're done, it's over."

So yes, all things considered I could do with a boost this morning. But as I carry my bike down the steps to the rack where I lock it up, I can see Jean in the secretaries' room clearly waiting for me. Prepare to be made to feel small, Harry. When I step into the building she follows me upstairs to my office.

"I've made a list of the things you need to do about Mr Andersen's estate. I've drafted some letters to send out. If you are happy with the contents then I can pp them."

I think she's psychic. I was expecting some sort of chastisement, although I'm not sure why, and yet she's as nice as pie. And I'm not sure why I bother reading them; I certainly won't find a mistake, there's no way I will be able to correct her grammar and we both know she knows more about law than me. No, strictly that's not true – what Jean knows is practical law, the sort that really matters and helps the clients, not the esoteric crap that I learnt by rote at the College of Law and try as I might I can't forget and replace with anything more useful.

I'm going through the motions, reading the sixth letter when the phone rings. Jean has disappeared to call the Coroner's court about getting a death certificate and I can answer without feeling as if I'm being assessed.

Gloria. "Hiya, shag bunny. I have a call for you. Sounds like whoever it is is at a race track." Gloria is unhelpfully cheerful for a Monday.

There's a click and indeed a lot of calling out and shouting in strained voices. Finally, just when I'm about to give up, I recognise the caller. Jeremy.

"Harry? Can you...?" There seem to be fireworks between him and me.

"Where are you?"

"Akiri."

"Where?"

"Akrotiri." Suddenly the line clears; it's like he's just landed next door. "The British Army base at Akrotiri. It's in Cyprus."

"Why are you there? I thought—"

"Stop asking inane questions Harry and get Jean."

"It's okay. I can help."

"Don't be daft. Jean will know what to do and I don't need you fucking everything up."

"But I've been looking after—"

"Rubbish. She has. Just get her, will you? That gormless lump Gloria put me through to you when I specifically asked for Jean."

Reluctantly I fetch her. She has Gloria re-route the call. I go back to the draft letters but the phone goes again.

"Police this time. You been a naughty boy?" I can hear in her tone that Gloria can't help smirking.

There is a click, followed by, "Mr Harry Spittle? My name is Detective Constable Sharon Wallace. I believe you are a friend of the late Sven Andersen and you saw him…" I hear a scrabbling like papers being shuffled. "On Thursday 18th?"

"Yes. He came to the office."

"To make his Will?"

"That's right."

"Do you have it?"

I look at the single sheet that seems to fill my desk.

"Yes."

"Would it be all right if I came round and saw it?"

"Yes, of course."

"That would be immensely helpful for our enquiries. Thank you. Would it be all right to ask you a few questions at the same time?"

"Sure. Um, can you say how he died? All I've heard is he was found under Wandsworth Bridge."

"Yes, his body was caught in some netting by the bridge. As to how he died, we are still awaiting the forensic report."

"Suicide?"

"Would you consider that likely?"

"I really don't know."

"We are keeping an open mind at this time. Can you tell me who the executors are? We will want to talk to them."

"Er, Mr Jeremy Panther of this firm. And I. Me." I say this last bit as softly as I can.

"You? Excellent. Will you both be in today?"

"I… I don't know. I will, but it seems Jeremy is still abroad. He's due back but he rang just now to say he's in Cyprus."

"Not making a run for it, is he?" the policewoman giggles. "Sorry, inappropriate. Speaking with you would be a great help I'm sure. Shall we say 11ish? I'm coming from Wandsworth and it depends on the traffic."

I have to agree. As soon as I put the phone down I head for the door to speak to Lucinda. Jean blocks my way. "Will he be back today?" I blurt out.

"All flights were routed to Cyprus yesterday. Some Saharan sand storm blew across the Med and Akrotiri is the only place with the radar facility to bring the planes down safely. There's an international incident blowing up. The Israeli defence minister is on one of the 747s and the Egyptian Head of the Army is on another. Seems they have history from the time of the Mandate. Jeremy says the officials there are in a flap and want those two out first; it is possible his flight won't take off for a couple of days. Still, we will cope Mr Spittle. I... Harry, what is it?"

I've started leaning against the door and begun to slide to the floor. It is all too much. Jean listens to me explain about the police and helps me to see Lucinda. She tells me, in no uncertain terms, that I must co-operate with DC Wallace and stop moping. I return to my desk chastised and no less miserable.

***

Detective Constable Sharon Wallace could be Jackie's twin but for the bob haircut (Jackie's is short, quite boyish) and the fact she is nearly six foot compared to Jackie's five and loose change. Her eyes, nose, mouth – they all come from the same mould. She insists on Sharon and calls me Harry without asking.

"So, talk me through what happened when he came to see you."

I do; I don't hide a thing but try to make it sound like there wasn't any violence involved in him being helped into the car. DC Wallace sees through it. "And you say you recognised one of the men?"

"I think so. I'm pretty sure it was Stephen McNoble. I don't know where he lives but he works for Miles Tupps."

"Mr Tupps? Really. Now that is interesting."

Oh fuck. I stare at her profile, her chewing the inside of her cheek as she makes a note. "It's probably nothing but his name has come up in the course of our enquiries." She narrows her eyes. "Do you know Mr Tupps?"

"A little. He's married to a friend, a close friend of mine. I went to their wedding and I see Miles from time to time."

"Do you know if Mr Andersen and Mr Tupps knew each other?"

"Yes, I understand that is the case. Mr Tupps was at Mr Andersen's Father's funeral." I hesitate. She's like a terrier.

"What is it?" She smiles. "Let me be as candid as I can. There are certain elements concerning Mr Andersen's death that make us interested in looking into it further."

"Oh?"

"For instance, while we await the forensics I can say preliminary results suggest he may have been dead before he entered the river. We find that unusual in suicides."

"Jesus. You mean…?" I can't say 'murder.' The word isn't a real one. It belongs in books and films and TV, not real life.

"It might be that someone wanted it to look like suicide. Maybe he had an accident and they were embarrassed to have him with them. A lover perhaps." She pauses. "However, it would seem to be a little suspicious to go to all that trouble. Perhaps we can have a look at the Will. It would be interesting to see who stands to benefit, given the circumstances."

I want to die. I will die, probably in prison. I hand the sheet over. Carefully D.C. Wallace reads the typed Will and then the handwritten part. "Which is the effective will? It looks like the handwritten one?"

I manage a nod, which is pretty impressive in the circumstances.

"And you're the Harold Spittle named?"

"Yes. I didn't know he'd planned this. The Will I drew up has his sister as the beneficiary."

"Please run through what you understand happened. Even if it's the same as you just told me. Including when you found out about this… gift."

I do. I'm shaking so much I pick up a pencil to try to do something to still my hands and nearly take her eye out with it.

"Harry, calm yourself." She takes the pencil from me and puts it back on the table. "I won't say this isn't curious, but it would be odd, don't you think, for the person named to be involved in, er, something suspicious. You'd need to be a psychopath or something."

Great. She thinks I'm a homicidal nutter.

She turns the paper over, peering at the typed side. "Marita is his sister?"

"Yes. I don't know where she is."

"No, we've tried to trace her too. We know she left her aunt's a few days before Mr Andersen visited you." She begins to collect her papers. "Can I have a copy?"

I hand her a sheet; Jean made four, just in case.

"Thanks. Look, please don't worry. You're his executor and you'll need to be getting on with that. I assume you've spoken to the Coroner's office? There will almost certainly need to be a hearing into the cause of death."

"Oh. Yes."

"As Miss Andersen is unavailable and I believe his Mother is abroad, will you be identifying the body?"

"Christ no." I catch myself and laugh nervously. "I think I'd faint or throw up or something."

"Hmm. Someone has to. You won't get the interim death certificate without it. Didn't the Coroner explain? He was waiting for the toxicology results before deciding on a hearing. You will only be able to plan the funeral once that is sorted; the forensic people are still working on it but there's a bit of a backlog just now." I'm vaguely aware she moves towards the door; it takes me a few moments to realise she has not gone.

When I look up she says, "It's hard the first time."

"Um?"

"Losing someone dear to you, especially with the uncertainty." She turns to go.

"Detective, er, Miss, er…"

"Sharon."

"Sharon. He wasn't that close. I don't even know where he lives. Lived."

"Isn't it on the Will?"

I glance down. "That's his family home. In Hampshire. I'm sure he had a place in town."

"Why?"

"I don't know. I just… I sort of got that impression."

She pauses, almost like she's checking with herself and then pulls out her notebook flicking through a few pages. "Avocado Buildings, Wapping. Flat two. That's why it's odd, him being in Wandsworth. We need to know what he was doing there. We're just finishing up our investigations at his flat. I'll let you know when you can have the keys."

"Me?"

"Since you're to be the executor. There may be papers you need."
She leaves me staring into the middle distance, thanking my lucky
stars she hasn't asked for my home address, since it's a little too close
to Wandsworth Bridge for comfort. It's only after she's gone, and I
realise I desperately need a pee, that I make the connection. Flat two,
Avocado Buildings is in the same block as Natalie's flat.

***

Jean, I've decided, is like my first headmistress at my primary school,
Mrs Pantcan. She married a Sri Lankan man she met while teaching in
Colombo and south Hampshire was scandalised that she should teach
us children with such a background. We didn't care. We loved and
feared her in equal measure. She had this way of getting you to do
things you absolutely hated, but made you feel good about yourself for
doing it. In my case, it was cleaning the blackboard, singing in
assembly and eating shepherd's pie. With Jean, it's making me realise
I have to go and view Sven's body before my meeting with Lady
Isabella.

I'm having kittens at the thought when Jean says, "Isn't there a
friend you can ask to go with you?" and a light bulb flickers on. Jackie
– she'll be used to dead bodies. I call the nurses' home before I can
stop myself. While I wait for my call to be answered, I begin to lose
my nerve. I'd told myself I wouldn't ring or meet or anything until I
was absolutely certain it was over with Penny. After all, while she was
angry enough to want to chop me up and feed me to the pigeons, that
doesn't mean she wants to break up. Does it? Just because she said it
was over doesn't mean it is? Maybe?

My agonising comes too late as Jackie answers the phone.
"Jackie? Hi, it's Harry."
"I wasn't expecting you to call."
"You weren't?"
"No, I... look, why have you called? I'm just going to work."
"Why weren't you expecting me to call?"
"You hated it when Gary made it clear he thought you were a shit
for having sex with me and you didn't tell him we hadn't nor tell me
why that might be an issue. You just stood there like you'd been
caught peering through the keyhole into the girl's changing room."
"I..."

"You've not really broken up, have you? You're trying to find yourself or some such nonsense. Is that your excuse for letting me give you a blowjob?"

I check that no one is listening and hope to heaven Gloria isn't eavesdropping. "It's not like that."

"Harry, I'm not 12. You have a girlfriend who you want to be with rather than me. That much is obvious. It's also obvious that she might not think the same. I like you, but we've gone a bit beyond the 'let's just be friends' stage, don't you think? Right now I can't be doing with a bloke who's happy to have sex but then agonises about the guilt. I, for one, have better things to do with my time."

"It's not like that." But she's right. It is exactly like that. "I'm sorry. This thing, me, with Penny. That's her name. It's over. I'm pretty sure. I think. Maybe."

"Call me when it is, and you are, but don't leave it too long. It's not just kettles that go cold if kept off the stove."

What an odd analogy. I'm staring at the phone when another face comes to mind. I call the flat below ours and five minutes later the lovely Mr Jones has fetched Dina. I explain what I need and she agrees to meet me to view the body.

Chapter Nineteen

In Which Dina Helps Harry and They Find a Clue

Dina really does the identification. She's met Sven a few times and confirms it is him. "He looks very bruised," she says to the mortuary attendant, "is that usual?" Uncle Fester refuses to say. I stand back but even seeing his blue-grey waxy chin at a distance nearly makes me gag.

A young man sticks his head around the door and says, "Mr Spittle? Your office rang. Can you call Miss Sampson before your next appointment?"

Dina waits while I use their phone. Jean tells me D.C. Wallace has rung; I can collect the keys to Sven's flat from a Constable Kruis if I go now. "I've phoned Lady Isabella's confidante. She will expect you at 5:30." Jean confirms the address. "And she says to apologise, but dinner will have to be another day."

Dina wants to come with me to the flat. I'm pleased, if truth be known; we use the train and tube journey to Tower Hill station and the walk to go through what I heard from Sharon Wallace and to speculate a little about the fact he had a flat in the same block as Natalie. "I wonder why she didn't tell me."

"She might not know. But that's got to be unlikely, hasn't it? Anyway, everything about Natalie has always been odd. Did this police woman tell you not to leave the country? How exciting that you're their chief suspect!"

"I'm not. Look, stop messing about. This is serious."

"Okay Mr Big Shot Lawyer. What do we do when we get there?"

I try to recall what was on Jean's list of things I needed to do. "We have to find any bank statements and other financial papers, such as share certificates or letters from stock brokers. Deeds to property and leases, that sort of thing. I suppose I'm going to have to organise a funeral so I'll need his address book if he has one."

Constable Kruis is South African with a thick accent and thicker neck, beady black eyes, short blond hair and the most genial smile imaginable. He hands me a bunch with four keys on it, two large and two small. The largest – a Yale key – is to the main door to the block while the Chubb is for the flat itself. He tells me one of the smaller ones is for the flat's letterbox, which stands in the entrance hall. "I don't know about this one." He points at the other little key. "It's not a spare. Maybe he has a safety deposit box or something. Do you need a hand with anything?"

Dina smiles at him. "Have you taken anything? You know, evidence?" She adds, "It's just this place seems pretty empty."

He nods. "Yes, that's what we thought, like he'd only just moved in. No, nothing taken by us. Shall I make tea while you have a look round? There's stuff in the kitchen and it would be a shame for the milk to go off."

Before I can decline Dina has thanked him and pushed me towards the sitting room. When he's left the room, I hiss at Dina. "Why'd you do that? I want him to go so I can look around."

She hisses back at me. "Oh, chill out H. He's a darling and I want to get to know him better."

"What? But you're with Jim."

She pulls a face. "I'm not any more. Oh H, we tried, really, but he's... he loves the New Forest, his home comforts, the garage and his beloved cars. It's not for me. I needed to get away."

"But you love the lump."

"And you love Penny, but it's not got either of us very far, has it? Jim and I are having a break. I may decide he is for me and I will always love him as the Father of George, but as a long-term commitment? Nah. It was never going to work."

I have to admit I'm not surprised. My sister, for all her many failings, is one of the cleverest and brightest people around. And Jim James really isn't. I'm pondering how even that little piece of certainty can be invalidated, gone, past tense, when Constable Kruis returns. I can't help noticing how he looks at Dina or how she's standing in a way to make him look.

"Constable," she says, as she takes a cup of tea from him, "while Mr Spittle checks for financial papers can you show me the flat's layout?"

The smile is easy. She is soooo transparent. The flirt. What a tart.

The flat is laid out like Natalie's. Mostly open plan with a mezzanine floor for the bedroom space and separate kitchen and bathroom. As Dina pointed out it's almost empty of possessions. I head for a bureau that sits by the picture windows overlooking the river.

The top section with a roll-top holds a file with my name on the front. On the inside of the cover someone has written: 'Will.' The only contents, though, is not a Will, but two photos and a pencil drawing.

The first photo is a garden. There's a lawn and flowerbeds leading to some trees. In the centre of the lawn is a table and, to one side, some sort of ornamental thing, maybe a stone urn. It's vaguely familiar.

The second photo is a parade of shops. I recognise them immediately. They are next to the railway station in New Milton, a small town near my family home in Hampshire. Near to Sven's family home for that matter.

The drawing is the more interesting document. It comprises two people, one sitting and one standing behind the first. The one sitting is me, only the me that I was when I first met Sven, with a lot longer hair and a waiter's uniform. I can see some cars just beyond where he's positioned me and realise it's meant to be the car park at the hotel where we met. Hemingways in the summer of 1976. Beyond that is a house that could be my family home, but that detail is only sketched and I might be wrong. Anyway, in real life there's no house there, just acres of New Forest heathland.

The second person is Sven's sister Marita, who to my certain knowledge never saw me at the hotel. I've met her a few times and I'm pretty sure it's her. She's looking over my shoulder at something in my lap, which I also seem to be looking at. A book or a sheet of paper, maybe.

Behind her to the right of the picture, I can see a church and further away a tall building, which might be the Post Office tower but why would the artist – who I assume is Sven – put me in a Hampshire car park with Marita yet draw in some obscure features that may include London buildings?

I put the drawing and photos back in the folder and slip it into my briefcase before opening the drawers. There are three on each side. On the left there are bank statements going back two years, the last of which is a month ago showing he had about £700 in his current account and another with £400. These accounts join the pictures and photos in my case. In the next drawer is a set of letters and papers about the flat; it is on a lease that expires in three months. The tenant is a company called Andersen Properties Limited. There's nothing in the bottom drawer. The right-hand side drawers are full of writing paper, envelopes and biros. Many packets, half-used and then tucked away like he forgot he had one, started another and then moved on to yet another. There's no address book or anything personal, such as letters he had received.

Constable Kruis makes me jump. "We found nothing, sir."

"Call him Harry, Jan, or he'll get ideas he's important."

Jan Kruis smiles at Dina. "We looked everywhere but that's about it. A few clothes in the bedroom, toiletries in the bathroom. Hardly any food. No booze. A little cannabis," he glances at Dina, "which we've taken, sir. Feels more like a hotel." He holds out a hand, "Oh, and there's this."

"What is it?"

"A car key. I'm pretty sure it's a Porsche 911. The registration details are on the tag."

"Is it Sven's?"

He nods. "I checked earlier. It's registered to Mr Andersen."

"Do you know where it is?"

"No, we don't sir. Since there's no evidence of theft, we haven't put out the details." He glances at Dina, as if for support. "I could ask my guvnor if you like?"

I manage a nod.

Constable Kruis has to go; I'm pleased because I can't think with him around. Dina insists on seeing him to the front door of the building. When she returns, she makes a sort of growl. "My God, he is magnificent. That voice goes right through you."

"I'll give you that, it is deep. Seems like a nice bloke."

"I'll let you know. We're meeting for a beer when he gets off this evening."

"You're quick. I suppose you asked him?"

"I teased it out of him but, yeah, I suppose. You men are hopeless. Find anything?"

We sit on the sofa to enable her to look at the drawing and photos. She studies them and then the bank statements. "When did he draw you and Marita?"

"He never did. Not together. Look at the length of my hair. That's me back when we first met. But when I first met her, also at about that time, she had much shorter hair. Hers is a more recent drawing, I guess. And I'm at Hemingways while I think she's in London – that's the Post Office tower there I reckon. Why's he put us together like that?"

"And what are you doing? There's something on your lap and she's looking at it."

"A book? Paper?"

Dina peers at the drawing, shaking her head. She goes back to the file itself. "What's with the cover? Do you think there was meant to be another Will in here?"

I shrug and pick up the bank statements. "There must be more. Natalie said he was selling off his Father's businesses. They had to be worth more than this." I tap the line that shows the balance.

"Maybe he's already given it to her. Maybe this is all there is." She shuffles back through the earlier statements. "No. The maximum balance seems to have been just over £1000 about four months ago."

I look at the drawing and the photos. "No, he's more devious than that. These were left deliberately for me. I just need to work out why."

She stands up. "Do you think there's a garage here? Maybe we can find if that car is there?"

I smile. "There is. I saw Miles drive out the other day."

"What's up?"

"Sorry?"

"You're frowning with that 'my brain hurts' look you get when you're trying to be clever."

"I think he was driving a Porsche. It was red. Damn, I wish I knew more about cars. I've no idea if it was a nine-whatever-he-said."

"911." It's her turn to frown. "There are loads around. Maybe they both had them. It doesn't follow he'd be driving Sven's."

"No, I suppose not."

To my surprise she does a little dance. "This is great."

"Glad you're enjoying it. My head really is hurting."

"Better than being bored by small village life."

"If these are some sort of clues for me, then it means he knew something might happen to him, doesn't it?"

She nods, the smile replaced by her serious face. "You need to be careful, H."

"Don't be melodramatic." Sadly, any suggestion of confidence that I really think she is overdoing it is lost as my voice comes out in a panicky squeak.

"He might have been killed."

"Stop it. Did the policeman say something?"

"No, but it's all rather odd if he wasn't."

"I really don't want to think about it. Let's go."

"What about the car?"

"Another time. I can't drive it without insurance and anyway I'm not sure I want to drive a Porsche."

"The sooner we sort this out, the better H."

I shrug. We have another check around, but there's nothing more to find. It's Dina who says, "Where is everything? I mean, you'd expect a few more clothes and stuff. Maybe his drawing things. And books. I suppose he has another place somewhere."

"There's Hampshire, I suppose."

"We need to go there, soon." Then she stamps noisily on the floor.

"Why did you do that?"

"It's solid, at least. No floorboards to hide stuff under. Go check the bedroom."

Nothing.

She puffs out her cheeks, mirroring my frustration. "Come on, let's go. You fancy buying me a drink before I meet Gorgeous Jan?"

I glance at my watch. "Shit. I have to meet Lady Isabella. God, what a fucking nightmare. Can you make your own way home?"

"Who says I'm going home?"

Chapter Twenty

In Which Harry Meets a Formidable Woman and Learns He is to be Grown-Up

I am late for the meeting but Izzy, as she absolutely insists I call her, is rather distracted. Dinner is off because she has a crisis to deal with. She hands me over to her confidante, a woman of about 40 with steel-rimmed spectacles and a cold mechanical manner who I must call Mrs Soderberg. She is to take me through the business proposition Izzy wants me to help her with.

"It is straightforward, Mr Spittle. We need a company formed – this one will be called Izzy Ventures Number Six. Buy one off the shelf with a general administration and property investment Memorandum of Association and change the name. You will be secretary; Lady Isabella will own 99 shares and I will hold one as nominee for her. You will then draw up an agreement under which Lady Isabella will allow Mr Sean Latterly to—"

"Sean?"

"Indeed. The 'Close Friend' of Sir Penshaw." She says 'Close Friend' with the same lack of affection with which Brenda/Vera says 'Maggie Thatcher' when she's having a rant about the 'fascist hegemony' in Downing Street. "He is setting up his own theatrical agency with Lady Isabella's help. She will allow him to acquire up to 49 percent of the business. He will start with 20 percent when he signs the agreement and—"

"Agreement?"

She peers at me over the top of her glasses. "Mr Spittle, please do not interrupt my flow. Surely you understand a Shareholders' Agreement? Questions are welcome at the end but I assure you, you will have none." She gives me a fraction within which to nod, which I do too late – she has already returned to her notes. "Lady Isabella…" She stops and looks up. "Are you taking notes?"

I manage a blink and show her I'm holding a pencil and have my pad out.

She tuts. "Please just listen. I will give you comprehensive written instructions after I have explained and your notes will therefore be redundant." There is a tiredness in her voice that I find utterly intimidating.

By the time she has finished, the idea seems pretty straightforward and I'm grateful when she hands me her notes.

"Questions?"

I shake my head, confident that is what is expected. She looks disappointed. "You think you can manage this?"

I smile and conjure a look that says I'm confident. I haven't the first clue what she is talking about, but I know that Lucinda will. "I do have one question?"

"Yes?" She is in the process of putting her folder away in her bag and pauses.

"Why is Lady Isabella doing this? Rather than Sir Penshaw?"

"Mr Latterly has a compelling business case. He knows a lot of the best people in the entertainment business who have lost faith in the current West End theatre establishment. It is a closed shop, and, in the spirit of the times, Lady Isabella wants to help Mr Latterly break that down. Anything else?" She stares, and I am sure I'm meant to say something.

I begin a spiel I've heard Jeremy use. "Clifford Risely & Co. will be delighted to act on this exciting—"

I'm interrupted by her closing her bag with a snap and standing up. I hurry to mirror her.

She looks at me and sighs. "Lady Isabella understands Clifford, Risely & Co. are technically her lawyers but expects you to fulfil the role of her adviser and act as company secretary. Is that understood?

"Yes, yes of course." Some chance, I think. I will check every dot and comma with Lucinda, not that I tell Mrs Soderberg.

"Good. Now, I'm sure I don't need to tell you it's crucial that there is complete confidentiality. Others in the business, if they hear about this before it is launched, might try to damage it. Kill it at birth, as it were."

I know this bit. "It is of the utmost importance to us at Clifford, Risely & Co. and—"

I'm quoting Lucinda, but Mrs Soderberg doesn't let me finish. "That includes Mr Latterly, insofar as the profit sharing is concerned. Good. You will meet Lady Isabella at Lord's Cricket Ground on Thursday with the draft documents. You will be her guest in the Warner Stand. Be at the Grace Gates at 10.15 and do not be late. And wear a tie."

I smile, making a mental note to check up on Izzy Ventures numbers one to five.

Chapter Twenty-One

In Which Harry Learns More about Brenda/Vera

As I climb the stairs to my flat, my mind turns to Lord's and whether I should wear my suit. The upcoming Royal wedding has infected London with a kind of posh-itis. When I asked Jean, she suggested 'smart-casual' would do, but my one suit is well past achieving smart status, and if I'm honest my attempts at casual tend more towards the scruffy. Why does Charlie boy have to get married? Can't he just reflect the modern world a bit? I mean, who really cares? As I push open the front door, I hear an explosion of girly laughter. Briefly my heart jolts at the idea that it's Penny, back home and remorseful, but then I realise it is Brenda/Vera and another woman whose voice I don't recognise. They are in the kitchen. Brenda/Vera has this woman bent over the sink and is working something into her head.

"Hi Harry. Won't be a moment. Keep still Mum, for fuck's sake."

"Brenda, mind your language please. You are not on stage now." Zenda's voice is lost as Brenda/Vera splashes water into her mouth. There's a brief struggle and Zenda stands, a line of green dye running down her cheek. 'Hello Harry. Sorry, but Brenda insisted. She thinks a light green tint will suit me." She waves vaguely at the mossy-coloured paste on her hair and shrugs. Both Mother and daughter appear very happy with whatever is going on.

I say, "I'll make tea, shall I?"

Zenda makes a noise that sounds like 'thank you' while Brenda/Vera ignores me, pushing her victim back to the sheep dip or whatever it is she's doing.

By the time I've made a brew Brenda/Vera has disappeared to her bedroom and Zenda, stained towel around her shoulders, has joined me at the table. She shares another beaming smile. "I never had the chance to thank you for making me see Brenda. You were right about her presence." Her face clouds a little. "She has her Father's tendency to show off and an uncomplicated way with Anglo-Saxon words."

"He's a judge, right?"

She wrinkles her nose. "That's her step-Father and he's what's called a Master, sort of a junior judge."

I pull a pained expression. "God, they're an articled clerk's worst nightmare. They eat us alive."

Zenda allows a neat eyebrow to rise a fraction, causing my stomach to feel hollow.

"Oh heck. Not that yours will be one those, of course."

Zenda smiles. "Oh no, Reggie would fit that mould exactly. I imagine he is an absolute bastard. Not the most sympathetic of men where youth and inexperience are concerned."

I think for a moment. "Where's he based? I don't think I've come across a Master Silverman at the High Court."

"You wouldn't. Silverman is my maiden name. Her Father is Jack Single, a twinkly-eyed pianist I met when I was too young to know any better. Brenda refuses to use either his or Reggie's name. His surname is Rother."

If there is such thing as a thought-vampire, my brain has just been bitten. Blood drains from it like it's been exsanguinated. Rother. No wonder Brenda/Vera hates her step-Father.

Zenda must see how I've paled. "He's been a complete horror to Brenda if I'm honest. When she decided to give up on her articles it was the last straw. I should have stepped in." She stops, looking at the door behind me.

Brenda/Vera stands, framed by the hall window, staring at her Mother, angry tears splashing her cheeks. "I'm really sorry, Mum."

Zenda goes to her daughter pulling her into a hug. "Silly. I should have stood up to him. It'll be different now. You and me." She eases Brenda/Vera to a chair. Her face is now rather green and Zenda dabs it with a towel. "You look like a wood-sprite."

Only a Mother could see some sort of faerie folk in Brenda/Vera's furious countenance.

Brenda/Vera says, "Harry, is it okay if Mum stays here? Do you think?"

"Where?"

"Tim's room?"

"What's Dobbin said?"

"He—"

"Actually, Dina's using it."

Brenda/Vera glares at me. "Your sister? Since when?"

"Dobbin suggested it."

"That's ridiculous. Anyway, Mum will pay the rent. Is Dina paying anything?"

Fair point, but I'm not about to give in so easily when Zenda stops her. "Darling, don't. I'll find a hotel."

Brenda/Vera's face hardens. "No, you are staying here. Dina is Harry's sister. She can share his room. Or use the sofa."

"Hello? If you think I'm sharing with my skanky sibling you are much mistaken."

"Stop." Zenda holds her daughter's wrist as Brenda/Vera looks like she might reach across and gouge out my eyes. "Harry's the tenant, Brenda, and he was here before you. And I'm not dispossessing his sister. I can find somewhere."

"NO, Mum." Brenda/Vera looks forlorn as she turns to me. "Harry, he'll kill her when he knows she's left him. Like he tried to do with me."

"Shh. Harry doesn't need to hear this. And anyway, that's an exaggeration."

"Yes, he does. She has to stay here, Harry. I need to make sure she's safe."

I'm finding this conversation very hard to believe, given it was me trying to get her to contact her Mum only a couple of days ago. And while I know Master Rother is a sod of the first order, then so are a lot of senior people in law and that doesn't mean they'll do anyone actual physical harm. Does it?

Zenda tuts, which seems to bring Brenda/Vera to her senses. "Let's talk about this later. When do you need to rinse out the dye?"

Brenda/Vera looks like she's about to argue then goggles at her Mother and swears in ways I've yet to hear from her. She eases her Mother over to the sink in silence and I sneak off to my room. I catch a sly glance a few moments later; Zenda's new hair looks like an advert for lime cordial although there's precious little that might be described as especially cordial in her expression.

Thursday, 2nd July 1981

Chapter Twenty-Two

Where Harry Goes to Lord's and Gets into a Fight

When I get to the office the details of Izzy Ventures numbers one to five are on my desk. I want to get off to Lord's but can't resist a quick look at what they tell me. Four are co-owned, with Sir Pen holding 49 percent of the shares; he is also named as a director along with Izzy. Two of those four are straightforward property businesses, one is a management company and the fourth runs events. The other, Izzy Ventures Number Two, is very different. It is 99 percent owned by Sir Pen and the memorandum is decidedly odd, covering dealings in commodities and entertainment. Sir Pen is not a director, Lady Isabella is listed as one as is Mrs Soderberg and two people I don't know, but both have addresses in Belgium. It appears the company has done a lot of business; the charges register suggests a number of loans have been recorded and cleared. I wonder if this is part of the 'millions' owned by Sir Pen that Izzy mentioned at the party.

As a result of my perusals, I am rushing already and damp and uncomfortable as I emerge from the tube at St John's Wood. My attempts to achieve a balance in my outfit sees me wearing one of Dobbin's pink-striped shirts, a tie my parents gave me when I graduated that has small elephant motifs on it and which I've never worn since Penny suggested it looked like they were giving each other blowjobs, but which I decide would do now she's not there to take the piss, and my suit trousers, embarrassing side-stain and all. My shoes are highly polished, mind you. Dad would be pleased.

Notwithstanding feeling like I'll be a laughing stock, I am ludicrously excited. I have never been to the Home of Cricket for any game let alone a Test Match versus the old enemy, Australia. Here I am, outside the Grace Gates looking up at the statue of Dr W. G. Grace while I wait to be met. It's overcast but already a warm day. The gates opened 15 minutes ago and a stream of members, universally clad, it seems, in outrageous red and yellow striped blazers, matching tie and jaunty hats have wandered past. They are between ancient and possibly dead.

As I hop from foot to foot, hoping I've got the day right, an old boy with one of the silly ties catches my gaze. I smile and he nods.

Moments later he's next to me, fingering my tie. "Looks like they're having fun, eh?"

I nod again and smile.

"Boys' games, eh?" he says enigmatically and gives me his *Daily Telegraph*. "If you're here at six and fancy a sherry at my club then just show my chauffeur this." He points at a part-completed cryptic crossword and then at a capped man standing by what looks like a Bentley. "Enjoy the day."

The crossword has some answers filled in: a name, 'Bingo'; the address of a club in Pall Mall; and a number, which, if it represents money is nearly twice my monthly wage. I watch him meander through the members' entrance, waving in a desultory way to the saluting flunky. Maybe I'm giving off some sort of gay pheromone and I don't realise it.

The queue is growing, but there's still no sign of anyone I know, and in the heat my mind begins to wander. I'm glad of the relative peace and quiet because it's been one heck of a week so far.

Jeremy returned yesterday, and I surprised myself by being disappointed to hand things back to him. Two and a bit weeks looking after his work made me realise that I can do a lot, especially with Jean by my side – or is that the other way around? In fact, I can see that he is not much better than me, a fact that Jean has been hinting for some time. When I told Jeremy about Sven's Will and him being joint executor with me he said 'fuck' under his breath and told me I could do the work and he would sign things off. I didn't mention that I was the beneficiary.

Lucinda thinks the opportunity with Lady Isabella is too good for me to miss and helped me draft the agreement. Jean had the company formed in a trice, and we held a board meeting to approve the change of name and the issue of the shares. I sent that paperwork to Mrs Soderberg, confirming that I will have the draft agreement with me today (which I have). Lucinda's only advice: 'Don't get drunk.'

Nothing new has happened with Sven's Will or his body or the estate. On Lucinda's advice, I called the aunt who sounded completely fed up about Sven and Marita and told me, in no uncertain terms, to 'do what I like with the body.' In that connection, Jean has heard from the police that they may release it shortly and has begun to pre-plan a cremation, provisionally booking at date in Bournemouth on Friday week. Jean has an announcement that will go out both locally to his flat here and the family home in Hampshire, if we get the all clear.

145

We've told the landlord of his flat and the bank, promising to send a death certificate once we have one. D.C. Wallace has not called. Dina tells me that Jan Kruis is still helping with enquiries. They are looking for Sven's car. She tells me she has been 'getting to know' Jan between visiting the London universities about her change of course, although it already appears to be that the 'getting to know' equates with a Biblical 'having knowledge of' if the squeaks from Tim's room are anything to go by.

At home, the Zenda experiment of sofa sleeping lasted one night. Well, it was never going to work. After all the sisterly love between Mother and daughter, Brenda/Vera rather ruined it when Dobbin came home. She announced she wanted to have sex on the small balcony outside their bedroom as 'the sunset will empower my orgasms' and Zenda's face turned the same colour as her hair. None of us commented on the hue – it is an extraordinary shade of green like a metallic paint BMW have introduced – but it is clear she hates it. On Tuesday morning, she disappeared to use Mr Jones' phone, intending to source a nearby B&B; by the evening Mr Jones had offered her his spare room and she had moved in with him. She pops up to clean and cook but leaves pretty much as soon as any of us appear. I feel a bit sorry for her, wondering what she's going to do.

Dobbin's job has been going well and he is confident he will get the Hong Kong posting. He is, however, worried what will happen to him and Brenda/Vera if he goes. "She says she'll stay here but that's no good. Anyway, I need her."

I never thought I'd see Dobbin in love, but he is smitten. "Just wait and see if you get the job and then worry about her."

"I'm not worried about her; it's you."

"Me?"

"If she stays here then you and she will have sex and I will have to kill you both." He's joking. Obviously.

"I don't fancy her enough."

He refused to talk about it and sulked all yesterday evening.

Natalie rang me yesterday afternoon, but I haven't returned the call. I need to pick her brains, but I don't know how to broach the subject of Sven's flat. I'm sure she must know about it and wish she'd told me. I still can't fathom why she didn't.

Penny and I haven't spoken. I've no idea beyond confident guesswork where she's staying. I've not spoken to Jackie either. I'm sure I'm single. It's horrid, made worse by Dobbin and Brenda/Vera on one side and Dina and Constable Kruis in Tim's room on the other. When they creep away from the TV, they may be playing Scrabble or jointly knitting a scarf, but I doubt it.

"Mr Spittle?" Mrs Soderberg approaches me through the crowd. "Hello."

Her eyes go down from my face to my shoes and back up again. She gives the impression she wants to critique my dress, but in the end limits herself to, "I suppose that's the modern way, is it?" accompanied by, "Follow me."

She sees me through the turnstiles and I trot behind her towards the Warner Stand that sits, from behind, to the left of the Pavilion. It's a tatty 1950s structure and a complete contrast to the magnificence of the Victorian Pavilion. To my surprise, Sir Pen is standing by the door with Sean Latterly.

Sir Pen reaches in and pecks my cheek, before squinting at my tie. "Are they…? Brave choice, Harry. Now, since I'm the host I'll show you to your seat. After that, just nod at Robert here," a tall dour faced man in a white waiter's jacket and black trousers nods at me, "and he'll let you back in if you go wandering. Feel free to watch or whatever – the museum is excellent – but lunch will be in the Grace gardens," he points behind me, "at 12.45. We have some rather splendid prawns." He sounds jovial enough but his eyes dart to Sean who ignores him and me. When he touches Sean's arm, he pulls away and walks off while Sir Pen, after a moment's hesitation, sees me up two flights of stairs to my seat. Lady Isabella is already there, talking to a man in a Panama hat and large dark glasses seated to her left. I'm offered the seat on her right. She acknowledges me but goes on talking to the man next to her. We are not introduced.

I don't mind, in truth. It gives me a chance to watch members of both teams wandering across the ground towards the far end, the Nursery end, where they practice. At 10:30 the spectators have pretty much filled the seats and the toss takes place. When Australia wins it and insert England there's a knowing murmur around me. 'Good decision'; 'Alderman will love the atmosphere, it's sure to swing'; 'He'll cock it up – not used to the slope'; 'Boycott's having a shocker. Lillee has the Indian sign on him.'

I'm in love. With this place, the atmosphere, the genteel hum of people ready for whatever the game has to offer but knowing it will be a slow burn of excitement, with the occasional burst of energy. *Like good sex*, I think to myself and laugh.

I jump as a hand touches my leg. "Glad you're enjoying yourself, Harry." Izzy has an intense stare that is now fully turned on me. "A good joke?"

I take a moment before explaining. Her expression doesn't change and by the end I wish I'd stayed quiet. She takes a moment, still staring at me, to say, "Do you think about sex a lot?"

I can barely swallow. Sweat forms on my neck and saturates my shirt. I can hardly form a sound.

She bursts out laughing. "Harry, you are priceless! I apologise. It is unfair of me, your hostess, to tease you like that. We can talk about sex another time; I'm sure there's a lot we can teach each other. What do you think the lunchtime score will be?" There's a glint in her eye. "Terry there," she indicates a man at the end of our row, "is running a book on the score when the first wicket falls, who it'll be, the bowler, oh lots of little flutters. That's why I love this place. You can bet pretty much all day."

We natter for a while between watching the English openers keep the dreaded Lillee and Alderman at bay. There's an audible sigh of relief when Lawson replaces Lillee, but it brings a swift reward in Gooch's and then Boycott's wickets. At 12.30 Izzy leaves me to find the ladies and reminds me to go for lunch at 12.45.

I don't want to leave and miss a ball but duty calls, so I head for the grassed area. Mrs Soderberg is already there with Sean who looks sullen and has a Champagne flute in one hand and a bottle of Moet in the other.

"Do you drink?" He sounds aggressive as he glares at me. So much for his body being a temple. Once I've sat down and accepted a glass, Mrs Soderberg leaves. Sean ignores me for a while before he says, "Did you tell her about the Will?"

"I... no." I struggle to remember what I've said. Why would it matter anyway?

As he doesn't seem to want an answer I say, "I hope the new business goes well."

He shrugs and then turns to face me. "You don't understand, do you? You're just a... a..." To my surprise, he drops the bottle and grabs me by the tie, pulling me closer. "Fuck's sake you little shit, has she actually signed her shareholder's wotsit? Where the fuck is it?"

I'm not breathing too well and try to pull away. All I succeed in doing is to lose my balance and we tumble onto the rug with an arc of Champagne following me. When I look up Izzy and Mrs Soderberg loom over us. Izzy is laughing and Mrs Soderberg is apparently trying and failing to do the same.

"Don't let Pen catch you two wrestling or he'll be most upset."

Sean pulls himself away and tries to look like nothing has happened. He wobbles to his feet. Izzy goes to hold his arm, and something passes between them: him anger, her disappointment or something, and then he leaves without a word. Izzy whispers to Mrs Soderberg who goes after him. She pours a glass for herself. "I assume that was to do with the agreement? Do you have it?"

I pull it from the briefcase. "It is just a draft. I've added in some questions that need answering before we can finish it."

She nods absently as she reads it very quickly. "Can I keep this?"

I nod. "The company is ready. There are some papers to sign."

"Okay. Those can go to Soderberg. I'll let you have any changes and then we can sort out signing." She looks in the direction Sean has disappeared. "Assuming things don't explode before then." She shakes her head and looks at me. "Families. So complicated, eh?"

"He, Sean, asked if you had signed it. I… I didn't say either way. I didn't know what I could say to Sean."

"You're wise beyond your years. Yes, assume it is to be kept from everyone, even the very fact I've instructed you on it. Until it is live we need discretion. Especially from Pen." She looks away. "He and I used to do everything together. Recently not so much. We make – made – a good team."

"Yes."

She looks at me quizzically and I feel like she's caught me out. I add quickly. "I hope you don't mind but I looked at your other Izzy Ventures. The public stuff. They are all jointly owned, aren't they? With Sir Pen."

She holds me with her gaze. "You're an interesting young man. I'm not surprised you looked into the other companies, but I am that you told me. Bravo. Yes, that's mostly true. My brother is a rich man, although I wouldn't exactly condone all his business practices. I'm the cautious one to his reckless side – no, his instinctive side. I worry he'll lose that if he focuses on Sean as he seems intent on doing." She surprises me by putting her hand on my cheek and keeping it there. "Your honesty is admirable, Harry, but use it sparingly. You might just find people trusting you with too much. And that can be a burden, believe me."

I'm just about to ask what she means when a shadow falls across us. "Goodness Izzy, is he one of yours? Or Pen's?"

"Mine." Izzy drapes a hand around my shoulders. I stare at her fingers as they toy with the lapel of my jacket; two gold rings, neither indicating she's married or engaged, and luscious red nail varnish.

"Thought he was… the tie, you see. Gives an old buck like me ideas. Shame."

Izzy watches him totter away. She says, "You've met Bingo?"

"While I was waiting by the gate. He propositioned me with his Telegraph."

"He pays well. Don't let me stop you, although a word to the wise. You'll be plied with drink that will be spiked and you'll wake up tomorrow with your arse as sore as your head. If that's what you want?" The way she looks at me conveys there might be an alternative on offer.

I stare back at her, holding her gaze. I say, "My boss warned me about accepting drinks from strangers."

"What about from someone you know?"

"Even more unwise."

"Sound advice. Top up?"

I hold out my glass. In for a penny…

Friday, 3rd July 1981

Chapter Twenty-Three

In Which Harry and Dina Confront Natalie and Zenda Asks a Favour

Dina catches me just as I'm about to leave for work. She looks wrecked. "Sorry H. Jan and I…" She blinks painfully. "We overdid it. I meant to say – the police have finished the autopsy. Jan, bless him, let me have the details. Sven's heart gave out. It could have happened at any time. Some sort of congenital weakness. They've not found anything suspicious, no drugs or poison. Nothing suspicious in the death, other than he seems to have been moved after he died. You will get the death certificate anyway."

"So he was moved? DC Wallace said she thought as much. I wonder why? And who'd do that?"

"Jan's a bit coy about that bit."

"What did he say about his heart?"

"Just that it was a mess." Dina shrugs and rubs her temples. "I need aspirin. Shall we have another go at those pictures, see if they make sense? Tonight? Jan's working."

"Why not? I'm not going anywhere."

"Have you called Jackie? Asked her out?"

"No. And I'm not talking about her or Penny." I grab my rucksack and leave her to her recovery. I'm not discussing my failed love life with my kid sister.

Vern the postman is sorting out the mail for our block. "Harry. You need anything?"

"No thanks, Vern. Maybe next week."

"To be sure. Your sis is keeping me busy anyway."

He leaves me open-mouthed. Is that why she looks so terrible? Am I naïve enough to think policemen don't smoke weed?

At work, I finally return Natalie's call. "Harry? We need to talk."

"Okay. What about?"

"The usual. Me. Can I come to yours? Tonight?"

"Why not? The more the merrier."

"Pardon?"

"Dina – my sister – she's staying for a bit. She'll be around. And then there's my flatmate's girlfriend and her Mother. We're planning on solving a puzzle."

"I heard about Penny."

"What did she say?"

"7:30? I'll bring some wine."

***

Natalie is on time and brings a decent red. She looks rather pale and tired but greets Dina with warmth. Dina makes a show of reciprocating even though I know she thinks Natalie isn't to be trusted. After I've poured three glasses we sit at the kitchen table. I lay out the two photos and the drawing, although I've kept the folder in my briefcase. "Unless you want that word first, this is my puzzle. I got these from Sven. I think they are meant to help me with his Will."

Natalie picks up the drawing. "This is weird, isn't it? He's put you on some wall, yet Marita looks like she's in my flat."

I can't help the cough that turns into a rather disgusting splutter of wine. "Your flat? Why do you say that?"

She's still peering at the picture. "Is that the car park at Hemingways?"

"Yes it is. Why your flat?"

She nods slowly and says, "He's made it look like Marita's standing by my living room window, even though he's not shown the window itself. That's clearly the church in Wapping, and that tower is the Post Office tower which you can just about see on a clear day." She's frowning as she looks up at me. "Why would he put those two things together?"

"That's what we hoped you'd tell us."

"Did he leave any other clues?" Natalie carefully lays the drawing down.

"Only these."

Before she can turn her attention to the photos, Dina covers them with a hand. She leans forward. "Why didn't you say he had the flat below yours?"

"What?" Does she look guilty? Maybe.

I butt in before Dina gets too obnoxious as I can feel she's brewing towards an unconstructive intervention. "Dina is helping me so don't hold back on her account."

153

"What flat?"

There's an awkward silence that Dina finally fills with, "Oh come on. You were lovers. Everyone knows. Is that where you met?"

This time the silence is pregnant with meaning. Or maybe it's just that all the available space is filled and we can't breathe. I glare at my sister who shrugs. "You're too nice, H. Natalie, we can always ask Miles what he knows."

Briefly she looks terrified. Then she shakes out a cigarette but doesn't light it, rolling it on the table. "We weren't lovers." She pours herself another glass of wine. "He did propose, way back, mostly to try to stop me marrying Miles. He and Miles…" She stops abruptly.

After a moment I say, "You said he told Miles he'd withdraw from the estate agency business. Did they have other business dealings? Is that where the money is?"

She doesn't know where to look. "I don't know."

"What about the pub, where you took me the other day? Or whatever he's doing up north."

She hangs her head. "He goes to Leeds. I don't know why. Why does it matter?"

Dina slams her hand on the table. We both jump and stare at her. Dina smiles. "Do you normally lie to your friends?"

Natalie looks shocked and then furious. "Who the hell do you think you are to say that? You can't even stop yourself from getting pregnant."

I stand up, sending my chair skittering back across the kitchen floor. "Woah, ladies. You two are really not helping. Natalie, what do you know about their business dealings? Or what do you suspect?"

"You won't believe me, clearly." She glares at Dina who sticks her tongue out.

"Please Natalie." I make a note to strangle Dina later.

She doesn't speak for a moment, more interested in her wine. Then, "Does it really matter now?"

"Look, cards on the table here. Sven died of heart failure and—"

"Heart failure?" She looks genuinely surprised.

"That's what the police told us. But he was moved after he died – by whom we know not. And someone dumped him in the river." Why on Earth do I sound like a nineteenth-century legal eagle all of a sudden? "It's a mess and I'm meant to look after his affairs as I'm executor of his Will. I need help to make sense of this and so far you're the only person I can ask. Or trust," I add the last as an afterthought.

She leans back in her chair and puts the cigarette in her mouth. Still she makes no effort to light it. "Sven told Miles he was ending his involvement in Miles' businesses. Whatever they were. That really pissed him off." She looks at me. "Miles took it out on me. He always assumed I had some influence over Sven. But really I don't have a clue what those businesses were."

Dina wrinkles her nose into a sneer. "You should have chosen a decent bloke as a husband, shouldn't you?"

"Dina, please. Do you know who might?"

"Stephen."

"McNoble?" I glance sidelong at Dina, whose face is a picture. She says, "Tell me that son of a total bastard is not involved too. H, surely not McThug?"

I ignore her. "How is he involved?"

Natalie looks down and shakes her head. "I don't know." She's probably lying, not that I'm any good at telling. She starts again with the cigarette. "Okay if I smoke?"

I nod. "If you lean out of the window."

She moves to the open casement and lights up, blowing smoke towards the gas works.

Dina says, "Come on, Natalie. We need help. Or should we go to Miles?"

Natalie stares at her, hating her. "He mustn't know." She grinds out her cigarette. "It was not like you're suggesting. We just supported each other. It was never physical."

Dina, however, looks like she's got a large dollop of cream and wishes she had whiskers to lick.

I want to get Dina out of the way as I fear Natalie will leave if pushed too hard. "I'm really not interested in you and Sven and neither of us will breathe a word to Miles. I just need to know about these businesses."

Natalie shudders. "That morning you came to my flat, Harry? He'd accused me of having an affair with Sven just before you arrived. Said Sven was trying to ruin him, and he wasn't going to let him do that and shag me as well." She shudders again.

I say, "Do you think he might have moved the body? Maybe had something to do with his death?"

155

She shrugs. "Anything's possible with Miles if he's in one of his moods. It wasn't murder then? I did wonder…" Natalie rubs her hands together like she's cold.

"What do you know about the day he died? The Saturday I saw you I think."

"After you left, that Saturday morning I tried to call Sven. Someone answered his phone. I think it was Stephen."

"McNoble? Did he speak?"

"No but he has this cough, like there's a tickle in his throat he can't get rid of. Miles came back at about one and stayed all Saturday afternoon, mostly on the phone. I went out shopping for a bit, just to get away from him. I wanted to see Sven ask about the Will, why he was involving you but I didn't dare try, not with Miles about." She pauses, dragging on the cigarette. "We went to the club later. Everyone was there. Sven too, but I couldn't talk to him. That was the last time I saw him. There were always a lot of people about."

"McNoble?"

She nods.

Dina speaks first, which is just as well as I'm still trying to process all this. "You'll have to tell the police. About their background, just in case it was Miles who moved him."

Natalie sighs deeply. "I can't. You don't know what he'd do. Anyway, if Sven died naturally what does it matter?"

"We could still tell Miles about the flat?"

She locks glares with Dina but then smiles, although in a rather cold mechanical way. "You said I can lie, well, that's what I'll do. Sven's gone so if I deny it, who's Miles going to believe? You?" She picks up her wine glass and finishes it. "I'll just tell him to go ask Harry. He's going to be more interested in you now."

"Me?"

"You'll be in charge of implementing whatever Sven planned with Miles' businesses, won't you? As part of his Will."

Shit.

"Dina, if you try to dump me in the shit you can kiss goodbye to any help."

"As if you've given us any so far."

Natalie wrinkles her nose before tapping the drawing. "For what it's worth, that picture of Marita could be in Sven's flat, not mine. Do you know why he's drawn you two together?"

I shake my head. "You should think about that shelter."

"I'll stick with Miles. For now. He spends a lot of time away on business, so at least I get a break." She points at one of the photos, the one of the garden with the table and the urn. "That's out the back of Sven's bungalow, isn't it Harry? You remember the swing where we shared that joint?" She smiles in a way that lets me know she remembers what happened as clear as I do. The bit after the joint.

"Yes. Yes, you're right." I stare at the picture to hide my face; I can feel a blush rising to the surface.

She bursts out laughing, so unexpected after the previous conversation. "You've gone pink. Are you worried about your baby sister finding out what we did there?" She glances at Dina. "We had some fun on that swing. Both as high as a mountaintop on that super weed you had. You know, it's such a blur I can't even remember if we had sex. I think we did. I hope we did. It certainly feels like we did. Happy days, eh?" She stands up to go. "I don't know anything about the other one, the shops I mean. I'd better go."

"Wait. You said you wanted to talk about something."

She nods. "It'll keep." Enigmatic as ever.

***

After she leaves, Dina keeps staring at the photos. "Do you think Sven's Dad owned those shops? Maybe that's why they're here."

"Fuck. Frank."

"I'm sorry? Who's Frank, and why do you want me to fuck him?"

"Ha. You remember the pawnbroker? Worked for Sven's Dad?"

"Vaguely."

"I'm sure that's his shop. Was." I point at the third unit from the left.

Frank was really scary when I needed to pawn some stuff to raise money to pay McNoble. How long ago was that? 1976? It still horrifies me to this day. In the picture, the shop is boarded up.

Dina pours us the remnants of the wine and finishes hers in one mouthful. "You should check it out, shouldn't you?"

I nod. "His bungalow, too."

"You know what this means?"

I nod again, with a shrugged embellishment. "A visit home. I suppose we have to stay with Mum and Dad?"

But we both know the answer to that.

***

Dina goes to bed at 10:00 citing tiredness. I'm about to do the same when Zenda appears. Her hair is tucked into a scarf, which she fingers absentmindedly.

"Harry, do you have a moment?"

"Sure."

She fiddles with a loose strand. "I look ridiculous, don't I? Brenda said it would make me look trendy, but I feel like mutton dressed as lamb."

"You know what, Zenda? Around here no one will notice. Let your inner punk blossom."

She laughs. "You think I should get a Mohican? And a safety pin through my nose?"

"I'm not sure your family is made for body piercings."

"No, well, true." She coughs and puts her hands on the table. "Can I ask you to keep this a secret from Brenda?"

"I guess." I'm intrigued and not a little worried. Grown-ups confiding in me is a new and rather disturbing experience.

"I'm going to divorce Reginald. It will be my second failure, which I hate but really it's inevitable. He won't like it, not at all." She stops as a shudder runs from her shoulders down through her whole body. "I can't face telling him, not yet."

I guess the horror of what I'm thinking is written across my face.

"I'm not asking you to call him or deliver a letter or anything like that. I need a law firm and, well, you are clearly a very sensible young man. Does you firm do divorces?"

"Yes. Lucinda, my principal, is very good at it."

"It won't be pleasant. I guarantee Reginald will try to bully you and your firm. But there will be a decent fee, I expect."

I sat in on a new client interview about six months ago when we were first instructed. The woman had said something like that and Lucinda had taken her hand and said, "We will be here for you, come what may." The client had been so grateful.

I do the same, but in this case Zenda shifts from her seat and pulls me in for a hug, sobbing into my shoulder.

When she lets me go, she says, "I can't tell Brenda. Oh, she wants me to divorce him but this new Brenda, she'd be the first to go to tell him. I wouldn't put it past her to turn up at the court and barge in on one of his sessions, just to cause the maximum humiliation."

Now that would be worth the entrance money.

Saturday, 4th July 1981

Chapter Twenty-Four

Where Harry Cleans His Bike and goes for a Pint with McNoble

I wake at 10:00 and no one is up yet. Having nothing better to do, I take a bucket of soapy water down to the courtyard behind the flats to clean my bike and check its vital signs. When Dina is awake we can hitch to Hampshire and see if the family unit is still intact.

It is therapeutic, sponging off the grime, oiling the gears and checking the tyres. I still don't really know how bicycles work, but I'm very grateful when they do. It's like some mechanised act of devotion. Maybe I should form a new religion, paying homage to the humble velo.

I've just emptied the bucket of filthy water over some ill-looking geraniums out front when a car pulls up. I glance across, as you do, expecting a neighbour. When I see who it is my blood chills. The window on the driver's side slides down. "You free for that drink, Harry?"

McNoble.

"What do you want?" To my disquiet, he climbs out, spinning the car keys around his index finger. How does he make such a simple action look so intimidating?

"You need to get over yourself mate. The days when I wanted you dead are long gone. Don't you realise I don't care? Now, with my Dad it's different. He'd happily have you hung, drawn and quartered for fucking up his plans with your Mum, but not me. That's over. Can't we try to be civilised?" He offers me his hand.

I hesitate, then take the meaty paw. "Bit early, isn't it?"

He shrugs. "Then we can have a nice little chat until the boozer's open, can't we?"

I know I need to do what he says, get over myself, so while doing my best to hide my shaking I say as I turn for the front door, "I'll wash and change. Be down in five."

"If your sister's about, bring her too."

"Why? And how did you know she's here?" I narrow my eyes. "Did Natalie say?"

He taps the side of his nose before leaning on his car and beginning to clean his nails with his penknife. I'd guess it's the self-same one with which he stabbed me in the thigh when we first crossed paths. I hope my old rancid blood poisons him.

When I knock on Tim's door, Dina opens it a crack. "What?" I can see Jan Kruis' naked arse on the bed.

"Sorry. McNoble's appeared and wants to go for a drink. You're busy?"

She glances back. "Oh shit. Okay, give me five minutes." She only has a sheet wrapped around her and it barely covers those bits of one's sister a brother should never ever see. I leave quickly and head for the bathroom.

After a quick wash, I return to the hall to wait for Dina. I'm staring out of the window at the back of McNoble's square head when Brenda/Vera emerges, also wrapped in a sheet. At least Dina covered her breasts. I make a show of shading my eyes. "You know, seeing them on stage is one thing, but do you have to be quite such an exhibitionist? I haven't eaten yet and your tits are playing havoc with my breakfast choices."

"Don't you like fried eggs?" She opens the sheet completely revealing her pubes trimmed in the shape of a heart. "You're a total prude, aren't you? Do women's bodies intimidate you? Is it our essential fecundity, our Venus-as-dominatrix that worries you?" Happily, this speech is accompanied by her covering at least most of herself up.

"Please, Bren—"

"Fuck, Harry, they're just flesh and muscle wrapped in skin."

"Dobbin will have kittens, okay? Cover them for him."

She's not listening, just staring out of the window down at the street. As she does so she heaves the sheet back up and I can breathe again.

"Dina and I are off—"

To my surprise she steps back quickly, hugging the sheet to her. "What?"

She looks at me, her brow knitted.

"I was only going to ask if you or Dobbin could get some milk. We're going to Hampshire and may not get the chance."

Her voice seems to come from far away. "Milk?"

"I'd go, only we're having a quick drink with… with an old acquaintance first. Then we really need to be heading off."

She's staring out of the window again, although a pace back from the sill.

"You okay?"

She shakes her head hard and spins round to stare at me. She does look even more pale than usual. "Milk? Yes, of course. I'll go and get some."

But she doesn't move. Why's she being so odd?

"I'd better get on. Tell Dina I'll wait for her downstairs."

"NO! No." She grabs my arm, incidentally exposing her breast again. "Please wait. I… I need tea. Sweet. Two sugars. Would you? I'll… milk, yes, milk."

And she's off, butt-naked running for Dobbin's room, her oddly droopy arse jiggling with the sheet flapping behind her. Dobbin might be right. Much more of this and I could imagine her and me—"

"You ready?" Dina appears, holding a rucksack.

"I'm not sure. Vera wanted me to make her a cup of sweet tea, like she was about to faint and then she did a streak for her room."

"She's bonkers. That's what too much sex does to you."

I glance at her. "Does it? You're the expert."

"Ha ha. Come on, let's get this over with."

Just then Brenda/Vera reappears wearing a T-shirt and shorts. No shoes. She grabs the door handle. "You making that tea, Harry? Please. Won't be a mo. Milk. Yes – milk."

The door slams and I look at Dina. "Yep, bonkers. Hang on, I'll make a pot for her. It won't take a moment."

Dina stays in the hall, clearly thinking I'm soft. Really, I'm just putting off having to deal with McArse.

She's staring down at the street as I finish boiling the kettle. When she turns to me, she's smiling. "Now why would Vera have anything to say to Stephen McNoble?"

I join her. McNoble is back leaning on his car. There's no sign of Brenda/Vera.

"She's just gone, I guess for the milk. But she had a very, hmm, vigorous conversation with that lump of gristle. You want to wait and ask her why?"

"Nah, let's just get rid of him. He's making the street look messy."

As we leave the flat Dina, who is wearing a denim jacket and a pink flouncy short skirt, does a twirl. "You like it? Jan gave it to me last night. It's a ra-ra." She twirls again this time showing her knickers.

"Lovely. Come on. And try to keep your pants to yourself."

"She's right, you are a prude."

"Oh, come on. It's not normal to go flashing your tits and arse at your flatmate."

"What have you got against the female form?"

"Nothing at all."

"Exactly. If you could get yourself up close and sweaty against the female form you might not be so inhibited."

"Oh do shut up."

"You're jealous."

McNoble is waiting by the junction of our street with the main road. As we approach I say, "I didn't know you knew Brenda."

"Who?"

"The woman who came out of our block and spoke to you."

"Her? She gave me an earful about parking here. Told her to fuck off. Come on, let's find somewhere for a pint."

He lies well, which is hardly a surprise, but I'm sure he is lying.

While I'm contemplating calling him out, he turns to Dina. I don't think Dina has seen McNoble since we fought in our kitchen back in 1976 and he punched her to the floor. If that was the last time, either they've both forgotten or she's decided to forgive, because she reaches up to kiss him and he hugs her back. "You've put on some weight." She taps his belly.

He smiles. "Resting muscle. You're all woman now. Nice skirt. Suits you." He nods appreciatively. "Where shall we go?"

I suggest a pub by the river called the Ship. As we drive, Dina chats to him and I try to work out why he's lying about Brenda/Vera.

The pub has only just opened yet it is already quite crowded and boisterous. McNoble buys us drinks. No one seems keen to talk. Eventually McNoble says, "Miles Tupps thinks he's a clever business man and entrepreneur, but he had nothing on Sven Andersen. That man was a fucking genius."

I nod and sip the second half of my pint.

"I heard you have his Will."

I keep my face as neutral as possible.

"This cop, Wallace, mentioned it. A bird, not bad looking if she would only dump those trousers. She'd look great in your skirt, Di."

He smiles at her and she smiles back. It's only then I realise this is all for show and she still loathes him. That pleases me.

She says, "Stephen, stop mucking about. What is it you want?"

He nods. "The cop told me you have his Will, it's legit and you are the executor. She'll almost certainly tell Miles the same thing. And he'll want to know what it says. Pronto. He won't put up with nods and enigmatic smiles, Harry. That's all."

"Really?" Dina pushes her glass at him. "Thanks for the tip. If that's it, we'll be off."

He pulls a face and suggests we should stay while he gets another round in. While he's at the bar, she says, "I get the feeling he might be helpful."

"Him? He never finished off our fight. I think that one has a looooong memory."

When McNoble returns with the drinks, I say, "The day Sven came and saw me about his Will, you hustled him away after I'd taken the instructions. Why?"

McNoble rarely smiles but this is one of those few occasions. "Yes, that was strange, wasn't it? All a bit convenient."

"Convenient?" Dina sounds as perplexed as I am.

"He called me, asked me to pick him up and make it look like we were putting him under pressure to hurry up."

"You knew why he was there?"

"Nope, not a clue. But, yes, I knew it was where you worked. Catching up for old times, maybe? He didn't say."

"He didn't say?" Dina sounds incredulous. "And you didn't ask?"

"Of course I asked. He was in an odd mood, not that that was unusual. He said, 'It's just as if the stars aligned so I took advantage of the celestial serendipity.'" McNoble shakes his head. "Wanker. I wrote that down because I had no idea what the fuck he meant. Still don't."

"He nearly lost me my job butting in on my meeting."

McNoble cocks his head to one side. "Yeah, he said. Some old boy. A Knight or something."

"Sir Penshaw Grimsdale."

"Yeah. Grimsdale. You must be doing well Harry if he's a client."

"You know him?" I'm sure I sound suspicious.

McNoble takes a moment to answer. "You can't not know him, can you? He's always in the papers these days. Anyway," he changes tack, "Miles believes, and I don't know how true this is, that Sven owed him a large amount of cash for ending their arrangement when he did. Sven told him to piss off, but he'll come after you for it when he knows you're in control of things. He needs funds pretty desperately and if it's not been left to him in the Will he'll be after whoever gets the money from it."

"If he can show he's owed money, he just has to make a claim on the estate and then…" I peter out.

McNoble is shaking his head. "We're not talking legit, Harry. There aren't contracts unless they're of the 'taking a contract out' kind. You know what I mean?"

Dina says, "But he'll have to prove he's owed the money. Won't he?"

I nod. "And there needs to be assets from which to pay him. Did Sven have much?"

McNoble smiles. "Sven was very rich, but I've no idea where he kept everything. I'm sure it will be safe." His smile widens, and I decide I really need a pee. He carries on. "I doubt there are many bank accounts or share portfolios. Knowing Sven's love of showing off how clever he was, there'll be some sort of subterfuge. A puzzle maybe?"

Since when has McNoble used words like 'subterfuge' correctly? It then occurs to me I told Natalie we were trying to work out a puzzle. She has to have told McNoble. Fuck her.

McNoble says, "I know he had the flat under Miles and Natalie's and I know she and Sven were having an affair, not that Sven wanted the sex, but he knew it was the only way to keep Natalie reasonably safe, keeping her close. He told me he felt bad about that, about misleading her but he needed Miles to behave while he got ready to dump the news on him that he was pulling out and he felt he could do that better if he had Natalie reporting back on Miles' moods and plans."

So she was having an affair. Dina was right, not that she shows it. She'll no doubt save the smugness for later when we're alone. But it doesn't feel right, the idea that Sven would string Natalie along. He was many things, but I didn't think he'd do something like that. "How do you know all this? If it's in fact true," I ask.

"We were sort of partners. How do you think a foppish Noel Coward impersonator was going to realise his Father's criminal empire without someone who understands the ways and means? Someone who the other side might believe wouldn't take no for an answer? We talked about it at the funeral, just in outline and it's gone from there."

I stare at him and his piggy eyes stare back. I say, "You're Sven's muscle? I don't believe you. Why would he work with you? He hated the criminality of his Father. Why link up with you?"

He sighs. "Because he had no choice once he decided to wind things up rather than just abandon everything. I know you don't believe me. I wouldn't believe me in your shoes. But think about it. What other choice did he have? Anyway, we had things in common."

"Like what?" This comes from Dina.

"A loathing of our Fathers. Okay, I learnt things from mine, which Sven avoided with his but both of us grew up hating what they were." He finishes his pint in a mouthful. "Sven felt he should have done more, and sooner, to stop his Father. He ruined his Mother's life – Sven always felt he was the reason she died – he made his step-Mother's existence hell and if Sven hadn't stepped in to protect Marita God knows what might have happened there. While, yes, he hated what he had inherited and wanted out, he wasn't just going to wipe his hands of it. He was determined to unpick it and then do something with the cash. He understood he couldn't do that alone. So, okay, yes – I wasn't the ideal choice for a business associate, but I was useful. And because I wanted to screw my Dad too, he believed me when I said I'd help him. It worked well while it worked."

"It stopped?"

"Sven wasn't usually moody like he was recently. Something worried him. And that worried me. It was like he was planning something that he knew I'd try to stop. He'd pretty much finished what he set out to do, but then Marita goes missing, he gets you to make a new Will and then he dies. All a bit odd, too much of a coincidence."

I really really want that piss now. Dina says, "He'd already made a Will? You said, 'new Will?'"

"So he said. He was always thinking ahead." He coughs, like something is stuck in his throat. "Does anyone other than Marita benefit in this one? It won't be his step-Mum. Anyway, even if it was she can look after herself, but I know it won't be her. Is there anyone else who needs to be warned? It could get a bit nasty for them."

"Who else would benefit?" Dina is frowning hard while I'm trying to open my throat and breathe.

McNoble smiles and points at me. "Him. That's exactly who Sven would give it to and that's why I'm here to warn him. And help him."

With that I piss myself ever so slightly.

***

When I've tidied myself up, he explains. "Some time ago we talked about making sure the money was safe. Selling these business interests usually means you don't get cash but another business opportunity, which eventually leads to cash. That has to be kept somewhere safe, sometimes laundered, before putting it into a bank. Because it's a large sum, that causes some suspicions. It doesn't help that we're so young. No one expects us to have money. Not legally." He shrugs like he sees the irony, but I still can't believe McNoble has the wit to understand irony. "We needed somewhere or someone who was utterly trustworthy. If he wanted to protect Marita from the Mileses of this world, and they'll be a few others even nastier than Tupps, he needed to put it all in the hands of someone he really trusted. That was when Sven mentioned you. He said he'd never met anyone as moral as Harry Spittle, someone who would bend over backwards to do the right thing. We did some thinking. Give it to you and once Miles & Co. were sorted and the money clean and free of traps and any possible danger to Marita, it could go to where he really wanted it to go. Marita and me, so we can use it to do some good."

It's such a fucking nightmare it could well be true. I say, "He wanted you to have the money? You said, 'Marita and me?'"

McNoble's smile damages the concept of enigmatic; there are dozens of possible interpretations. "Is that an issue?"

"It's... why not give it to you now? I certainly don't want it."

That smile again. "You'd have to ask Sven. Maybe you can find a Ouija board? I have my suspicions. So you are the beneficiary?"

Dina says before I can answer, "He probably didn't trust you."

I'm still pondering where McNoble learnt the word beneficiary? Five syllables for God's sake. He says, "Maybe, although if you get to speak to Marita she'll tell it differently. It's more that if I'm in control then it'll be more difficult for Marita to be troubled."

"Troubled? Who by?"

"So are you the beneficiary, Harry?" he asks again.

I nod. It seems pointless denying it. Dina sucks on her straw noisily, like a five-year-old. She pushes the bottle of Coke away and says, "If Harry is the beneficiary, how do we know it is really meant for Marita?"

McNoble nods like that is a fair point. "Harry knows it. Sven will have made it clear. Hasn't he Harry?"

He's right. Sven had made it plain in several ways.

"Maybe." Dina has on her Sherlock Holmes face. "But what's to stop Harry—"

"Besides me?" McNoble smiles.

Dina nods. "Granted you could pull off his fingers easily enough but really, with the money you are hinting at Harry could get himself some protection."

McNoble's face suggests he's getting bored. I recognise the signs; he will soon revert to type and extract one of my vital organs to chew on. He says, "First, Harry's not like that. Second, Harry wants to be a lawyer. But the problem is, he's holding a handwritten Will that supersedes a typed one and leaves him everything. He's an executor with another lawyer from whom he needs a helping hand in his career, a lawyer who has some significant money issues of his own and—"

"Does he?" Jeremy in debt. That has me interested.

"You have no idea. He likes a bit of a flutter, stupid sod. Anyway, the Will allows Harry's firm to fleece the estate for its fees and given the only people involved are Harry and Panther that will be easy-peasy. But what will the Law Society's professional standards people say? Sounds a little like abusing client money and hardly complying with his fiduciary duties. And that's before they hear the client died and oddly ended up very close to Harry's flat when he had no reason to be in that part of London. If the death turns out to be a mite suspicious…"

I goggle at him. He's not even smirking. "You set all this up, didn't you?"

"I'm just pointing out what it looks like. Third – and most importantly – I can help. If you tell me where the money is, how he's hidden it, I can make sure it gets to the right place and you retain the ability to walk to the toilet and piss standing up."

Dina is still in super-sleuth mode. "You knew all along, didn't you? You didn't need to ask him if he benefitted."

He nods. The smug shit.

Dina is patently very cross. She is beginning to sound like Mum. "How'd you know all this? About the Will?"

"Detective Constable Wallace is rather careless. She leaves all sorts of things lying around. And I've always been able to read upside down. Another drink?"

I want to give in. Maybe he knows about the mystery pictures too and can help, but Dina stops me. "You know as much as we do. We've no idea what he has or where it is, beyond two ordinary bank accounts totalling a few hundred quid. We thought Marita had it already."

It's his turn to pull a sour face. "No, she has nothing. Look, it's easy to tease Harry. He still thinks I want to chop him up and feed him to the pigs."

"Don't you?"

He looks exasperated. "For fuck's sake Spittle, no. Once, maybe. Back when we were at uni, I thought you were a wanker whose Mother was a gold digger after my Dad's money. Maybe she was but you stopped their plans and I'm grateful for that. Not that you'll ever believe me. And I'll be the first to say I don't have Sven's hatred of his Father's illegal money. I'm much more pragmatic."

There he goes again, spitting out the dictionary. It can't be him. He's acquired someone else's brain somehow.

"But Sven was good to me. He helped me with some issues I had with my Father." He looks uncomfortable. Charlie Jepson tried to set my Mum up by buying Hemingways, the hotel where I met Sven, Penny and Natalie, and unwittingly I stopped it. With a fair bit of help from others, including Sven's Dad who I then nearly accidentally killed when a lorry's worth of silage filled the car he was in. McNoble was and probably still is an oily slime-ball.

Dina finishes her Coke. "What'd he do? To save you from the Evil One?"

"It doesn't matter. Thing is, we didn't finish what we started, and, in his memory, I want to make sure we do. Miles is one place to start, but there must be others."

A thought occurs to me. "Why did your Father go to prison?"

That startles him. "Where'd you hear that?"

"My Dad."

"Yeah, your family. That makes sense. He never could leave well alone. He ran these hotels in various small towns along the coast. Brothels really. Someone gave him away – living off immoral earnings, not paying tax, using violence to control things, that sort of fun and games. Then there was this fraud over holiday insurance. He lost a lot when he was inside and... yeah, well, the shit is still just about managing to wriggle out of his past. Once upon a time that would have been my career all mapped out."

I stare over Dina's shoulder at the Thames shimmering in the heat. Somewhere the faint sound of the cricket commentary floats over to me. An Australian wicket must have fallen. How long ago was I at

Lord's, in the company of peers of the realm, talking about Shareholders' Agreements and company formations? That's the world I want to inhabit – a world of integrity, honest dealing. A world of lawyers and bankers. Not this sleazy subsection of the criminal underbelly.

McNoble has stood up, looming over me. "I don't want the fucking money, okay? It's for Marita. I just want to see through what Sven and I started."

Somehow, I stand. "I don't want it either and I don't particularly want to finish what he started if it's all the same to you. I don't have to accept either it or the appointment as executor. I can resign. Let Marita sort it out with your kind assistance."

I turn to look from McNoble to Dina. They both stare at me like I'm mad. They both have the same incredulous expression. They both say, "You can't do that."

Sunday, 5th July 1981

Chapter Twenty-Five

A Visit Home Reveals Very Little but Still Causes Tension

A Vicar from Basingstoke picks us up in Wandsworth and drops us at Fleet Services on the M3. Almost immediately a couple stop in their little sports car and offer to let us squeeze in the back. The girl has a mane of stunning Titian hair. "You two in love like us?" She doesn't seem to want an answer for which I'm grateful because I have a strong feeling Dina will say yes to ensure we get to keep the lift.

"We're going to Bournemouth to see Gary Glitter and make love on the beach."

I glance at Dina and we have difficulty not smirking. Both sound painful and rather gritty. The girl, whose name is blown away by the wind as we hurtle down the outside lane, stares adoringly at her beau. Abruptly she leans over the back of her seat to make sure we hear. "Have you ever tried this?"

She grins and swivels back, bending over the man's lap. It doesn't take much imagination to guess what's happening. Especially when he goes rigid and presses back into his seat. Unexpectedly we leave the M3 and head off down the A303. Somehow, despite the fight he is putting up he manages to re-join the end of the motorway before we hit some traffic where the three lanes merge into one. As the car slows so much the woman surfaces, breathless with pink cheeks and shiny lips. "Do you want a go? It's such fun."

I'm incapable of saying anything but Dina manages to hiss, through gritted teeth, "just let him drive you stupid bitch," which gets an astonished look from her and a guffaw of laughter from him. They drop us a mile or so from home and we walk the rest of the way.

Home is a large whitewashed five-bedroomed house on a busy junction just inside the New Forest boundary. It's one of three houses in a small cluster, miles from anywhere. Utterly idyllic except when you are a teenager. We both hated living there with its lack of reliable transport and acting as a buffer between our warring parents. For the last seven or eight years, the middle part of the house has been given over to guests of the B&B business, while Mum has increasingly turned the garden over to growing vegetables as part of her own self-sufficiency plans. She has green fingers and a poisoner's way with

173

cooking. We both know the risk we are taking arriving in time for lunch.

"Don't look shocked when you see the state of the place." Dina's expression has hardened since we started walking. "And Dad said she's keeping rabbits. For food."

"Is Mrs Ohja still helping with the B&B?"

Dina shrugs her ignorance. For a few years after they moved in in the summer of 1976, Mr and Mrs Ohja – Ravi and his wife Pritti – were the major reason why the B&B remained a going concern. Lately they've been less involved, but at least until recently Mrs Ohja still did most of the cooking in Mum's various absences. The Ohja's live at Hemingways these days, where Ravi is general manager, a role once earmarked for Mum as part of the Charlie Jepson takeover plans that I thwarted. The Ohja's loyalty to my parents is extraordinary. Ravi and Dad found a mutual interest in their love of Elvis Presley and mechanical gadgets while Mrs Ohja – I'll never feel comfortable calling her Pritti – and Mum battled over the kitchen for a month until they came to an understanding of sorts after Dina found out she was pregnant. Despite their patent differences they make a good team. The Ohja's have two children: a girl called Noor, who must be 15 now, and a whirlwind of a boy called Sajid who would be 12. I hope they're about as they are the best ice-breakers.

I ask, not really expecting an answer, "How do you think Dad's coping with Mum back home? He's had it to himself for a while."

"It has to be two and a half months since she left Aunt Petunia's." My aunt and uncle Norman own the family garage business they inherited from my Grandfather and which Dad mentioned was up for sale. "I guess they are massing their troops for a final assault."

"I wonder how the garage sale is going. If they get some cash, it'll ease some of the tension."

Another disinterested shrug. We are walking down Mothball Hill – so named for the unusual smell that no one has ever isolated but is redolent of old ladies' wardrobes – and are a few hundred yards from the garden. Dina stops abruptly and says, "Let's just make sure we have the story straight. You're doing Sven's Will. You need to pick some stuff up from his bungalow so can we borrow the car? After we're done and we drop it back home, we need to get back to London therefore we head for the station to catch the train home."

"I can't afford—"

"Shut up. Of course we'll hitch but if we say we're going to Mum'll get huffy and insist we need to stay and go tomorrow and that'll mean at least two unnecessary meals. Is your lower intestine ready for that sort of punishment?"

"She'll make us stay and eat anyway."

"Well, if she tries I'll say I'm going to Jim's for tea with George."

"Bugger. What am I going to do? Can't I come and see my nephew?"

"No. Anyway, things might get a bit tense with Jim, you know." She pulls a face.

"Jan?"

"No. Uni. I need to explain."

I stop and eye her suspiciously. "He doesn't know you're planning on going? You've had a place for ages."

"I know, all right? It just hasn't come up." She strides off again.

I stay put and call after her. "So why does he think you're in London? Please tell me he knows you're in London?"

She spins back, glaring in my direction. "Stop being a fucking know-all and come on." And she's off again, leaving me with my mouth hanging open. She never, well almost never, swears. She calls back. "Don't mention it to him, please. Okay?"

I catch her up. "We could try to see Frank, maybe? I mean, it is a clue and a pretty neat excuse."

Her mood has changed and she's barely able to look up from her shoes. "I really do need to see Jim and George. It is only fair."

She's probably right.

***

The last few hundred yards drag and we are both rather introspective when we turn the corner and hear a hubbub of conversation. The garden is full of people and the gate at the end of the garden is locked. That's new. As a result we make for the front of the house, catching glimpses of people in bright casual clothes and a fair bit of lively chatter. Surely my parents aren't having a party? They never have parties. Rounding the corner, we peer through the side gate; we can see about 15 people from small children to Asoka, Ravi's Father and known to all as Papaji, who must be approaching 80.

"God," Dina looks thunderous, "since when do they have garden parties?"

175

"Harry! Dina!"

Noor Ohja, who is now nearly my height but still pencil slim, bounds over and hugs me and then Dina. We are aware of the guests turning and smiling. Any moment a hurtling mass of humanity in the shape of her younger brother will crash into my testicles. But there's nothing. "Where's Sajid?"

Noor's fantastic teeth light up Hampshire and counterpoint her furry eyebrows, which beetle at the mention of her brother. "Inside, listening to some punk band. They've been banned on Radio 1 but he's utterly hung up on them. You may know them. The Twats?"

"Oh God. Yes. But, hang on, they can't have a record out."

She shakes her head. "He's in with this bad crowd. One boy, they all call him Roach, no idea why, he gave Sajid a tape. A bootleg of some concert. He loves the girl singer but she just screeches and wails. Mum hates it, so he's gone upstairs to sulk." She grabs Dina's hand. "Come on. Mum is in the kitchen with your Mum, and Dad is in the shed with your Dad. Nothing changes, eh?" She endows us with another huge smile and the world feels an infinitely better place.

Dina waves at the crowd. "Who are all these people?"

"Dad's people from the hotel. Well, some of them. He's introduced a summer party for staff and their families. Half one Sunday and half the next. To help your folks he's hired here." She looks serious. "Things aren't so good, you know. You hear about the rabbits?"

I nod. "Some food business of Mum's."

"Yes, but you heard what your Dad did?"

We shake our heads.

"He released them, and they've decimated your Mum's crop of carrots and beans and parsnips and all the brassicas. They're not talking, and the rabbits have been given a death sentence. I love those little bunnies. I hope your Mum isn't really going to go through with it."

She clearly doesn't know Mum. Ruthless is her middle name.

As we wander amongst the people I look to see if there is anyone I know from when I worked there. I spot Magda, the East German receptionist with her hard efficiency and soft heart. She still has the face of a chemically enhanced sprinter but the rest of her looks stunning in a red slinky dress displaying a lot of her performance-enhanced breasts that I've dreamt of summiting for years. Before she had edges; now she has proper curves.

176

I also see the head waiter, Terry the Terrible. He looks exactly the same. There's no way he will remember me. He turns and makes a beeline for us, hand outstretched. "Harry? Goodness you look grand. How are you?"

I'm flummoxed. He hated me.

"Tragedy about poor Sven. Did you and he spend much time together?"

"Not really. I—"

"And do you see Nancy? And Persephone? The two girls? Lively souls."

"Yes. Natalie and Penelope."

"Of course." He wraps an arm around my shoulder, cutting Dina out of the conversation. "Now let's see who you know here."

While he drags me to a small group I see Dina and Noor link arms and head indoors.

Magda beams at me. "Zo, 'Arry. How izz ze beeg lawyer? You still vith Penny?"

I shake my head and smile. Her smile grows as she says, "Zo! Now ve 'ave sex, ja?" She bursts into laughter and the others in her group look nervously at me and then her. They must be new and still at the terrified stage. At least two look pasty and spotty enough to be students. I take her hand and press it against my chest, in close proximity to my heart. "I will always be yours. Shall we try Dad's shed? Or the gazebo? Whose turn is it on top?"

Magda's eyes widen, the laughter increases, and she throws her arms around me before giving me a firm, deep and rather metallic-tasting kiss. "I could eat you, 'Arry Spittle. We make babies later okay?" She rubs my groin with her tungsten thigh and grins.

I keep my arm around her shoulder and look at the astonished faces. "If you haven't worked it out yet, this woman is the most important and generous person at Hemingways. When I was there years ago, I would have been in so much trouble if it wasn't for her help." I pull myself free. "Now I must find my Mum and Dad. Take care, Magda."

"Ja, 'Arry and zere vill alvays be a bed for you at 'Emingvays."

I shake away inappropriate thoughts that involve me taking up that offer and wander to the house as Mum appears at the backdoor. I watch her scan the crowd until she sees me. The way her face lights up as she strides forward makes my stomach jolt. If there's one emotion

177

Mum can trigger in me with just one look it is guilt. I let her approach, marshalling my defences.

Close up, I can't miss how dark the rings under her eyes are. "Harold. So grown up! Am I pleased to see you?!" She hugs me, holding on for longer than I am expecting. When she releases me, she turns half away and blows her nose. "Let's sit on the swing," she waves down the garden to where the old gazebo sat – Dina and I used to sneak there to share a joint when family life got us down. Now it's a wooden thing like a bus shelter with a swing under it.

Rascal the family cat is sleeping in the sun. I'm very wary of him but Mum just pushes him to one side and he makes no attempt to fight her off. "Poor old thing. He can barely get up here now." She pats the seat next to her and says, "Things have changed quite a bit."

Before I can even frame a question, Mum asks, "Your Father said he'd spoken to you. What did he say?"

"We didn't speak for long, but he wrote a letter. The garage is going to be sold and you'll get your money back to use on the B&B." I want her to be the one to mention my money. I still don't believe she intends to try to keep it.

She speaks in a low monotone, as if we'll be overheard. "He has such grand ideas, your Father." She sounds bitter.

"How so?"

"He thinks this sale is the answer to our prayers. *His prayers.*"

"And you don't?"

She smiles, rather as she does when Dad's trying to make a joke that is inappropriate for the company they are in. Trying to be tolerant, but at heart just embarrassed. "He means well." Her eyes dart at me, like I've said something unexpected. "He doesn't realise…" She peters out and I follow her gaze; Dina is approaching with Noor in tow. "Later."

Mrs Ohja also comes over; she is all smiles.

Mrs Ohja is what Mum once described as a sparrow of a woman; she seems if anything smaller than ever, more wren-like. Her eyes, dark impenetrable jewels, still twinkle like she knows what I'm thinking, and are still with that hint of a ferocious love that makes you want her on your side. "Harold Spittle. The important lawyer! Come and give me the hug I deserve."

I glance at Mum. Once she would have bristled but now she smiles with genuine warmth. Mrs Ohja takes the seat I have vacated and the two women link arms.

Mrs Ohja says, "Has Veronica explained the plans for the B&B? Aren't they exciting?"

I sort of nod, peering at Mum for guidance. She's looking over the fence, away from me. "Not in detail."

"Your Father has taken his time to understand the benefits, but Ravi has been encouraging him to see sense."

I force myself not to look confused, nodding slowly like I know this. Mum still won't look at me.

Mrs Ohja changes tack in the beat of a hornet's wing. "Dina says you have work to do. I have given her my car keys and we will expect you for roti at six. I have checked the trains and there is one from Brockenhurst at eight – and before you say anything, I will pay for the ticket if it means we can share a meal. Take Noor. She needs to get away from all these boring adults."

"What about Sajid?"

She frowns but merely waves at the front of the house.

Mum has turned to me, looking confused. "Work? What work?"

"Come on, H," Dina pulls me away, "we need to get on."

"What work?"

"I'll explain, Veronica. Off you go," Mrs Ohja says.

I catch Mum's expression as she listens to Mrs Ohja while I'm bring dragged up the garden.

Dina says quickly, before we catch up with Noor, "I told Mrs Ohja and she said it's best if she explains. You know those moths you said Sven gave Dad? According to Mrs O, when Mum found out where they were from she went barmy and tried to throw them out. I don't think she's forgiven the Andersen family for what happened back then. I think Pritti is the only person who'll make sure Mum doesn't have a fit of the screaming abdabs."

"Who's Sven?" Noor is skipping in a way I can no longer imagine ever feeling relaxed enough to manage. What it is to be young and innocent.

Dina keeps pushing me forward. "We'll explain on the way."

Chapter Twenty-Six

Dina and Harry Make a Discovery and Realise that, Yes, Sven was an Arse

I haven't been back to Sven's house in over four years. As we turn into the drive some powerful memories are evoked. Sven had several parties here during the summer we worked together. At one Natalie and I got stoned on a swing when she tried to give me a blowjob but I was rather too quick for her; at another Penny and I made love in the small wood between the garden to Sven's bungalow and the main house, then occupied by his parents and Marita, before we were chased away by a ferocious dog. When we managed to reach safety, we realised we'd left several items of clothing behind, much to my embarrassment. Penny, who's never minded who sees her starkers, loved it.

All together the house, bungalow and grounds cover several acres and include within the boundary a small Roman hill fort and an ancient deciduous wood. From the top of the rise where the hill fort sits you can see the Isle of Wight and the merest sliver of sea.

To reach the bungalow you turn left at the top of the drive; to reach the main house you go right and through the wood. The gates are shut and rusty but not locked. I'm all for thinking twice but Dina directs Noor to push them open and I let the women dictate.

"It's a mess. Doesn't anyone live here? Are there ghosts?" Noor is so excited she bounces across the back seat to see out of each side.

The lawns are more like meadows and the drive is full of weeds. Dina drives us up to the front door. "It would be good if there was key under the mat."

There's no mat, nor a flower pot by the front door, nor a key on the door frame.

"Let's try the back, shall we?" I lead the way around the side of the house. We peer through the French doors that are also locked.

"Not much by way of furniture."

The room at the back of the house stretches all the way across – a sort of kitchen, dinner and living space combined. "It only ever had that table and six chairs. Not much inside either, if I remember right. One bed and a stereo. Sven hated having to live so close to his Father."

"I'll try the windows." Noor skips away.

Dina rubs her chin. "Do we break in?"

"Not yet. I think we're meant to have a look there." I point away from the house to the large ornamental urn in the middle of the lawn. "It's in the picture he left."

Dina smiles and mimics Noor by skipping across to it. It's easily four-foot high and when you add in the concrete plinth it's at least seven foot off the ground. "Can you climb up?"

I walk around it. The urn sticks out from its base giving it a rather intimidating overhang. Cautiously I reach for the lip and try to pull myself up. The urn wobbles violently. "Shit." I leap back and sit down hard on the grass, expecting the bloody thing to topple over on top of me. It comes to a rest back where it started. "We need a ladder."

"Where's the picture?" Dina digs it out of my briefcase. "There. The table. That's why he's put it in. You use the table. Where is it?"

Just then Noor appears. Dina says, "Have you seen a table?"

She nods. "It's around the side. I used it to have a look in one of the upper rooms. It's full of pictures."

That makes us really determined to get inside. We hurry to fetch the table. When it is in place and before I can stop her, Noor jumps up. She's so graceful.

"What can you see?"

Noor gingerly peers over the edge. We've warned her not to put her weight on the urn. "There's a bag, I think. At the bottom." She looks back. "I need something to hook it with."

Dina goes back to the picture. "There. What's that?"

Leaning against the wall is a broom or something. "Did you see anything?"

They both shake their heads.

"We'd better check." We head for where it was shown to be leaning. "There's nothing… wait." I tug at the rampant geraniums. Lying tangled in some foliage is an ancient garden hoe. I yank it free and take it to Noor.

She goes fishing and in next to no time the three of us are gathered around the table with an old leather satchel facing us. Noor is bouncing with excitement, firing off questions that I don't want to answer but to which Dina patiently responds. I start on at the first strap when Dina's hand stops me. "What about the police? Should you tell them? Let them open it?"

Noor squeals. "Police? You're not serious?"

I'm a bit irritated with them both. "He died of natural causes, okay? I'm his executor and this is his house." Her caution is probably sensible, but after 18 months of being exposed to the bullshit of the legal world I'm learning the art of self-justification and ex post facto reasoning. "If they thought they should search here they would have done it already."

She shrugs.

"They know this address from the Will, don't they? I have a duty to assemble the estate's assets."

For a moment, Dina looks about to argue; then she grins and nods. "Carry on, sergeant," she says in her best Captain Mainwaring voice.

Inside is an old box. I'm gobsmacked. "For fuck's sake, how did he get that?"

Noor giggles, embarrassed at my language while Dina looks at me, demanding an explanation.

"It's Ruth's box. Or maybe the one like it that Monica Jepson owned. This is so weird."

Dina says, "Sorry? What are you on about?"

By way of an explanation I turn the box over and after a bit of a struggle, trigger the secret compartment. "Ruth James, Jim's cousin, stole a box from Jim's Dad. Remember? The one with the illegal diamonds in?"

"That one? Bloody hell, is this it?"

"It might be." I look at Noor. "About the time you came to Hampshire, back in the mid-70s, I was going out with this girl called Ruth. Her uncle. Jim's Dad?" Noor nods her understanding. "He didn't trust banks so kept valuables around his house, in boxes and vases and things. One like this had a load of diamonds in it that he'd illegally imported. I met this woman when I worked in Hemingways with the man whose bungalow this is. She had a box just the same and showed me how to open the secret compartment." I look at Dina, "Monica Jepson, Stephen McNoble's step-Mum. I found the diamonds. And here we are again, courtesy of Sven Andersen and his little games. I told him all about the box. This was meant for me, wasn't it?"

"Did you doubt it?"

Yes, I think I did. Or at least I wanted to. Not anymore.

To cover the increasing sense that Sven's ghost is actually watching me, I poke my fingers in the open drawer. There's a key. I also find something stuck to the roof of the slot. I carefully unpick it; it's is a sheet of paper with something like a crossword puzzle grid written on it, but there are no clues. The grid has seven lines of empty squares, each of a different length. Then there is a space and a final line, but this line is edged in thick black ink, as if each square is important. This line has eight empty squares.

Dina takes it from me. "He's having fun, isn't he? The sod."

Fun, yes, I suppose it is. I say, "Bastard."

***

Inside, the bungalow is very musty with cobwebs hanging from the ceilings and the door to the kitchen very stiff. "God, what's that stink?"

We can all smell it and it isn't good. Dina goes and opens the French doors. "Smells like something's died."

We have a look but can't find anything. We check the other rooms; nothing. "Where are these paintings, Noor?"

"Upstairs."

Dina looks confused. "Upstairs? But this is a bungalow. Show me."

While the two girls go back outside, I stand in the hall. When we had parties, Sven used to say, 'And if you get lucky, go up there.' It comes back to me – a collapsible ladder to the roof space. Noor and Dina return. "What she didn't say was having climbed on the table she then shinned up the drainpipe to see through the dormer window."

We study the hall ceiling; there's a hatch that's not at all apparent if you aren't looking for it. Dina has her hands on her hips. "How do we get to that?"

Noor heads back outside. "The table."

I follow. "No, the hoe."

Dina stays put, looking sceptical but the hoe once again proves its worth. I manage to dislodge the hatch and pull down the chord that frees the ladder. "Ta-da." As it opens the stench increases.

Dina catches my look. "What's up there? A body?"

"Don't be daft. Noor just saw pictures." But even so I'm a touch concerned as I climb up.

From below, she says, "He went to a lot of trouble, H. He must have known someone was after him."

The seriousness of her tone makes me shudder, but Noor is buzzing; she's up after me, pushing me to hurry along. She quickly finds a light switch. Inside there are the drawings Noor told us about and some bits of furniture. On the floor, and probably explaining the smell, several birds lie dead. A small window is open, which maybe explains how they got in.

The pictures Noor saw are hanging on two walls. One set is of different people. Not exactly portraits. The other set appear to be motorcars. Dina goes to the pictures of people. The first is Marita and the third is me. We are the only ones that are full face; in the rest the features are hidden and in some cases not much is shown of the person.

I go and stare at my picture. I'm sitting on the swing in his garden with my head down staring at my lap. No one else would know why, but I do. I'm wiping up the aftermath of my failed attempt to have sex with Natalie. I go to the little window. Sure enough, you can easily see the swing from here. The shit was spying on us. Not that he ever said.

Behind me, Noor has opened some cupboards; Dina says, "Well, the mystery of his stuff is solved." Boxes fill the bottom with a rack of shirts – the stupid jolly prints he loved – hanging from the top.

Noor picks up a paint box. "He's got some awesome stuff."

I'm still staring at the pictures. "I don't suppose his car is in there too?"

Dina moves down the line behind me. "Do you know these other people?"

I shrug. I'm still wondering what this is about when she moves to the other line and I follow. She peers at one. "Isn't this an advert for that German car?"

"Yes, I think so. They might all be adverts. Isn't that a Jap car?"

She counts them. "Eights cars. Six people."

Noor is by the table. "There are photos of each picture here. Plus, one of the whole room showing both rows. And, look." She points at the table. "There was one here. Another person. You can see the dust has settled around it." She wipes her finger twice. "Although it's been gone for a while because there's dust where it used to be too." She grins at me. "I watch too many cop shows."

Dina moves quickly to the line of people and peers at the space after the last one. "There was one here, too. I can feel where there was a picture hook; the paper's rough and, see, there's a faint line like someone outlined it." She lifts the picture next to her. "No outline here. Or here," as she moves to another. "I'd say whoever took it wanted to let you know how big it was. It's a different size, isn't it? I wonder who took it."

"So maybe there were meant to be seven people?" I check the photo of the room on the table. There's nothing where we think the missing picture belongs. "Whoever took the photo did so after the last painting was removed."

"That's really odd. Why take a picture of the whole room, showing everything but leave out number seven deliberately? Gosh, he's a real tease, isn't he?"

I say, "Arsehole, more like," under my breath, eliciting a giggle from Noor.

Noor has moved in front of Marita's picture. "I've seen her. Do you know her?"

"Sven's sister. Marita."

"She's pretty."

"Where did you see her?"

"At Daddy's hotel last week."

"Hemingways?" I can't hide my shock.

"Yes. She's a waitress or something."

I cover my face with my hands "Tell me she wasn't at the party at our house?" I can't believe it.

"No, she wasn't there. I think she left. Why has he done this? It's very cryptic." Noor walks across the first line and then down the other side while Dina looks at me.

I nod. "Exactly." I pull out the crossword grid. "There are seven lines, and then a gap for the eighth. In that line, the letters are edged like they're special." I check the pictures. "If we assume this grid has something to do with the pictures, we have eight car adverts and eight lines in total. Maybe each line is the names of the cars?"

Dina picks up a photo. "This one, the German one, is an Audi. I saw it in a magazine in the dentist recently. Jim's always saying he wants an Audi. Are they special?"

I shrug.

"The Audi is picture number five, yet the fifth line has eight letters, so it isn't Audi. And the sixth is a Honda."

I peer at it.

How does she know that?

"The sixth line has nine letters, so it can't be 'Honda.'"

Noor comes to look over our shoulders. "Maybe the seven people are the first seven lines. Marita is line one and she's six letters."

"Yes! Line three is six squares and that's you, Harold." Dina squeezes Noor on the shoulder and the two girls grin.

"Could be?" I'm less certain.

Dina frowns, "Did he call you Harry? That's five letters."

"Nope. It was always Harold with something unflattering to begin with." I check the others. "If these are names of the people in the pictures what's the last line for? Eight letters, all bold. He's made it like it's more important. And what's that?"

I'm in front of Marita's picture. Across the top are a set of symbols.

Noor says, "Is that a bird? A hen, maybe?"

Dina taps the pile of photos. "I bet he assumed we'd need to take these away to work out what it all means. I suppose we leave the originals here." She stares at the images. "I've seen these somewhere before. Damn." She moves to the second picture. "See, each picture has a symbol or two, although Marita has the most. You've got the Olympics."

She's right. I've got the Olympic symbol painted a bright green. I've no idea what he meant by it. I say, "We need to check to see if it really was Marita at Hemingways. I don't see how it can be; she was living at her aunt's up north somewhere until she disappeared. Come on, let's lock up. We can look at these later."

Dina's holding the photos. "Do you think we should we take everything?"

"Where would we put them? And if the police do come here, it might be best if we've not moved much."

"It will be easier with the originals, they're clearer." Then she nods. "But you're right though. Let's leave well alone. At least until we understand things better."

I'm ridiculously pleased that she agrees with me.

Chapter Twenty-Seven

Harry Makes Two Social Calls and is More Confused than Ever

We visit Hemingways. Terry is by his credenza, folding napkins as obsessively as ever, no doubt dreaming about the tip box. "Hello, Harry. What—?"

"Marita Andersen. Did she work here?"

"Rita? Yes, left on Friday. She's a good—"

"Did she leave a forwarding address?"

He frowns. "Why would she do that?"

Good question. "Sorry. I just hoped, you know, if she was still around I might get a word."

He shrugs. "No, sorry. She didn't stay here if that's what you were wondering. I assumed she'd be at the Andersen place."

Damn. The big house. We should have checked. He is still frowning. "I'm pretty sure she said she was going to London. Yes, she had a case. Maybe Magda knows."

She doesn't. And she's busy sorting out some crisis so we leave her to it.

Noor is still imitating Tigger. "So what now?"

Dina waves the car keys. "I'm off to see Jim and George. You two want a lift home or back to Sven's?"

"No point if she's gone to London. Drop us at home. I'll go and be nice to Dad. You coming back for dinner?"

She wrinkles her nose. Noor must see because she says, "It's okay, my Mum's cooking."

"I might have to stay, you know?" She looks at me. Difficult conversation time.

"Sure. If you're not back by six I'll ring and let you know when the train's due to leave."

She doesn't reply, her mind clearly composing what she wants to say. Halfway back, I change my mind. "You drop Noor off and then drop me by the station. I'll go and see Frank's place."

"What's Frank's place?" Noor asks excitedly. I can feel the car begin to bounce.

"You've had enough excitement for one day, young lady."

"Ohhh." But she doesn't protest when we let her out.

On the plus side the shop is indeed the one in the picture, but it is shut and looks like it has been for a while. There's a sign on the door that has faded but may have once been a forwarding address. Being a Sunday, the other shops are closed too. They are all next to the railway station entrance and I head for the ticket office. The man behind the counter is working at the back of the office and I have to cough to make him turn round.

"I'm sorry to disturb you but—"

"Harry? Harry Spittle?"

I peer at the man through the glass. He looks vaguely familiar. An old school friend maybe?

He gives me a moment to recognise him and then says, "Cool dudio, Harry is the MAN, yer dig. You groove the lurve, Harry-O."

"Christian?"

"The same. Although I'm not quite the free spirt of yesteryear."

More like a prize wanker, I think uncharitably but immediately regret it. Another old acquaintance from my time at the hotel, Chris was a completely ippy-dippy hippie mostly because he ingested more drugs than a world-class hypochondriac. He had a ponytail back then, but now he has the sort of haircut my Dad thought was the business in 1955. I say, "I thought you were going to be an actor."

For a fraction of a second his face hardens. "Yes, well." Then he smiles and his usual good nature returns. He was always on my side when most of the others thought I was a spy for my parents, who, they believed, planned to take over the hotel and have all the staff sacked. He carries on, "You rather scuppered my lucky break, didn't you? Trying to kill off Mr James."

I'd forgotten that. Chris was going to work with Jim's Dad on a cruise ship as part of the entertainment crew, but Mr James had that accident with a lorry load of silage – the same load as did for Sven's Father – just before being arrested. Many people thought I had planned it. As if. Christian never appeared to hold it against me.

"You see much of the old crew? Amos? Natalie? Penny? Her nipples still orange?

Hmm, the fact that he got there first and teased me with his knowledge of her unusual colouration has always grated on me. Another thing I'd forgotten. "I saw Amos the other day. I think he has a new boyfriend."

"Alan? Or Tom?"

"Gregory, I think he said."

Christian shrugs. "I'm out of touch. I should go and see him. You too. Maybe try my luck again. On the stage. Working in a ticket office isn't exactly helping me pull the birds. Still, I have my hopes. The odd plan, you know?"

"Acting?"

"It never paid enough and I've a kid these days."

"You're married?"

"Nah. Just responsibilities. Jake's great but, well, it doesn't help either. Having him I mean." He sighs. "Play the cards as they fall. That's what my old man says. This is it, my man, this is my life. You dig?" He waves around his cubbyhole of an office. Some of the old lingo still lingers but I can tell his heart isn't in it any more. "Do you need a ticket?"

"Right. No actually, a bit of info. You know those shops, by the entrance? There used to be a pawnbrokers there. I wondered—"

"Frank? Sven's man? Or his Dad's at least."

"That's it. I wanted to see if I could speak to him. Frank. Any—?"

"None. He's been gone for a fair while. I think I heard Sven had seen him right, but where he went God only knows. Sven might know, I imagine."

"You've not heard? Sven's dead. Just over a week ago. If you want to come we're having him cremated at Bournemouth cemetery this coming Friday at 2:00 pm. You'd be very welcome."

Chris looks stunned. His mouth slowly opens but nothing happens, no noise emerges. Then he says, slowly, "The prick can't be dead. He can't do this to me."

"Sorry?"

For a moment, Christian looks like he's only just noticed me, such is the surprised expression on his face. Then without warning he pulls down the leather shutter and disappears.

Chapter Twenty-Eight

In Which Harry is Surprised and Dinner is Served

I walk to the main road and hitch a lift back to the family home. The sun has been in and out most of the day, but as the afternoon draws on it's become very close and I'm sweating a lot when I walk through the gate. I can hear voices from round the back so follow the path to see who is about.

The guests have gone; in their place Mum and Mrs Ohja are sitting in deckchairs while Sajid and his Father Ravi perform some sort of weird dance-cum-slow-motion play fight. Sajid is a stocky boy with none of the tall genes of his Father and sister. He has the darkest complexion of all of them and a look of fierce concentration on his face, making him appear to be on the verge of violence. In contrast Ravi towers over him, smiling gently and moving gracefully.

"What's the play?"

"Harry? Dear chap." Ravi takes two strides and grasps my hand; as ever the anaconda in him dislocates several bones before he lets go.

I look at Sajid who immediately looks away. "Hi Sajid."

He manages a little nod and shuffles from foot to foot.

Mrs Ohja raises her gaze to the sky. "Sajid, come on. Trying saying hello nicely."

His expression goes from fury to a grin, "Hello nicely. Dina said you've heard the Twats? They're mental, aren't they?"

Mum frowns. "Does he mean the Twits?"

I laugh. "I saw them live a few days ago. They did their new song."

"Yeah? What's that?"

I look at the understandably confused but trying to be interested faces of our Mothers. "Let's say it's anti-Thatcher in sentiment."

Ravi says, "We'll not hear a word against Mrs T here, thank you. And don't you dare buy it Sajid. I warn you, if I find—"

Mrs Ohja pats the seat next to her. "Of course he won't." She looks at me. "And you won't send him a tape, will you Harry?"

"Absolute not. He can come and stay and tape his own."

"HARRY!" Mum looks gratifyingly horrified.

Mrs Ohja shakes her head. "Sajid, be a good boy and go and make some tea, would you? There are some sweets in the red tin under—"

Ravi coughs and looks sheepish. "There were sweets. I might have taken them to work."

Another exasperated look. Mrs Ohja sends her son just for the tea. As he passes he says in a whisper, "What's it called?"

I check no one is listening. "Maggie Has No Cunt."

He almost expires trying not to laugh.

Left with the grownups Ravi asks about work. I check with Mum who lets her eyes roll upwards. "It's all right Harold. Pritti told me about the Andersen boy. I didn't approve of him and certainly not his Father but if he's dead and he trusted you to act for him then of course you must honour your professional commitments."

While she's speaking her expression suggests she has also swallowed a strand of particularly spiky barbed wire.

I can see Ravi looking from me to Mum and back, unsure what to say. Mrs Ohja saves me by standing and saying, "Noor says you found what you needed at the poor young man's house."

I manage a nod. "Just some papers."

She nods. "These things are mostly paperwork, aren't they? I'll just go and check on dinner. About 20 minutes?"

Ravi smiles, relaxing a lot. "I'll go and let Papaji and Arthur know." He scurries to the shed, clearly delighted to get away. Alone with Mum, she asks, "Why are you involved with that boy? It doesn't have anything to do with Charlie, does it?

Charlie Jepson is McNoble's Father and Mum's ex-lover, both Ancient and Modern.

"Charlie Jepson? No, why would it?"

"Because he and that boy's Father were in each other's pockets. There was something going on there. And the Andersen boy has had a run in with your uncle. Several in fact. He's part of the reason the garage had to be sold."

"Did his Father lend Norman money?"

Mum shoots me a glance. "Who told you that?"

"No-one. But that's what Robin Andersen did. Get his fingers into other people's business and then rip them off."

"So why are you working for them, Harold?"

I really can't hide how tired this makes me. "Sven asked me to make his Will. That's all I really know. It's my job." I sound defensive to my ears but she doesn't react, just sits picking at a loose thread or a fraying hope or something. "Now he's dead we – by which I mean my firm – have to sort out his estate. You can see that, can't you?"

"Well, I wouldn't trust him even if he is dead." Mum won't look at me. "If Sven or whatever he's called has anything to do with his Father's business dealings, then somewhere along the line it'll involve Charlie-bloody-Jepson and it's sure to be illegal." The bitter tone is unexpected, but the fire in her eyes as she speaks dies as quickly as it appears. She looks exhausted, pinching her nose like she's developing a migraine. "Harold, we need to talk before you go. I need your advice." She adds, as an afterthought, "Please."

Before I can express my reaction to this discombobulating statement – my parents have never shown the slightest inkling that they are aware I have any judgement, let alone trust in it – Dad emerges from the shed followed by Papaji. There's no sign of Ravi. Dad makes straight for me and holds me in a surprising hug. He's smaller than me, and his head is on my chest; I think he might be a little emotional. When he steps back I can see him clearly for the first time and after Mum's look of defeat the fact he appears to be really rather chipper is a surprise. The dark eyes of my last visit have gone and his face is flushed with what could be excitement.

"You're looking good, Dad."

"Yoga, Harry old chum. Asoka has me in positions I only dreamt of a few months ago. I've promised to show Veronica."

Is Dad being smutty? Mum tries a little smile, but it slips off her face. As Dad plonks himself on the swing and Papaji – Asoka is his real name – solemnly kisses the top of my head and shakes my hand, Mum stands and mumbles something about helping Mrs Ohja.

"How's the law business? Lots of death and destruction then?" Dad massages his thighs with a clenched fist.

Clearly he hasn't heard about Sven as he isn't usually so tasteless. I toy with telling him but I'm loathe to upset my unusually ebullient Father.

"So, has your Mother told you about the plans? This place will be the best B&B in the New Forest when the next season begins. It'll be great."

"Marvellous."

Dad nods, his expression telling me he has all the answers to my no doubt unspoken questions. "It's all sorted, Harry, my best mate. That's the beauty of it. All the previous weaknesses will be dealt with. We will have three extra bathrooms so no sharing, a new dining room just for guests, TVs in every room, the kitchen will be upgraded and," he leans towards me and says in a transparently stage whisper, "your Mother promises not to cook." He waves a hand indicating the garden. "We'll even landscape this wilderness now that Veronica has realised she cannot make us self-sufficient. A few exotics, maybe, and the fruit of course, but spuds and cabbage are a thing of the past."

"And the rabbits?"

Dad's expression clouds a little. "Their presence is no longer required. It's all part of the plan." As if to reinforce the strength of his intentions he motions towards Ravi, who is coming over to join us. "Ravi's been giving us, me, the benefit of his expertise. I pointed out that there are some obvious tie-ups between Hemingways and here that have yet to be exploited. Ravi agrees."

"Sounds great. Like what?"

Dad looks positively regal as his little legs make the swing move. He waves like he's batting away a fly or some implied objection to his scheme. "We are working through the details. It'll be fabulous now that your Mother is back and we have the cash."

"Great. And you and Mum? All okay?"

He won't look at me. "Grand. Splendid." He pauses and blinks hard. "I won't deny it's been difficult. Very difficult. That man..." I just know he must mean Charlie Jepson, "well, he did his best to destroy us but he's long gone now and we won't hear any more from him. Our time apart, it lent us... we gained... we achieved..." His optimism is withdrawing rather rapidly as he struggles to find the right word.

Ravi looks at me and gives an almost imperceptible shake of the head to warn me. He says, "Perspective, Arthur. You gained perspective."

Dad beams. "That's it. I – we – gained perspective. A new horizon. The summit is in sight." Dad is looking straight into the lowering sun; to me and, I think, to Ravi he looks like a man clutching at a very fragile last remaining straw, and he knows it too. Poor old sod. I want to hug him, say it will be all right, but I can't get emotional in front of someone who would not know how to cope with it. He looks like one of the rabbits caught in a strong headlight and unaware of what fate has in store for him.

I'm saved from having to do or say something we will all regret by Dina, George and Jim arriving. Mrs Ohja waves to us and we head indoors. Somehow, she conjures up a feast that is both delicious and extremely hot. George is his usual delightful self, climbing up and down me much like Sajid used to do, not that Sajid is happy to be reminded in front of everyone. I notice Dina talking to him and him looking at her doe-eyed. I wonder what he'd make of Brenda/Vera. What wouldn't I have given to have met someone like Brenda/Vera just as I was becoming aware of girls? I rather shock myself by thinking what it might be like to get to know Brenda/Vera now, seeing her running naked in my mind's eye. That is just what Dobbin was worried about and here am I having a rather cosy and risqué little fantasy. Dobbin's right; just now I must not be left alone with Brenda/Vera for any length of time.

Imaging Brenda/Vera naked is all very well, but I have other priorities when it comes to women. The relative quiet as I wrestle with George allows me a moment to try to get my feelings for Penny, Natalie and Jackie in some sort of order. I force myself to be honest as I list the current state of play.

One. I would like to have sex with each of them. Probably Jackie is top because I've had limited opportunities in the sex department with her so far. Two. Natalie is easily the most difficult one to envisage having sex with. Jackie is the keenest. Penny, I just don't know. It feels like it's over, but it's never actually been said and I really don't believe she has suddenly decided she's a lesbian. It all feels – I look across at Dad chatting happily to Jim and Ravi – just a little bit like she's living in a fantasy and sooner or later reality will bite. If it does, do I want to be there on the rebound? I never manage to get to number three as I'm brought back to reality by Mrs Ojha.

"Harry, what are you doing to George? Please don't squeeze him like that, even if he likes it."

I put my nephew down and he runs over to his grandpa and begins climbing up Dad's legs.

The truth, as I stare at Dad, is staring back at me. It's obvious but I refuse to see it. Penny has moved on, and probably already moved out. Sure, I have a lot of affection – did I really say 'love'? Maybe that's what scared her off? – for Penny but I want Jackie, I want to get to know her better and there is nothing, least of all Penny, stopping me. I didn't like it when Dina said, "Face it, H, either she forgives you for groping Natalie and getting caught or she doesn't, but right now she's not even thinking about you. Why should you think about her?" That's the truth right there. I've held off because I didn't want to admit I was in the wrong with Natalie, that really I went into that cupboard hoping

194

something might happen and the only person I'm fooling is me. I want Jackie, she wants me, Penny doesn't want me. I need to stop thinking about the what ifs and—

"Dinner."

Chapter Twenty-Nine

In Which Harry Has to Become a Man and Charlie Jepson Casts a Shadow

"He must have been ages doing these, don't you think?" We are sitting at a table on the train to Waterloo. The carriage is nearly empty. Dina is studying the second portrait, the one that Sven placed between Marita and me. "Why not show us their faces? This is a woman but that's about all you can see. Not that young, either."

I pick up my portrait. "Sven was really quick. I sat with him once by the tennis courts at Hemingways and he did four or five to about this level of detail in an afternoon. See here? He loved putting in things that tricked the viewer. Like one of those false lead thingies."

"A trompe-l'œil?"

"Yeah. Maybe. What's a trumped oil?"

"A trick of the eye and it's called a c.l.u.e. He probably wanted to help you."

"Help? Bloody funny way of going about it."

She giggles. "They won't be particularly difficult either, not if he wanted you to work them out." God, she can be smug. She puts her finger on something sticking out from behind the shrub that's in the background of my portrait. "Anyone who knew you would recognise your awful bike." She goes back to Marita's image and stares hard then points. "See there. That's a scarf isn't it?"

"Yes! It's a scarf. She wore that at the croquet game where I met her first. Bloody hell." We look at each other. "It has to be meant for me, doesn't it? These are things I'd know."

Dina sits back and waves a hand over the photographs. "Yep. Off you go, matey. Your turn."

"What about this one? He looks like a priest? I don't know any priests." The man – I'm sure it's a man despite the longish hair – seems to be praying. This is going to be a real struggle and even if we guess who's who it doesn't explain why Sven's drawn them.

Dina has numbered each photo, even though we have the one of the whole room so we can work out their order if they become muddled. She's copied out the grid and put in Marita and my name. "Maybe we have to take a letter from each of the names we insert in lines one to seven to make up a word in line eight? No, that doesn't work. There are eight letters in line eight."

I leave her frowning. For a while we have been sitting at a signal outside Hook, sweating in the sultry evening air. I lean back and close my eyes. I need sleep right now; my brain is melting like my face.

Sleep won't come. It would be good to report it's because I'm excited: about the puzzle, and about my plan to get together with Jackie now I've sorted out who's first on my list. But really it's because I can't stop replaying the conversation I had with Mum just before we were driven to the station. Talk about leaving a bitter taste. And Mum didn't even cook.

After dinner she insisted on showing me her vegetables, at least those not decimated by the condemned rabbits. We'd just stopped by some weedy looking carrots when she said, "He came to see me. I didn't call or anything."

"Who?" But I can guess.

"He turned up when Petunia was away. I'm sure he was watching. Or he had a spy. I was in the office at the garage." She stoops to pull up some weeds that seem to be doing better than anything else and to have avoided the scorched earth rampage of Hyzenthlay, Fiver and the rest of Watership Down's elite troops.

"Jepson?"

She stretches up, grimacing as her back clicks. "Your Father… you saw him, he won't understand. With Nanty gone and Petunia devastated at having to sell the garage, they expect me to be strong. He, Arthur, thinks that now we are back together and focused on the B&B I can sort it all out." At that she looks at me, sad, searching. I don't want to think about what she isn't saying.

"The plans sound very exciting."

She digs her fists into her eyes. "I've ruined everything, Harold. Everything."

I think she expects a hug or something, but we aren't a touchy-feely family and a shoulder pat is the best I can manage. "Come on, Mum. Selling the garage may not be what Uncle Norman and Aunt Petunia want, but it'll realise some cash for you and… Mum, what on Earth's wrong?"

Her nose is running and she's dabbing her eyes. Mum just does not cry. Ever. Surely it can't be hay fever.

"I won't get a penny, Harold. No one will. There won't be anything left."

For a moment, I feel acid in my stomach, anger at the idea the money I was forced to invest all those years ago might have gone. "How can that be? Was there a mortgage?" I just about manage to sound calm.

She straightens up, then looks at me red-eyed. "Five years ago, the garage was about to go bust and I put in the money from Grandpa's estate. Then, last year, they needed more money, another £5000."

"Is that where Nanty's money went?"

She blinks at me. "Edna? What do you mean?"

"Didn't Nanty leave you some money?"

"Barely, and that went on sorting out the electrics here." She laughs. "If he'd sold then, when your friend wanted him to, it wouldn't have been so bad."

"Sven?"

"Yes, bloody Sven-bloody-Andersen."

"What did he do?"

Mum has always had this habit of smoothing down her skirt when she's ordering her thoughts. She's reached the seat by the gazebo and sat down. Now she's almost setting fire to the material with the friction she's generating. "I knew Norman did a lot of work for the old man Andersen, before he died, customising his cars, looking after them, that sort of thing. He had a lot at one point, very expensive foreign ones. Norman's useless with paperwork and the Anderson boy said there wasn't any evidence of the work so he wouldn't pay for it. The trouble was Norman had borrowed from Andersen and had not told either Petunia or me."

"Surely they'd set the loan off against the cost of the work?"

"Norman thought he could bully your friend but he's an Andersen through and through. I don't think he handled him well. That young man comes across as all genteel and rather fey and I think Norman's plan backfired a bit."

That's true. Not many people would bully Sven.

"Your friend made it clear he expected the debt to be cleared or the garage would have to be sold. Norman wouldn't hear of it. He'd rather have driven it into the ground."

I tried to imagine the conversation between uncle and Sven. Sven must have been really angry to want to force a sale.

"Is that why he's selling then? Sven made him?"

"No." She blows out air. "Norman believes it's him, Sven, demanding the sale, him and his 'people,' the thugs, but… but actually it's me."

"You're not making much sense, Mum."

I let her take her time. "Your uncle and aunt have had a rocky time of it. He's a fool, Norman – that budgerigar woman he went off with a few years back was a mistake and he knows it – but Petunia took him back, goodness knows why. Family, I suppose. They'd been back together for a few months when this nonsense about selling came up. I… that is your Father and I… we wanted to help, since they were making a go of things. But we can hardly pay for this place, we didn't have any spare money." She drops her gaze; her shoes seem to hold her full attention. Suddenly she stands up and begins pacing around.

"Do they expect you to let them off what they owe? Not repay you? Is that the issue?"

She stops and stares at me, like I've started speaking Welsh and it's really very rude of me. She shakes her head hard and looks mad-eyed, like she might explode then flops back into the swing and covers her face with her hands. "I have been an utter fool. When the garage is sold, they'll be… there won't be…"

I can't help filling in the gaps. "You'll get no money back?"

Another vigorous shake.

Frankly I'm completely at sea. "You will get some money, but not—"

"Harold, just shut up." She sits forward. "Please. You see, Charlie…" She loses her thread.

"What about him?" My stomach has begun to melt again and not in a good way.

"He offered to help."

"But Mum, you know he's a crook. And I thought he was in prison?"

"Don't say it like that. He's not a bad man, Harold. Misguided." She picks at something in her lap. I will her to look at me, so I can show, by my horror, how deluded she is, but she won't oblige.

"It was before he went inside. Charlie called me out of the blue. Just after Petunia told me the garage was on the verge of ruin. Again. Because of your friend. He made me an offer. I couldn't ask your Father. Charlie told me he felt dreadful about that thing with the hotel when you worked there. He said he knew he'd let me down, how it wasn't your fault really because you were too young to understand. He admitted he was angry when it all fell through, but he blamed Robin Andersen and his own son, Claude. He wanted to make up for his behaviour."

"It's Stephen. Not Claude." Listen to me, defending McNoble against my Mother. She ignores my interruption.

"It didn't surprise me, but that wife of his, Millicent—"

"Do you mean Monica?"

"Probably. The tarty one who never wore underwear."

Yep, that's Monica.

"He said she wanted to divorce him, and he felt he had to make a clean start and that meant apologising to me."

I have been feeling sick and the nausea is growing. I am certain she is going to do something completely gross and disgusting like tell me she started another affair but instead she says, "He was insistent that he wanted to help me, us, financially. I don't know how, but he seemed to understand the state we were in, the problems with the garage."

That had to be McNoble, although why would he tell his Father if Sven had confided in him? I tune back into Mum.

"He made it very easy. He asked how much we needed, even proffering a figure that was more than enough to pay off your friend. The next day a man arrived with a packet containing... a lot."

"How much?'

"He didn't want anything, no agreement, nothing. It was so generous."

"What did he give you?"

"He said it would help him if I kept it. He indicated he wouldn't want it back for at least five years." She glances at me and then away, "And we needed it."

"Christ."

She takes her time speaking. "I'm not naïve, Harold. He's a little dodgy, as your Grandfather would have said. He likes to cut some corners. I was flattered by his attention and... well, that's in the past and we needed the money. So I took it."

"How much was it, Mum?"

She breathes heavily. "He's been back in touch now that he's out. He says he needs the money. He apologised that it wasn't five years yet but was quite insistent. Somehow he'd heard we were selling the garage and assumed that meant it would be fine."

I'm trying to keep my mind focused but it's going every which way. "He's out of prison?"

She looks startled. "You know about that? He said it was a mistake."

"I doubt that. I bet he was hiding the money from the authorities, not Monica."

"You had a thing with her, didn't you? He said you did but blamed her. It was her… her loucheness."

Loucheness? Where does Mum get them from? I know I'm going pink but living away from home for a few years has given me the semblance of a backbone. "I was 19 with incurable spots, Mum. Do you really think a sophisticated woman, albeit one who didn't invest in pants, was likely to be attracted to me? Of course not." Mind you, there were a couple of moments in that small meadow when she was sunbathing naked after Cyril the gardener started a bit of solo sex with a tub of Nivea. "My point is he might have been hiding the money from the police or other creditors. Nasty people, probably."

She's seems flummoxed by this suggestion. "Why would he tell me a lie? He didn't need to. Anyway, it hardly matters who he was hiding it from, given he now wants it back."

I rub my eyes. "You're right, it doesn't. Will the garage sale cover it? Is that the problem?"

She swallows and then finally looks at me. "The garage will be sold for around £29,000. There's barely any goodwill and the buildings need a lot of work. After the bank is paid what is owed there will be about £19,000. I owe Charlie nearly £25,000 when you add in interest…"

"Jesus." It's my turn to stand and walk in circles. "Shit."

"Harold, please don't swear. Or blaspheme. You are a professional and should have higher standards."

"Mum, for fuck's sake—"

"Harold!"

"What are you going to do?" I shudder. "What's Dad going to say? You can't do anything here, can you? Not with that hanging over you?"

She turns and heads off down the garden. Our lawn tapers to a point. In the triangle at the end, there is a sort of working compound with compost bins and old flowerpots and netting and canes. Years ago Dina and I used one of the compost heaps to hide some weed she had stolen from Reggie James, Jim's Dad, before we sold it when I was in

201

debt to McNoble. That's when he stabbed me. If the Law Society knew about my past they'd never admit me to the Roll of Solicitors.

Mum is standing in the apex of the triangle, staring down the lane. On the other side of the road is a bungalow where Ms Glebe once lived. Everyone thought she was a lesbian but she was probably just a spinster. If anyone was less like Penny. I shake the thought away.

I follow and stand behind her. Maybe I should hug her again but twice in one decade seems like an indulgence. "What are you going to do?"

Mum turns. "I wondered if you could speak to his son. See if he might put in a word? You seemed to know him."

If only she was joking. How can I tell her she's utterly and completely off her trolley if she thinks I can put in anything with McNoble, other than something sharp and stiletto-like?

Fortunately, she goes on, "Pritti, Mrs Ohja found out and wants to help. She caught me just after I received Charlie's ultimatum, I told her… well, most of it. She is a good woman. A bit of a know-all, what with her bloody degree and everything, but good. She offered to lend me the money to pay him back. I can't take it, but it's good to know I have friends." She looks at me and the accusation is not lost – if the Ohjas can help, why can't I?

I can't stop blinking. "She will loan you the money? Well, that's good."

Mum looks cross. "I can't be beholden, Harold. I just can't. Not again." To my surprise and horror Mum deflates, slowly like a leaky balloon, sinking to the ground. I catch her and help her up.

"Come on, Mum. We'll find a way. Really we will. Somehow."

She faces me. Once upon a time she looked me in the eyes, but she must have shrunk as she is looking up at me now. She strokes my cheek, like she used to; then it was bloody irritating, especially in front of my friends, but now it seems light and gentle. "You're all big and grown up now Harold, doing important things. I know it isn't easy to realise that your parents can't solve all the world's problems and always be the strong ones. Sometimes that is going to have to be you from now on. Your sister will need you – I mean, she's done amazingly well to overcome having a child so young and still get to university, but they're only just starting, her problems, and she'll need you. You're going to have to be our rock, Harold." She pats me on my arm and turns back to the house. "I'll tell Dina we should be going in about five minutes if you want to catch that train."

The train is slow and noisy, and I wonder if we will ever reach Waterloo. It's been a long day; hot, sweaty and I've been on enough of an emotional rollercoaster without being told that I'm the person on whom this family will, in future, rely. I know I should be touched, proud, uplifted by the confidence shown in me. I hurry to the toilets where I vomit up Mrs Ohja's roti; I don't feel any better.

When I return to my seat, Dina says. "Why cars? He's fixated with bloody cars."

All I can think about is the garage and how Sven precipitated the family crises by demanding the money back and then refusing to pay for the work on his Father's cars. He was probably in his rights and Jepson is the real villain of the piece, but I can't help hating him.

"There." Dina pulls me out of my gloomy reverie. She's pointing at a poster on a station wall where we've stopped. Farnborough, for yet another unexplained delay. She shuffles the photos and pulls one out. Sven has painted the same poster, advertising the Audi. In every detail his is the same save that at the top there's a gap in his painting where, on the advert on the station wall, it says 'Original.' "Is that a clue? Why's he left out the word Original?"

"I've no idea."

She stares at the poster and the picture. "'Original' is the only thing he's not included in his painting. He left that word out for a reason, didn't he?" She squints at the photo. "He's included the small print, at least as some squiggles, but not the main slogan." She turns the photo over and writes 'Original' on the back, then looks at another car advert. "There's a gap on this one."

I'm too tired to care; let her solve the bloody puzzle.

203

Monday, 6th July 1981

Chapter Thirty

In Which Harry is Given a Gift and Learns about the Cost of Flowers

Mondays are traditionally the most hated day of the working week but this one starts well. To begin with I have no one trying to harass me out of the shower, there is plenty of hot water and no more of Penny's self-control rules. I am mid-polish when the doorbell goes.

Cursing I splosh to the front door but it's Vern, the postie. He hands me a sachet of weed. "My birthday. Share the love, Harry." Underneath the herby wonder is an envelope, looking rather like something threatening from HM Government but is in fact a £10 premium bond win – Nanty gave Dina and me £50 of premium bonds on our 18th birthdays. While she cashed hers – admittedly to buy things for George – I kept mine. This is a first.

Back in the shower, I'm ready to finish what I started when the door goes again. This time I'm rather less sweary. Just as well as it's Mr Jones from the flat below. He eyes my dripping torso and then his gaze drops to the tenting that my recent efforts have caused to my towel. One eyebrow rises a smidge. "A young lady called. She left a message." His gaze dips again. "Possibly just as well. A Miss Jackie asking if you can meet her this evening at 7:30." He looks me firmly in the eye. "She suggests Nelson's Column."

We part awkwardly. Somehow I know our relationship will now be different but in what way I cannot quite fathom.

Back in the shower, everything has settled down somewhat and it seems wrong to start again. Maybe I won't need to. A tenner and a date. Things are definitely looking up.

As I leave the flat, a nervy Zenda is hovering outside Mr Jones' front door. Does she check me out too? No, I'm getting paranoid. She launches straight into what she needs. "If it's all right, can I come to your office today? As we discussed?" She pushes a package at me, something wrapped in silver foil. As I take it, she cups her hands around mine and whispers, "Thank you." She squeezes mine together. How can Brenda/Vera and Zenda be related?

The package contains a sandwich with a pinky-orangey fish in it. I'm a bit suspicious but try a nibble. It's delicious. We agree she should call the office at 10:00 and fix a time to come in. I rather hope Lucinda will be about, but today I'm feeling as if I might manage the first interview alone.

At work, I lock my bike in the lightwell and head to the gents to wash the sweat from my armpits before changing into my suit. Jeremy isn't in yet, which allows Jean to take my dictation. Words flow easily. We have the letters to let people know about Sven's death and the arrangements for the cremation are all set. As Jean is sweeping up the paperwork prior to making some amendments, she asks, "Will you be offering the attendees a cup of tea somewhere? Maybe a sandwich? I can look into possible venues nearby. Or perhaps your parents could help?"

"Mum? I can't see it."

She smiles benignly. "No harm in asking, is there?"

She doesn't know Mum but since this has been officially declared a 'good day' I give home a call. Mrs Ohja answers.

"Yes, Harry, I'm sure Veronica will want to help."

"I think you'd better ask, Mrs Ohja. She has had some issues with him in the past. When he was alive."

"That's the thing, isn't it? He's gone and the least we can do is be hospitable and help you. I assume it is something you should do as executor?"

"Yes. Well, I suppose." Is it? Jean made it sound normal. "Can you let me know what she says?"

I can almost feel her smiling. "Why don't you assume it's a yes and let me know the likely numbers so I can sort out the catering? If Veronica is against it then I will speak to Ravi and he will find space at Hemingways. The young man worked there, didn't he?"

"Yes. That's where we met."

"Right. So that's a plan. It will be here, after the ceremony, or at Hemingways. But assume here unless you hear to the contrary."

I sit back, wondering what just happened. Have I slipped into a parallel universe?

At 11 o'clock, I've just gone through some post and – glory be – spotted a mistake in Jean's typing. That's a first. There are a few calls I need to make but I decide to head to the secretaries' room to point out my masterstroke and perhaps sneak in an extra coffee on the way.

I suppose it's the power of hubris or Sod working his magic. If only I had decided not to make a coffee. The rules about beverages are strict. Edith makes coffee in the morning for everyone and brings it round. Jean does tea in the afternoon with a biscuit. We can make one ourselves at lunch time. That's it. However, if Edith is out (as she is today) you can sneak one extra in if you are careful.

In the kitchenette, Sandra and Gloria are having an earnest conversation. A sixth sense tells me not to interrupt but some cavalier part of me overrides instinct and I push open the door. "Hi." I try to sound breezy.

For a second, they both freeze, certain I suppose that Edith is about to catch them in the act of granular larceny. "Only me." I smile at Gloria, avoid eye contact with Sandra and head for the cupboard with the mugs. Behind me I hear a door slam and I'm alone with Gloria.

"What's this?" Gloria sneers very effectively when she wants to. "Making your own coffee? I thought Mr High and Mighty would have his staff do it for him. Oh, sorry, you're only the articled clerk, aren't you? You're not that important, are you? Even if you think you are."

I can feel my blood rise to my face but decide ignoring her is best until I know why she's having a go at me. "Nice weather."

"Did you see her face?"

"Face? Who?" I turn to the kettle. It's steaming from having been recently boiled but before I can pick it up, Gloria intercepts it, resting her hand on the handle.

"Sandra, of course. You just looked away, didn't you? Embarrassed."

"I… no. What?"

"You just don't care, is that it? Do you know how she feels?"

I'm on quicksand and I have no clue where firm ground might be. "Can I use this water?"

"No, you can't. I need it." She lifts the kettle and empties it into the sink. "You never ask, do you? That's the trouble with you lawyers. All lord of the manor. We keep this firm going and you lot swan around – well, apart from Lucinda and maybe Christine, they know – but you men take the credit and for what? You don't even talk to us like we're human."

I make a grab for the empty kettle, but she snatches it away. There's a dangerously soft note to her voice. "You remember the party, do you? At Christmas?"

I nod.

"You looked at her then, didn't you?"

"Yes." Since this is about Sandra I think my toes are beginning to feel the bottom. I make another go for the kettle but she holds it high and way out of my reach. "What are you on about? I was the one who took her to the hospital when Mr Risely buggered off home."

Gloria surprises me by clapping, even though she's still holding the bloody kettle. "Quite the hero. Or was it a guilt trip?"

"I... no. Why would it be?"

She looks furious. Scowling, she fills the kettle and plugs it in, then stands with her back to me, blocking my path to it. "She was just 17 and hadn't drunk alcohol before. She told you, didn't she?"

"Not exactly. What she said was, 'Oh Harry, I don't normally drink.'"

"You plied her with booze so you could have your way with her."

"No, I didn't. Mr Risely was in charge of drinks. He topped her up."

"Only because you asked him too."

We are now dancing with me trying to get past to the kettle and her still blocking the way.

"Don't be daft."

"Did you or did you not snog?"

"Well, yes. We—"

"Did you grope her arse?"

"I..." Vague images of a dark booth with Sandra pushing me back, her extraordinarily wet lips locked on mine and her hand hunting for my fly as I tried to hold her back. I suppose I might have had to put my hand somewhere near her bum to get her to stop.

"And grab a handful of her boobs?"

"No, definitely not. I—"

"I saw you! You were damn near milking her." She slides away, letting me get to the kettle.

I, however, am staring at her. "She was all over me! I had to fight her off."

Gloria folds her arms, causing her boobs to froth out of her low-cut top. "Really? I think we all know what the office thinks. If she hadn't been so unused to the booze you forced on her you'd have taken advantage."

"What? I was the one who—"

"Mr Risely hailed the cab. And he paid for it."

"She had passed out on the pavement. He asked me to see her to the hospital because he had to get home."

"That's not what Edith says."

"She wasn't there."

"No, but she speaks to Mr Risely and he was."

"He can't be saying what you're implying. It's... it's wrong."

She pats my cheek and takes the kettle. "Coffee? One sugar isn't it?" She stirs the water into the granules before adding the sugar and milk. "You rang her Mum, even though she told you not to. You know what that cost her?"

"She didn't say not to call. She was unconscious and the hospital wanted a next of kin." I found her home phone number in her diary in her purse and rang. Her Mum was fine. All she said was, 'not again' before telling me to go home. "I even waited with her until her Dad turned up."

Gloria hands me my cup and I take a sip. It's only then I realise the water she's used hasn't boiled and it's utterly repellent. I know better than to show it.

"Have you ever asked her how she is? Did you check she was okay? Talk to her after that? Go and have a word? Be friendly? You seemed friendly enough at the party. You have a girlfriend, don't you? High and mighty," why does she love that expression so much? "Penny. You try to have a bit of nooky on the side, but can you be civil after? No, you bloody can't."

"What's brought all this one? It was six months ago."

"She's suffering, moron. She's sure you hate her and now you won't even give her any work, not now that Jean is fawning all over you. Can you imagine what her self-esteem is like? Have you explained to her why you've dropped her?"

She does have a point. The truth is, after the embarrassment of her attack and then collapse I rather assumed she was the one who didn't want to mention it. And I haven't told her why Jean is now happy to do my work. But this whole nonsense about me trying to have my way, like I'm some sort of dastardly Victorian villain, what's she trying to achieve?

"I'll have a word sometime."

"Now."

"What?"

"Talk to her now. Better – buy her a drink, flowers, something, anything. Just make her feel worthwhile."

"But Jean's there. I can't just—"

"Are you a complete wanker? I'm not asking you to shag her across the desk, am I? That is exactly your problem and you can't see it, can you?" She snatches the cup back, slopping the oily contents on the drainer. "And don't be a prick and pretend you can drink this shit. Come on. You're going to do the decent thing."

"Decent thing?"

"Oh, grow up Harry."

I know better than to object. As we step out of the building and into Beauchamp Mews, I sense people looking. Gloria is a presence, there is no doubt about it. She's eye catching, like a dhow with a leopard-print sail tacking against the drab crowds as we head for Wigmore Street.

"Where are we going?"

"The florists. You are going to spend a ludicrous amount of money on making her birthday memorable."

"I didn't—"

"No, you didn't know because, as we have established, you never ask." She stops abruptly and glares at me. "One day you may be a partner and responsible for staff. If you want to be a good boss and have people that are loyal to you, you need to treat them like human beings." Off she goes again.

Walking a pace behind you can see the expressions of those ahead as they focus in on this force of nature. It's far too hot for her coat, the coat is far too loud for the environs and yet the faces light up, people nod as if in the presence of something in equal parts magical and dangerous and give her a wide berth. She doesn't stop talking either, throwing her philosophical musings over her large padded shoulders.

"You need to understand that you cannot just spend time with someone, snog them inside out, get them thinking you are interested and then ignore them and expect them to be all smiles. You need to find out if they are okay."

"But I looked after her—"

Gloria turns again and glares. "Only when the poor kid was pissed beyond help and only because your boss was present. She should never have ended up there in the first place." She sighs, like the weight of the world is on her shoulders. "Harry, Harry." She cups my face in her hands, which is pretty unappealing given how sweaty they are. "She's only just told me the full story, you know. She's been through hell because of that night and you ignoring her, then dropping her has totally undermined her confidence. You've walked into their room how many times do you think since that party? 50? 100? And what have you said to her, beyond some instruction about typing?"

"I... I didn't realise she…"

210

"Do you think she fancies you? After that? Don't flatter yourself, kiddo. You have her tongue licking your spleen it's so far down your throat and you think it's what? Charity work?"

"No, but… she never looked… she never said…"

In a millisecond, Gloria squeezes my cheeks making my eyes water. "You are how old? 23? 24? And she is 18 today. You've been where, exactly? Uni, College of law? She's been to Clacton-on-Sea for a holiday. Christ Harry, you're meant to be the grown up one here. Poor kid thought you at least liked her but oh no, she gets the complete cold shoulder. And then dumped as a secretary. And you know what she thinks, Hercule-bloody-Poirot? She thinks that you were embarrassed by what happened. By the kissing, by having to help her to hospital and calling her Mum on the phone. She was mortified."

"Why didn't she say? Why didn't anyone say?" I know I'm whining but I can't help it.

Gloria has set off again. "You know what happened yesterday, the day before she comes of age? Her boyfriend dumped her. So of course she thinks she's worthless. I'm the only friend she has got, and it took that for her to say something. Poor kid has been bottling this up since December and it just exploded. Then you march in, won't look at her as usual, all cheery and she crumbles. So you are going over there," she waves at the florist, "and you are going to get her the biggest bunch of flowers available."

Gloria folds her arms and waits. I can feel my date and my tenner dissolving as I hesitate. I sort of feel a shit, but part of me thinks I'm being punished for the mystery boyfriend who is the really guilty party in all this. I head for the florist.

We are now on Portland Place; the florist is part of the mansion block where Lady Isabella has her London apartment. As I study the displays, waiting to be served, I glance across the road at the entrance. My flat is also in a mansion block, but that's where the similarity ends. Mine has cracked external red brickwork, peeling paint and a vague smell of piss in the hall while this is a grand affair in creamy Portland stone, with gargoyles and Grecian-style carvings on the facade, a liveried porter standing sentinel in the marbled hall and highly polished brass numbers everywhere.

I accept the inevitable and buy a bouquet of summer flowers that fills my arms. I have to hold it close to my chest to get through the door. Gloria is on the other side of the road looking at shoes in an expensive shop.

211

Just then the gates to a basement car park slide up and a car emerges from the Stygian depths. It's a dark coloured BMW being driven by Mrs Soderberg and, nearest me, Sean Latterly has his head resting on the passenger door window. He looks like he's in a trance.

If I wasn't so encumbered I would wave but instead I glance in the back. It is difficult to see but from the outline it looks like Sir Pen although his head seems to be lolling back at an odd angle. There's someone next to him, leaning over him but I have no idea who. There's something unsettling about Mrs Soderberg's grim face and Sean's lifeless expression that makes me wonder if they are off to hospital or something.

Gloria takes my elbow. "Wow! She will love those." Somehow, she manoeuvres her head past the foliage and kisses me on the lips.

***

"Harry?" Sandra looks up as I approach her desk, horribly aware that Jean and Gloria are watching.

"Hi. I… look… the thing is… last Christmas… I never realised… I've been a fool… and your birthday—"

I'm thrown by Sandra, quite literally. She leaps, there's no other way to describe it, at me and grips me and the flowers hard. We're enveloped in pollen. Everyone begins sneezing. I put the bouquet down and back towards the door while Sandra studies each bloom, making a little mewling noise as she does so. Jean makes a big thing of shuffling some letters and disappears upstairs. I'm sort of aware of something unspoken between her and Gloria.

"I… look, it's… are you okay?"

She's started crying. "I can't Harry. I know you've been mucked about by that bitch Penny. Glor said but you know Kev." Her eyes go up sort of indicating something about Kev, whoever he is."

"Kev's your boyfriend? Your ex?"

She nods. "I mean, we've broken up but we're always breaking up and if you and me went out, if Kev thought we was having sex, he'd cut your nob off." She smiles sweetly and pats my cheek. "Shame. Maybe one day." She looks at Gloria and sniggers. Gloria won't meet my glance. "We could have a drink, though. After work. That'd be nice."

I calculate my date with Jackie. "Yes, okay. One drink. Big birthday, 18."

"Yeah, I can get pissed and it's legal."

"And vote."

"Yeah? What for?"

Happily, we can say no more as Jean reappears and makes it clear without words that I need to go. Gloria follows me upstairs. As I break off to go to my room she says, "Do you still want that coffee? I'll make you one if you like."

I manage a smile and head for my room vaguely aware I've been had, but not sure exactly how. Gloria calls up the stairs. "Oh, and someone called Jackie rang. Cancelling your meeting. And Mrs Silverman wants a word. She says she'll be a bit late. The hair stylist is taking longer than she thought. There's a number for her if you need to speak."

I kick open the door. And things were going so well. As I sit at my desk I wonder about Sean. Was he unwell? Should I call him or Izzy? I shake my head. It's not like they're family or anything. Instead I turn my hand to drafting a conveyance.

***

Zenda Silverman enters with a quiet class that I just know Lucinda will love. Her hair has been cut very short and dyed a silvery blonde that still has notes of the green about it. It's made her seem both younger and sadder. She can't seem to stop touching it. After the pleasantries and establishing that no one wants any tea, Zenda coughs and says, "I'm not sure how much Harry has explained, but I want, no – I need a divorce. I've been married to Reginald for 10 years and I should have divorced him 10 years ago. Better late than never."

"I realise this must be difficult but is it all right if I ask some questions? Your husband is Reginald Silverman and—"

"Rother. Reginald Rother. I've decided I want to use my married name by my first husband."

"Rother?" Lucinda stops writing and frowns. "And he is…?"

"He's a judge."

Lucinda caps her pen. "Harry, can we have a quick word?"

Outside, Lucinda paces up and down. After a minute, she stops and stares at me. "Reggie Rother is a friend of Philip's. School or university or something. I'm pretty sure Rother was godfather to Philip's son."

"Does that mean we can't act?"

Lucinda pats me on my cheek. "Oh no. The man is a bastard. He groped me at the christening. No, we need to do two things. First, keep this from Philip for as long as possible and second, set up a new client file right away. Once Zenda is a client, Philip will be conflicted from acting."

"Won't he mind?"

"Mind? Good grief no. Rother patronises him appallingly. I think Philip fagged for him. He'd feel obliged to act and charge the old sod bugger-all. This way he'll be able to decline gracefully. Off you go and get that file opened."

Chapter Thirty-One

In Which Harry Dodges a Bullet and Walks Home

In the pub Sandra is sitting at a table with one spare chair. She has what looks like an orange juice in front of her. There is no sign of the flowers.

"Hi. I—"

Sandra nods violently at the bar. I turn and Jean smiles back at me. She finishes her order and walks briskly across the pub. She says, "I was just asking about her sister's pregnancy. As a twin that must be exciting." She looks around. "Where are the flowers?"

Sandra leans over and picks them up off the floor.

"Oh no. You need to take more care. Here, let me."

While I find another chair, Jean fusses over the flowers.

Jean smiles when I return with a half-pint of lager. "Meeting someone?"

"Sorry?"

"I thought I heard Gloria talking to your friend about your date. At 7:30?" Jean smiles at me, but there's a degree of frost involved.

"She cancelled."

Jean sips what looks like a white wine and raises an eyebrow. "Really? From what I could gather she was anxious to make sure you had the time right."

I look from Jean to Sandra and back. This is a game and they are both playing while I haven't been told the rules. Jean carries on, "I don't usually come here," she looks around at the gold leaf and flock wallpaper, "but I spotted Sandra coming in and thought why not? She can see me to my train that way. Can't you, dearie?" Jean doesn't pursue my evening plans but instead chats inconsequentially about commuting, the Essex countryside and the difference between town and country pubs. After about 30 minutes she looks at her watch. "Well, we girls ought to get on or you'll be late. Have a good evening, Harry."

I watch them go. Sandra looks defeated, Jean triumphant. The door has been closed for about 30 seconds when Jean returns and picks up her scarf from the back of the chair. "I want to talk to you tomorrow. Come in early."

I'm confused. Pleased – no, relieved – but confused. Why has Jean stopped Sandra and me from having a quick drink? I finish the dregs of my beer and head for Trafalgar Square – the walk will take half an hour and gives me time to ponder how my day has been a not unusual rollercoaster. I should know by now not to judge its quality until it is over.

As I turn the corner at the end of Lower Regent Street and head for Trafalgar Square, I'm convincing myself that Jackie won't be there. Instead I spot her immediately leaning against a lion, watching some children chase pigeons into the air.

"They are filthy, aren't they? And look at that one." She points at a pigeon that is limping across the paving. Its right foot is just a lump. "You know what causes that? Lead in petrol. The little particles gather in the dust on the ledges and stick to their feet. Think what it's doing to those children's lungs. If I have kids, I'm bringing them up in the countryside."

"They'll hate you if you do."

"What do you mean?" She links arms and manoeuvres me towards the Strand. "Shall we see what Covent Garden is like? I've not been since they opened it up as shops and restaurants."

"I went last year with Dobbin. Overpriced. And parts still smell of rotting veg. There are some decent pubs though. I grew up in this country idyll and until I was about 13 I thought it was great. Then I discovered there was nothing to do and no place to go to and no pubs or discos or cinemas or anything. Just me and my sister and my parents and the TV. It was DULL. I even enjoyed my homework as it gave me something to do."

"What about girls?"

"Saw them at school – they terrified me – and that was it until I got to uni."

"Who was your first girlfriend? Proper, not just a snog at the end of a disco?"

It's not hard to remember. "None at school, not even for a snog. It was at uni, a girl called Dessie, second year French and Politics student. We had three dates, and I never got further than the wall outside her hall, having a snog and a fumble. I was arrested after one, too."

"What? Why?"

"I fitted the profile of some serial flasher and they hauled me in. Utterly terrifying, even if they let me go after about 20 minutes."

"That was lucky."

"More like humiliating. They had me show them my willy. Apparently, the suspect had an unusual kink and I didn't. The sods just laughed."

"What about Penny?"

I squirm. "She worked in a hotel with me at the end of the first year. I had a girlfriend at the time but that was always destined to be another failure. Can we maybe not talk about her?"

"So not many then?"

"Oh, I've lost count."

I know she's smiling even though I'm staring ahead, trying not to think about Penny. She says, matter-of-factly, "My first boyfriend was called Alistair. He was 16 and I was 15. We had eight dates before he decided that seeing me interfered with flying his model airplanes. Then it was Simon. God, he was a great kisser. But he had an odd smell, which put me off and he liked the Stones who I couldn't stand. I put up with it for about two years though. No one really serious after that."

We've just reached the old Rhodesian embassy building on the Strand, which I guess will become the Zimbabwe Embassy now the war has finished; it's a formidable slab of architecture that looks very neglected and has been shut for ages. The entrance is in shadow, even though it's still daylight and a pleasantly warm evening. I pull her to the door and manoeuvre in for a kiss. It is wonderful. After God knows how long we surface for air; her face is flushed.

"You know what?" Jackie has a very serious face on. "Let's skip the drink and go back to yours, shall we?"

We do. We kiss twice on the way to the bus stop. Pretty much all the way on the bus to Chelsea and once in the middle of Chelsea Bridge we stop and lean on the parapet for what seems like an age. Even though it's still daylight she's squirming around my leg and moaning. When we reach Battersea Park, I say, "We can cut through. There's enough time before the gates close."

"You don't think we might get distracted?"

God, I'm torn. Would she understand if I said I wanted to get back for the test match highlights first before we resume? I decide not to risk it. Today needs something to end it on a high note.

217

Tuesday, 7th July 1981

Chapter Thirty-Two

Where Harry Receives the Wisdom of the Ages

Christ, I am sore. It's just before 7:00 and I'm in the toilet seeing if there's some cream or something. Jackie woke me about 10 minutes ago and made it clear she wants to go again before work. Unless I can find something, I'll be joining her in A&E.

Everywhere stings. My nob, it seems to be bruised it's so purple. My bum and my knees aren't much better from the grass near the running track and then the carpet in the sitting room. And my thigh throbs where I nearly kebabed myself on the railings when we climbed out of the park. I'm actually grateful my bike is at work and I don't have to cycle. I've never wondered if you can have too much sex but that thought crosses my mind and I stare at the door and compose excuses.

It's all right for Jackie as she isn't on duty until 2:00 pm. She has time to recover.

There's a knock at the door. "Harry?"

It's her. I open it a crack and she skips in, dropping the sheet she has wrapped round her. "Come on, let's have a shower." She glances at my wounded tool, now bathed in the harsh bathroom light, "Oooo, did I do that? Shall I kiss him better?"

Half an hour later she's snoring in bed. I kiss her bottom and she squirms. I'm torn but the need to keep earning and give myself time to heal helps me drag myself away. On the kitchen table there's a note from Dina. *'You sounded busy! I think I've worked out a few of the clues. You up for trying to work out the rest tonight?'* Since Jackie won't finish until 10:00 – she promises me she will be right round as soon as she can get away but doubts it will be before 11:00 – I scribble 'Okay' and stick it under her door.

I'm not looking forward to seeing Jean but she's smiling when I walk in. She still has her coat on and has just finished speaking to Gloria, who isn't and hasn't – smiling and coat-wearing, that is. "Come on, Mr Spittle. We mustn't be late."

Jean marches me out of the office to the café we visited the last time we had a chat. Same table. Syrupy black coffee for her, thin milky for me. She takes off her coat and gloves – Christ, how does she wear so much in this heat? It's been like a Turkish bath for the last week – and plants her hands on the table either side of her cup. "Harry, I don't need to ask, but I will anyway. What are your intentions towards Sandra?"

I blink. "None. I mean I don't have any."

She waves me quiet with a finger. "You wouldn't be the first young man to keep a light in each port."

I think she means a ship in each port. Or maybe a light in each window, not that I'm about to correct her. I wait.

After a sip and a grimace, she says, "I know Sandra's type. You would be quite the catch with the career you have ahead. Now it is up to you, of course, but if you start down that road, don't think it will be easy to extricate yourself."

Jean has the wrong end of the stick, but from her expression it's clear there is no point explaining and I just nod, keeping my gaze on my cooling coffee.

"You are a grown up." She says this without trying to hide the doubt she has in making the statement. "But you are so naïve." Suddenly she beams. "That's why I like you Harry. Despite the career you have chosen you are patently honest. Unlike Mr Panther." She shudders. I had no idea she didn't think well of him. I'd like to ask why, but she's speaking again. "You are just the sort of young man that the likes of Gloria and Sandra aim for."

"Me?"

Another warm smile. "You have a degree. You may be paid less than a church mouse now, but you will be on £30,000 before you are 30."

I goggle at her. She is pulling my leg although she looks deadly serious and I have yet to know Jean make any sort of joke or even exaggerate.

"They know it. Currently Gloria has her sights on Mr Panther…"

"But he's engaged? He just went to Greece with his fiancée."

"And where does he go every Tuesday and Thursday after work?"

"He plays squash with a friend."

"Really? If only that were true. He and Gloria go to the Monmouth Hotel. They stay for two hours before he goes home. Ms Latham, his fiancée, has become suspicious and Greece was a way for Mr Panther to prove to her she was being silly. But Gloria is the source of her suspicions and they will grow and fester and in time only Gloria will be left and Mr Panther, frankly, will have no chance. If she wasn't

220

already plotting about how to snare him, she may well have turned her attention to you. That's probably why she left the way clear for Sandra to have a go."

"How do you know all this?"

Jean shakes her head. "Because, Harry, I come from where they come from. Marrying well has always been a way out if you don't have the brains to get an education. Now, with the pill, she can spread her legs as well. Not an option in my day." She takes another sip. I am horrified at the notion. "I don't blame her, Gloria I mean. Her family is very, hmm, traditional. Religious. I believe she has a younger sister who has suffered somewhat because of Gloria's modern ways. There's some issue…" She looks away, into the far distance then back to me, smiling. "Still, all that needn't concern you. Poor thing will need help, though. Now, promise me you will be more careful."

I'm still struggling with the reference to the spreading of legs, but manage to say, "I promise not to make the same mistake."

"It's fortunate she had too much to drink at Christmas. If she had remained upright, you might already be having Sunday roasts in Basildon. And don't believe what she says about a boyfriend. I understand that is a fiction." Jean finishes her coffee and begins to put back on her outdoor clothes. She looks at me as she readies herself to go. "You must have a guardian angel."

I think about Mr Risely circulating with a bottle, always topping up Sandra and encouraging her to drink, while often failing to fill my own glass. I remember being annoyed, not that I could say anything as he is the boss. Mr Risely as a guardian angel? Now that's an image to hold on to. It's like a crazy Mills & Boon story.

Chapter Thirty-Three

In Which Harry and Dina Focus and Dobbin Fears the Worst

Dina has put the photos on the kitchen table in the sequence they were found in the loft. The crossword grid is in front of her. She doesn't look up. "How's work?"

"Weird. One of the secretaries wants my baby and I can't seem to stop bringing in new clients."

"Is that normal for Mondays?"

"First time ever."

"What does Jackie think? About the secretary?" She looks at me and smirks.

"We haven't done much talking."

There's a pause before she says, "Penny?"

"What about Penny?"

"You're not over her, are you?"

I'm about to argue, get angry, say something mean but I know she's right. Having fun – all right, having sex – with Jackie is exciting, but I still feel guilty about it, like I'm cheating even though Penny's last comments to me were how she thought I was a cretin. Or words to that effect. "All her stuff has gone. God knows where. I think it's fairly clear it's over," I say.

"Still, if she walked back in now what would you do? And would you tell her about Jackie?" Dina taps the nearest picture. "Forget about it, H. I saw her when she collected her last bits. She admitted she was harsh, but she said you both needed a break."

"What did she say? She didn't say we'd broken up then? Where is she staying?"

She turns and stares at me. "Don't. She's the one who's moved out. You're better off focusing on Jackie. Come on, let's think about these clues."

"What about you? Jan? Jim?"

"I told Jim we needed time apart and I was seeing someone else. He told me he was too, but I think that's just bravado, male pride." She shakes her head. "I felt really warm towards him at the weekend, you know? Seeing him with George. He's a good Dad, but…"

222

"But?"

"That's not enough. He doesn't want to come to London. Hell, he finds Southampton overwhelming."

"And George?"

"Ah, George. I don't know what to say. I feel rotten if I say I enjoy the time away from being a Mum. I'm not very maternal. Is that bad of me? Evil?"

"Probably. We're a right pair, aren't we? What about uni? Heard from Kings? Imperial?"

"Imperial said they'd decide soon. Come on – to work, Horatio." Dina goes back to looking at the pictures. "I've focused on the people. The motor vehicles have me utterly confused. Why would he be fixated on cars?"

"Maybe he's not. I heard his Father had a collection of flash motors. Maybe he thought he'd leave me those. I guess they're worth a few bob. Anyway, what did you work out about the people?"

She grins broadly. "First up, that first drawing. The one of you and Marita?"

"Yeah? What about it?"

She pulls it out of a folder we are using to hold all the photos and pictures. "What do we know about it?"

"I… come on. You know I'm no good at puzzles."

"Not true." She's smirking, and I really really hate her.

"Di…"

"What are you doing? In the drawing?"

"I don't know. Staring at my lap?"

"Look at what you're holding in your hand? You can just see a pencil, can't you? And see how you've crossed your legs. You don't do that mu—"

"Shit, a crossword."

She claps. "Exactly. You used to do the cryptic one if you could, didn't you? You'd make a table of sorts by crossing your legs. And she's watching you. In fact, look at her mouth. I think he's drawing her talking to you. Helping you with the clues."

I peer at the little pencil marks. She's right, Goddammit.

"I think this is a really important picture. See the settings. Home, Hemingways and the flat, near Natalie's. These are all important. I think he's giving you pointers to where you'll find answers."

I want to hug her. Of course I don't."

She's not stopped grinning. She pulls out a photo of a portrait – the person who's at number five in the line. "Who do you think this is?"

I stare at the image. It's an outdoors setting with loads of greenery. The subject, a woman, has turned away from the artist and is holding her hands to her face... no, to her mouth. "Christ, it's Mum. How'd I not see that? She puts her hands over her mouth, doesn't she? When she's shocked. How'd he know about that?"

Dina nods. "I noticed her shoulders, the way they lift asymmetrically. And the clincher is what she's looking at. On that table."

"A courgette? Or... oh God, you're not serious?"

She giggles and says, in a singsong squeaky voice, "They grow willies!"

I have to laugh with her. When Sajid Ohja first arrived as a small boy, with his accent and squeaky voice, he found Mum's veggie experiments in our garden. She's managed to grow a courgette in the shape of a willy. In a way, it helped Mum and Mrs Ohja to begin to tolerate each other.

Dina asks, "I've forgotten. Why did Mum try to make them look like penises?"

"She wanted to get on That's Life and be Cyril Fletcher's guest with her phallic vegetables. Goodness that is a lifetime ago."

She adds, "You must have told Sven."

"I think I told everyone at the hotel one lunchtime, but yes, he'd have known about it."

"He could have just painted her face, couldn't he? You'd have recognised her easily."

"As would anyone else who knew her. He's not hidden Marita's face, has he? Not really. Nor me. We said these are clues for me and me alone, but what if they are also for Marita? If only I could speak to her." I point at the grid. "And 'Veronica' fits for number five."

Dina's face clouds. "The real question, is why is Mum included? What has she to do with Sven or the Andersen empire?"

The bloody garage. It has to be, doesn't it? Does this mean it's a list of people who owe him money or something? Although that excludes me and Marita. Another bloody puzzle. "I guess we just need to sort out the clues and hope they'll make sense when we've got all the answers. Did I ever tell you how much I hate him?"

She holds my gaze for a moment; bugger it, she reads me like a three-year-old's picture book, but then bends back to the photos, moving number six forward. "He's dead, H. You could be a little more sensitive." She grins. "Though he is an arse. I wonder if he was worried someone else would find them. That's why he felt he had to hide who's who. I wonder who he feared might go digging. Stephen perhaps?"

"Or Miles. Or Jepson, McNoble's Dad."

She still has her index finger on number six. It's another view with the subject mostly hidden by a pillar. You can see some of the man's hair and his back. He's looking across a high street and you can sort of see a reflection in the window opposite. "What's that reflected in the window?"

"Could it be a car?" The grin is back.

"Yes! Well done. It's Christian, the hippy I worked with way back when, isn't it? Those boy racer stripes. The shag-wagon."

"I was so jealous when you went off to the beach in it once."

"Christian's nine letters on the grid, too. I saw him when I went to check out Frank's shop on Sunday. He works in the ticket office at New Milton station. When I told him Sven was dead he became really angry, like Sven had let him down."

"We need to ask him why, don't we? Why these people?" Dina realigns the images. "Now we know number one is Marita, three is you, Mum is five and Christian is six. That leaves us two and four to sort out."

"And seven, if we can find the missing one. You're brilliant and I'm bloody starving. Anything to eat?"

"There's a shepherd's pie in the oven."

Tentatively I open it. It smells great. She says, "Serve me some?"

"Where did you learn to cook? Not at home, that's for sure."

"Jim's Mum. She thought it essential I knew how to keep Jim happy and the second-best way is through his stomach."

"Ha ha."

She takes the plate. "The first way is to let him watch the motor racing and not interrupt."

"Seriously?"

"No, it's sex you nit. Motor racing is about sixth. Sven must have had a reason to make this a game; he had to know it would take time to unravel."

"Too clever for his own good. But yes, he had a reason."

She eats some of the pie. "Okay. I'll leave you with the missing people. What about the cars? If 'Original' is right, then maybe we're looking for words that describe these others that he hasn't included in the drawings?"

"That'll just be a load of adjectives, won't it? What's that going to tell us?

"I guess it'll all become clear when we work them out. I did have an idea. Jan is a car nut and—"

"You didn't tell him?"

"Not exactly. He has this awful mag – Custom Car – with these half-naked girls everywhere. You'd not know it was about cars most of the time, it's really just porn."

"I've seen it."

"You do surprise me. Anyway, it has these adverts and I thought I might be able to identify the cars. I managed to spot two – a BMW where the missing word is 'Incredible' and a Mercedes where it's 'Newest.' That's when I had this brainwave."

"Why does that make me feel a little sick?"

"Silly. I showed Jan the photos—"

"Shit. What—?"

"…and he identified the cars, although we couldn't find the actual adverts. I suppose we'll need to go trawling through car magazines."

We peer at the grid, but the two words Dina has found mean nothing. After a few minutes we give up. "This is pointless. We don't even know how this grid relates to the people's names, do we?"

She wipes her finger round the plate to make sure she doesn't miss any of the gravy; she'll make a perfect student. "Shall I try to see if there are other car mags with the missing adverts?"

"What we need is someone who works in advertising." I can't hide my smile. "Which happens to be Natalie."

"Won't she recognise Sven's style? And she'll want to know why? And what if she's really working for Miles and isn't planning to leave him?"

I hadn't thought of any of that. Damn her. "Okay not yet, but using her remains a possibility."

"Is Jackie coming round tonight?"

"She said 11ish. Just time to watch the cricket highlights first. What about Jan?"

Dina doesn't answer and goes to the kettle. I can tell I'm not meant to press the subject.

***

226

I'm watching Ian Botham trudge back to the Lord's Pavilion, dragging his bat like a naughty schoolboy having been bowled around his legs by Ray Bright for his second duck of the match. The commentators are glorying in his fall from grace, talking about him being sacked. It is painful to see such a big man broken. That's when Dobbin comes in. If Dobbin has been on the piss, normally he goes to the kitchen and drinks at least a pint of water. Not tonight. He heads for the sofa and flops down, putting his head in his hands like he's got the Mother of all hangovers already.

"What's up with you?"

He just shakes his head.

"Is it Vera? Where is she by the way?"

"Out with her Mum, and no."

"Tell Uncle Harry. What happened? You've got an awful dose of the clap? The condom split and she's up the duff? She wants you to—"

"Why the fuck is it always about sex with you? Jesus, you're obsessed, like some pervy pest." He is livid. Dobbin never gets angry. Then he starts to cry. Dobbin never cries.

"Shit." I look desperately at the door to the hall, wondering if I can fetch Dina as she'll know what to do better than me. "Mate, what's up? Is it your family?" As far as I know his parents, two brothers and twin younger sisters, are all in rude health.

"I've fucked-up Hong Kong."

"How?"

He swallows and leans back, rubbing his eyes. "Since I started I've been so keen to do well I've been sweating more than usual. On Friday one of the secretaries said I had BO. I can't risk that getting about. I took in a clean shirt. I reckoned I'd have a wash at lunchtime, put on the shirt and Bob's your uncle. The gents are amazing. Fresh towels, scented soap and talc and Eau de Cologne. Today, I go and wash and splash on the scent and the talc, only the talc sticks to my hands because they're wet from the scent. I have to get to a training session. I dash out of the toilet and bump into my boss, Lee. He's with this ancient Chinese chap, Mr Wong or something, who Lee introduces as some big cheese from Hong Kong. We shake hands while Lee says these nice things about me. Oh God." He sobs again.

I say, "What's wrong with that? It sounds great."

"What's wrong is I watched them walk away. Mr Wong looked at his hand then sniffed it. He damn well nearly threw up on the spot and looked back at me. He couldn't have been more disgusted. I'm done for. He thinks I'm some sort of scented fairy. He'll never have me out there now."

"Oh, come on. It's not going to be decided on a stinky handshake. And even if you don't go this time, there's always next. And it'll give you more time with Vera."

He slumps even further. "She's the other problem. She's wants to get married."

"Hardly fits the image, does it?"

"She thinks if she's married and divorced inside a week she'll have something no one else has. She even said if I could die of a heart attack while we are screwing on our wedding night that would be even better, but failing that divorce will do."

"She was joking?"

"Who the fuck knows?"

"She's nuts. Does she want to split up or something? After the divorce?"

"No. Although she says she'll need to have sex with another guy soon or she'll get stale."

"She is completely nuts."

"But I love her, Spittoon."

"Yeah mate. I know."

Friday, 10th July 1981

Chapter Thirty-Four

In Which Brenda/Vera and Dobbin Explore the Facilities and Everyone Says Goodbye

Cremating Sven is going to be awful. I tried to ignore the reality of it but crushed in the back seat of Dobbin's Mum's Austin Allegro it comes rushing over me. Jackie offered to come – which is sweet, given it's her day off – but as Natalie and Penny should be there, I suggested it might not be a great idea. She's okay about it. I think. Still, not having her there means I can avoid some awkward conversations.

The countryside around Farnham rushes past as I contemplate what part of the day will be worst. First up it's got to be seeing Penny, because she will know about me and Jackie. She'll smell the sex a mile off. Dina and Dobbin have both promised not to mention Jackie although Brenda/Vera was less than forthcoming when I asked for some discretion. As in, "I don't see why you don't ask if she wants a threesome. I tried with Gary but he's a prude."

"You said the third person was Bullet from the band."

"See what I mean? It's not like it's with some random stranger."

Then there's Natalie. After the awkward conversation in our kitchen, I've not heard from her and I've no idea what state she'll be in. Add to that the possibility of Miles being around and making a scene about the Will and everything will probably go pear-shaped.

And as if that's not enough to worry about, there's always McNoble. He'll want to know what we've found out since our cosy riverside chat. It'll not be easy if he sees Mum and Dad. I wince at the sudden thought that we might have Charlie Jepson popping up. Christ, this is the work of Satan.

I'm brought back to the moment when Dobbin swears and swerves, just missing some scurrying creature. Once the equilibrium is restored Dina tells the story of the couple we hitched with and the woman who gave a blowjob to the driver, making him leave the motorway rather abruptly before deftly re-joining it.

Even before she reaches the punch line, Dobbin is holding Brenda/Vera back; she is trying to get into his lap. Dobbin's performance is a tour de force. As the Fleet services appear shortly after this wrestle starts he pulls in.

"You're mental. You drive. I can't fend you off all the way to bloody Bournemouth."

Brenda/Vera is kneeling on her seat, ignoring Dina and me goggling at her from the back. "But I need sex, Gary. Per-leeeeeease... I can't go all day without a tiny little shaggy-poos."

"Don't be rid— get the fuck off! I'm wearing black."

"I'm warning you, Gary. If you won't then Harry will have to do. He's game."

"Me?"

"Him?"

Dina jumps out of her side and yanks Dobbin's door open. "For pity's sake, Gary. Take her to the bogs and give her what she wants. We'll get the teas in."

It is an unlikely fact that in such circumstances Dina is the voice of reason. While a reluctant Dobbin and a skippity-hoppity Brenda/Vera disappear round the side of the grey flat concrete services, Dina and I head inside and buy four hot drinks. We've barely sat down when they reappear.

"Done so soon?" Dina sips her brew.

Brenda/Vera nods. "It'll have to do. Shame the disabled loo was locked or we could have—"

Dobbin screams and she looks at him blankly. "What?"

"Can we talk about something else? Like how long this is going to last? Who might be there?"

"Boring. I bet Harry and Dina would like to talk about how far we might—"

Dina stands, swigging down her hot tea and grimacing. "I think I'll just pop to the loo."

I follow her, not really needing to. "Meet you by the car." I leave Dobbin with Brenda/Vera wondering if they have time to pop to the woods that line the side of the motorway.

As we are walking back to the car, Dina puts the icing on my cake of anxiety. "You'll have to say something. If none of his family are there and you're his executor, it will be down to you."

I suppose she's right. I spoke to the local vicar who knew Mrs Andersen. It seems Sven's Mother was a regular churchgoer, part of the Baptist Congregation in Lymington where Sven was christened. Mrs Andersen gave them a bit of money a while back, enough to make

231

the vicar happy to take the service. Although when he asked for some anecdotes about Sven I drew a blank beyond his drawing and the unwinding of his Dad's criminal empire. Actually, I didn't mention that last bit.

The crematorium is a bland brown building surrounded by landscaping and alcoves for urns. We're early – there's another service ahead of us and we are dispatched to look at the flowers. Dina leads the way, giving a commentary. "These are from his aunt. Will she be here?"

"No idea."

"What about his Mum?"

"Step-Mum. They never got on, and from what I heard she lives in Sweden. The only address we found was in Stockholm and there's been no reply. His real Mum died a long time ago."

"These are from Mum and Dad."

"Given they disliked him and his family, that's nice of them." She sneers. "Bit cheap, though. This one is from the hotel."

"Ha! Terry signed it 'your dear friend.'"

"Terry?"

"Head waiter. He was a nightmare to all the students. At least he was to me, but he and Sven hit it off. Anything from Marita or Frank?"

Dina checks again and shakes her head. "Come on, let's find Dobbin and Vera. She's probably trying to get him to screw her over some gravestone or in a coffin." As we wander away she asks, "Any word about Marita? Did the hotel call?"

"Nothing. I rather hoped she'd be here. Or at least at the nibbles after."

The service is due to start at midday. We sit at the front, where family would normally be seated. With a couple of minutes to go, I turn around and see the room is half-full with maybe 20 people. Mum and Dad haven't come but Ravi and Pritti Ohja are there, sitting next to Terry and Magda, the receptionist. She briefly acknowledges me but looks too upset to do much more than that. Towards the back, Amos has arrived and is speaking to someone who I can't see from where I'm sitting.

The vicar wants to start, so with a final check of my watch, I wave him on.

It's a pretty dull and unemotional affair. The vicar 'Call me Rodney' keeps to the few facts there are. After five minutes or so, we stand for a hymn and George decides he wants to be an aeroplane.

While I stare, hugely embarrassed, and Rodney makes faces of disapproval, Jim, Dina and Mrs James ignore him. It's Brenda/Vera who takes charge, marching forward, bending to speak to the boy and leading him out the back. I wonder what she's said.

When it's my turn, I feel pretty unsteady. The lectern is slightly raised and when I stand on it I can see the congregation better. Amos is next to Natalie who is next to McNoble. There's no sign of Miles, which is a relief. I look for Penny but there's no sign of her either. It's then I jump; seated in the far back corner is an old man with scruffy long hair and a thin white beard. Frank. He's ignoring the service and appears to be writing. Next to him is a much younger man with a floppy fringe. He is wearing a purple blazer and yellow tie. He catches my eye, smiles and nods like I should know him. I nod back and look to the other side of the aisle. The back two rows are full of what appear to be a group of heavyset black-suited bouncers.

My few words go without a hitch; at least I assume so because I barely notice I'm speaking. The group of beefy men, all apparently about to burst out of their suits, watch me with an unsettling intensity, although one dabs at his eyes with his sleeve. I hope I'm not upsetting him. He doesn't look like he's naturally of a forgiving disposition.

When I finish, Rodney takes over. "Before we say our last farewells I'd like everyone to note that there will be drinks and nibbles at Mr Spittle's house after the service," he reads out the address of my family home, "and everyone is welcome."

There's not a lot more to say. When the little curtains part and the coffin slides forward it barely seems possible that this is the end of Sven, a man I've known for a short while and who I never really liked much. Oddly, after worrying about how today will go, this bit, while sad, is also calming. It's done. He's gone. It's over. I'm in the middle of some morbid thoughts when Dina tugs at my sleeve. "I think they expect us to go first."

It seems so wrong, me leading the way out. Dina seems to understand the etiquette and heads for the alcove with the flowers. I'm more interested in trying to see where Natalie is to ask her about Penny when Dina says, "Look. There's something from Marita."

That makes me turn. A simple white rose with a card that says, 'My Rock. When will I see you again? Your loving sister.' I'm certain it wasn't there earlier.

Dina lifts the card. "It doesn't say where they're from. I wonder if the manager knows." For a moment, she hesitates before she says, "I'll ask. You never know. Meet you by the car."

Dobbin comes over. "Vera's gone ahead with Mrs James and Jim. Seems George has taken a shine to her and she's keeping him amused. I think she wants to have children." He shudders. "Who knew sex could be so damn complicated?"

"I think you'll find that was the original idea of sex, having babies."

"Really? How quaint. I said I'd drive you and Dina. You ready to go?"

"Dina's just checking something. I'll wait here till everyone's gone and meet you by the car."

"Okay. I think I'll wander around the gravestones, see if anyone died of excessive sex. The Victorians died in their sleep a lot, you know. Maybe we Elizabethans will be the ones to pop off while coupling." He seems to sag into his suit and walks away.

A few of the bruisers wander past, inscrutable behind their mirrored sunglasses, and they make me think about Frank. I'm pretty sure I've not seen him go so I head back towards the hall. Another service is being set up. The only people still inside are Natalie and Amos. She takes my hand. "Thank you. That was so lovely."

Amos nods. "Very nice. You've grown up, Harry. You couldn't have done that a couple of years ago."

I manage a smile while casually glancing around, not wanting to be rude but anxious to find Frank. But he's gone. Damn.

Back with Natalie I notice how red her eyes are. Sad eyes, flushed cheeks. God, she's adorable. "Are you coming to mine?"

She shakes her head. "Miles wants to get back."

"He's here?"

"Outside by the car. He said he was too upset to come in."

"Okay. Well, I'd better—"

"Do you think anyone really loved him, Harry?"

That catches me off guard. "Maybe Marita. And you."

"You didn't, did you?"

"No, not really. I never knew him well enough to be honest."

"He was very kind to me, tried his best to protect me." She shakes her head. "Did you see Marita? She was here briefly."

"No, sadly. I wanted a word. Do you know where she's gone?"

"She said she couldn't stay. Stephen gave her a lift to the station."

"Bugger. Where's Penny?"

That triggers a rather furtive glance at Amos, who won't look at me at first but then beams. He says, "I spoke to her last night. She said she had a job on and couldn't shift it. She's really upset to miss this."

"Oh."

"She said to say—" but he never finishes as Miles' head appears round the door.

"Come on doll, time we get going. I've got be to be heading north by four." He disappears.

"I'd better dash." She pecks me on the cheek and squeezes my hand, whispering in my ear, "We need to speak. Soon," before disappearing in a cloud of Chanel and anxiety.

Amos follows. "Sorry, I'm getting a lift. We should grab a drink, yes?"

I follow slowly but even so, Miles is on his own and leaning on his car when I reach the car park. It's a red Porsche. Miles glances at me and then returns to his fingernail cleaning. He says, "Nice speech. Sven would have *hated* it." He laughs at his own joke. His laugh ends as abruptly as it began. "Found where he's hidden it yet?"

"Hidden what?"

Miles affects a laugh. "You really don't want to play clever with me, Harry. We all know you'll be rich if you can find what he's done with it all. Won't you Harry? You lucky lucky boy. I didn't know he liked you so much. He certainly hid it when he talked about you. What did he call you? The Wet Wanker, wasn't it?"

I know he's lying. Sven may have hated me, he may have thought me useless, but any nickname would have had more class than that, even if the sentiments were the same. To change the subject, I say, "Nice car."

He smiles at that. "Yeah. She's a beauty. I'd not go anywhere without her." He pushes himself off the car. I glance where he's looking. Natalie is standing by Dobbins' car taking to Dina. "Sorry we can't stay. Keep in touch, Harry. All of us are interested in what you find out. We all feel a connection, know what I mean?"

Soon enough, there's a roar of the engine and they're gone.

I stare at the dust cloud kicked up by the tyres. "Jan Kruis said Sven had a Porsche."

Dina says, "I'd forgotten that. You think that's it?"

"We should check when we get back."

"Do we know the registration number?"

"It's on a piece of card attached to the keys. They're in my room."

Just then a Ford Cortina pulls into the car park and stops next to us. McNoble. He winds down the window. Dina blows him a kiss. In response he grins – I really didn't know he could do that – and blows one back. Amos is sitting in the back. He waves at us. This is all very jolly. McNoble leans towards the back and says something. Amos laughs and McNoble says to us, "We'd better go. Say thanks to your Ma for the invite but I don't really think she wants me at yours, does she?" He doesn't wait for a response.

As they drive off, Dina says, "Shame they're not coming back. Be good to pick their brains about Sven."

"Do you think they have any?"

"Oh yes. Stephen for one is far cleverer than you give him credit."

"Bollocks."

Dobbin is alone in the car. He says nothing as we climb in, just sits, staring ahead, gripping the wheel hard.

After what seems an age, I say, "In your own time, Mr Dobbs."

He sags and slowly bangs his head on the horn, jumping back at the noise. "Oh, fuck."

"What's cheered you up?"

"Bloody Vera. You know, I just don't understand her."

"Agreed, this fixation on sex is—"

"I don't mean that. It's her mood swings. One minute she's bouncing, the next she can't get away soon enough, biting my head off. Bloody hell. She said she might even catch the train back if I stay at yours for the afters."

"Why? Mum's not done the catering. Mrs Ohja has."

"I don't know, but something's got her goat." He peers across at me and I nod, which is followed swiftly by a clip on the ear from Dina.

"Ouch! What was that for?"

"That was because you were thinking 'it's her period.' Sexist pig."

"I wasn't," but we both know she's right.

Dobbin sighs and we drive off in silence.

Chapter Thirty-Five

Where Harry Sits with Frank and Stands Up to Mr Lewis

The three of us are in our own little worlds as we walk around the side of my parents' house to be confronted by a sea of faces looking at us. I scan to see who's there and it's a jolt to spot Frank sitting on my parents' old swing with the same smiley faced young man from the cremation. Mum has set up a couple of trestle tables, probably borrowed from the WI, for the occasion and she and Mrs Ohja are manning the tea urn (another WI loan) and sandwiches and I know I should go and say thank you but I don't want to miss Frank again so head there first.

Frank is still doodling. When the young man sees me, he stands up and straightens his jacket. He looks very uncomfortable, like wearing a tie is unusual, or perhaps the colour combination, which to be fair isn't usual for a sad occasion like this, isn't his choice. His smile puts me in mind of the Sunday school teacher I had when Mum and Dad sent us to Church to allow them to have a free Sunday morning. All he did was smile and say 'No, children' while we tore about until the vicar slammed in, bellowed at us to behave and left. It felt rather as if the bellow was aimed at Mr Smooting as much as at us.

"Mr Spittle? Beautiful service. You did him proud."

"Thank you, Mr... er?"

"Stammer. I'm from Sunnysites Nursing Home." He glances back at Frank. "Mr Smedley, Frank, was determined to come. He's been looking forward to it." Mr Stammer goes pale. "Oh, that's dreadful. Of course he was your friend. I didn't mean…" His apology peters out and he rallies. "Frank has a few lucid moments, one of which was when we heard of Mr Andersen, that is the younger Andersen – I mean Sven." He stops abruptly. "Frank insisted we came. Frank said he was a very fair-minded employer. And, well, we do what he wants. Of course." Mr Stammer looks across at the group of human rocks who came to the funeral in their black suits and ties and who are now sipping tea in a circle next to Mum's camellia bush. He laughs mirthlessly. "Obviously."

"Did Mr Andersen—?"

"Which one?" He smiles at my confusion. "Maybe I should explain. Robin Andersen had his own ideas about loyalty that were different to Sven's. When Frank had his stroke – that was the start and now it's the beginnings of dementia – shortly after Sven's Father died, Sven set up a fund for his Father's old employees. Whatever their role, he made them comfortable. He pays – well, paid – for everything." He nods at me. "He told me about you last March, well the March before that, of course, it seems like it's just the last one but time flies and…" he stops then rallies again. "That's when the fund was finalised. He said you'd be sorting everything else out, but he wanted the staff dealt with properly. They're very loyal to him. His death was a real shock." At that he folds his hands and drops his gaze, apparently relieved to be able to stop talking.

I'm thinking that it couldn't be correct that Sven had my involvement planned in March and certainly not back in 1979. I mean if so why wait until this July to make the Will? As Mr Stammer is talking we both look at the group of big men, obviously his Father's former employees. They look sombre and from their glowering expressions it almost looks like they are planning something nefarious. It is only as I watch that I notice two of the five dabbing their eyes again and one who cannot look up from his shoes. Only one stares at me. I shudder.

"Would you like some tea? I'll leave you and Frank for a moment while I fetch some cups. Milk? Sugar?"

I place my order and sit down. Being next to Frank is quite unpleasant. The swing has always had a bad smell, courtesy of Rascal the cat, but now the cushions feel damp and mildewy too and there's something coming from Frank that I really don't want to inquire about or become any more familiar with it than I am already. Frank doesn't seem to mind, and I swallow any queasiness. "Hi Frank. Remember me? The young man who—"

Frank stops me by grabbing one hand in a vice-like grip and proffering his sheet of paper with the other. I glance at it and smile. "What's this?"

The clench tightens, and while he makes it clear with his now free hand that I should cover the sheet or something, he hisses with barely disguised anger, "Shut the fuck up, can't you?"

I nod and he presses the sheet again. "What is this?" I whisper although why I'm not sure since there's no one close enough to hear.

By way of an answer, Frank holds my gaze in a way that threatens all sorts, before opening the corner of the sheet with a finger and pointing at one figure amongst several where he has written: '70SB.'

"I don't understand. What—? Ouch!" The pain shoots up my arm as my fingers are bent back. How come someone debilitated by a stroke is so strong? It's only then I grasp what he's trying to get me to do: put the sheet in my pocket. As I do so, I follow his anxious nod. Mr Stammer is approaching. I manage to stand, my hand in my pocket covering the sheet and smile at the younger man. Behind me I'm aware of Frank slumping back into the swing's cushions. I glance back and, bugger me, he winks before closing his eyes.

"Tea? Your sister is lovely, isn't she? If you've finished with Frank, shall I introduce you to the others?" Mr Stammer holds out a cup and saucer.

"I was hoping…" But when I glance again at Frank he is, for all the world, fast asleep.

"It happens." Mr Stammer's smile grows. "He goes just like that." He snaps his fingers, but Frank doesn't stir.

As he is happily snoring, I follow Mr Stammer to the group of trolls filling one corner of the terrace. They are oddly similar, even though the tallest is easily a foot and a half bigger than the smallest (and he's still taller than me). They each have the same lumpy eyebrow line and noses than appear to be the experiments of a primary school pottery class.

"'arry? H'im Grant. Grant Grate" The speaker is the only one capable of knotting his tie tightly at his neck. "These hare my bruvvers." He points at the tallest before working his way round in size order. "Graham, George, Gray hand Grew honly 'e never did."

The five stare down at me like vultures round their prey before this rumbling sound emerges. It takes a moment for it to become apparent that it is from them and another to realise they are laughing. Grant throws his arm around my shoulder. "It's what hour hold pa would say. Hon haccount hof 'e's the smallest." I wonder why he adds an 'h' to every word beginning with a vowel. If it's an affectation I'm not about to mention it.

"Yes. Hof course. Of course." I laugh to cover myself and hope to all that's holy they don't think I'm taking the piss. Happily, they don't seem to notice.

"Not that this his the time to laugh, right?" Grant's face is close to mine; it's not the sort of face you argue with.

"No. Yes. Sorry?"

"We won't stay. Just wanted to give 'im a send-off. Thank your Ma, will you? Hand hif you need hanyfink hat hall, 'arry, just give hus a bell, right?"

Each of them nods in turn before peeling away like formation gorillas and heading round the side of the house. Before Grant, the last in line, disappears, he presses a card into my jacket pocket and pats it.

Once they've gone it feels like everyone else releases a collective breath and relaxes. I look at Mr Stammer and say, "I wouldn't want to be on the wrong side of them."

"Actually, Grant was the accountant, George the cook and Grew the gardener. Graham and Gray drove and provided secretarial services."

"I think I remember Graham when Mr Andersen came here once."

"His accident? Yes, Gray mentioned that earlier. Very unfortunate but Mr Andersen, Mr Sven always said you weren't to blame. Someone called James, I think. They are loyal and hardworking men."

"Really? I'm sorry. I assumed…" I shrug. "Why does Grant drop all the aitches and then add an aitch on every word beginning with a vowel?"

"Does he? I can't say that I've noticed."

"Oh. Ha h—"

Mr Stammer holds my gaze. I don't think he's joking. While I question both my hearing and my sanity, wondering at how much more surreal today might become, he says, "Of course, they'd also beat you senseless if that was needed. Look, Mr Spittle, we all know the background, but the thing is Sven was a good man. He didn't hide what his Father was like, nor what these people did, but he knew if he abandoned them they'd probably go off and do worse." At this Mr Stammer closes his eyes and brings his hands together like he's praying. It seems a familiar pose. "He didn't judge and believed in redemption. He and his sister were clear that these people should be cared for and they would only lose the support of the trust fund if they did anything criminal again. Mr Lewis is the trustee of the fund and he wouldn't countenance a slip."

"Is that where Sven put all his Father's money? In the trust?"

"I'm sorry. I don't know. Maybe Mr Lewis might."

"Is he the solicitor? In Lymington?" If so I know him from a while back. I'm surprised he's still alive, in truth. He seemed ancient then.

"Yes, that's right. He did most of the Andersen family legal work. Clever man. He will be around somewhere I expect. He was intending to be at the ceremony. Now, I'd better take Frank home. He likes to eat at set times or he becomes cranky and his diet is rather specific." He smiles weakly. "Mostly cabbage."

That might explain the smell. I feel in my pocket for the note; it's still there. "Could I have a word with Frank before you go?"

He shakes his head. "Not worth your time, in all honesty. He'll not say anything more for a few hours. Why don't I take a number where I can call you and when he's in the right frame of mind we can fix something up?" His look can only be described as beady. "Assuming it is that important?"

***

Mr Lewis was old and desiccated when I last saw him at my aunt's old house one never to be forgotten Sunday when Mum gave aunt the money she needed to keep the family garage business going, even though it now seems there had to have been several other cash injections since then. It was the beginning of a rapprochement between the sisters and the cracking of aunt's marriage. Now it seems things are rapidly reversing, with aunt and uncle back together and aunt and Mum barely talking following the decision to sell the garage. The lawyer is talking to Dad and Asoka Ohja. Dad waves me over when he catches me looking. He's not very happy.

"Who were the Flintstones?" His tone is sharp and even his good eye seems to glare at me like his glass one does most of the time anyway. When Dad did his National Service back in the fifties he had an awful accident that resulted in him losing an eye and some of his hearing. This was when he and Charlie Jepson were fellow soldiers and competing for Mum's affection. I've never really found out what went on back then, but I heard Mum and Charlie boy had an affair, which was why I thought I might be his son.

I try a smile. I'm beginning to realise I shouldn't have let Mrs Ohja convince me she would be able to persuade Mum to host this wake or whatever these post cremation refreshments are called. "The Flintstones were part of Robin Andersen's old staff. I hear Mr Lewis has a trust fund he runs for their benefit."

Dad makes a growling noise, but I ignore him and concentrate on Mr Lewis. He is, if anything, more wizened than I remember. The only things about him not grey are his lips and tie, both a similar scarlet. He smiles, if you can call the expression he makes – more a twitch at the corners of his mouth – a smile. He catches me looking at his tie. "Such a tragic loss of your friend, Harry, not that I realised you were so close. I hoped I might catch you. The funeral home told me you had organised the service. I assume you did that on behalf of Marita? I really do want a word with her if you have current contact details. There's a lot of work to sort out."

Perhaps Dad senses a tension between Mr Lewis and me because he makes some daft comment about Mr Lewis' red tie and launches into an anecdote about a similar tie he had when demobbed and how it caught on fire. When Dad pauses for air, I say, "I hoped for a word with you, Mr Lewis, about this trust fund?"

It's difficult to say if I detect a flash of annoyance in his expression. I've probably been reading too many crappy crime novels. Whatever, his expression morphs into a simper. "Oh Harry, and you training as a lawyer too. Surely you know about client confidentiality?"

I'm still, at heart, a callow youth but over my few years on the planet I recognise well enough when I'm being patronised and condescended to. And I really, really don't like it. Even though heat flushes my neck and ears and I imagine I look rather like I'm turning into a flamingo, I can't hide the irritation in my voice. "We weren't friends, not really Mr Lewis. But since he named me executor in his Will, the body was released to me and I felt I had to organise the funeral. Consequently, I'd like to know how, if at all, the Trust works alongside the Will."

The simpering stops, and he says, "What are you talking about? I have his Will."

I'm conscious of Dad and Asoka staring at me. Dad says, "You? Why you?"

I manage a croaky, "He wrote a new Will, a few days before… before he died. I'm an executor, as is Jeremy Panther – he's a partner in Clifford, Risely & Co. where I work and—"

Mr Lewis is no longer pretending to be friendly. He glares at me with undiluted contempt. "That's ridiculous. It must be a fake. Who benefits?"

Boy, do I not want to answer that. There's an awful pause before he leans in and says in a sort of stage whisper that carries to everyone else who's listening – which is everyone else – "Well? Who?"

It's then Dina, who is standing behind him, chimes in with, "Client confidentiality, Mr Lewis."

He glares at her, then turns back to me. He holds my gaze while he speaks to her, "I see. As your brother well knows, Miss Spittle, the Will becomes a public document as soon as probate is granted, and the executors can do nothing with the estate until then. I will find out." At this he looks at her. "As will anyone else who might be interested. And there will be a few of those, I expect."

He turns to Dad. "Arthur, I'd better go. Busy, busy, you know. Love to Veronica. And pop by when you want to talk about the loan. Sooner the better." He shakes everyone's hand before coming back to me. "Harry, we need to speak, clear up this, erm, confusion. Can you come to my office later? I'll be there until seven tonight." He doesn't wait for an answer, sure that I will do as he asks.

When he's gone I realise Dad has fixed an uncomfortable stare on me. Agog would be a good word. For a moment, I assume he's proud his son has such a high-profile role, but it quickly becomes clear he is horrified. "What are you thinking, Harry my son? We just thought you were being nice to his sister, doing the funeral. But surely you're not really working for him, are you? The Andersens are crooks. Everyone knows it." He glances nervously towards the tea table. "It's bad enough giving those thugs their tea. Whatever you do, don't tell your Mother. She'll be horrified. After what that Andersen boy did to Norman's hopes."

Dad has always seemed lacking in some basic understanding of how life works, seeming to go around in a fog of uncertainty. But maybe he knows more than Mum gives him credit for if he knows about Sven and the garage sale.

Chapter Thirty-Six

In Which Penny Re-enters the Plot in an Unexpected Way

About two hours later all the guests have gone. I'm relieved Charlie Jepson hasn't turned up, and I imagine Mum is probably the same, not that we have spoken about it. Mum has offered to make dinner – under the watchful eye of Pritti Ohja I hope – and I want to go and see Mr Lewis. I go to find Dobbin, who I've lost track of what with everything. I did wonder if he'd left given what he'd said about Brenda/Vera, but I find them both sitting on the sofa talking in low voices.

"Hi. I need to go into Lymington to see a lawyer about Sven's estate. You can go if you want. Dina and I will catch the train home. Or hitch."

Dobbin glances anxiously at Brenda/Vera but she's all smiles. "No, we'll come too. There'll be somewhere to tick off the list."

"List?"

She smiles and he shakes his head hard so I don't pursue it.

Around 30 minutes later the four of us set off for the harbour town of Lymington. It is a twee place and a ferry port accessing the Isle of Wight. Its High Street is on a sharp hill that leads to the harbour. As we approach the town centre, Brenda/Vera says she wants to see if they can find a boat where they can have sex. "I've not done it afloat yet. I've still about 30 places to tick off."

I'm sitting next to Dobbin, who grips the steering wheel tightly.

"Is that on the list?"

Poor bugger nods once. She'll probably kill him off at this rate. I keep quiet, sure he must be hating this, but Dina has no such qualms. She asks what else is on the list. Brenda/Vera points at the church we are just passing. "If we can't find a boat we could try to see about the pulpit. Churches are great. Bell towers, vestries, maybe an undercroft."

"It's good to see you happy again."

Brenda/Vera looks at me, her eyes narrowed a little. "What do you mean?"

"You seemed a little, erm, downbeat at the crematorium." I can feel Dobbin tense and wonder if I've said something I shouldn't.

"No, I was fine."

"Good. That's good."

"What made you think—?"

Dina interrupts. "Here's fine, Gary. Come on H. Let's get this over with."

We leave the young lovers to their fun and games. We are about 200 yards shy of Mr Lewis' offices, which are in two adjacent houses in the middle of the High Street that have long been converted to work spaces. As we walk she says, "You're an arse, you know. Couldn't you see how Gary was squirming?"

"Yes. That's what our friendship is all about, making the other squirm."

She looks at me with an expression that says clearly, without words, 'you are mental, you know?'

At the offices we head for the furthest front door as the first has planting in front of it making it clear it is no longer in use. The receptionist takes our name, and immediately, or so it seems, there is Mr Lewis, smiling broadly. "Harry, Dina, come through."

We have to sit, in my case anxiously, while Mr Lewis goes through the rigmarole of ordering tea, giving instructions to his secretary about letters and calls to be made and then taking his seat opposite us.

"So you're the wealthy man, are you Harry?" He smiles, loving his knowledge. "I called your fellow executor and he told me all about the Will. Handwritten? Two days before he dies?" Mr Lewis shakes his head. "And you benefit. All very convenient, isn't it?"

I'm already sweating. "We don't know why he changed it, but I'm trying to ascertain that." Despite trying to sound confident, I want to tell him everything, hand everything over and run away.

He says, "And the police? They are happy his death was of natural causes?"

"Heart attack."

"Goodness? In one so young? That must have raised some questions?"

Dina says, "You're not surprised, are you?"

Mr Lewis shakes his head, surprising me at least. "No, relieved. I feared for a moment that they had got to him at the last hurdle and he'd been forced to give it to them."

I look confused and manage. "It? Them?"

For the first time, Mr Lewis' smile disappears. He frowns, removes his little gold-rimmed glasses and rubs his face. The result is he looks about 1500 rather than 100. "Sven wrote a Will a while ago bequeathing everything to Marita and she did a mirror Will. That was before they realised both the extent of their inheritance and the, erm, strings attached, shall we say? My worry was he had succumbed to the pressure he was undoubtedly under. Clearly not. What did he tell you?"

"Me? Nothing. I—" I stop as Dina's kick sends a searing pain shoot up my leg from the shin.

"Really? That's unlike him. He was meticulous in his record keeping, who deserved what and when. Mr Stammer told you about the trust fund, I suppose? A generous but prudent gesture. As for the rest, well…"

"There is a 'rest' then?"

"Oh yes. Several hundreds of thousands I shouldn't wonder." He pauses and shuffles some papers. "You will understand that I never knew what Mr Andersen senior was doing when I acted for him, setting up companies or buying and selling properties, yes? It came as a shock when Sven indicated that some of his businesses were, shall we say, less than completely kosher?"

Dina is leaning forward. It's like she's trying to read upside down. "Did you stop then? When you realised?"

Mr Lewis lets the silence lengthen. "No. I decided that, given Sven's and Marita's honourable plans to do good with the money, it was better to turn a little blind eye to the past."

"And that way no one asked questions about your former role?"

A flicker of a smile crosses his face. He says, "I'm being candid now, but I will deny anything and everything. Sven even signed a short document absolving me, for what it's worth. Once Mr Andersen – Robin – passed on and it was clear what Sven and Marita wanted, we unwound as many businesses as we could as quickly as possible."

"What happened to the money?"

"Well, I've mentioned the trust. And there were some immediate debts on the estate. Not," he laughs but not in a happy way, "what you'd call legal debts, not ones that are set against the estate assets for the purposes of probate. And we knew there would be others lurking. Sven's idea was to meet all those as soon as possible and then deal with the residue quickly."

"Where did you reach? Have all those businesses been sold?"

"All bar two, I believe. And I think the last couple were more like investments – loans probably – rather than businesses he owned outright."

"Who—?"

"I don't know. Really. I refused to know. Just that there were two he intended on sorting out when he went up to London that last time. If there were others he didn't confide in me."

"You really have no idea?"

He sighs. "No, no idea. I know Marita had plans but whether they were new or dealing with existing issues…" He spreads his hands wide. "Only she will be able to help you there."

We all sit, in our own little worlds, before he says, "I could challenge the Will, really. On behalf of Marita. I mean, if she wanted to. But I suspect he knew exactly what he was doing and if I'm not much mistaken, so do you. Just be careful, Harry. You too Dina. I've no idea what he planned exactly but he must have had a reason to choose you. It could be because he thought you were safe. Or safer than Marita. That's the best I can do."

We leave about 20 minutes later. I say to Dina, "Two businesses remaining. That'll be Miles and McNoble."

Dina says, "He said he believed it was two. I'd not be too sure about those two either. At least not McNoble. I really want to believe him, and he never said Sven owed him or the other way round. More likely his Father, don't you think? Whatever, the answers have to be in those pictures, don't they?"

"Why?"

"Oh, come on." Her tone is that of a tired bored teacher who has explained an idea to a class once too often. If Dina could give detention, I'd never see daylight.

Outside leaning against the wall are Dobbin and Brenda/Vera. Brenda/Vera is smoking – I didn't know she smoked and wonder briefly if it's a joint, but it's a Marlboro. Dobbin looks flushed like he's just been jogging. I refuse to ask why.

Brenda/Vera asks what we've found out. I didn't really say much about why we were seeing Mr Lewis on the way over and for some reason her curiosity, which is probably just her being polite, irritates me. I snap back, "I seem to be involved with some unlovely people. I hope you enjoyed yourself."

Dobbin stands and heads for the car. He says, "Harry seems to attract thugs just now. Those heavies at your parents and that prick

247

McNoble." He glances at me. "The sooner you're shot of this Will, the better."

I nod. "I agree. If only it were that easy."

When we arrive home, Brenda/Vera suggests to Dobbin they go and sit in the gazebo and 'have a chat' and I go to find Mum to ask about dinner. In the end I find her reading a book; Mrs Ohja has taken over the catering, thank heavens. When she sees me she says, "Oh, there you are. Can you ring your friend Natalie? It's urgent apparently. The number is by the phone."

I can't help wondering if there's been some sort of payback for Natalie from Miles, but as soon as she answers she blurts out, "It's Penny."

I can barely hear the next couple of sentences as my head spins in all sorts of awful directions. It only stops when she says, "Police custody."

"What? Sorry, Natalie. Bad line. Can you say that again a bit more slowly?"

"Penny's been arrested. She wasn't making a lot of sense but it's something to do with the people she was visiting."

"Sean Latterly? Maggie someone? Sir Penshaw Grimsdale?"

"Yes. Him. How do you know? Never mind. He's dead and she and a few others are all being held."

"He's dead? Sir Pen?"

"Yes, that's what I was told."

"Christ."

"Harry, that's not what matters. Penny is being held by the police. You will help her, won't you? Call them and explain she's not some murderer—"

"He was murdered?" I can hear the incredulity in my voice.

"I don't know. For heaven's sake, you're the lawyer! You can call, find out. I know things haven't been good between you two, but you can't just abandon her. Not now."

"Yes, okay. Where is she?"

She slowly dictates an address and a number. "You are really sweet. I'll wait by the phone. You will let me know what happens, won't you?"

"Miles?"

"He's travelling north. He won't be back until tomorrow."

I sit staring at the handset for several minutes, unsure what I should say or do. I need a story. I pick up the phone and call the office. Gloria tells me Jeremy is out with clients, but she has a number if it's urgent. "He's made a mess of a conveyance and Christine is trying to sort it out for him. He wasn't happy, but he did leave a number. Should I give it to you?" It's her best teasing voice but I don't have the time or energy for her games.

"Sir Penshaw's dead."

"Oh no! He was such a lovely old boy. Hang on. Have you a pen?"

She dictates the number, which I call. Jeremy is fetched. He is not best pleased but listens to me. "Are you sure he's dead? I mean it's not been on the news or anything?"

"I heard it from a friend."

"Well then. It's probably some stupid rumour."

"I thought maybe I could call the police and find out, say I'm calling on behalf of you as his lawyer. Makes it sound official."

I can tell he's thinking this through, probably calculating the benefit of his doing it if it's true against sounding so important he has one of his people make the call for him. Just then a voice calls his name and he says, hurriedly, "Okay Harry. Do it," before ringing off.

I may be stupid, I may miss the obvious, but I'd recognise that voice. Miles Tupps calling Jeremy's name and saying, "It's your deal." What is he up to? Natalie said he'd gone north.

The police are more helpful than Jeremy. Someone who says they are Detective Sergeant Pattinson tells me that Sir Pen is indeed dead and they have just had him officially identified by his sister, Lady Isabella Grimsdale. She also confirms that three people are voluntarily attending the station for questioning in connection with the death as there were some circumstances, which she cannot yet disclose, that requires something more than a doctor's attendance and may well warrant an autopsy. When I tell her I'm also Penny's solicitor she becomes suspicious, insisting on taking my name again and that of Jeremy. Now I'm petrified she's about to insist on calling him; instead I suggest I visit in the morning so that we can discuss details in person. I also agree that Penny needs her own representation and having me acting for both Sir Pen's estate and Penny would be unwise. At least she has confirmed Penny is indeed in for questioning, even if voluntarily so far as the police are concerned.

I find Dobbin stretched out on the lawn with his hands cupped a few inches above his flies, which are rather obviously open. "Are you wanking, Dobbin?"

He jumps but keeps his hands in place. When he sees it is only me, he flops back. "She's insatiable, Spittoon. I can't go on. And now she says if I fail her again she'll definitely find someone else." He twists to look at me with a face like a chastised puppy. "I'm fucked either way."

I flop down next to him. "Well and truly by the sound of it. You know you're living every man's dream, don't you?"

"It's some sort of Faustian fuck-pact. Either I manage a stiffy every two hours or so or she'll get a new bloke. I'm rubbed raw."

"How about if I say I need you for a very important job tomorrow, one needing you in a suit and able to walk without grimacing?"

He tries to smile but his heart isn't in it. "If I survive the night. What's the job?"

"You will become Garfield Dobbs, solicitor to the highest courts in the land. It's a criminal offence but only a small one and no one will die."

"Why not? I've buggered my chances of Hong Kong and I can't cope with Vera just now. Do you know how many places in that bloody church she wanted to—?"

"I've got to call Natalie. Thanks mate. Try Calamine lotion. It's good for burns. I'm sure Mum will have some. And no – if you have blisters you can drain them yourself."

Saturday, 11th July 1981

Chapter Thirty-Seven

Where Dobbin and Harry Talk to Penny and Veronica Makes a Sauce

Because of the 'Penny situation,' as it has become known, we all stay at Mum and Dad's overnight. It is a long drive to Swindon where Penny is 'helping' with the enquiries. It's good Dobbin borrowed the car for the weekend. To kill time, Brenda/Vera and Dina decide to go to Bournemouth to sunbathe. Mum suggests Milford but when Brenda/Vera hears it's just pebbles she turns up her nose. For an anarcho-syndicalist with Maoist leanings, she's remarkably precious. She has taken a shine to Asoka as well, which is worrying Dobbin.

"How old is he, Spittoon? I mean is he, you know…?"

"Too old for sex?"

"Yeah. She sort of let me off last night but only because I cried."

"Yeah?" I don't want to be interested, but I can't help myself.

"I told her about when Noor first saw your Mum's veggie patch. 'They grow willies!' She insisted we pick a courgette."

"Bloody hell."

"We'd already stolen a cucumber from across the road. Frankly her fanny must be made of leather."

"Thanks for sharing that." I'm really not interested but… "Don't you, you know, need something?"

"What?"

I wish I hadn't started this. "You know. To help. Er, some sort of cream?"

"Oh. Yeah. Yoghurt."

"Yoghurt?"

"She says the bacteria helps her oojit or something. Your Mum has loads in the kitchen. She said to help ourselves."

"Are you telling me you…? No, I had some for breakfast. Let's move on. When we get there, you need to let me do the talking. Your firm is?"

"I'm not stupid."

"Humour me. Address?"

Dobbin runs through the plan. I'm pretty certain it will look odd if I try to sit in on his meeting with Penny. At least we have our suits from the funeral and look the part. As it turns out I needn't have worried. Penny isn't arrested and when we check in she walks out to meet us, and we head into the centre of Swindon to find a café where we can talk. If she's concerned about Dobbin as her lawyer, she doesn't show it.

We talk for an hour and I make a few notes. 1. Sir Pen died of asphyxia. Or so she's heard. 2. Backtracking, Penny agreed to meet Sean about getting work via his new talent agency. The plan was to meet in London on Wednesday, but Maggie told her that Sean had gone to stay in a friend's cottage outside Swindon and they would see him there. 3. Just before they left on Wednesday morning, Maggie took a call, said she had to go to an urgent meeting and would come later. She gave Penny money for the train and taxi fare. 4. When Penny arrived on Wednesday afternoon, Sean was out of it – possibly on drugs. A woman she'd not seen before was looking after him. She gave Penny a drink after which she doesn't remember anything until later in the evening or maybe early on Thursday. 5. When she awoke Maggie was there and the police were on their way. 6. They told her Sir Pen was in a bed upstairs, he had been dead for at least 24 hours and Sean was in hospital though she didn't know why. 7. She'd planned on being at the funeral but couldn't because of the police. She was mortified to miss it.

When she finishes, no one speaks for a moment. Then I ask, "This woman, who was there. Was she five ten, short hair, severe face?" I try to remember what I saw through the windscreen of the car as it left Sir Pen's mansion block. "Was she wearing a red spotted blouse?"

Penny looks stunned. "Yes. How did you know?"

"Mrs Soderberg."

"Who?"

"Izzy Grimsdale's confidante and assistant. That's Lady Isabella – Sir Pen's sister. She's a client of my firm. I saw her driving a car with a sick-looking Sean and Sir Pen in it on…" it takes a moment to recall, "Monday. I think. She was wearing that blouse then."

Penny frowns. "Monday? Do you think he was dead?"

"I didn't get that impression. You ought to mention her name." She's grabbing her hands, squeezing them together and frowning at something. "Do you want me to? I should tell the police, I guess."

Penny doesn't react. I ask, "Do you think they suspect you of anything?"

She looks at me, horror on her face. "Me? Why? I mean, I passed out. I told them I think I was drugged." She says this with a desperation in her voice. "I was. I had to be!"

Dobbin smiles and takes her hand, holding it still. "If they thought you'd really murdered him they wouldn't have let you go."

She snatches her hand away. "Murder? You think he was murdered?"

Dobbin looks contrite and I don't know what to say. Penny goes on. "Maggie left for London ages ago. I don't know about Sean. I guess he's still in hospital." Her bottom lip wobbles. "My Dad is abroad just now and Mum is recuperating from a knee operation and can't drive. What shall I do?"

"I'm here." I hold her gaze, feeling a complete fraud.

For a moment, her look is so hopeful it could melt icebergs. Then she spoils it by shaking her head and looking down. She stands. "The policeman said be back by two."

"Shall I come?" Dobbin looks very nervous.

At last Penny manages a watery smile. "Thanks Gary, but they've arranged for a local solicitor to help. Probably best I have someone who actually knows the law."

"But I told them I'm your lawyer."

"I explained to the detective. He thought you two were very sweet, if misguided."

I ask, "Is there anything we can do? Anyone we can talk to?"

"Maggie, I suppose, although I'm sure she will corroborate what I said. She was in shock when I saw her; she could barely speak." She swallows hard. "What about the funeral? That go okay? I so very much wanted to come…" She trails off. Oh heck, she's about to cry.

Dobbin envelopes her in a hug. "It's all right, lump, your boy did him proud."

It takes a moment to realise he means me. She smiles and reaches out a hand for me to take. "He wouldn't have minded, would he? He would have understood?"

How the flip do I know? "Of course."

She hugs both of us. I try to read something in the hug but fail miserably.

Dobbin, practical for once, asks where she'll stay if she's voluntarily helping the police. He says, "If you need to crash, you can come to the flat. Right Harry?"

"Of course." Though I think we all know that isn't likely.

After she's left I say to Dobbin. "I'll meet you by the car."

"Where are you going?"

"To tell the police the little I know."

***

It is as we are driving back that I remember Frank's drawing in my wallet. His writing is tiny and it's difficult to read the numbers and letters. I'm squinting, trying to decipher the details when Dobbin asks, "What's that? A code?"

"You remember the old boy on the swing at the wake? He gave it to me. I have no idea what it's all about." I show him. "Any ideas?"

He barely glances at it. "Nope."

"Thanks."

"Who is he?" We've slowed right down and he looks across. "And why'd he give it to you?"

"Keep your eyes on the road, you loon. He worked for Sven's Dad. Ostensibly as a pawn broker but more like he provided money laundering services. I'm guessing it has something to do with Sven's estate."

"Something Sven pawned, maybe?"

I look again. It's not a receipt. "Possibly I suppose."

"Did you ask him?"

"I'm not sure he can speak much. He had a stroke. Although he didn't want his helper to know I had this."

Dobbin yawns. "I expect Dina will work it out."

"I wish someone would." I add up all the numbers. 267. And he's used a different coloured pen for each line. The 70SB – the line Frank was at pains to point out to me – is in blue, for instance.

Dobbin says, "Maybe that's where Sven kept his Dad's money. With Frank. Maybe to launder it?"

I think about Frank, the supposedly frail old man with no speech and barely able to stay awake, yet who can talk, point, crush my hand like a wrestler trying to get at the last little bit of toothpaste and wink to order. Would Sven have entrusted everything to him? Probably, but if so why change and give everything to me?

***

I have to put up with the third degree when I return. Brenda/Vera has spilled the beans not only about Jackie but also about Dobbin pretending to be a lawyer to help Penny. Having pissed me off she then tells Dobbin, "Papaji's amazing. Did you know there's this incredible Indian philosophy where they make love for six hours at a time? If you can centre on your inner spirt you can find the strength to maintain your love-making for that long."

Dobbin looks ready to commit suicide.

I leave them to discuss her lurid plans and go to the kitchen.

"Where's Dina?"

Mum is at the stove working under the watchful eye of Mrs Ohja. "Just a little milk, Veronica."

"You know Harry, I never realised you could make a white sauce without lumps. I thought there was some magician's trick to it. Look…" Mum begins to hold up the pan but Mrs Ohja restrains her.

"Just finish stirring first, Veronica. Harry can see the end product."

I tense, certain that Mum will snap, but she grins sheepishly and puts the pan back. It's clear who's in charge, at least in the kitchen.

"Dina? Anyone know where she is?"

"With Jim and George. They decided to meet at the beach. Brenda went with them, but she came back early." Mum looks at me suspiciously. "There's something I can't quite place with that girl. She spent ages with Asoka and then sat on the lawn quivering and shaking. When I asked if she needed an aspirin or something, she said Gary would anoint her something or other with the cream of his wotsit – really, the nonsense young people speak." She pauses. "That's not some sort of drug, is it?"

I meet Mum's gaze. "No, not drugs."

"Good. There's nothing worse than that."

I wonder if Dobbin agrees. "Do you know when Dina's home?"

"I don't. She might stay there. They haven't seen each other in a while. Maybe they need to catch up."

I can't stop myself sighing, but I know I'm being churlish. She needs to sort out things with Jim.

"Macaroni cheese?" Mum looks apprehensive but not as much as me. Mrs Ohja claps her hands. "It'll be macaroni paste soon if you don't add the cheese."

Mum nods and turns back to the stove. I leave them to it.

Monday, 13th July 1981

Chapter Thirty-Eight

In Which Harry Plays at Being Competent and Has a Brainwave

I'm glad to be going to work. The journey home was grim: Dina pretended to be asleep and Brenda/Vera and Dobbin bickered in whispers. As soon as we reached the flat, Brenda/Vera and Dobbin disappeared into their room, Brenda/Vera leading and Dobbin dragging along behind while Dina went to Tim's. About 20 minutes later Jan Kruis turned up. He didn't say anything when I opened the door, just nodded like I was the hired help. If the atmosphere was tense last night, it is not much better this morning. I should have called Jackie and said I was home, but after seeing Penny it didn't feel right.

I think I'm beginning to get the hang of lawyering. Jean, of course, is a major reason for this. I've begun keeping a list of things to do and I ensure there are at least two items on it that I have already done so they can be crossed through. "You need to feel you are making progress, Mr Spittle," Jean had said when she told me to add them the first time.

Today I add 'Sir Penshaw's estate,' 'Penny' and 'Frank's code' to my list. It already contains 'Sven's probate.' I take my first dilemma to Lucinda.

"What do I do if I think there are assets in Sven's estate, but I haven't found them yet?"

"Are you certain or making an educated guess? And, if certain, do you have any idea of value?"

I wobble a hand. "More guess work so far and I've no idea about value."

"Then go with what you have. You can always add them in when you finalise the estate accounts in due course. You really need to get probate; then you can collect the assets, those you know about, pay the debts and distribute the net assets. These other assets – what makes you think they exist?"

"I know he inherited some, erm, assets from his Father."

"Is it likely he'd have much? He's your age, was – sorry – wasn't he?"

I nod. "His Father was, er, well off."

"What sort of assets? Shares? Property? Something else?"

I shrug. "I really don't know." I suppose Lucinda works out how uncomfortable this is for me as she says, "Is there anything else you want to tell me, Harry?"

I want to tell her everything, but it all sounds so implausible, almost like a stupid childish prank. I hesitate. Sven's smartarse games with paintings and quizzes, which up to now seemed really clever now fill me with an unexpected fury. I begin to squirm under Lucinda's gaze. "Harry, you are going to be a good lawyer and will do well in whichever field you choose but there's a lesson here that you need to learn and learn soon. You will make mistakes, you will be asked to do things by clients that feel wrong, you will come across behaviour by other lawyers that you think is questionable. In each case, you will feel the pressure we all feel to run and hide, to look for the easy way out. If you have the courage to share the worry when it's barely formed in your head, you will have a far more comfortable career than if you ignore your instincts. So, with that in mind do you want to tell me anything?"

I fight the urge to confess. I want to tell her what I suspect but constantly Miles' mean face and McNoble's heft fill my vision and behind them are Natalie and Marita, depending on me to make the right call.

Lucinda looks disappointed. "Okay. The time's not right. Just think about it, hmmm?"

***

Dina rings me while I'm having lunch. She sounds exhausted. "You left a note?"

"Yes, half a mo." I'm up to my eyebrows in piecing together a set of property titles, trying to make sure the farm a client wants to buy is all covered by the little bits of land shown on six Land Registry plans. It's like being back at nursery school, doing some cutting and gluing, the only difference being if I'm wrong I don't have to go stand in the corner, but rather the firm is sued for several thousand pounds and my chances of a job on qualification take a hit. "Have you just got up?"

"And?"

"What?"

"Are you making a stupid point about me?"

"No, but… never mind."

"Just fuck off, okay? JUST FUCK OFF."

She never swears; she's always hated it. "Di, what's up?" I can't stop checking the door in case either Jean or Jeremy appears and hears her.

A voice, somewhere in the background, says something to Di. She mumbles something to whoever it is – I guess she's in a phone box and startled some passerby as much as she did me, or it's poor Mr Jones or Zenda worried by the outburst. Her voice is a dead calm when she comes back on the line. "I've got to go. I—"

"Wait. You know the old guy who sat on our swing at the funeral? Frank Smedley. The pawnbroker?"

"Yes."

"You remember what I pawned, back when I was desperate to pay off McNoble?"

"No. I need to go, not play 20 questions."

"Diamonds. They were in that box, the one Ruth stole from Jim's dad, Reggie James. What if his list is a list of diamonds? Maybe the letters are a code for types. Back then Frank told me the ones I'd stolen and pawned with him were Sierran Blue – 70SB. Frank pointed me to that one specifically. He'd know it meant something to me. What if this is where Sven's hidden the money? Can you do some research?"

"Okay. But I really need to go."

A male voice with a thick East European accent says, "You go fuck, yes?" and the phone is slammed down.

I stare at the handset. "That would be nice," I say to no one in particular.

***

I'm tidying my desk when Gloria comes on the line. "What have you done? A Detective Inspector Simpson from Swindon police wants a word you naughty boy."

"Mr Spit?"

"Spittle."

"Spittle?"

"Yes." I add, "It's Scottish."

There's a cough and a scratching sound and possibly a snigger. I think he says, "Unlucky," but before I can question it, he adds, "You are Sir Penshaw Grimsdale's solicitor, correct?"

"The partner here, Jeremy Panther, is. I'm his, um, assistant."

"Is Mr Panther about?"

"No, he isn't in today."

"I see. Perhaps he can call me."

"You can tell me, officer."

"DI Simpson. I wanted to let you know that we will not be releasing the body at this time. More forensics are needed. There's an autopsy scheduled, too."

"Do you know how he died?"

He speaks slowly, as if talking to a half-wit, a tone with which I am sadly very familiar. "That's why we need to do the autopsy."

"I heard, um, he was asphyxiated."

There's a long pause. "Did you? And where did you hear that?"

"Is that not the case?"

"Maybe." He speaks cautiously. "We need to keep an open mind."

My stomach converts its contents into a liquid form and I desperately want the toilet. It was exactly how they described Sven's death before deciding there wasn't anything suspicious.

DI Simpson carries on, "Our enquiries are ongoing. We can't rule out an accident, suicide or…" He lets the spectre of a grisly alternative hang between us. "We need a toxicology report and then we should have a better idea. I was ringing in the hope you could tell me about his Will. I understand he may have changed it recently? There's some confusion about this."

"I suppose I can."

"It'll be public soon enough."

It takes a moment to realise the ambiguity. "The death?"

"Exactly. We're holding a press conference this afternoon and those jackals will be all over everyone. Can you help?"

"He changed it, apart from some fixed bequests to his children; everything goes to his, um, partner. Sean Latterly"

All I hear is a thin whistle and some muttering in the background.

After a minute of understanding only the odd word, DI Simpson says, "Right. Thanks. Someone will need a statement. But that's all. For now."

"Do you think—?"

The buzz tells me the line has been disconnected.

Have I done the right thing?

Chapter Thirty-Nine

In Which there's a Race and Harry comes First

Jackie meets me at the newly refurbished cinema in Elephant and Castle. We go to see Chariots of Fire, which she's already seen but wants to see again, and I missed when it came out in March and I would be happy to miss again, but a couple of hours in a dark place with no one to hassle me seems like heaven just now. The cinema is almost empty; an elderly couple sit at the front eating sandwiches and a spotty young man shuffles in after a few minutes to sit three rows behind us and to one side.

I'm vaguely aware of some men in their underwear running around a quadrangle when Jackie startles me by putting her hand on my nob. Well, on my fly but it's pretty clear what she's after. When I look at her, she's staring intently at the screen but there's a smile on her face. I instantly become steel-tipped.

On the screen, someone is agonising about the sin of running on the Sabbath. Back in the fourth row, I'm agonising about the sin of coming in the ABC cinema. Her fingers are tugging at the zip and every ounce of my energy is focused on her struggle. Like the athletes on screen, I strain every sinew. It's agony.

"Jackie, I can't…" My voice is as hoarse and as urgent as I can make in a whisper. I glance at the young man; he's engrossed in the action. On the screen.

"Shh." For a moment, I fear someone is behind us but it's Jackie, smiling at me; she expertly slips her fingers inside my pants. My eyes are screwed tight as I fight for control and then, to my amazement, her warm lips cover my embarrassment.

Harold Abrahams wins the 100 metres and punches the air. Jackie grins and settles back into her seat. She says, "Amazing." I don't flatter myself that she means me.

When the lights go up, I realise the young man has gone.

Later, sitting in the communal hall where the nurses are allowed to entertain guests and drink tea, I tell her about Sir Pen's death and the possibility of asphyxiation. She nods. "He's gay, right? It could be some kind of accidental bedroom shenanigans."

"How do you strangle yourself?"

She smirks. "We've had a couple of cases recently. There's this idea that if you deprive the brain of oxygen it increases arousal. Apparently it's quite the thing in the gay community."

"That's mad."

"Is it? You stopped breathing in the cinema and it worked for you."

"That was incredible. Did I say thank you?"

"I think you might have made it clear. Non-verbally."

"I wonder if a cinema is on Vera's list."

She smiles and frowns at the same time; boy, is that a sexy combination. I explain about the church and the boat and the greenhouse and the vegetables. By the time I finish she's in fits. "Ask her if she wants to try an operating theatre. I may be able to swing something. What about you?"

"Me? I'm more for comfort and discreteness, thanks." For some reason an image of Penny in jail comes to me.

Maybe my expression changes because she says, "You'd better go. I need to change for my shift." Am I reading too much into her swift dismissal?

Wednesday, 15th July 1981

Chapter Forty

Where Harry and John Thomas Combine to Make an Impression

I'm being followed. I'm sure of it. And it has to be one of Miles' henchman. I suspected on Monday when I went to buy a sandwich with my 15p luncheon voucher. That buys one slice of bread and a crust and to get the basic cheese sarnie means I have to find the other 15p from my paltry wages. I asked Heather, the part-time bookkeeper at Clifford, Risely & Co., why it is only 15p and received a withering look. "Don't they teach you any tax law?" Apparently 15p is tax free as a benefit in kind. "Not very kind, if you ask me," was my rather smart response, which came back to bite me when Heather told me I'd been recoded for my PAYE and wouldn't be receiving any pay that week. I was in a panic for three days until, with a smirk, she said it had been a mistake. I know she did it deliberately. That woman has too much power.

While I queued for the sandwich, I noticed a man staring at me through the condensation-covered window. He was wearing a brown trilby and shapeless black Pac-a-Mac, despite the sun shining brightly. Something about him seemed familiar.

Then today, this morning, he was outside the office reading a copy of the Evening News.

Now I'm on my way to the High Courts of Justice to issue a writ for Mr Risely and he's there again. It is a shock to realise my suspicions are justified. What am I going to do?

On the central line to Chancery Lane, I can see him one carriage down. It's like he knows where I'm planning on alighting because he's ahead of me on the rattily old escalator up onto Holborn. Because he appears so harmless, part of me wants to confront him, but knowing he's working for Miles makes me hesitate. Instead I wait to see which exit he takes and then take another, hurrying for Fetter Lane. I'm delighted when I'm sure that I've lost him.

Inside the Royal Courts, I pause and wait to see if he's caught up. Nothing. Relieved, I head for the Bear Garden. Outside the Masters' rooms I spot John Thomas in the same chair as last time, head once again in his hands. "Hi John. Illegitimi non carborundum."

"Oh, hi Harry. What's that mean? I never got beyond *Up Pompeii!* where Latin is concerned."

"Don't let the bastards grind you down."

Not even a flicker of a smile. He is in a bad way. "You couldn't do me a favour, could you? My principal got the defendant's name wrong and when I tried to amend it they said I'd have to see the Duty Master as today all amendments are being checked. Apparently there's a real queue and he's eating us alive."

"Master Rother?"

"Who else? Normally I'd just go back and blag an excuse, but my principal told me if I came back without the amendment then I might as well not come back at all. Do you think you could, maybe, you know…? My nerves aren't up to the Rother just now."

A voice says, "When are you on?"

John and I look at the speaker. I'm startled to see it's the man in the Pac-a-Mac, my shadow. I realise I know him from seeing him around here, one of the old hands who chums up to the Masters and other staff and always gets what he wants.

John says, "Ten past."

Pac-a-Mac man holds out a hand. I can't help noticing the tattoo on his exposed wrist. It looks like a dagger. "Give it to me. I'll get it for you."

For a moment, John hesitates before hurriedly digging out a scuffed yellow file with 'Martin v Martin' typed on the white label on the cover. The stranger takes the file and heads for the Masters' room.

"Bloody hell, what's got into him? He's never been friendly before."

"Who is he?" I watch the retreating back, the black plastic creaking with each step.

"He does loads of stuff here. No idea who he works for, but no one refuses him an order or anything. All the Masters joke with him and he gets his judgements and executions, no problem." John rubs his hands. "Looks like I'm still in work. You fancy a lunchtime pint?"

"I need to issue a writ but after, sure. Do me a favour – find out who he works for, will you?"

"I'll try. The George in half an hour?"

**

267

John is leaning against a pillar by the door to the public bar. "I thought I'd wait until you got here."

Seeing his smile, I remember why I never really thought of John as a friend. He never bought a round ever, having the shortest arms and deepest pockets of anyone at uni. "Did you find anything out?"

"What?" His face falls momentarily before he twigs. "Oh, the creep? Yeah, he said to give you this." It's a small white card with 'Impressions' written on one side and an address in Highbury and phone number on the other. "He said he'd be there every evening between six and seven, and..." he's trying to smile but his lips lose out to gravity, "...and he said to make it clear that you need to go and see him. Sooner the better." Having passed on the message, he brightens up. "Pint then?"

Chapter Forty-One

Where Harry Finds Out All Sorts of Things but Really is None the Wiser

Dina has left a list of diamond types on my bed. It's complex; they are distinguished by colour, clarity, cut, carat and size. If Frank's list is to be believed the code seems to refer to colour and size. She has made a stab at decoding his list and from what I can see she's probably right. Maybe I should go and see Frank to see if he can confirm it. I wonder where she got the information. There's an asterisk with a comment: 'there are blue diamonds, but we have no idea where the 'Sierran Blue' comes in.' We? Who's we? And the Sierran Blue was Frank's name. Probably winding me up.

At the bottom, she has added, 'I don't understand why you think this has anything to do with Sven's money.' Blind guesswork, in truth.

First things first, I call in on Mr Jones in the flat below to see if I can use his phone. As ever he insists I take tea and try his homemade biscuits. Today these are coriander, chocolate and cheddar – 'I'm focusing on the Cs, Harold.' Like Mum, he is a rubbish cook, but he's such a lovely man I don't hold it against him. And Zenda, who is out, is clearly delighted to be here. Thinking about her, I wonder what Lucinda has done about making sure Mr Risely is happy for us to act for her. Another thing I should probably check.

Eventually, duty is done and I get to use the phone, although the call is short. Penny is no longer at Swindon police station. I try Natalie but reach the answer machine. I leave no message; I don't want Miles hearing my voice. Penny asked me to try to contact Maggie, but I don't know Maggie's address or phone number. I try Izzy Grimsdale and, of course, get Ms Soderberg. "I can't possibly give out Ms Margaret's number Mr Spittle, but if you come round I expect Lady Isabella will put in a call for you."

Since I saw Izzy in the car with Sean and Sir Pen I'm not keen, but I have to find Penny to make sure she's all right. Even thinking that makes me feel guilty about Jackie but I've already convinced myself that once I'm sure Penny is okay, I'll be able to concentrate on Jackie.

"Would you like to take some with you? I've wrapped them up," Mr Jones says while proffering biscuits. I accept them, wondering if the ducks and pigeons fancy a snack.

***

As I look up at the mansion block, it dawns on me that Sir Pen's flat is in the same block as Lady Isabella's. Funny I'd not made the connection before. As I wait to be let in, it's hard to think of the old boy as dead. A maid shows me into a library full of timeworn leather-bound books. A painting of a distinguished gent with a walrus moustache and twinkly eyes looks down on me from above the fireplace. He looks a lot like Sir Pen.

"Our great-grandfather. Did some significant favours for the Liberals in the years before the First World War."

Izzy is wearing all black with red stilettos, which is a pretty sexy combination emphasising her full figure. She's wearing a necklace of black stones that clack together as she moves.

"I'm ever so sorry about Pen," I say.

She holds up a hand. "He's gone. He chose badly. Sean was always going to be a liability. I suppose he'll pay. Well, someone will."

"Do you know how he died?"

"I believe he was strangled." Her voice is seriously cold.

"But was it, you know, unlawful?"

Her look is the epitome of condescending. "Such a lawyer's way of describing murder. How else do you get strangled? The police haven't said for sure but that's my understanding." She pauses holding my gaze, almost daring me to say something contradictory, "I'm not sure if it was Sean or if Sean's lover was involved."

"Lover?"

"Oh don't play smart." She walks to the fireplace and takes a slim cigarette from a silver box on the mantelpiece. She holds it up and studies it. "Sobranie Black Russian. I don't suppose you've ever tasted anything so exquisite." Picking up a lighter she gives it to me and leans close so I can light it for her. I can smell a mix of scent and sweat from her and can't imagine feeling more uncomfortable.

I carefully take my time putting the lighter back on the mantelpiece. When I turn to her she says, "I don't know what happened, but I understand there was a game that went wrong. Pen didn't do games. I suppose I was naïve thinking Sean would be

270

sensible, after our business planning, but the lure of Pen's money was too much."

"Could it have been an accident?"

She looks at me coldly. "He was handcuffed. I don't see how that's an accident. I imagine your employers will be delighted."

"Sorry? Why?"

"Fees, Harry. The Will must be undone. As executors, Philip and Lucinda will be over the moon." She blows out smoke. "I should have made you tell me he had signed it, rather than play Pen's game. Had I known for sure I might have stopped him." She grinds out the cigarette before walking up close to me, pinning me against a small sofa. "Are you very clever or very stupid? You brought that woman to his party. Did you have any idea what she'd do? I understand desperation, infatuation – but this?"

"Penny?"

"Is that her name? Somehow the police haven't seen the obvious picture, but they will. Eventually. Are you here to plead for her? That at least would reveal your stupidity."

I can only stare. Eventually I manage, "Sean was a homosex—"

"He pretended. Maybe he was bisexual. The facts are, this woman was desperate for theatre work and Sean could give her her dreams. For that, she helped him. I expect he thinks she will take the fall for this, but I'm going to make sure they both suffer."

"But Penny was with Maggie?"

"Maggie? Maggie is Sean's closest confidante. She does what he wants. I imagine she just gave them a cover, a place for them to meet. You know that farce of a wedding? Did you wonder why is was so discreet? Only six people, wasn't it? Sean. He didn't want it, not to be kind to Pen, but because he knew he'd be dumping him soon enough. And didn't I tell you your friend was enjoying herself in the hot tube? Well, it was with him and Maggie. Quite the threesome."

My head is spinning. I can barely form a sentence. Izzy lights a second cigarette. She says, "It's my fault. I thought Pen would realise his mistake. My stupidity was assuming if I gave Sean what he wanted – his independence – he would be satisfied. I shouldn't underestimate greed and the stupidity." She sneers as she looks at me. "You keep strange company, Harold Spittle. This Penny woman and the Andersen boy. I should have wondered when I heard that."

My anger is overcoming my fear but is mixed with my confusion. "Sven?"

She moves quickly to the door and holds it open. "Why don't you leave? I think we've spoken enough, don't you?"

There is no chance the Penny I know would be so stupid or so callous as to hurt anyone. Before I get thrown out I need to find her. "Do you know where Penny is? Or Maggie?"

She looks nauseous. "If I were you, I would distance myself from that girl pronto. You'll only be caught in the crossfire. Maggie's devastated by this. She trusted them both and feels awfully let down. I believe she's gone away for a few days. As for your friend, no, I have no clue, but I imagine the press will be all over her if they can find her."

Around 20 minutes after I arrive I'm back outside, staring at the crowds of tourists meandering along Regent Street. Gravity pulls me across town to where Natalie lives. It's beginning to rain and there's no answer when I ring the bell. Having tried and failed three times I step back and look up at the windows to her flat. It looks dark and uninviting, but to my surprise the one below has a light on. I fumble for my key ring; the four keys Constable Kruis gave me are there. Shaking a little, I let myself in.

***

There are voices coming from the mezzanine level. They continue as I cross to the bottom of the stairs. Whoever is there hasn't heard me. Rather than startle them, I cough loudly. Silence.

"It's me. Harry."

Penny's face appears at the top of the stairs. "How'd you know we'd be here?"

"I didn't. I just got lucky. Who's we?"

First Natalie and then Marita Andersen appear, both looking sombre. I look at the three of them, reminding me more of the girls in the playground, staring me down. But this time it's me who feels in control.

When Penny has made us a coffee and we are sat around the dining room table, I say, "Okay, who wants to explain what's happening?"

Natalie starts with, "The police are bloody stupid."

"Maybe. Though it may not be easy to prove." I hold up a hand as she tries to interrupt. "I know Penny's not done anything wrong and will do all I can to prove it."

"You will?"

"Of course." I explain what I heard at Izzy's flat. "Lady Isabella is obviously upset about her brother, but that may be guilt for not doing more to protect him. In one way she encouraged Sean and probably feels guilty."

Natalie is outraged. "Are you defending her?"

"No, just trying to understand why she's acting the way she is."

"Because she's a first-class bitch?"

I don't want to argue with Natalie right now so ask Penny, "Have they charged you with anything?"

She shakes her head. "They talked about conspiracy to murder and aiding and abetting and perverting the course of justice and… oh, I don't know, it seemed endless. The lawyer – Mr Jefferson – said it was a classic police tactic, but it really scared me. They let me go eventually on police bail. They said they would need to question me more, but they were very interested to talk to the other woman, the one you mentioned Harry. Mrs Soderberg or whoever it was. If only she or Maggie would tell them the truth. I was only there because Maggie wanted to go, really."

"You said there was some notion of a part in a production?"

She looks down. "Well… Maggie asked me not to say the real reason. She was Sean's lover you see. They had rekindled their affair. She said he was going to break it off with Sir Pen but didn't want to hurt him after that stupid ceremony."

"Did you tell the police this?"

"Yes, but…" she begins chewing the inside of her mouth.

"But?"

"I tried not to. At the start. But the lawyer told me I needed to tell them everything I knew and. . and when I did they were cross I'd hidden it. I'm not sure they believed me. At least they made me feel like they thought I was lying."

She looks so unhappy. I want to hold her, but with the others there I just can't and anyway, Natalie is squeezing Penny's hand. I want to ask about Maggie, about the kiss I saw, about her anger at me, about us, but know this really isn't the right time. Instead I say, "I'll talk to your lawyer, tell him what I know. Hopefully that will help."

"Will you get in trouble? They're all clients of your firm, aren't they?"

"Probably, but I expect I'll survive." I look at Marita. "How long have you been here? I'm guessing you're staying here with Natalie?"

She nods. "Sven told me, once he was dead and buried – cremated, I mean – I should stay here until you sorted out the money side."

"You knew he was going to die?"

Suddenly Natalie seems to perk up. She reaches out and takes Marita's hand. It's looking a bit like a séance. She says to me, "We've known he might die for a while. He said it was a matter of months, probably weeks. He'd been diagnosed with this congenital heart problem, aortic valve stenosis I think they called it. They said that any sort of stress was a real risk. He should have had an operation to fit a valve but he refused. I…"

Penny looks stunned, as I assume I do.

Natalie holds Marita's gaze. "If I'd accepted his proposal."

"Did he really propose?"

Natalie gives me what I think is called a wry look. "Is that so strange?"

Penny gets in first. "You bet it's strange. Since when did he fancy you?"

Natalie and Penny glare at each other and for a moment I actually think one of them might punch the other. If so my money is on Penny. Marita, however, steps in and says, "He wouldn't have gone through with it, would he? He wasn't the marrying kind." She looks at me. "I know he wanted to tell you what he planned, but in the end he never had the time."

I take a few seconds to watch the three women. While Penny seems to realise her reaction was too extreme, Natalie won't meet anyone's gaze. Not one of them speaks and I just know something is off. I say, "I don't think he did, Marita. I think he knew exactly what he was doing by not telling me." Another thought, "He staged McNoble kidnapping him, didn't he? At my office. The driver – the heavy – was Grant Grate, one of your Father's old henchmen. I think Sven called McNoble to pick him up and then made it look like he was being forced. He wanted me to worry about him, about you. If he'd told me what he'd planned, he knew I'd have run a mile. He had to make me feel responsible." Like everyone else, I think.

Marita won't look at me. "He never told me much about that side of things."

I don't believe her. "Okay. If you say so." I turn to Natalie. "And why didn't you tell me you knew he was going to die soon? Even when I told you he'd been found under the bridge you said nothing. You let me believe it might be suspicious."

"He made me promise—"

"He was dead. Why did it matter then?" But even as I say this I know why; he had a way of making the promises stick. "I'm going now. You three console yourselves, but I've got a lot of thinking to do." I'm just standing when another thought jostles into place, something I've been meaning to ask for a while, "What exactly is McNoble's role in this? Do you know?"

Marita scowls. "He's out for himself, Harry. I know he and Sven worked together, but I'm not sure Sven really trusted him."

"Is it really all about his Father? Screwing him?"

She nods. "Yes. I think that part is true. He hates Mr Jepson for how he treated his Mother and his step-Mothers. Even Monica, although she's hardly an angel. Mind you, she stood by him while he was in prison. If Stephen has a plan it's to make sure his Father doesn't get back into his old businesses." She glances at Natalie and something passes between them, but she says no more.

"Is there a phone here? If I need to ring you?"

She nods and scribbles down a number.

I'm nearly at the door when Penny stops me. "Harry, I'm sorry for getting you involved in this."

My heart does a little dancey-skippy thing and then settles. For a moment I want to hold her, tell her it'll be all right, tell her I still love her, but then it's gone and I just feel like she's a friend who I'll help if I can but I'm not going to try too hard. Something may just have died a little.

On the way to the bus stop, I find a phone box and call Jackie. "Hi. Any chance you can come round?"

She hesitates a fraction. "Okay, but it'll be nearer one than midnight. Any particular reason?"

"I really really want to sleep with you, if that's okay?"

Chapter Forty-Two

In Which Harry Goes to the Police and Leaves Them Confused

Dina is still up when I get back. "Jan needs a word. He says it's urgent."

"Jan? Is he here?"

Before she can answer, Jan appears. He looks more serious than usual. "My boss wants a word. It won't take long."

My watch says 10:15. I say to Dina. "Jackie's coming round at 12ish. Can you keep her company?"

She nods but won't look at me. That makes me suspicious. "What's this about, Jan? Sven's death was due to natural causes. What's there to say?"

He holds open the door and repeats, "It won't take long."

***

Ha! I should have known better. We go to the police station in Earl's Court where DC Sharon Wallace is accompanied by an Inspector Thistle, a bulbous-faced man with little to no neck. Throughout the interview, he sticks a finger inside his collar to try to free it from where it is clearly pinching; it certainly doesn't help his mood.

"You've been a busy bee, haven't you?" Rhetorical questions are the usual way TV detectives make their victims squirm and it works a treat on me.

"I… have I?"

Inspector Thistle does something that might have once been a smile but is nearer a sign of tortured pleasure. "One, Sven Anderson – the son of a rather nasty crook who has been working assiduously to collect a lot of money – turns up at your offices, apparently having not seen you in months and makes a Will that appoints you executor and leaves all his worldly good to you. No trust – all yours to spend as you like. Shortly after this he dies and his body is found close to where you live, having been moved. Funny that. Not at all suspicious. You then

276

have him cremated PDQ so any plans we might have had to exhume him have—"

"Exhume?"

"Obviously we can't because he's just bloody dust, but it might have been nice to have the option. Given all that's happened, we would have liked to have done some more tests, but we can't now, can we? As I say, all very suspicious, don't you think?"

"Suspicious?" I'm thinking fast, which usually means my brain smashes into a wall, but this time I have a response. "It's hardly sensible, if I was involved in something unlawful, to dump his body close to where I live, is it?"

Thistle does manage a grin this time. "You're a clever sort. A double bluff. Or bloody unlucky. Maybe you moved it further away from where he died and not nearer but it then got caught on the bridge near you? Who knows? Maybe you've really annoyed some God or other."

I can believe that last bit. "But that's daft. If I wanted to move it further away I'd make a better job—"

"The point is it could have been you." He leans right forward; his breath is oddly spicy, like he's chewed a cinnamon stick. "What about the fact that while Mr Andersen is making his Will, we understand you were having a meeting with him and Sir Penshaw Grimsdale—"

"A meeting? Sir Pen was redoing his Will and it just happened that's when Sven appeared—"

Thistle's face is wreathed in smiles. "Serendipity, was it?"

That rings a bell. Who referred to 'serendipity' recently? I can't think straight, sure I'm missing something.

"Sir Penshaw is now dead and your girlfriend, who you cunningly introduced to him, was present at that death. I'm told the evidence points to strangulation and there are indications that your girlfriend was involved in some way."

I look desperately at DC Wallace. She seems embarrassed although whether it is for me or for herself in allowing Sven to be cremated I can't really be sure. I say, "But they're two different things. I don't understand."

"No? Really?" Inspector Froggy keeps on a'marching. "We have received information that suggests there may have been some links between Mr Andersen and Sir Penshaw Grimsdale—"

"What? They didn't know each other. Did they? I mean, I introduced them and they showed no signs that they knew each other."

I rack my brains. Someone asked about Sven, didn't they? Or am I making that up?

"So you say. Was anyone else present at this introduction to verify they were strangers?"

I can't bloody remember that level of detail.

"Two Wills, recently made, two unexpected beneficiaries and you at the centre of it all. Look at it from our point of view. You'd be curious, wouldn't you? And when we're told there may be links…" He takes his time, a sort of twitching of his mouth indicating humour as he says, "…less than kosher links, I may add, it's only right we ask some questions Mr Spittle." He says my name like he's about to vomit. "What happened between them in your office? What did the three of you cook up? Was Sir Penshaw leaving his estate to Mr Sean Latterly somehow tied into Mr Andersen suddenly deciding to leave his to you? If so, what was intended?" He checks his notes and then looks at me. "We have obtained a warrant to search Mr Andersen's Hampshire property, which we will do tomorrow, but I understand you may have visited recently. I do hope you haven't removed anything important."

His stare is somewhere between beady and downright malevolent.

He doesn't mention the flat. It occurs to me they may go back there, but he doesn't mention the warrant that he'll need to do that. My head is in a complete state, but only one thing makes any sense. Somehow, somewhere behind all of this, is McNoble. He said something, I'm sure, which puts him at the centre. Although why and how I have no idea. I tell the Inspector I will let him know everything I know, but I need to gather my thoughts. It's as I'm leaving that I remember Lady Isabella saying something about Sven, although I can't recall what. Was she involved with him? Maybe she knows something, not that she's likely to talk to me just now.

Thursday, 16th July 1981

Chapter Forty-Three

In Which Dina Swears and Jackie Gets Some Sleep

It's two in the morning when I get in. Dina meets me at the front door. She looks exhausted. I say, "Jackie?"

She nods at my room. "Asleep. I said you had to go out. I didn't say where."

Right now she's the least of my worries, but the idea that she'll think I've let her down again makes me want to cry. Dina then does something she's done on less than four occasions previously. She hugs me. "He wouldn't tell me what was going on. I trusted him and then he does that. Bastard."

I think of how Jan looked so awful, handing me over and how he was still there to bring me back after. "I'm pretty sure it was the last thing he wanted to do. Don't blame him, Di, just doing his job."

She is furious. 'Well, I do blame him. Come on, tell me what happened." She seems to want me to convey the story of my night there and then in the hall, but after a pause she turns and leads me to the kitchen.

Over tea and toast, I explain what happened. She's as amazed as me at the suggestion of some links between Sven and Sir Pen. I tell her about my meet-up with Lady Isabella and then Penny, Marita and Natalie and how they knew Sven had a terminal illness. I say, "It explains the timing of the Will, although why they didn't say beats me."

"What could these links be?" Dina frowns. "Assuming it's not just some bullshit."

"When did you start using the word 'bullshit?'"

"Since I spent time with you. Come on, what do we know about Sir Wotsit's business interests? Or his sister's?"

"Not a lot. There are the companies – Izzy Ventures. I have details at work."

"Okay. I'll grab them tomorrow and do some research. You call Marita and see what she knows about her Father's empire. I suppose we could ask McNoble although it sticks in my craw to ask for his help."

A light goes on in my head. "Hang on, you're right. When I asked McNoble about collecting Sven from my office on the day he made his Will, he said something about Sven being in an odd mood and saying it was serendipity. I remember it because there was a time when McNoble couldn't have even say the word, let alone know what it meant. Then earlier, the Inspector used the same word about the supposed meeting between Sven and Sir Pen. McNoble has to be their source. He's winding them up to put pressure on me. It's bullshit, but if I'm scared enough I might just turn to him for help. And then he gets a lead on where the goodies are."

She's not convinced. "From you, that sounds very clever and until the bit about you turning to him for help it's almost believable. Let's keep it in mind. We need to know more about Sir Penny-Wenny—"

"Please. Call him what you like but not Sir Penny."

"How was she? Did she tell you why she's been mucking you about?"

"No. She was grateful I was helping, that's all. Anyway, you're right about McNoble. We should leave him out of this if we can."

She nods. "I think you need to quiz Marita and Natalia a bit more about Sven and what he's been doing. They have to know more than they've let on. I… oh, hi."

It's Jackie, wearing one of my T-shirts and looking like a dopehead from having surfaced from a deep sleep. "Hi. You're late."

"Long story."

She rubs her eyes. "You still want to come to bed?"

"Yes, but only to sleep."

She sighs. "You're far too sensible." She turns on her heels and heads back to my room. Why do I feel like all the air has been punched out of me?

I glance at Dina, but she's avoiding my gaze. Feeling very flat, I follow Jackie. When I push open the bedroom door, Jackie is standing by the bed wearing nothing but her nurse's cap and a stern face. She holds my gaze for what seems an age while I try and hold hers and not look at her perky and come-hither nipples. Then she tilts her head to one side and says, "You're tired? Seriously?"

I begin to form some sort of response but she doesn't wait and yanks me onto the bed.

Chapter Forty-Four

Where Harry Meets an Old Acquaintance and Asks Some Good Questions

We make love. Twice. I'm quite proud of myself but, frankly I'm grateful when she turns over and falls asleep, soon snoring like a diesel train. I lie on my back, stare at the ceiling and sleep won't come. It's well after four and I'm still awake when I go and make tea, falling asleep across the kitchen table while the kettle boils. Back in bed at just after six, I fall straight to sleep and wake at eight to the alarm and no Jackie. She's left a large red lipstick heart written on the back of a letter from Lloyds Bank offering me one of their new cashpoint cards. That makes me smile even if I feel like I've died.

Part of me is desperate to ignore the alarm and go back to sleep but I drag myself to my bike for a slow and unsteady ride to work. In fact, I'm going so slowly I might well end up falling asleep while riding when I reach Hyde Park. It's then that a man steps out in front of me, causing me to have heart palpitations. "What the heck?"

It's Pac-a-Mac man from the Courts, the one who followed me and gave me the card for Impressions and who I've avoided seeing since. I realise I don't know his name and he doesn't introduce himself as he says, "I told you. You needed to get in touch and now the police are after you, right?"

Part of me just wants to push him away – he's not exactly heavyweight material – and get to the office to hide. But instead I just stand there, straddling my bike. When he doesn't speak, I say, "I don't know what you know or why you are so keen to talk to me, but I'm meant to be at work and I need to get a move on."

"Nah, I called in. Said you'd had a minor biff and were off to St Tommy's and you'd call later to update them. Your receptionist was really worried. She must like you a lot. Gloria, is it? Come on, we've 30 minutes at least for that chat. I'll buy you a crap coffee."

I want to go, but just now I want to know all I can about what's going on. If he is working for Miles, as I surmise, or maybe McNoble, I want to find out. The café in the park is pretty empty and the coffee is indeed rubbish, mostly because the water is barely warm and the granules don't dissolve properly.

'Look, Harry. I represent an interested party who wants to offer you the chance to assist them in returning what is rightfully theirs."

I'm becoming fed up with so many people knowing what's going on apart from me. "You know what, Mr… whoever you are. I don't give a hoot. Unless your client speaks to me him or herself then I'm not interested. You tell him – I assume it's a him – that."

The weasel shrugs. "You can tell him yourself." He points behind me. Sitting at the table in the corner is Charlie Jepson, Mum's old lover.

When Jepson sees me looking, he jumps up and hurries over, neatly blocking any thought I had of escape. "Harry. Good to see you. You well? Your Mum said you were quite the legal eagle these days."

He's all sticky syrup and soft soap, but I know from before how quickly that can change. I decide to stay silent and wait to find out what he wants. He seems to take the hint as he pulls up a chair and settles down to face me. He always had this direct stare and this time it's really boring into me. To stop myself looking I decide to focus on the oily brown lumps in my coffee, trying to decide what they most look like.

"See, I know you and Claude are close." Claude is what Jepson calls his son, Stephen McNoble; it's his middle name and calling him Claude is sure to wind McNoble up. "He's been looking after some of my affairs while I've been away and it's proving a little tricky getting hold of him. I wondered if you might be able to help."

The lump nearest the right edge is like a headless sheep. I push at it with my spoon.

"Once we get to have a really good chat we'll have everything straight. I don't think he knows how keen I am for that conversation. So would you be able to help?"

The one opposite is more like Dobbins' ear, or his ear if someone had tried to melt it.

"There's quite a lot of money and I really need to get hold of it, see."

I look up. He's clearly desperate. Last time I saw him, just before Mr Andersen and Jim's Dad were covered in silage, he was sporting a Brian May poodle-perm look. Now his hair is grey at the temples and short on the back and sides. Did I know his eyes were green? I go back to staring at the coffee. The top right lump is morphing slowly from some vaguely familiar image of Lady Di that filled the papers at the weekend into a walrus.

"I heard you might be working with Sven Andersen, helping him sort out things. Did you know he owes me money too? Well, his Father did. I imagine he's getting ready to pay me back."

I've had enough. "Why are you hassling Mum for some money you lent her?"

He looks genuinely distraught. Well, he's acting genuine. "Your Mother? She said she and her sister are selling the garage so I said it would be good if she could return the money I lent her. She didn't suggest there was any issue. Is there?" A flash of the old, mean Charlie scuds across his face.

"It's taking longer to sort out. I imagine she'll let you know."

His expression suggests he has just realised he has backed the winning horse at the National at 100 to 1. "Of course, if you can help me with Claude I won't need to bother your Mum quite so much."

"You know I'm not friends with Stephen. But yes, I have been in contact. If I see him, I'll tell him we spoke. Is that helpful?"

I jump back as he grabs my elbow and digs his finger and thumb into the joint. It's agonising. Creepy man looks anxiously around in case we are being watched but he doesn't intervene.

"Listen, you little shit. You well know the Andersen boy and 'Stephen,' as he insists on being called, are out to screw me. They think that just because Robin's dead, they can take over. New generation in charge and all that bollocks. Well, tell them from me that ain't happening."

"Sven is dead, Mr Jepson. You know that. Surely."

"Dead? No. When?" He does look perplexed. "How did he die?"

"I don't know for sure. It was a surprise, but he had been ill."

"When did he die?"

"Just over three weeks ago."

His face is a picture. "When, exactly?"

It's my turn to frown. "Well, I heard on a Sunday." I do some mental gymnastics. "That would have been the 22nd, no. 21st June. Although it could have been he died on the Saturday."

Jepson is shaking his head. "Shit. I saw him…" He struggles a bit, "It might have been that night or maybe the Friday before. Anyway, he wasn't looking too hot, that's for sure. He'd been in one hell of an argument with Miles Tupps. You know, the one married to that Natalie woman you're friends with?"

"Where was that?"

His smile isn't pleasant. "The Pretty Flamingo."

"Sorry, but I've no idea—"

"It's a club – a discrete and rather special club – that's mine. Was mine. Right now Andersen says it's his but I'm the reason it exists and if Claude hadn't been a stupid prick I'd still be running it. Miles manages it for Andersen."

"I..."

"Yes?"

I'm struggling to remember where I've heard this before. Was it Natalie? Or McNoble? My brain slows to a crawl, not sure what I should say that doesn't get her into any trouble. The best it can manage is to repeat, "Miles runs a club?"

"Yes, Miles runs a club. Christ boy, aren't you listening? Andersen, the senior Andersen, stole it from me while I was... while I was away. Tupps runs it for Andersen, although Andersen wants to sell it. Wanted, I suppose, if he's now dead."

I am feeling rather faint. "And the night before he died Sven was there, arguing with Miles? Do you know what about?"

Jepson glances at Pac-a-Mac man, grinning as he does so. "No, but if Tupps killed Andersen that would be rather too perfect."

"No, no it was natural causes. But still, it would be good to know what went on."

"Why?"

"Erm, well, to tell Sven's sister. If I see her. She's keen to know, you see, what happened. Sort of to get a full picture. As you can imagine it's a tragedy. For her I mean."

Jepson shrugs. "I went with my brother-in-law. He's a member and he got me in. They'd not have allowed it if he hadn't blagged us past the doorman. We played the tables there. I'd intended to sort out the 'confusion' over my ownership once and for all – I'd heard Andersen was getting out, but the Andersen boy wouldn't listen and Tupps wouldn't talk to me. Then Andersen had a bit of a turn and Claude took him home."

"McNoble took him home?"

"Yes. So? My lad's dumb, a shit really, but he's no killer. Anyway, you said he died of natural causes."

"Yes, yes I did." I'm trying to compute all this.

Jepson is still talking. "It was quite a scene really. Andersen has this turn and then spews over another customer – some old boy, a peer. Bent as a nine-bob note. All rather unnecessary. Very unpleasant."

"Was Sven going to sell the club to Miles?"

"No. Tupps doesn't have that sort of money. Claude told me he was going to buy it, but I know that's a load of crap." He checks his watch. "What does it matter? I had a discussion with Tupps where we would jointly buy it back – Tupps would put in some working capital and I'd sort out the money Andersen owed me by taking back the club. That was before Claude said Andersen had agreed to sell it to him. That's why I went. To 'clarify' a few things. Not that I got the chance."

"The old boy you mentioned. Was that Sir Penshaw Grimsdale?"

"That's him. He's dead too, isn't he? Not healthy that place, clearly. His sister brought him I believe. She's a regular."

"You know them?"

"Only from the papers, not to speak to. But back to Andersen being dead?" He looks worried. "I suppose Tupps knows? He'll be anxious, like me, if that's the case. He's not easy, not when stressed. He's not going to be happy." It is like thoughts keep occurring to him. "What's going to happen to Andersen's money? I suppose that weasel Lewis will be dealing with things."

Time to change the subject. "Are you sure Sven planned on selling it to your son?"

"I don't see why that matters to you, but that's what Claude said, yes. If you see him, tell him we will need to sort out the club and the agency with Lewis as well as what Andersen owed me." He glances around like someone else might be listening and laughs. "I doubt there's much paperwork if you get my drift."

"Were you involved in the estate agency, too?"

"Of course. I set Tupps up a while back. But I was under pressure from Robin Andersen and I let him invest. Big mistake. In a way, Tupps is the son I should have had. He has a far more rigorous approach to business than Claude. That boy is too soft."

I can think of dozens of adjectives to describe McNoble, but soft isn't one of them. Even the fat around his waist ripples with hard-edged malevolence. "You introduced Miles to Robin Andersen, did you?"

He nods. "And now with your help, I will be restored to my rightful position and won't need to bother you. Or your parents for that matter." This last is said with what I suspect he intends to pass as a twinkle, but it comes across as more of a threat.

I'm beginning to sweat and need to get away sharpish. "If I see Stephen I'll tell him. I'm sure we can find a way out of this. Do you have a number that I can reach you on?"

He's clearly still working through what Sven's death means, but scribbles a London number for me on a serviette. He says, "Albert knows how to find you if needs be."

I realise he means Pac-a-Mac man. I manage a small smile for Albert's sake.

"Tell Claude I've been patient, but if Andersen's dead then we need to finish this. Soon. And tell your Mum not to worry. I expect I can give her another couple of weeks." He meets my gaze. "And Monica sends her regards. You remember my wife?"

I nod.

"We had a tough patch, shortly after that time down your way, but it's been okay since then. She's been very loyal, all things considered."

That is a surprise. She was determined to leave him, she said. He'd been violent towards her. Monica also offered to have sex with me, a sort of consolation shag as I recall, which still amazes me to this day. Almost as much as the fact that I turned her down.

Chapter Forty-Five

Where Harry Finds Out He, Zenda and Brenda/Vera have Mutual Friends and is Appalled

I sometimes wonder at my psychic powers. I'm cycling home after work, thinking about McNoble and pull up at a set of lights outside Selfridges on Oxford Street. The cricket is on a TV in a shop window and the images playing are of catches being dropped. I can't at this distance make out who is doing the dropping, but my heart says England. I'm straining to see if the latest error is Botham's when I'm yanked onto the pavement. McNoble.

"Well? What's happening?"

My mind is rather scrambled and I'm balancing the risk of his wrath if I tell him I've seen his Father with keeping both schtum and my arms, when he glances past me, does a double take, turns on his heels and hurries away. When I look where he was looking I see Zenda Silverman staring at us. As she realises I've seen her, she too turns away and disappears inside the department store.

I take the journey home carefully, hoping to miss Zenda. Unfortunately, I'm just dropping my bag in the hall and heading for the sitting room to catch the cricket highlights when the front door opens – it's Dobbin, followed by an anxious-looking Zenda. He says as he moves past, "You coming tonight? To the gig?"

"I don't—"

We're interrupted by Brenda/Vera's voice. "That you, Big Boy? We need to get going."

Dobbin hurries to their room, leaving Zenda staring at me.

"Hello, Harry. Can we talk?" She looks determined.

"I was hoping…" No, I can't fob her off just for the cricket, not with her looking so ill at ease. "Shall we grab a cup of tea?"

In the kitchen, she perches on the edge of a chair, hands gripped in her lap. "I saw you earlier. On Oxford Street."

"I wondered. You seemed in a hurry."

"I… that man you were talking to? What was he saying?" She looks at me, like she's pleading. "Was it about me? Or Brenda?"

"I'm sorry?"

She looks very upset. "It's… I know him, you see. He might be working for my husband. Was he asking about me?"

"No. No, he wasn't."

She looks relieved.

"Why would Stephen McNoble be asking about you?"

"Stephen?"

She's looking as confused as I feel. A cold finger runs down my spine. "Or Claude?"

"Oh God. How do you know him?"

"How do you?"

She swallows. "His step-Mother is my half-sister."

"Half…? Step…?" That takes a moment's untangling. "Do you mean Monica Jepson?"

This time I think I've nearly caused her a heart attack. "You know her?" She breathes out the words like they're her last.

"We met five years ago. Her husband – Stephen's Father, Charlie Jepson – and my Mother were old friends. Sort of. They nearly went into business together back then, but it didn't happen in the end."

She's frowning hard. "How come he's talking to you now?"

"I'm looking after the estate of a mutual acquaintance. He was asking how it was going."

She manages a laugh. "It looked to me like he was threatening you."

I take a sip of tea. "Yes, well, if you know him at all you'll know that's how he asks for things. The man is a violent psychopath."

"What's going on, Harry? It can't be a coincidence, can it?"

"I wish I knew. Look, I don't trust him and if I can get him out of my life I will. Why do you think he might be working for your husband?"

"He threatened me, a while ago. You see, my husband and Charlie did some business together. I don't know what. Claude was trying to find out when Charlie… you know he's been in prison?" She rubs her face, like it might eradicate an itch. "Oh God, why did Monica marry that crook?"

"I won't tell him about you being here if that's what's worrying you. Honestly, I want shot of him as much as you do."

She stands very quickly. "Thank you, Harry. That's very helpful." She leaves me staring at the door. What was that about? My watch says the highlights have 20 minutes to run, but first I have to go to find Brenda/Vera.

Happily, Dobbin is in the bathroom and their bedroom door is open. Brenda/Vera is sitting on the end of the bed plucking at her hair, making it spiky. She's wearing a pair of ripped tartan dungarees and a torn T-shirt that is failing to hide her right nipple. I say, "We need a word."

"Can it wait?"

"Not really. Your Mum just told me she's related to Monica Jepson? By marriage."

"So?" But she does glance at me quickly.

"You saw him the other day. Stephen, aka Claude. He was waiting to meet Dina and me. You shot downstairs and said something to him. What was all that about?"

She doesn't say anything, but I'm sure her breathing has altered.

"Vera?"

Still nothing.

"When I tell your Mum you knew he'd come round here... when she knows he knows where you're staying...? How that's going to go?"

She looks horrified, standing and reaching past me to slam the door shut. I should probably be concerned, given her worried expression, but I'm more conscious of her right boob jiggling in and out of the shirt and how soon Dobbin might return. It would be easier all round if she showed more decorum.

"Christ no. Harry, you mustn't."

"Of course I won't. She's just told me she's terrified he's working for your step-Father and might pass on where you're living. Given that, what the fuck are you playing at?"

Her expression is a mix of wildly swaying emotions, but she pulls herself together. "It's nothing to do with you so why don't you piss off? I have a gig to get to."

"We'll talk later then."

She's gone over to the mirror and is adding another layer of mascara. "You know I don't need this shit right now. He's trouble and I'm not dealing with this."

"Where are you playing? Maybe I can catch you in the interval."

"You don't want to come. The Jug in Camden. Rough crowd. I'll leave your name on the door if you really want some raw meat tonight."

If Brenda/Vera thinks they're rough, then they're probably borderline bestial.

She turns back to me, the momentum exposing both breasts completely. "Do I look okay?"

Of course, that's the moment Dobbin comes back in. He looks at her, then me and then her.

She smiles and walks past us both. "I'll see you downstairs."

"What's going on, mate?" Dobbin does look genuinely confused.

"Nothing. Have fun."

Poor sod. He hasn't a clue what's going on. But then neither have I.

Chapter Forty-Six

In Which Harry has a Thought and Gets Confused

The cricket is over. I'm staring at the TV when Dina comes in behind me. I didn't know she was home. I ask, "Any news? From Imperial?"

She shrugs. "Not yet." She's not able to make eye contact. "I'm sorry, H. About Jan. Last night. I shouldn't have trusted him."

"Drop it, okay. I know you're on my side. God knows no one else is."

"Jackie?"

My turn to shrug. "I'll call her later. Maybe. Come on, I think there's some muesli in the cupboard. I thought about that pasta, but I think it's probably toxic by now. Unless you've a better idea for dinner?"

While I dig out some bowls and look for the muesli, Dina spreads out the pictures. I tell her about Zenda and Brenda/Vera and McNoble.

"If Jepson and McNoble know Zenda and weirdy Vera then I'd just feel sorry for them. Bit of an oddity, mind, isn't it? Them knowing those thugs and you too?"

"Pfft. I'm beyond trying to work out how the world works. It's no more weird than Sven leaving me his bloody estate."

The cereal has been pushed to the back of the bottom cupboard and the paper bag it comes in is torn – Mum bought it from Lymington Saturday market and gave it to me – 'It's high in fibre Harold, and will be good for you motions; Dr Parsons says you need stools that are floaty and fluffy' – there are times when I wish Mum would focus on the length of my hair.

I sweep the horse food into the bowls; Dina regards it warily. As I hold it up, she wrinkles her nose. "I think I'll have toast."

Maybe she's right but I don't earn enough to throw food away. As I pour on the milk and add some sugar I explain about Pac-a-Mac man and Charlie J in the park; about the gambling and how Sven was at the same place as Miles and Sir Pen the night he died. "Maybe Sven and Sir Pen met there, although it sounded as if Izzy was the regular, not Pen."

Dina mulls this over and then says, "They are both Grimsdales, right? The police might have confused Sir Pen with Izzy when it came to them having a business links with Andersen."

"Yes. That makes sense. It explains why they wouldn't have recognised each other in my office." Another thought hits me. "Izzy knew Sven now that I think of it. She mentioned him when I went to talk to her about Penny." Absently I pick at some of the oats. "There's something we're missing, you know. I mean, how many coincidences can there be? Sven and Sir Pen and Izzy and…" It's like my head explodes. "Shit. Lewis."

"What about him?"

"When I was trying to get my articles, Dad asked Mr Lewis if he knew anywhere and he recommended Clifford Risely. He was at school with Philip Risely. And Risely knows Rother, that's Jepson's brother in law, from school. I'll lay a pound to a penny that Lewis also knows Sir Pen. And that would link up with Andersen and Jepson and McNoble and the rest."

"I think you're getting ahead of yourself."

"Probably."

Dina tries to maintain her thoughtful countenance, but like me she's also confused. As she runs over what we know I look at the pictures for the umpteenth time. At the far end, she's added a blank sheet. When I ask why, she reminds me about the missing picture – number seven. I'd forgotten about that. It's then I have a revelation.

"Number two. It's Monica. Monica Jepson. Ha ha, bloody Sven. See there, that tub? It's Nivea, right?"

"Yes. Did she use it?"

"No idea. But there, behind it, that's not a tree – it's a silhouette. It's the gardener from Hemingways. Cyril. He used to watch Penny and Natalie when they sunbathed topless. And… well, you know. See to himself." I cough in embarrassment.

She tilts her head and giggles. "He wanked, you mean?"

"Yes, well… I stopped him."

"You? How?"

Oh, dear God, I can't tell her about the Nivea and the cactus spines. "It doesn't matter now. Let's say he got the point and stopped. Thing is, he was perving on Monica Jepson when he learnt his lesson. She was naked. I must have told Sven. Yes, I did. He covered for me. I nearly got the sack about that, but he saved me. I wouldn't have recognised her profile; it's ages since I saw her.

Dina smirks. "Especially if she's got her clothes on here." She's checking the grid. "Number two is six letters. 'Monica.' It fits."

I laugh dutifully but the image of her standing up, facing the hedge where Cyril and I were hiding comes roaring back to me. It was the first time I'd seen a woman's pubes. I force myself to eat some cereal and look at the remaining picture. "I still don't know about this one. Nor what those symbols mean. And seven is missing and I need to ask Natalie about those car adverts. Maybe if I showed the pictures to her and Marita they might know something."

Dina nods. "Probably have to, won't you? We need to know." She breaks the toast in two; it's like chipboard. "Maybe I will have some of that horse food."

I wash up my bowl. "Vera's on stage in Camden tonight. She said she'd leave my name at the door if you want a drink and a pair of ruptured eardrums."

Dina is crouched down, peering into the cupboard where the muesli lives; she reaches in and wipes her finger, sniffing the tip. Then she carefully picks something up between her fingertips. The forensic way she's looking at whatever it is makes me feel very queasy. It's when she picks up the paper bag and inspects the tear, a tear that now looks like it might have been chewed, that I feel distinctly unwell. She meets my gaze. "I think you might have mice."

It's while I'm clutching the great white telephone and revisiting the cereal I ate earlier that Mr Jones appears to say Jackie has rung and wants to know if I'd like a drink.

Friday, 17th July 1981

Chapter Forty-Seven

In Which Harry Meets Karen and Copes with a Tuna Sandwich

It wasn't until late yesterday when Gloria reminded me I'm on a course today that I realised I would be out of the office. At the time, with a heap of work to do and the inevitability it will all be waiting for me on my return on Monday, I must admit to feeling somewhat depressed at the prospect, but today, what with my head spinning as fast as my stomach, a few hours listening to some dullard explain the Solicitors' Account Rules and basic book keeping does appear to be heaven sent. With luck I might even manage a kip.

We definitely have mice. And they have definitely crapped in my muesli. Or peed. Or both because I was up and shouting Ruth and Hughie into the porcelain speaking tube on four occasions last night. Twice I found myself sharing it with Brenda/Vera, whose alimentary problems were grain-induced from what she managed to communicate. Dobbin, sympathetic sod that he isn't, even stood by the door and shouted at us to vomit more quietly, like we had a choice. I admit it must have sounded rank, because it was pretty appalling being involved.

John Thomas is on the course as is Karen Himcol and a few others from the College of Law days. Karen seeks me out during a coffee break when I'm balancing the urge to hide in the toilets with the need to drink as much water as possible to avoid being completely dehydrated.

"Hi Harry. Look, sorry I never called back."

I think I must look blank because she seems annoyed. "John said you wanted a word and then your office called, and someone asked if I'd snogged you. I thought that a bit strange."

"That would be my sister. She was acting for a third party."

Karen laughs and looks a bit like one of her horses. "Incredible. Was that some sort of joke? I don't remember you being very funny."

"No. Right. I had your number in my wallet and she found it. I guess it was a joke. She can be weird." It's then I remember she knew Brenda/Vera and that's why I took the number. "You remember Vera? Sorry, Brenda Silverman?"

"Sure. I heard she dropped out of her articles. Some problem with her Father."

"I think. Not sure."

She shrugs and looks a little embarrassed. "I don't mean to gossip, but I'm sure there was something about how he'd got her the job and then the firm she was with refused to act for him over some debt, so they made it clear she needed to think about leaving. Poor thing, like it was her fault."

"Where did you hear all that?"

"My principal was at school with her Father. It's still a small world, isn't it? Although we're qualifying at the right time, aren't we?"

"Are we?"

"Harry, you always seemed to be away with the fairies, but even you must read the papers. When Maggie deregulates the City – this 'Big Bang' they're all going on about – they're going to need loads of lawyers."

"But surely they were just banging on about how there are too many solicitors?"

"God, you are so behind aren't you? My firm are already asking us if we know any good lawyers qualifying. What about you? Are you placed yet? What areas have you specialised in?"

My head is about to implode. I manage to say, "Well, I've done lots of conveyancing…"

"Right… that's it? Was it commercial? Shops and offices?"

"Houses and flats and some estate work. It's pretty leading edge with a lot of tax—"

"Tax is good. They need tax lawyers. How long did you spend in the tax department at your firm?"

"We don't have departments. We just do what comes into the partners."

"Surely they specialise?" Her expression tells me I don't need to answer. She pulls out a pad from her bag and writes down two names. "These are recruitment agencies. Put your name down smartish. That's assuming you're not planning on staying put." The tone of her voice tells me she thinks I'd have the wit of an amoeba to even think of staying in such an antiquated firm. "We'd better go back in. Some of us are having a liquid lunch; this is so boring, isn't it? You want to join us?"

I sort of nod and head for the toilets. Assuming I get that far.

***

It's during the last session in the morning when we have a lecture on ethics that I realise this place is just around the corner from Natalie's office. The perfect excuse to nurse my stomach through to the afternoon and not spend all my hard-earned with Karen and her overpaid mates at these City outfits. Mind you, it would have been good to hear a bit about this legal explosion; I really should try to read something more newsworthy than Dobbin's tattered NMEs.

When I enter the reception I can see a TV on in a room to the right. Men in shirt sleeves are gathered round the door. As I walk to the reception, two of them walk away. Both look miserable. Another bad morning for the cricket, I suppose. Why do England's cricket fortunes seem to mirror my own?

I suppose that, because I'm in a suit and not sweaty, this time the excessively fragrant receptionist actually calls Natalie who seems to be with me in seconds. Having taken my elbow and steered me outside towards Red Lion Square, she asks. "Have you eaten?"

"I don't think I can."

"Why?"

"I've got food poisoning."

"Geez. Is that your sister? Does she cook as badly as your Mum?"

"No. I think I ate some mouse turds."

"You...? How...? No, don't tell me. Let me grab something and we can talk."

In the Square, she picks at her tuna pasta or whatever it is. I don't like tuna. It's the smell. A boy thing, I suppose. I start talking before she can, "Were you there? At Miles' club when Sven took ill?"

She hesitates, then takes a mouthful, like she's using it to give her time to think.

"I think you were. You knew he was ill, and you saw him with Stephen, didn't you? The night he died?"

She shakes her head hard. She can't swallow quickly enough. "No. No, it wasn't like that. I heard him and Miles arguing but he'd gone off with Stephen by the time I found out what had happened. They said he'd been taken home because he had too much to drink."

"He barely touched a drop."

"I know. But... Miles scares me, Harry. Really. I don't argue with him. And I try to stay away from him on club nights."

298

"So what went on? It was the night he died, wasn't it?"

She looks so forlorn. The tuna thingy remains on the seat between us. "Miles didn't know Stephen's Dad was coming, I'm sure of it. When he turned up, Stephen went ballistic and Miles asked me to try to calm him down while he spoke to Stephen's Father. Then Sven turned up and there was this argument. They disappeared into Miles' office – he told me to keep the other guests happy." She made a face. "That was my role. His bloody poodle."

"Who else was there?"

"That peer who died. The one Penny was with. Him and his sister."

"Lady Isabella? You knew her and didn't say? Why…?"

"It's not like that, Harry. They use pseudonyms. But I've seen them in the papers. After. There was a lawyer, too; he came with Mr Jepson."

I'm shocked when my mind screams 'Jeremy.' But I immediately realise it makes sense. Someone said he gambled, had money problems; he knew the Grimsdales too. And I heard Miles' voice when I called Jeremy about Sir Pen's death. "Jeremy Panther?"

She struggles to remember. "I think his name was Rupert. Older guy, tall and broad shouldered. Booming voice. He, Sven, Miles and Mr Jepson were in the office, then it was just Miles and Sven."

"Oh." I'm oddly disappointed it's not Jeremy, who doesn't match her description. "What about Sir Penshaw and his sister, Isabella? Were they with Sven?"

"I don't know. Maybe the woman. She's a regular."

"Did Sven talk to him? That evening? Or earlier, on a different occasion?"

"I don't know. There are private rooms so it's possible."

"What were Sven and Miles talking about?"

"I don't know, okay? I know you think I'm hiding things, but I'm not. I'm worried about Miles. If he finds out I'm talking to you I'll be in so much trouble. Sven had some interest in the club. I think it involved Mr Jepson and Stephen. You know Stephen hates his Father?"

"Yes. Yes, I do. You could have told me all this, you know, before. It might have helped."

"I didn't know it mattered, did I?"

"What about other businesses? The estate agency and that pub?"

"Pub? What pub?"

"You took me there, said he had a half-share?"

"Did I? I don't remember."

"And Leeds? You said—"

"I don't know, okay?" She's really annoyed but then her voice wobbles. "Oh Harry, it's been awful. I…" She covers her face. "I just want to get away, but how am I going to? Sven was my only hope."

I take her hand and hold it; it's rather sticky, I think that may be from the tuna, but I concentrate on quelling my rippling stomach. "We'll do something. Trust me."

She nods and mouths 'thank you.' Then, frankly to my amazement, brushes off her skirt, picks up the residue of her pasta and eats it. She tells me she has to go back. But she stays sitting, watching some young Mothers push their buggies round the perimeter path.

"Where is this club?" I ask.

"A large basement under a pub over in Bermondsey. It's near Butler's Wharf, really seedy on the outside but very swish inside. Miles wants to do things his way, but Sven – this is what I heard – Sven told him he had to clean it up or he'd close it down." She slows to eat another mouthful but clearly regrets it because she looks ill when she swallows it. Maybe it's not just a boy thing after all. To my horror she holds out the residue to me. "You finish it."

The smell is truly appalling, and my head has joined my stomach in a free-fall. "No thanks. I need to get back, but can we talk about this more?" I'm still wondering what happened that night. "Does Marita know McNoble took him home?"

Natalie looks sick. "No. The other day in the flat when she said Stephen was out for himself, when she made it clear she didn't trust him, I couldn't say it in front of her. Do you think…? I mean he didn't do anything, did he? It was natural causes, wasn't it? That's what the coroner said."

"God knows. We know McNoble hates his Father and if Sven was selling up in a way that gave Jepson a way back in, then McNoble might want to stop it."

Natalie is shaking despite the heat. It's only then I realise the danger she must be in if she knows all of this. "Are you sure you're safe, staying with Miles?"

She scuffs her heels in the dirt. She doesn't speak for a while. "You know, I think I actually loved Sven. I want you to find his money and finish what he started, Harry. Miles thinks I'm stupid, that I don't know what's going on. And if he has his club, well, I don't think he'll miss me really. He's not exactly a faithful man, after all. All his 'business trips.' Ha! He's all show. None of it – the wealth, the life style – none of it is real. He doesn't own the flat or the Porsche, that's Sven's and—"

"It belongs to Sven?"

"Technically it was Mr Andersen's, so Sven inherited it. He had several cars, I think he got rid of most of them but he kept the Porsche. Sven used it a few times but mostly he let Miles drive it. Miles loves that bloody car. He goes everywhere in it." She takes my hand and massages it. "If I'd made more of an effort with you, back when we first worked together, we'd not be here now, would we? And sorry I snapped."

"Is the club members only? Is there any way you can find out who uses it?

"Would that help?"

"It might. You sure the Porsche is Sven's?"

"Yes. And maybe I could get hold of Miles' Filofax and copy out the contacts. I told you the clients used pseudonyms at the club and only Miles knows their real identities? That will help if I can find them, won't it?" She's shaking as she says this.

"You sure? I mean, don't take any risks—"

"I don't have a choice, do I? We have to finish what Sven started or…" She picks at the corner of her eyes, blinking.

We are about to part company when I remember the other reason I called round. "On the subject of cars, any chance you can help with some adverts?"

"Sorry? Is this to do with Sven's Father's cars?"

"Sort of, maybe, yes. I have some of his pictures – I think they are Sven's interpretations of some recent car adverts – and I need to compare them with the originals. If I show you the pictures – I can give you the list of the cars to be getting on with – could you see what you can find? I think the adverts are British and from the last two years. That would limit the search."

Natalie remains confused for a moment and then smiles. "Do you know why they matter?"

"Not really. I'm clutching at all the straws."

"You're not asking much, are you?" she smiles. "Okay. How many adverts?"

"Eight."

"Can't you get me copies of Sven's drawings? It would be easy that way."

"I suppose. It's just difficult to get to use the copier at work, that's all."

"Give me the originals and I can get copies made here."

I must pull a face because she says, "You don't trust me with the originals?"

"I... I need to keep them in case I have a brainwave. You know, they're part of his estate. They, erm, shouldn't really leave the office."

She nods slowly. "Okay, Harry. I'll do my best."

I grab a pad from my briefcase; it should be full of notes from this morning but has one line saying 'double-entry' underlined four times and a cartoonish picture that could be anything but is in fact my attempt at a naked Jackie in profile. The face is rubbish, but I've nailed her boobs.

As I copy out the list on a clean sheet, she says, "That is so typical of him. This is about the money, isn't it?" She looks excited and just for a moment I wonder if I've done a stupid thing by telling her. What if she's still on Miles's side in this and is going to tell him?

As I head back to my afternoon of lectures, I have to ask myself if things can get any more complicated. And what on Earth is McNoble playing at?

Chapter Forty-Eight

Where Brenda/Vera Reveals a Phobia and Penny Goes to Bed

I'm feeling rocky when I get in, having been dragged off by Karen's friends for a drink that turned into several back at some bloke's flat near King's Cross Station. Penny, Dina and Brenda/Vera are talking in the kitchen. They seem embarrassed when I walk in. As I make tea I can feel I'm being watched, no – studied, like I'm some sort of zoo animal. God, that is so intimidating. "So how was last night, Vera? You were in a right state," I say, not making eye contact.

She grimaces. "I was shitfaced. Groin, he's the new bassist, he had these greeny pills. Meant to make you fly – sort of acid on acid – but they just made me belch. Although the whisky kicked in a lot harder and quicker than normal."

"Groin? Any reason for the name?"

"It's all he thinks about. He needs to fuck, like, every six hours or he loses his muse."

We all look at her, waiting, wondering. She becomes aware she's now the exhibit. "Me? How the fuck do I know? I was shitfaced."

Thank heavens Dobbin isn't about.

"You weren't much better, Harry."

"Yeah, but I'd been poisoned."

Penny looks aghast, but Dina gets in first. "It's okay. It's not by the crooks he's spending his time with."

Brenda/Vera looks up sharply. "Crooks? Who?"

Dina laughs, like she's made a great joke and carries on, "A mouse crapped in his cereal and he ate it."

It's fun watching Brenda/Vera's head spin from Dina to me and back. Finally, she manages, "Where?"

Dina has barely lifted her arm to point at the cupboard when Brenda/Vera leaves her seat and climbs onto the table, scattering the cutlery and breaking one plate as she does so. But the thing that catches all our attentions is her scream. It is extraordinary and nothing like her singing. In a way it is a thing of beauty, even as it perforates beyond the eardrum and seeks weaknesses in the brain. "Get the fucking thing out of there!" Slowly she sinks into a foetal squat, eying the cupboard suspiciously.

Even Penny appears uncomfortable, lifting her feet onto the seat. Dina gawps, then shakes her head. "It's long gone." She pulls open the cupboard. "See? Nothing."

Indeed, the cupboard is empty, but Brenda/Vera isn't about to move. If anything she pulls herself tighter into a ball; Penny, meanwhile, puts her feet back on the floor.

"You threw it out?" Brenda/Vera sounds aggressive, but her face still shows the residue of terror.

Dina glances at me. "Yes. Of course. Anyway, it's tiny."

Reluctantly Brenda/Vera gets down from the table and disappears to her room. Penny looks at Dina. "You didn't, did you?"

"I've no idea where it is. Who cares? She's being childish." She yawns, twisting her face in several directions. "Time for bed, I think. See you in the morning."

Left alone Penny and I drink some tea in silence. Then she says, "I've been stupid, haven't I? Do you think I'll be okay?"

The truth is, of course, I've no idea, but I nod and that appears to help as her face relaxes a little. "I was shitfaced, like Vera. I took something Sean offered us, something he said he swears by. That's the problem. I have this huge gap where I have no idea what happened."

"Have you heard anything?"

"The lawyer told me Pen's blood test is inconclusive. There were signs of drug use, but not enough to kill him or render him incapable. I told him what you said. About the sex games. He said he'd pass it on but assumed the police would know anyway."

I wonder if she knows about McNoble and Sven and what happened at the gambling club. Maybe she was there. I should ask her, but I can't; it seems like another way to make it look like I don't trust her.

She surprises me by saying, "Can we go to bed? I'm exhausted."

"Don't you want the sofa?"

"I'd prefer a real bed; that thing makes me want to weep. I'll not touch you if that's your worry." She does look shattered.

"No, it's okay."

Like strangers thrown together we change separately and slip into the bed sticking to our sides for a few minutes. Then she snuggles in close and curls round my back. Her hand rests on my hip and of course

I get an uncalled-for erection. That has to be Pavlovian, right? It can't be what I really feel. We've moved on and it's Jackie I'm falling for.

Sleep, when it comes, is oddly untroubled. I don't know what to make of that either.

Saturday, 18th and Sunday, 19th July 1981

Chapter Forty-Nine

In Which England Follow-on

Thank God for weekends. When Penny wakes she leaves quickly before the rest of the flat stirs. She says she's going to her Mum's for the weekend, but who really knows? Jackie has a half-day on Saturday afternoon and we end up at the Imperial War Museum because she has this idea we can trace her great uncle who fought at Amiens in 1918 or something and her Mum has asked her to do some research. I'm waiting outside while she buys a postcard, standing by the huge guns and imagining Brenda/Vera wanting to squeeze inside with Dobbin when McNoble strides past the railings heading towards Waterloo. He ignores me, but I'm completely shaken like it can't be a coincidence, and if it isn't then he's following me and I don't even realise it. I need to be more vigilant. Jackie suggests an ice cream and then we end up back at the flat with sun pouring through the window while we make love several times. Each time it feels wrong and good at the same moment. I am officially a mess. After she leaves for her shift I settle down in front of the TV. England has followed-on and are staring at defeat. I am officially depressed.

Monday, 20th July 1981

Chapter Fifty

Where Harry Saves the Day and Puts His Bike Away

Monday's are of course dire, especially with England likely to lose and go two-nil down in the series. This one starts like it will be doubly so because Mr. Risely has cocked up an Order 14 Summons. This is a quick way to obtain a court order enabling our client – a gruff Italian man by the name of Pellegrino who runs various garden centres in Bromley and Beckenham – to force his cactus supplier to pay back some money he owes. Mr Pellegrino is what Mr Risely describes as 'flamboyant' and who Lucinda more aptly calls 'dangerously volatile.' When I told him we couldn't enforce the judgement because we didn't actually have it, he flipped. The noise he made – something between a wail and a lamb excreting a hedgehog – brings everyone running, the assumption being some mammal was being eviscerated or the office banshee had returned. Lucinda, as ever, has a solution but it involves me in a dash to the courts to try to see a Master on an emergency application for relief. I know, with the cold hard certainty that tells me Sod runs the universe on Mondays, that Rother will be the duty Master taking emergency applications and I'm dreading what I have to do – which is tell a load of 'porky pies' as Gloria rather neatly puts it – but Mr. Creepy von Pac-a-Mac is there and agrees to my plea for help. Another Faustian pact; another moment I will live to regret.

Anyway, having obtained the forbidden fruit of a dodgy Order 14, I'm actually quite chipper as I hop off my bike and fiddle with the lock before I carry it down to the lightwell.

"Harry. Just the man."

Shit. McNoble. He is definitely following me.

"Any news?"

"No. I saw Mr. Lewis. You know, the old boy…"

"Yes. So?"

"He doesn't know what Sven might have done with any money he raised beyond what he put into the employees' trust fund."

"That's it? What did Frank say?"

"Frank?"

"Don't be smart. Why'd you go and see him?"

"Politeness. I saw him at the funeral and Sven was clearly keen that he was looked after."

He nods. "Just being polite?"

Maybe I've got away with it. "Yes. Anyway, he's pretty dependent on help these days, not the best conversationalist."

McNoble nods again. "Yeah. Poor sod. Miles was asking. He's getting itchy. He wants a resolution."

My turn to nod. "Much like your Dad. He's equally keen to talk to you about Miles and his businesses."

His expression changes from an occasional risk of showers to imminent biblical thunderstorms. "When'd you speak to him? I told you I'm dealing with him. Just stay away."

"He found me. He thought, given we're such 'good friends,' I might put in a word, ask you to get in touch."

"Really? Stupid sod."

"Me or him?"

"Both of you if you think I'm helping him back into play. Just get a move on with Sven's money. We need this sorted."

He's really pissing me off. I say before I have a chance to think twice, which I really should learn to do, "Tell me, when you helped Sven home from the club on the night he died, how was he when you left? Because it's a miracle he made it to Wandsworth Bridge from his flat, don't you think? Maybe he floated on the tide?"

It's like it used to be with McNoble, watching his face adjust to a new reality and the cogs turn oh so slowly as he tries to process what he hears. It's rather cheering to realise he's unsure about me. Surprisingly he tries a conciliatory tone; it really does not suit him. "Harry, you didn't ask for this and you're really not cut out for it, are you? But you're involved, so a word to the wise. Try not to make it any more difficult for yourself. Or your family. Okay?"

Oh dear. He can't resist a little threat. I tilt my head, wondering for the first time if the ready violence of five years ago is in fact a thing of the past. Do I want to push him to find out? "I should tell the police really. They are keen to understand what happened that night. What do you think?"

"They know. That woman Wallace asked when I last saw him and I told her I took him home. Sven had a heart condition. It killed him. The coroner found out as much and he's now been cremated. I think that ends any chance they might wonder if anything else caused his death." He pauses then adds, "If that is what you are suggesting. He was alive and kicking when I left him."

Before I can answer – not that I want to – he turns and begins to walk away. He's lying. "Where did you take him? What address?"

He hesitates before turning. "As executor, I'm sure you have his address – all his addresses." With that he's gone. Does he know about the flat under Natalie's? It seems unlikely. And why didn't he react to me knowing about the club and his involvement with Sven? Maybe it was innocent. But if so, where did he take him? And what's with the stuff about other causes of death? Is he teasing me?

I'm still pondering what he means and whether he's actually suggesting there was some other cause when I open the door to my office, the one I share with Jeremy. He's standing by the large sash windows, staring down the road and jumps as I enter. "What was he saying to you?"

"McNoble? Do you know him?"

"Yes." Jeremy sounds more than a little anxious and I realise his hands are shaking.

"It wasn't anything to do with you."

He checks the window, I suppose making sure McNoble has really gone and then grabs his jacket and leaves. Moments later Jean comes in to ask if I know where Jeremy is. When I tell her he left without a word, she looks annoyed and then rather worried.

Chapter Fifty-One

Where Harry Uses Marita's Knowledge to Good Effect

Rather than go home I head for Wapping and Sven's flat. I ring and when there's no answer I let myself in. Marita is on the mezzanine level, terrified. "Can we have a code or something so I know it's you? You could telephone first, maybe three rings then ring off? Do that twice and then on the third time I'll answer. Do the same with the doorbell."

"Sure, if you think it's needed."

"Please. I want to get away, but I can't go to my aunt's and I don't have any money so I've got to stay here for now."

"Nothing? Didn't he leave you any money?"

She looks totally washed out and slips onto a creamy coloured sofa. "A little. Enough for food but not a hotel. He said you'd deal with everything. I know it's difficult and I will be patient."

Great. I'm the delegated hero, am I? It's not like I'm rolling in lucre and can bung her a couple of twenties.

She pours herself a glass of water and sips it, eying me carefully. "How are you getting on?"

It's an innocent enough question but I don't know who to trust other than Dina. Blowing out a breath I open my briefcase. "When I found out about this flat and came here, I discovered this picture." I lay the sketch of her and me, me in the Hampshire car park and her in this flat. "It didn't make much sense, not at the time."

She stares at it. "Where are you? I'm here, aren't I?"

"I think so. Or in Natalie's flat upstairs. I'm in the car park at Hemingways."

She frowns. "Is that the car park?"

"Not today. Back in 1976 when he and I worked there. See I've something in my lap? We're both looking at it."

"It's not clear, is it?"

"No it's not. But I found other clues that took me to his Hampshire bungalow and I found more pictures there. I'm making progress with them but I think he wanted you to help me work out the answers. I accept it's a guess but…" I shrug, not sure what I can do.

She takes another couple of minutes studying the sketch of the two of us. Finally she puts it down. "Where are the other clues?"

I'm holding my briefcase to my chest. "I have to be honest with you. I don't know who to trust and—"

She looks horrified. "You have to believe me. I only—"

I stop her with a flat hand. "No, wait. Hear me out. Sven never told me anything but I keep finding out more and more. And so many people apparently want to help me but they may have their own agendas."

"Stephen? Miles?"

"Yes, that's obvious. Stephen's father too. But can I trust Natalie?"

"Natalie? Sven wanted to help her. Why—?"

"She's married to Miles. Okay, maybe she hates that but it's possible he's controlling her."

Her horror has morphed into anger. "Natalie has been treated awfully! How can you think she'd help Miles?"

I open my hands in what I hope is a gesture of uncertainty but it doesn't lead to any softening of her expression. "Okay, but if I show you this clue will you promise me not to show it to anyone else or say anything about it?"

She glares at me. Oh sod it, I give up. I have no choice but to trust her. Before I change my mind I pull out a copy of the photo of the woman bending over a table, her face hidden by her thick hair. Number four. I swallowed my worries and made copies on the office Xerox machine. Totally against the rules but I'm beginning to lose my natural terror of doing the wrong thing. Thanks, Sven. See what you're turning me into? "Sven painted this and some others and left me this photo of it. Sorry the copy is rubbish but it's the best I could do."

She turns it round and stares at it. "It's his style, isn't it?"

"I think if I can identify who this is, I might be able to find out what he's done with the money he realised from selling your Father's businesses. I wondered if you knew who it might be."

She smiles to herself. "We both loved puzzles and quizzes. Typical of him to do this." She peers at it closely. "It looks like one big woman. He's made her look huge against that dresser, hasn't he?" She looks closely. "Where is that dresser? I recognise…" She glances up. "Just a moment."

Before I can object she picks it up and moves quickly to the bathroom, locking herself inside. She flushes the toilet twice and a minute or so later there are three quick taps on the front door. I still trying to get my head around what's going on when she unlicks the door and in seconds Natalie is inside. She hands Natalie the print. "Where's this?"

Natalie stares at me, ignoring the copy. "Harry? What are you doing here?"

Marita ignores me; she taps the picture. "Any idea who this is? It's a clue from Sven."

Great. If she is working for Miles then I'm sunk.

Natalie takes the briefest of glances. "The club, isn't it? That chest is in the smoking room. What's this about?" Her glance goes from me to Marita and back again but neither of us speak. Natalie looks at the picture, studying it. "Whoever this is they're doing a line. Mind you, the club isn't really laid out like that." She points at one feature. "There's no table in the smoking room to do a line on. Artistic license perhaps? What is this all about?"

Marita folds her arms, her focus on me. "He'll explain."

"Oh bloody hell. Marita, I hope you know what you're doing?"

She turns away and moves towards the kitchen. We follow her.

"Sven painted the picture and left it for me, but I've no idea what it means."

Natalie puts it on the table and we stand back, all looking at it. "Is it like those car pictures? Some sort of clue?"

I nod, aware that Marita is looking at me. I spread my hands, "Yes, okay, I'm a hypocrite. I already asked her about those."

"What cars? Harry, why won't you tell us what he's done? We can help, really."

Natalie leans over the picture. "What are they meant to be?" She points at the odd symbols along the top that Dina and I had noted, but without any idea what they were.

Marita looks where Natalie is pointing. Then she leans in next to her and picks the copy up, squealing, "They're from that Christmas game!"

"Sorry?"

She shakes her head, like she's trying to order her thoughts. "Maybe you didn't play it when you were young. We had this game we played as kids. With Dad. We only got our presents if we won enough gold."

Natalie looks at me and then Marita. "You're not making much sense."

314

"It was a card game based on the 12 days of Christmas. They used symbols like these." She taps the picture. "That's the symbols for Swans a'swimming and that's the French hens. Here," she goes to the desk and finds a sheet of paper and starts drawing. "This is lords a'leaping – I loved that and…" She hesitates, pen poised. "The five gold rings were like this." She draws the Olympic symbol. Then she puts her pen down. "I wonder why he included those. We used it as a code, sometimes." She has a beady stare and I feel she's trying to read my mind. "Come on, Harry. You know, don't you?"

"Nope, not a clue. You're the first person to have any idea about them."

She smiles. "Well, it proves you were right about the first picture. Come on, show Natalie."

I pull it out. She taps it. "We – that's me and Harry – have to work out his clues together. Only…" she folds her arms again, "Only you don't trust us to help, do you?"

I refuse to rise to the bait. After a moment while we compete to see who has the most expressionless stare, Marita gives in with, "He always drew. Tons of stuff, although he threw most of it away. It was like he wanted the perfect picture and if he couldn't achieve it, he couldn't bear keeping something he deemed unworthy. I'd love it if I had more of his stuff. He always had a way of capturing the essence of a scene." She laughs. "He'd have taken the piss out of me for that. He loathed any sort of artistic pretention. God, I miss him."

Natalie has the presence of mind that I don't and goes over to comfort her. I really want to leave and report back to Dina and tell her my idea that Sven did mean for Marita to help work out the answers. Maybe Natalie too. God, he is so annoying. Although that doesn't help us work out who Number Four is meant to be. That man was a pain in the arse.

Natalie looks at me over Marita's bowed head; her eyes are red, too. It strikes me that everyone really had a soft spot for Sven and I didn't, which makes me feel like I'm lacking something. To me, he was and will probably always remain a smug know-all.

She lets Marita go. "He left you more pictures, didn't he? I understand why you might be suspicious but you need help, don't you? She," she waves at Marita, "knew about the symbols and I knew about the club. And you want my help with these car adverts, too. Why not show us everything you've got and we'll pool our brains?"

She's right. Reluctantly I go to my briefcase and pull out the copies of the adverts. "I… I was going to drop them off. Soon."

"You overcame your reluctance to use the copier then?" Natalie takes them without looking at them, but holds my gaze. "We want to help, Harry. You'll have to trust us if you want to sort this out, won't you?" She taps the copies. "These will save a lot of wasted effort. I'll find the originals as soon as I can. Now, will you show us what else you have?"

Marita looks almost pleading. "Yes, please do. We did puzzles for each other all the time. I can help, really. Please."

They both seem so anxious to assist that I almost give in. Eventually I smile and say, "I don't have them with me." I know they're wondering about my briefcase and part of me is expecting them to make a grab for it but they don't move. "If you can help with those adverts that would be great."

They clearly aren't happy. Natalie is the first to react. "I found Miles address book. I'll copy what looks useful and let you have it."

"Thanks." I feel guilty but I worry I've taken too much of a chance already. "I'd better go."

Marita surprises me by hugging me. "It's okay, Harry. I understand why this is difficult. If you need help, just ask."

Natalie follows up with a hug of her own, but it's more perfunctory. As she lets go, she says, "Did you hear about Botham's heroics? The boys at work were purring over it."

I glance at my watch. Of course I've missed the bloody highlights. "Did England lose?"

"I don't think so?"

Oh well, I think as I head home. *It's just a temporary reprieve.*

Tuesday, 21st July 1981

Chapter Fifty-Two

In Which Harry Has a Philosophical Moment and Zenda Cries a Bit

I catch snippets of excitement from office windows and shop doorways as I pass, having been sent out on a variety of errands from mid-morning onwards. Something dramatic is happening in the cricket and I'm stuck in queues at the Probate registry and the writ division of the High Courts. I'm late returning from having a title transfer stamped at Bush House and Zenda is already with Lucinda, so my hopes for a quick glance at Mr Risely's TV are thwarted by Gloria hustling me upstairs. When I knock and enter, Lucinda gives me a warning look; Zenda is seated with her back to me but the heaving shoulders give away her emotional state. Lucinda coughs, causing Zenda to glance up and, when she sees me, she turns away to hide her tears. Noisily, she blows her nose.

"I was just explaining to Zenda that I've had contact with her husband's lawyers and they are insisting their client meets with her to discuss a reconciliation before—"

Zenda's howl is nerve-shredding. "I can't. I won't!"

"Of course you won't. I'm sure there is absolutely no point. However, I need to report to you what they said. They were rather... aggressive."

Zenda nods but only I see Lucinda's expression. It clearly communicates her distaste.

She continues, "My strong impression is this is all about money. Does that sound correct?"

Zenda takes another moment to compose herself. "I have family assets. I'm sure that's what attracted Reginald now that I'm able to admit it. But it remains in a trust and the trustees have always been cautious about how they release both capital and income."

"That suggests foresight."

Zenda smiles. "Well, my brother never liked Reginald and when he – my husband – had his financial problems a couple of years ago the trustees were especially unsympathetic to his demands for money. Looking back, that's when I realised our future was strictly limited."

"Financial problems?" Lucinda looks up from her note taking.

Zenda looks over to me and holds my gaze. "My husband gambles. A lot. Not just a flutter on the horses either. To start with, early in our marriage, I let him have money that I now regret. Then, he was introduced to a club by a family connection and through that person he became involved... I don't know the details, but he's had problems as a result." She looks back at Lucinda. "I know he's really regretting it now. I think he always assumed that, in extremis, I'd make sure he was bailed out." She shakes her head, but whether at her own stupidity or his isn't clear.

Lucinda is a sharp woman. She moves her gaze slowly from me to Zenda and back. "Am I missing something here?"

Zenda looks exhausted but manages a nod. Feeling sick, I say, "I think I know this club. And the relative." Lucinda begins to look shocked so I hurry on, "I mean, I've heard of it. I found out recently that my friend who died, the one who made me and Jeremy his executors – he inherited an interest in this gambling club from his Father."

Lucinda makes a few notes, slowly and rather deliberately. After what seems like a long pause, she says, "You do lead an interesting life, Harry."

Zenda shrugs. I copy her.

Lucinda carries on, "As a Judge, a Master, he can hardly find himself owing money to, erm, unsavory characters. That might be interesting if we could find out anything." Once again, the look she gives me is like a clear unspoken instruction. I suppose I manage to look like I understand, but in truth I would prefer chewing off one of my toes than to go asking about Reggie Rother and his gambling debts. It is only as I'm showing Zenda out that it occurs to me I might have some help close at hand.

Before I can say anything, Zenda's cold hand takes mine, making me jump. "He mustn't find me. Really. I don't trust him and I worry about Brenda. She's vulnerable right now. She doesn't know what she wants and all this, er, experimentation, well it's just a sign of her struggles to find herself." She hesitates by the front door then asks, "Can you see me to the Underground?"

I could weep; twice I heard Mr Risely cry out as if in pain during our meeting, but whether it's an exquisite agony of unexpected success or the shattering pain of real disappointment, I have no clue. But the cricket must wait, I can't really refuse her. We set off for what turns

319

into a funereal stroll to Oxford Circus. After a while I say, "When did you find out that Charlie Jepson lent Mr, erm, Master Rother the money?"

"My half-sister told me. I mentioned Monica is my half-sister, didn't I? It's ironic, really, because when we met Charlie, when we met at their wedding, Reggie hated him, called him a spiv. Such a dated word. I knew Reggie was badgering Greg – that's my brother – for money but he wouldn't say what it was for. Monica warned me Reggie was getting in too deep but when I asked him he refused to see it that way or tell me what he'd done. Stupid man." She stops abruptly causing me to turn to face her. "It's not a surprise to me that Charlie's been in prison, but I worry... I think he might have tried to get Reggie to do him some sort of favour, given his position. Reggie really is naïve. For all his bluster, he really doesn't know who he's dealing with." She tries to relax her face. "He's not a bad man, whatever Brenda thinks. His temper, his anger... it's mostly aimed at himself. I suppose it's disappointment, really. He had such hopes when I first met him."

"He's Brenda's step-Father, isn't he?"

She nods. "Her Father died of a complication from a stupid knee operation. Reggie was the barrister who got us compensation. He was so kind, went well beyond what he needed to do. But then he didn't take silk and had a bad three years with pneumonia – that's when he became a Master, when the stress of the bar proved too much." She looks sort of wistful. "I did my best but the gambling is so corrosive."

We walk on. She asks, "Have you seen Claude again recently?"

I nod. "He's not spoken about you. Or Brenda. He's after information about something different."

"Claude told me about the gambling club, about how Reggie was helping Charlie with it – I don't really know how, he didn't say but even I understood it wasn't legal advice." She forces out a smile. "Claude wanted me to find out, but there was no way I could say anything. He was so insistent. He said it would be in both our interests if I found out what was going on." Her laugh is what might be described as hollow. "You know, the way he said that – 'in our mutual interest' – made it sound like a threat. Then again, most things he says sound like a threat. Horrible little worm."

I love Zenda. Yes, that sums him up perfectly. "Did you find out anything?"

"No, but Greg – my brother – said he wanted several thousand pounds from the trust and I assumed it was gambling debts but it may have been something else entirely." She shakes her head slowly, her forehead wrinkling. "He would have asked me had it been legitimate. He knows I can usually get Greg to do what I want. I just don't know."

We walk on in silence a bit more before she says, "You know, I really think Claude might be – might have – mental health issues. He hates Charlie and anyone who helps him. I think he assumed I did too and therefore I'd help him." She shudders. "I never want to see him – either of them – again."

She doesn't look very well while she talks about McNoble. For a moment I think she might faint, which given we are crossing the bottom end of Harley Street is probably the best place for it to happen. We walk on in silence until we reach the steps down to the Underground station. As we pause, she smiles weakly and then kisses me on the cheek. "I think you are an exceptional young man Harry. I know that you – you and your colleagues – will look after us, Brenda and me. Thank you."

I watch her disappear and, as I look up, I see Albert Pac-a-Mac stare at me from across the road. He's seen Zenda, too. As she disappears into the crowds coming out of the Underground entrance, Albert hurries down the other stairs and disappears as well. It occurs to me that he is going to follow her. God, of course! He's Jepson's man. If he and Rother are working together he may want to know where she goes. Maybe he trailed us from the office.

Feeling sick, I run down the stairs. At ticket office level there's a crowd of foreign students milling about, blocking both my view and the escalators. By the time I've forced my way through to the barrier there's no sign of Zenda or Mr Creepy, and since I have no ticket there's no chance the ticket inspector will let me though to try to warn her.

Defeated, I return to the street and run back to the office. Inside I dart into Mr Risely's room. The TV is off and he has disappeared. Gloria sticks her head round the door.

"He's gone to his club."

"How was he?"

"Somewhere between astonished and appalled."

"I don't suppose you know if we won?"

"Won what?" She's knows exactly. "There's a message for you lover boy." It's from Natalie. She's sorted out copies of the car adverts

321

and promises to drop them round soon. I hope 'soon' is 'really soon' as I want to get to the bottom of this before my nerves get the better of me.

I head for the stairs when Gloria says, "We did. Win that is. I'd make sure you catch the highlights if I were you."

I should be delirious. History must have been made, but somehow I've managed to dodge it. That sums up my life just now. Good things happen to other people. I feel miserable. All I do is let people down as the world drops me in the do-do.

Thursday, 23rd July 1981

Chapter Fifty-Three

In Which Brenda/Vera Announces She Plans to Grow Up

Dobbin has some good news today, which is pleasing because I've had a hell of a time worrying about Jepson, McNoble and Miles Tupps. Pac-a-Mac man called but I didn't have the courage to talk to him. Gloria is getting suspicious, but I've nothing to say. It's always the same question they want an answer to: have I found Sven's money yet?

Dobbins' news is about Hong Kong. While he has been passed over for the first wave of new blood, he is still being considered. He announces this to Brenda/Vera, Dina and me in the kitchen. Brenda/Vera, however, barely reacts. After trying to catch her eye, Dobbin says, "I hoped you'd be pleased. You can come with me. If you wanted."

She looks very serious. In fact, I realise she's not wearing any piercings; at least none we can see. Dina asks her the obvious. "You okay?"

"I realise I need a job. Talking to Mum, about her divorce and everything, I have to take my life more seriously."

I think I detect a sigh from Dobbin, possibly of relief.

"What about your music?" If Dina wants to do the world of hearing a favour, she'll stop pressing the subject.

"Oh, I'll keep going with that. I think I have a real talent for polemical lyrics."

If that means they eviscerate eardrums then, yes, she has that nailed.

"No, I need to finish my articles and qualify as a solicitor. Not that I want to practice but it looks good on my CV."

Dina says, "Will you go back to your old firm?"

"I'm not going back to those crooks and windbags. No, I'm transferring." She holds my gaze, letting her head tip to one side like she's appraising me.

There's something foul in the air that I can't place.

Dina is the one to ask. "Where?"

Brenda/Vera's glance tells me before she says it, she looks so guilty

"Clifford, Risely & Co."

She cannot mean it. She just can't.

Dina and Dobbin both goggle at me. I manage to squeak, "My firm? Are you serious?" Another thought wallops me like a fly on a windscreen. "No. I'm not asking. You can't ask me to. It wouldn't be fair."

"No, of course it wouldn't be fair. Mum asked Lucinda. She explained the sexual assaults and the problems with Dad and she agreed to take me on. I know Mum will be able to channel some work their way, too. That probably helped. It'll be fun, won't it?"

It will be many things but 'fun' isn't in the top 20.

Brenda/Vera has moved to sit on Dobbin's lap. In a stage whisper, she says in his ear, "And they have a vault. With all these deeds' boxes. Just imagine…"

Dobbin's expression tells us he is doing just that and, if I'm not much mistaken, wondering if asking her to go to Hong Kong with him is such a good idea. All those junks and Buddha statues and whatnot.

After Dobbin and Brenda/Vera disappear to their room to discuss their future, I tell Dina about my meeting with Marita and Natalie. "It was a spur of the moment thing, showing her that picture and her realizing she knew what those symbols meant. She was supposed to help us. You were right."

"Gosh. Thanks, kind sir. You don't mind about Vera, do you? It'll do her good, give her some focus."

I think of Dobbin's expression when he caught us in their room with her boobs on show when I asked her about McNoble. Yes, he'll be delighted.

"Do you think Natalie's meant to help, too?"

She wrinkles her nose. "Come off it. She's as flaky as an old scab. I doubt that woman is going to do anything that doesn't put her own interests first."

"That's not fair."

Before she can answer there's a knock at the front door. Jackie has rung and left a message with Mr Jones. He's very apologetic as it seems she left the message yesterday and he forgot to pass it on. "She said to tell you she's away on a course. In Essex. She'll be back at the weekend and will get in touch then."

It's the most cheering thing I've heard in ages.

Friday, 24th July 1981

Chapter Fifty-Four

How Harry Jousts with a Thistle and comes Away Unscratched

Detective Inspector Thistle sits back in his chair, a very tired expression on his face. He seems less bulbous than the last time we met. "You could make my life so easy, you know. Do you get that?"

I shake my head.

"By telling me what you know. Even if it makes no sense."

I want to. I really do. "You already know everything."

"Do I? And how do you know that if you don't tell me?" He rubs his temples, loose flesh puckering as he does so. "You seem to be the one person who connects two strange deaths, maybe even suspicious deaths. You drew up a new Will for Sir Penshaw who dies with your long-term girlfriend present in mysterious circumstances and with her apparently having an affair with Sir Penshaw's bi-sexual lover..."

"An affair?" I know that's what Lady Isabella said but I still don't believe it. "Has she said that's what happened?"

"No. She denies it. Her story is that Sean Latterly is in a relationship with Margaret Cloud."

Maggie. "Yes, that's what she told me."

"See? You didn't know I knew that; why assume I did?"

"Who do you believe?"

He holds up a hand, forestalling me. "There is evidence that Sir Penshaw was drugged before he was strangled. There is a suggestion he was playing some sort of sex game and it went wrong. It is clear his body was moved post mortem." He stares me down for a few moments. "Just like Sven Andersen's body was moved. A young man, whose Will you also wrote. After a joint meeting with both him and Sir Penshaw. And you are the beneficiary. Have you discovered what the estate comprises yet? What ill-gotten gains are included in the legacy you'll now no doubt enjoy?"

"No."

"Those pictures in his bungalow? They're clues, aren't they? The cars and the people? There are prints all over them which aren't the deceased's. Yours?" He raises an eyebrow.

"Yes, mine. And my sister Dina and a friend. A young girl. I'd rather not say."

He leans in very close. "And I would rather you did, Mr Spittle. Please?"

I shake my head. "She's irrelevant. And yes, I think they're a puzzle for me to solve and when I do, that's where any money will be found."

For a brief moment, the Inspector looks interested. "Why would he do that? Make it so hard?"

"I think he was basically an arsehole, Inspector. It's the only sensible explanation."

He very nearly smiles.

I add, "Will you charge Penny with anything?"

He looks at me with a pitying expression. I suppose I'm not sure if he's pitying me or himself. "There's a lot not making sense right now young man, and if I find you are wasting my time then I will find a way to make you regret it. All I'll say is people with influence in high places are pressing for a swift conclusion to this matter. That's suits me too."

Eventually he gets bored, I think, and tells me I can go. I do need to tell him what I know but I'm more than a little concerned that if I do I'll only muddy the waters. Not that they are actually that clear to me. As I'm leaving he says, "I spoke to a Mr Lewis. Another bloody lawyer. He told me I could trust you and that you were honest. You related?"

I shake my head.

"Hope not. I thought him a right creep. But he was helpful. Which is more than I can say about you. Now bugger off."

Saturday, 25th July 1981

Chapter Fifty-Five

Where Harry and Dina Have a Picnic

It's Saturday morning and the sun is struggling to make an appearance, much like my flatmates. At 10 there's a noise, the front door closes and Dina appears looking a wreck. "Have fun?"

"Have you tried Sambuca?"

"No, what is it?"

"It's a contraceptive. I thought Jan and I might have some fun but my stomach just—"

"You want toast?"

"Okay. No Jackie? Or you back with Penny? Or both?"

"I was in bed asleep by 10:30."

"Buffing the bishop then. Oh well."

"You know, for a sister who doesn't swear and claims she doesn't like to drink, you are one major hypocrite." While I make some toast, she nurses a cup of tea. "I rather hoped we might have another go at those pictures and the clues."

"Yeah okay." Then, "Imperial want me." Her voice suggests she is about to have root canal treatment but her grin is a pleasure to see.

I can't help smiling as I face her. "Good. You deserve it."

"Do I?" Her face slips to something more sombre. "Jan said I should be with George."

"Bit bloody presumptuous."

"No, he's right. I'm a Mum, H. I can't swan around anymore. I need to go home and get myself, me and Jim and George, sorted. After that I can do uni."

I put down the plate and push it at her. "You need to do something for yourself."

She eyes me in a way that screams 'one hell of a hangover.' "Get you. The feminist. I want to go. It'll be amazing, but will I regret it, not seeing him grow up I mean? He's at a really interesting phase now, just about to start school."

"Is this really about you and George or you and Jan?"

She picks up the toast and stuffs it in her mouth. Through the crumbs, she says, "I can cope with H the feminist but please don't try to be a psychologist as well. I'm going back home tomorrow and I will decide after that." She wipes her mouth and says, "What happened with the police?"

I tell her and we talk about the pictures.

In the end, we decide to go and get some pork pies and tomatoes and have a picnic in Battersea Park. It's good, spending time with her. I would miss her if she doesn't go to uni in London. I never thought I'd think that but it's a funny old world.

We've brought a blanket and Dina spreads out the pictures in the order they were on the wall.

She leaves a space for the missing one, which I keep forgetting about. We stare at them for a while before she says, "Those symbols, the ones Marita said were the 12 days of Christmas. See here, there's three hens and six geese. That either makes nine or 18. Do you think they refer to the diamonds in Frank's list?"

"Assuming they are diamonds. Do the numbers match?"

"No." She looks at me quizzically. "Though there is the missing picture. We don't know what symbols there might be there. And anyway, what if Sven got in more money than he expected when he did the pictures? There'd be some left over."

"Okay. Let's assume you're right. How do we know which type of diamond goes where? Frank's list specifies different sorts of diamond, but this code is just numbers not types."

Dina squints at the first photo. "I think the numbers are in different colours but we need the originals. I think that's how we distinguish which type of diamond goes where."

"Maybe you're right, not that it makes much sense. Do you think Sven intended Frank to give me that list?"

She flops back and closes her eyes. "I don't know. It's just guesswork, isn't it? We don't even know if that's what Sven meant. He's not mentioned diamonds anywhere, has he? It's only because of Frank's list. And we are still missing who number four is and we don't have the seventh picture either. And the code might not mean the number of diamonds anyway."

I open a can of warm beer. "What about the car adverts?"

"Maybe they are vintage cars he owned. Some are really valuable, aren't they?"

"Where are they, then? And these are all recent models, not vintage marques. Although his Porsche might be worth a few thousand."

She checks the picture of the Porsche and frowns. "See there, the guy in the passenger seat leaning forward like he's looking at his shoes? Isn't that you?"

"Me? Why would he put me in the Porsche?"

"No idea, but most of his pictures are done for a reason. If we could see the original of this advert we'd know if it had someone in the passenger seat or if this is meant to be you."

"He did leave the Porsche keys in the flat, although Miles has it now so it's not like I can go and check it over, is it?"

A large drop of rain hits Dina square on the forehead making her sit up and glare at me.

When she realises it's not me being childish she bursts into laughter. "Come on. Let's get back. I promised Jan we'd have one more night before I go home and he wants to take me to this club in Neasden. Sounds really dodgy."

"Perfect. You sure he's not working?"

Chapter Fifty-Six

Harry and Dina Have Guests and Go to a Museum

We are still laughing when we enter the flat. In seconds, our laughter dies away as a small hardheaded bundle crashes into Dina. "George? What are you doing here?" She bends down and kisses him as he squirms about, trying to climb over her.

A familiar voice says, "I brought him." Dad. "Nice place, Harry."

"How'd you get in?"

"Your flatmate let me in. Made me tea, too." My Father is short and mostly round. At times of stress he seems to wobble a lot. That and his glass eye, which has a habit of slipping out of place, making him look like something out of a Hammer horror film. Today there's something of the jelloid about him, so shiny and wobbly does he appear.

"Gary?"

"No. Erm, Wanda?" He looks confused and glances over his shoulder towards the kitchen.

"Zenda? Or Vera? Or Brenda?"

"Brenda! Lovely girl."

I try to imagine how the spiky haired pincushion meets Dad's idea of a 'lovely girl' when a strange apparition appears. The pale face and raw spot on her nose where once was a safety pin tells me it's Brenda/Vera; her grey suit and mid-brown hair says 'stranger.' "Hi. What do you think? Will Clifford Thingy be okay with this?"

I snort out a laugh. "They'll be ecstatic. Not sure how Groin and the boys will take it."

Dad looks confused. "Groin?"

I walk forward and tap him on the shoulder. A manly hug seems a step too far. "Let's have a cup of tea and you can explain this surprise visit. Just up for the day?"

It transpires he's here to leave George with his Mother. Dina barely registers what Dad is saying, playing with her son on the sitting room floor. It seems he's is obsessed with trains and spends most of the time emulating his hero, Gordon the Big Engine from his Thomas the Tank Engine books, as he hurtles around the room and crawls behind the sofa peeping and tooting randomly. Frankly just watching him is exhausting. I never want children.

Mum has had a panic attack and is in Lymington Hospital because the doctors want to do some tests on her heart. When I press him, he says it's routine observations and, to be fair, he doesn't appear to be worried. If Mum really was ill he'd be falling apart.

Jim has shingles and his Mother insisted Dad took George to look after him while she coped with her ill son. As far as I can understand, Jim is not a model patient. Mrs Ohja offered to help, but Dad thought Dina would want to look after her son now she has her university place sorted out. Brenda/Vera also seems besotted.

Someone suggests we go out and someone else suggests the Natural History Museum, which is where the four of us head off to leaving Brenda/Vera to cook supper for us. As we are about to leave, she says, "You will stay Arthur, won't you? Dina can sleep in my bed and I'll crash on the sofa."

This is an awful idea, but all I can offer is, "What about Dobbin?"

She smiles, a real know-all smile. "On a course in Birmingham. It's only for the night."

I suppose I should be grateful that she doesn't offer to share with Dad, but maybe she's ticked the 'dull old git' box already.

The Natural History Museum takes me back to school trips of interminable coach journeys, disappointing sandwiches – mine lacked any of the pizazz of my contemporaries – and someone vomiting on the way home. I remember nothing of the museum itself and, actually, it's great. Dad keeps holding us back, moving at a snail's pace while he reads the small cards in the glass cabinets. Dina is constantly trying to marshal George as one might a cat who needs to go to the vet. Finally, Dad sees a sign saying 'Lepidoptera' and tells us he has to go and 'have a gander.'

"You'd better stay with him, H. I'll meet you by the entrance in an hour. Okay?"

I catch him by a cabinet full of moths. Death's-head hawk moths. "You know these are the only moths to make a noise. Like a mouse. A squeak."

"Yes Dad."

I thinking of the gift Sven gave him when he adds, "I'd love to hear that. A chap at the Wheel Inn says he's heard someone found a caterpillar in a potato field over near Milford. Had one when I was a child. I'd give my right arm…" He shakes his head sadly. "Not going to happen, is it? Asoka would like to see it too, I'm sure."

I used to love listening to Dad go on about his butterfly and moth collecting days, but it's getting a bit dull and I rather wish I'd left him to his own devices and joined George and Dina to look at the dinosaurs. "You should ask this chap, see if he'll let you hear it."

"That wouldn't do. No, can't do that. I barely know him."

He is exasperating. Never says what he wants to the people he should ask.

He peers closely at some other large moths as he says, "Do you know anything about the money for the work on the house? The garage sold last week but there's a hold up releasing the proceeds and your Aunt Petunia told me you knew why. I told her that was very unlikely." He manages to glance at me quickly, then away. "You don't, do you?"

"A hold up? Who says?"

"Lewis. The solicitor. I'm not the client and he won't tell me and, what with Veronica being ill, I'm having to rely on Petunia for information. Well, you can imagine how easy that is."

"When did Mum have her panic attack? It wasn't after the sale went through, was it?"

"Same day. She went into Lymington to do some shopping and sign some papers and next thing I know she's in the hospital."

"If you like I'll call Mr Lewis on Monday. He might listen to me."

"Why would…?" Dad stops. "No. Right. That would be great. Gosh, I never realised how useful having a lawyer was going to be. In the family, you know?" He moves like he's about to do something awfully demonstrative and then checks himself, saying, "We are so proud of you, you know?"

That amount of emotion is bound to take a toll and he wanders off quickly, dabbing his nose. I let him get ahead, dragging my feet and pondering if Mr Lewis has some sort of arrangement with Jepson to repay the money he lent Mum. It would explain any delays and Mum's need to avoid confronting Dad.

Chapter Fifty-Seven

Where Harry Is Pressed to Babysit and Asks an Awkward Question

Dad announces he is meeting an old friend for a drink and leaves us to go home. Back at the flat Dina drops her own little bombshell. "The plans have changed. Jan's taking me to the Police Benevolent Fund Ball."

"You what? What about Neasden?"

"It is in Neasden, just not that dodgy. Look, I know Jackie's not about and this is my last chance for some fun. It's why I planned to go home tomorrow, so I could have this date, kind of end it with him gently. I thought Dad would babysit, you know, when he appeared but… can't you?"

"I am not babysitting."

"I will." It's Brenda/Vera, emerging from her room, blankets in her arms. "I've made the bed for your Dad. Are you going out, Di?"

"With Jan. I think I'm breaking it off with him."

"Nooooo, don't do that. He's so nice and you make a lovely couple. If Harry is staying in then we can babysit together." She looks at me. "You can tell me about the other people at Clitoris, Arsehole & Co. I heard that Jeremy is really sexy."

It's a bloody conspiracy. But to be fair, Brenda/Vera is amazing with George. He's bored with trains and turns to cars, which makes me think of Sven's pictures. I bring out the photos and lay them on the table with the details Natalie gave me over the phone. I really need to see the originals. The Porsche catches my eye once more. Is that man in the front seat meant to be me, as Dina says? Why would he put me in a Porsche? Bored, I turn to my nephew. "Okay George, which one is your favourite?"

He mulls the question before pointing at the Audi. "That one. I like the colour Uncle Harry."

"And which one should Vera like?"

"That one. It's like her hair." The Mini is indeed a nutty brown colour.

Brenda/Vera peers at them. "Who drew these?"

"The guy who died. Sven Andersen."

"I heard you and Dina talking about him. He was a good friend, was he?"

"Better than I realised I think. I'm his executor."

"Goodness. I never thought about a Will. I don't have enough to warrant it. Why did he make one?"

"His Father left him a lot. I'm meant to find out how much."

"Have you found anything then?"

"Bugger all."

"Are these his Father's cars? You'd need a lot of garage space for that lot."

I have the most enormous urge to kiss her. My smile must give myself away.

"What is it? Harry, you've gone weird."

"Vera, you are a genius."

I'm stopped by the doorbell. As George is excited and wants to answer it, we head down the stairs to open the door to the block. It's Natalie, utterly drenched. "Who's this?" she says.

"This is George. My nephew. George, this is a good friend. Natalie."

"Is she your girlfriend?" the boy asks.

She holds my gaze and then smiles. I say to George. "Once upon a time I thought, maybe, but she's now found someone else."

Natalie squats down and looks at the thoughtful George. "But who's to say what the future holds, eh?"

Damn her, why did she need to say that?

She stands and steps inside. "Can I come in? I've found something you'll want to see."

In the flat, Brenda/Vera decides to take George off for a bath while I make Natalie and me some coffee. When I put the cups down on the kitchen table she pulls out a Filofax, which she covers with a hand. "I told you I'd got Miles' address book and I'd copy it. It's full of family and friends who I know. But he left this behind today – he rushed out for some reason after getting a call and rang me an hour ago to say he's off to Leeds for something or other." She opens it at the back.

Under a section headed 'Club' there is a list of names and a series of numbers, one crossed through and replaced by another. It's pretty obvious it represents money owed. As I scan the list I see Jeremy's name, Jepson and Reginald Rother. No surprises there. There's Sean and Izzy too, but no Sir Pen. Sven is there, although there's no number against his name. In all there are about 30 people, some famous celebrities like the actress Sonia Masden and the Tory MP Reckitt O'Doyle. Other names that ring some bells are Piotr Princip, the business tycoon, and Bernard Causeway, the theatre owner.

"Do you know who was there on the night Sven died?"

Natalie frowns, running her fingers down the list. "Miles, Stephen and his Father. A friend of Miles call Julian. Maybe a dozen others. The Tory chap, that actress and another couple of theatre people. Oh, and Princip and his wife."

"What about the lawyer you mentioned? Is he one of these?"

"I can't remember he's called. Anyway, they all used pseudonyms if they wanted to and only Miles knew their real names."

It occurs to me Brenda/Vera may have a picture of her Father but she pulls a face when I ask. Then she brightens. "Mum might. I'll pop down and ask."

Minutes later Brenda/Vera reappears. "Those two are watching Des O'Connor. They'll have to get married if that carries on. Here," she hands me a picture showing Zenda standing next to a ruddy-faced man, who is holding a fishing rod with a large catch on it. He is smiling broadly while she looks ill at ease. He looks nothing like the articled clerk-eating monster of the Bear Garden but Natalie instantly nods.

"Yes, that's him, the one who came with Mr Jepson that Friday night. He's..." She frowns in concentration. "Rupert. Yes: Rupert."

Brenda/Vera, who has gone from looking relaxed to perplexed, says to me, "Do you mean Claude's Father?" She takes in Natalie's confusion.

"She means Stephen's Dad."

"You know him?" Natalie says. "How come?"

When Brenda/Vera doesn't answer Natalie looks at me, as confused as Brenda/Vera a moment before. I really don't have the energy to explain. "I'll fill you in later." Instead I say to Brenda/Vera, "We are trying to solve a puzzle and one part seems to be that Jepson is involved in an illegal gambling club in which Natalie's husband has some sort of financial interest." I pause. "Your Mum told me your step-Father gambles. Seems he goes to this club."

Immediately she is serious. "Have you told Mum? About this club?"

"She knows they gamble together. It was her who told me. But maybe she doesn't know exactly what was involved."

338

She surprises me by grasping my hand. "Promise me you'll not tell Mum. Or at least let me tell her what you find. Please? She's very fragile just now. With the divorce and everything."

I nod. I get that.

Natalie waits until Brenda/Vera takes George for a wee. "Explain this link. It's too weird, her knowing Charlie and being related to this Rupert."

"Reggie. Reggie Rother. Zenda, Vera's Mum, is Monica Jepson's sister. I think Rother put some money into Miles' club when Jepson owned it."

"You are quite the detective, aren't you?"

I try to smile. I think she's about to give me a hug, but she slaps her forehead in a cartoonish gesture. "What a lummock. I've forgotten those adverts again. Next time, really. Do you think they're important?"

In a way, I'm glad she hasn't got them and I don't need to explain what they might mean. I've enough going on what with processing the news about Master Rother being involved in some way. If I'm totally honest, when everyone thought me useless and left me alone life was much simpler. Sadly, I know I don't have that luxury any more.

With yet another sigh I ask, "I need to find out if one or two of the others on Miles' list were there the night Sven took ill. Are you free tomorrow to be my super-sleuthing sidekick? You'll need to look smart."

"Why does it matter who was there? If he died from a dodgy ticker?"

I sigh, so deeply it must come across like I want to asphyxiate myself. "I don't know. It just seems like there was something about that final argument that's important. If I can unpick what it was actually about…" I shrug. "You really didn't hear anything?"

There's something in her expression, something like a deep pain that passes over her face. "He made…" She cuts herself off.

"Yes? Who made what? Someone made you do something?"

It's just a guess but her look of horror – no, terror – makes me feel sick.

"You know?"

"Know what?"

Brenda/Vera's head appears. "You want tea? George wants to make you some."

Natalie uses the interruption to wander over to the window.

When Brenda/Vera disappears to the kitchen she turns and faces me. "No, don't ask. I want to help so what are we going to do?"

"Let's meet at Oxford Circus about 10 tomorrow."

"Yes, Cap'n Harry. Now let's see how good George's tea-making skills are."

Sunday, 26th July 1981

Chapter Fifty-Eight

In Which Harry Hides in a Doorway and Looks at Some Photos

Natalie is wearing a white dress that clings to her with a zip up the front revealing lots of her legs and a generous scoop of décolletage. Her hair is loose and pushed off her face – recently she's worn it in a ponytail. She looks fabulous and is attracting a lot of stares. When she sees me, she does a twirl and then giggles. "You like?"

"You look amazing. But why?"

"You said look smart." She does an extraordinary thing. She nuzzles my neck, breathing on it hard and setting off a chain reaction of goosebumps. "And I wanted to impress my boss." When she stands back, she is flushed, as, I imagine, am I.

Before she has a chance to say anything else I turn around and head up Regent Street towards the BBC Broadcasting House at Portland Place. I need to clear my head. She's wearing heels; as she starts to trot I realise I need to slow down. When we are in step, she slips her hand through the crook of my arm and eases in close. This has all the makings of something very awkward.

To cover my increasing uncertainty, I begin to explain the plan. "First, we are going to a mansion block where Lady Isabella Grimsdale lives. With luck we'll see her and her assistant Mrs Soderberg. You know Izzy, don't you?"

She nods. "I know her from the club, now I've seen the code. And from the papers, of course."

"I'd like to see if you recognise Mrs Soderberg too. She's her assistant, her confidante as she calls it. We'll need to try to stay out of sight." I glance across at her eye-popping profile. "If we can."

Natalie is grinning. "How exciting!"

I smile back. "Did you remember the adverts?"

She stops abruptly and squeezes her eyes shut. "Shit. Sorry. Next time, really. I know it's important."

I try to look like it's okay, but I'm beginning to wonder if this is deliberate. Is she really working for Miles? I don't want to be suspicious, but it's difficult not to be.

There isn't a café, so we cross the road to stand in the entrance to another smart block of expensive flats. I can see a liveried commissionaire through the glass, but he doesn't seem to have noticed us. Natalie leans on my shoulder as I try to work out which are the windows to Izzy's apartment. I jump as Natalie kisses my ear. We are now facing each other. "Natalie…?"

She looks both excited and worried. "Vera thinks you're amazing."

"No she doesn't."

"She does and so do I. When I got back home – it was like a light going on – that I've been stupid for so long. When we had that moment, on that swing, back in Sven's garden, I wanted you then, Harry. And—"

"No, stop. Wait. That was five years ago. We were smashed and as high as spacemen. This is your rejection of Miles talking…"

She steps forward, slipping her hands round my neck. "No, it isn't. Like in that cupboard, when you squeezed here." She puts a hand on her left breast. "I thought I'd burst."

"You said you wanted to punch me."

"That was for Penny. I wanted to make love."

I goggle at her. This isn't how today is meant to work at all.

"You and Penny are over and I've seen who you really are at last. Can't we…?"

For years I have wanted this woman, desired her in ways that have made me look a complete chump. And now, when she's sober and sexy and trying to seduce me, I know it's not what I want or either of us need. Oh God, I hate being a grown up.

As her lips seek out mine I glance to the left. Never did I expect the Lady Isabella to save me. I whisper, "You need to look to your left as you kiss me. It's Lady Isabella Grimsdale. Just make sure it's the same person as you've seen in the club."

She stops and glances left and as she does I kiss her. It feels good to both take charge and kiss Natalie. It is also good that she's focusing on Isabella and not the kiss because her tongue stays sheaved.

After a moment, she pulls back. "Yes, that's her. That's Janet at the club. And the man she was with, John, that would be her brother? Silver haired. What Dad would have called 'dapper.' She knew Sven, too. I—"

"Shit." I lurch in for another kiss but she looks startled and pulls away. I grab her and pull her to me, just about managing to say before locking lips, "The other woman, the one on the steps, what about her?"

Natalie moves her head. "She's watching us. I think she recognises me. I don't know about the club – I've not seen her there – but she came to the flat once and had an argument with Miles. I thought it must be to do with the estate agency, not that I asked. Harry, she's following the other one. What shall we do?"

We are still pressed tightly against each other. I look at her gorgeous brown eyes and lean away. "This."

We kiss. Properly, like two consenting adults and, honestly, we could have continued if the commissionaire hadn't flown out of the marbled entrance and shouted at us to 'clear orf, pronto, yer dirty scumbags.'

We begin to run towards Regents Park in the opposite direction to where Izzy and Mrs Soderberg went. We are laughing and relieved and after a couple of hundred yards we stop, out of breath. She says, "Where shall we go? To the park? We could find somewhere, somewhere quiet…"

I pull her to me and we kiss again, quickly. "No. That's it. You know it and so do I. Neither of us needs this right now. Yes, I'd love to go and roll around with you in that amazing dress, but first I need you to meet someone and second I need you watching Miles. If we are going to sort out this mess, if we are going to help Penny…"

The mention of Penny's name makes Natalie step back, disappointment on her face. "I thought—"

"I have no idea about Penny and me Natalie. My head says it's over. My heart isn't so sure. Anyway, I have another girlfriend just now and I want to see where that goes. But if that flops, as well it might, and if you feel the same way in a few weeks, well, never say never – right?"

I'm rather pleased at how mature that sounds, but her face tells me I have utterly misjudged her. "Third on the list? You expect me to be third on your bloody list? Second fucking reserve if you can't get inside the pants of this woman and Penny won't have you back? In your bloody dreams, matey-boy."

One minute she looks like she's going to thump me and then she laughs and I laugh. "I've always misjudged us, haven't I?" I say.

"Too right you have. That was it. You missed it." She lurches forward and hugs me and then kisses me slowly, savouring the moment. Or so I think. "You're a crap kisser. If we do get together there'll be a few lessons. Come on, who is it I'm to meet? I hope they appreciate the effort I've made."

"Oh, he might but I'm pretty sure his girlfriend won't."

It takes us 30 minutes to reach Wembley on the tube and find the rather tired-looking 1930s house. I suppose I assumed all partners would live in the sort of posh flat occupied by Mr Risely or the country estate that Lucinda owns, but Jeremy is still a novice and working his way up the property ladder. As I approach the door, noting his car is a red Renault and in need of a wash, I feel very nervous. To cover it, I say, "Jeremy Panther is a partner in the firm I work for. He's been Sir Penshaw's lawyer for a while and I think he's part of the gambling club, probably introduced by Lady Isabella. He certainly knows Stephen so I think that's a link too. And he's on Miles' list."

Natalie shrugs. "His name doesn't ring a bell. Do you think this is wise? I mean, won't he sack you or something? If he knows you know?"

"I thought about that, but I think it's unlikely. And I think him knowing I know something he'd rather I didn't know might help us somewhere down the line."

I've run through a lot of possible scenarios in my head, but one I've not imagined happens. We ring the bell and see Jeremy approach through the frosted glass.

He opens the door and sees me. He says, "Harry, what—?" And then he sees Natalie whose eyes are widening in surprise.

He says, "You?" and goes very pale, but he doesn't faint. He then gets very angry and makes to grab her.

I'm in the way and stop him. His girlfriend Dale then appears wanting to know what's going on.

He manages to calm down and says that this is a client who needs urgent advice, which is why I'm with Natalie and we are shown to his study in no time, where he shuts the door. He looks very ill.

"What's she doing here?"

I look from one to the other. He looks fit to burst and Natalie is pale, red spots on her cheeks, jaw clenched tight. "You know each other?"

"Of course we bloody do. She's married to that crook Tupps."

"Was he there that night?" This from me to Natalie.

She stares at me. "How could you?" She whispers and then starts crying.

"Natalie?" I go to comfort her, but she waves me back and walks to the far side of the room, keeping her distance from both of us.

When she speaks, her voice cracks. "He was there all right. With a girl. Not the one downstairs. Large boobs hanging out everywhere." She narrows her eyes at him, clear loathing in her expression. "Gloria? I think that was her name."

"Bloody ridiculous." But from the way he won't meet her gaze I bet he did take our receptionist. She'd love it, too.

I think this is the first time I've really understood how feeble Jeremy is. "Why didn't you say you knew Sven? When you found out we were executors?"

"Why should I say? It wasn't like I had a choice."

"When I drew up his Will, I'm sure he didn't know who you were. Or he hid it well if he did."

Natalie has almost slipped behind the curtains, her arms folded tight across her chest. "Everyone used pseudonyms. He goes by the name Philip."

I can't help stifling a laugh. "Not Philip Risely?"

"Yes, that's it."

Jeremy looks annoyed.

"Do you owe Miles much?"

"Mind your own business."

"Funnily enough, it is my business. Sven inherited the club, or maybe a debt on it that I think he planned to give to a nasty piece of work. I suspect Sven acted as a brake on Miles being robust in pursuing what you owe but, if Miles thinks he's free of that control, well he or this other party might not be so forgiving."

Jeremy looks worse, if anything. Just then Dale appears, carrying a tray of cups. "Anyone want… Jeremy?"

As he registers Dale, Jeremy goes from pale to translucent with a hint of avocado and rushes out. Dale watches him until he disappears through a door then turns to me. "Is this about that cesspit?"

"Cesspit?"

"He's worried silly about it. Apparently, he missed it when doing the searches and the client sort of broke it when he got a contractor in to landscape the garden. It turns out it was both illegal and full of heroin."

"He's not mentioned it. But all he needs to do is tell the police and…"

"No, well, it's a bit late for that. He said he told the client to sell the heroin. He meant it as a joke, but the client took him at his word and he's now being pursued by some unsavoury crooks as well as the police. You won't say I mentioned it, will you?"

"No. No, of course. It's much more, erm, mundane. Really. Maybe he ate something. He doesn't look very well. We should go maybe?"

Dale is really sweet. She insists we stay and drink the coffee. After some desultory chat, she leaves us. As soon as we're outside, Natalie turns and slaps me. "You utter bastard."

I take a leap back and massage my burning cheek. "What was that for?"

"Oh, don't be naïve. You know full well. You and Stephen and Miles, you're all the same."

"Really, I don't know—"

But she's not listening and turns and hurries away. I race after her. Despite the heels it takes me two streets to catch her up and grab her arm. "Listen to me." She stands, her body language suggesting she's run out of fight but her expression is full of hatred. "That kiss. That wasn't fake. It... I... it's not the time but it so easily could be. I'd never want to hurt you though. Whatever Jeremy or Miles or Stephen has done to you, I'm not involved. I want to help. That's all." I let go of her arm and my voice drops. "That's all I've ever wanted."

She shudders as if with cold and then sits down hard on a garden wall. Behind her a hydrangea creates a sort of bluey backdrop. "That man. He's being..." She stops and starts again. "Your friend is being blackmailed by Miles."

I frown. "For what he owes?"

She shakes her head.

"It can't be for going to the club, surely. I mean it may be a bit dodgy but—"

The shaking stops me again. She swallows. "There are photos."

"Photos? What sort of photos?"

Another shake. "You and Jeremy?"

A nod. I suppose I can guess.

"He's not the only one. Janet too."

It takes a moment to remember. "Lady Isabella?"

A nod.

"With Jeremy?"

Natalie looks at me, astonished. "No. With me."

"You?"

"Me and some friend of hers. She brought him a couple of times."

"What was his name?"

"I don't know, do I? They were all fake. I think he may have been an actor or in the theatre business or something. He was so pissed, though. I thought you knew. Miles made me, told me I had to. Or he'd… they're awful. Degrading. At least I wore a mask with him. Your work colleague. Philip or whatever his name is. Oh God…" She holds her stomach, turns and throws up into the bush. I hope to God there's no one gardening.

"Christ." A thought occurs to me, a stupid, half-baked one but… "You stay here."

She doesn't look like she could move anyway. "Where are you going?"

"Won't be a mo." I turn away and then turn back. "Does he know it was you? In the photo? If you had a mask on? Or just that you were at the club?"

She shrugs. Maybe it doesn't matter.

***

I manage to make Dale understand it's important I speak to Jeremy, who's shut himself in his office.

"Jeremy, we need to talk," I say through the door.

"Go away."

"Now. About Natalie. And those photos."

He yanks the door open seconds later, dragging me inside. "Keep you bloody voice down, you moron."

"How long has Miles been blackmailing you?"

"What?"

"Natalie told me about Miles' blackmail. About the photos. How long?"

"I bet she loved that. Bitch."

"Of course she didn't. She was upset."

"Guilty more like."

"Guilty? She was made to do it."

"Oh, fuck off Harry. She's part of it."

"Do you have them?"

"What?"

"The photos."

"No"

"But you know what they show?"

If he rubs his face any harder it'll peel off. "He told me he had something important to show me. I couldn't believe them."

"What do they show?"

"You are sick, aren't you? Really sick."

He begins to reach for the door, like he's going to show me out but I push past him and stand with my back to it. "I think I can maybe make this go away. Don't ask how, you really don't want to know. But I need to know, or at least pretend I know what they show."

He doesn't look convinced.

"What's the harm? I know about them, so knowing a bit of the detail will..." I stop as he turns to a desk.

"Why should I believe you?"

"Miles expects me to pay him some money he says Sven Andersen owed him. There's no evidence though, nothing in writing so I could just ignore him, tell him where... what?"

He looks animated all of a sudden. "I'm an executor, aren't I? I could pay him, get the negatives. I don't need you—"

"We haven't got probate yet. And we don't know if there's any money in the estate."

He looks astonished and then sags. "You're not trying to hide the assets from me? Are you?"

I'm feeling on uncertain ground, especially arguing with a partner. Fortunately Jeremy's ignorance of the law is as deep and wide as mine.

"Oh, very well, I don't want anything to do with these crooked friends of yours. If you can trade the photos for some dodgy money, then great. It's your career that's on the line."

"I think it's possible. Many things are possible." Including my body ending up as part of some bridge crossing the new M25. Obviously I only think this last piece. I mean I don't want to worry him.

He looks like he'd happily operate on me with his paperknife, but in the end he unlocks the right-hand desk drawer and dumps a brown envelope on the table. "They left me this one. No faces, nothing to show it's me or her."

I do my best not to google at the graphic image. In the shot a masked naked woman is giving a man a blowjob. She's wearing a collar and he's holding a chain attached to it. There's something on the table next to where he's standing. I'm no expert but it looks like a little mirror with a line of white powder on it.

"The rest are clearly me."

"Didn't you think about the police? Miles' prints would be on the envelope. Maybe?"

The old, supercilious Jeremy returns. "Are you mental? First I doubt they would be and this is a dirty picture but it's not clear it's me, is it? It's not illegal, what's going on. But if the images got out Dale would leave me, the firm would sack me because I'd have to say where I was and how I went there in the first place and that would have dumped a client, a very important client, in the mire."

"Sir Pen?"

"Izzy. And it's an illegal club, Harry. The Law Society might remove me from the Roll if it got out. And then there's that bloody powder."

"You took cocaine?"

He glares at me. "Yes, I did a line or two. So?"

"Can I keep this?"

"You won't tell Dale?"

"No, of course I won't." No, of course she mustn't know. I mean, gambling and cocaine are okay in moderation, I suppose, but having your girlfriend knowing you've had a blowjob from a strange woman who you're holding like a dog is a step too far.

He sits on a stool, leaning forwards until his head is nearly on his knees. "Christ," he moans. Jeremy's pose is very familiar. He uses it in the office when something goes wrong.

"Were you drugged?"

"I told you, I did a line."

"I mean doped. How do you know it was Natalie?"

His look is like he's been caught out in a lie. He's not the victim here. "You knew it was her, didn't you? Did Miles offer her to you?"

"It wasn't like that."

"She wanted to be held like a bloody animal, did she? She asked for that, did she?" I slip the picture into my inside pocket; all I want to do is get out. I turn for the door.

He doesn't move but stops me with a question. "Did Izzy put you up to this?"

"Izzy?"

"She took me the first time, said I had to go if I wanted to be her lawyer and then this happens. This has all the hallmarks of an Izzy Grimsdale trap."

350

"No, not that I know." I hesitate a fraction before adding, "She's being blackmailed too. Compromising pictures."

"Really? How do you know this? You seen the pictures of her, have you? And what would 'compromise' a woman with her reputation?"

I think about Natalie's expression. "I'm sure she's also being targeted. Probably a covert filming like you."

He moves to the window and looks outside. "When she asked me to work for her businesses, I thought I'd really made it. After Martindale handed over to me. But she's a total shit." He throws his hands in the air. "Oh, what does it matter? I'm fucked any which way, aren't I? God, I wish I'd never joined Clifford Risely." He rubs his eyes like he's falling asleep, an impression he compounds by yawning. "When the old man bequeathed me his practice – everyone assumed it would go to Philip and Lucinda – I thought it was because he saw me as a worthy successor. Ha! It's because he needed me to get him off her hook. He encouraged me to go to the club – 'good client relationship building' he called it. I was so bloody naïve. He told me about everything a week before he retired. By then I had debts at the club and had been director of her shell companies for ages – my name was all over all sorts of transactions that turned out to be as dodgy as your friend's. Having Tupps yank my chain to ease off hers would be typical of her. She pays well, but we both know I can no more tell her I won't act as I can see my arsehole. She's got her claws into you now, hasn't she?"

"She said… she said she wanted me to act for her…"

"Yes, well, all bollocks I'm afraid. You were suckered by her flattery, just like me. You're no better. I expect having you suckered in was just extra leverage. Did you set up a company for her?"

"Yes. One of her Izzy Ventures." I'm feeling a bit sick now.

"And you're still a director even though she says she'll take over, only she's been too busy?"

"It's an investment in a hairdresser's business with Sir Pen's, erm, partner. Sean."

"Sean Latterly? Yeah, she took him to the club a couple of times. Total little wanker but there's no accounting for taste. You want to resign PDQ."

I'm wondering how this is happening to me. He actually looks sympathetic. "I know you think I'm a plonker and a shit and disloyal and useless and I am all of those things, but I don't have much choice, do I? It's what happens in small firms. It's how we keep afloat. Turning a blind eye. Why don't you go and find your friend? If, and it's a big if, you can get hold of the prints and negatives of those pictures then great. And if you can sort out Izzy, too, then you might even get her to let you go free. But I'll believe it when I see it."

I leave him dabbing his forehead like a Victorian heroine. The last person I need to see is Dale and I manage to leave quickly without her catching me.

Natalie is where I left her. When she sees me we just stand and head for the tube. She doesn't want to talk and I need to get my head straight. First, Izzy knew Sven. Sven met Jeremy and Reggie at Miles' club, but didn't know their real names. Maybe he never really appreciated how everyone fitted together. So when he threatened Miles with closure a lot of other carefully laid plans started to come apart. Second, it's not clear if Sven met Sir Pen before they encountered each other in my office but it's possible. In any event they really didn't know each other. And third, it is probably true that Izzy had some business dealings with the Andersen Empire. It would make sense if she knew Robin Andersen, too.

A thought occurs to me. Sir Pen and Izzy owned a company that dealt in commodities and the directors came from Antwerp, Belgium, alongside Izzy. And Antwerp is the capital of the diamond trade. Which may be where Andersen bought and sold the gems Frank dealt with. Suddenly seeing Frank again becomes very important; although if he is going senile, it'll probably be about as useful as asking Dobbin to do the shopping. He'd be just as confused. Something in that wink he gave me when we last met suggests I may have more hope there than I have a right to expect.

And then there's these bloody photos. "Natalie, can I ask you something?"

She says nothing, indicates nothing, just keeps walking with her head down.

"Jeremy showed me a photo of a woman in a mask being held by a chain on a collar, and she was giving him… satisfying him. There was a line of coke in the picture too. Were the ones with Lady Isabella the same? You and her and the friend? Was she, Isabella, giving him… doing…?" Why is the word 'blowjob' so hard to say?

She stops and glares at me. "Yes. So? You think I wanted to? Like I had a choice?"

"No, I don't."

"Why does it matter? Does it turn you on?"

A little, yes, not that I say it. "No, of course not. But if I'm going to get the pictures and screw Miles, I need to know what they show."

I think she nods but she doesn't say anything.

"Do you know who the friend is? Is it Sean Latterly?"

A shrug. "Who?"

"I'll try to find a picture of him."

Another shrug. "I don't care, Harry. I really don't." At the tube station, she manages to look at me. "I'm going home. Please don't follow."

I pull her into a hug. She doesn't reciprocate. Close in I whisper, "I will fix him, Miles. Somehow. I will get him out of your life."

She looks at me briefly before heading for the gate. It's pretty plain she doesn't believe me for a minute, but then again neither do I.

Monday, 27th July 1981

Chapter Fifty-Nine

Where Harry and Natalie Go for a Drive

I don't usually have problems sleeping, but then I'm not usually thinking about thugs and blackmail and diamonds at bedtime. If I've managed 20 minutes' kip in aggregate by the time it's getting light, I've been lucky. I start sweating as soon as I'm awake and I go and sit in the lounge and stare out at the dawn. Things are getting really serious. A blackbird flies onto the wrought iron railings around the little balcony. I don't want to have anything more to do with Sven and Mikes and all the rest of them, but I can't see a way out of it. I need someone to start telling me the truth. That's when I realise I must go and see Frank. He gave me the list of numbers that I think are diamonds. He's the only one who's offered anything other than Sven's stupid cryptic clues. He is the only person who seems to know anything about what Sven has done. Or at least – because I still think both Marita and possibly Natalie know more than they are letting on, and McNoble certainly does – he's the only one volunteering anything that might help me.

At seven, I make myself breakfast: a lettuce and ketchup sandwich – floppy but surprisingly flavoursome – which I'm halfway through when two things happen at once. First the front door bell goes; I'm on my way to answer it when George appears from Tim's room at high speed.

"Rats! There's rats! On Mummy's bed!"

Shit. I'd forgotten about the mouse. I assumed it had packed its bags. "George, go and wake Uncle Gary and ask him to answer the door. I'll go and have a word with Mummy."

Dina is in bed, staring at the bedcover and looking furious. "Bloody thing gave me a fright. It ran across my pillow and into my hair. We need to get rid of it before Vera has a heart attack."

Outside the room, I hear George talking to someone – I hope it's not Brenda/Vera. Seconds later the door bangs open and he runs past me and jumps on the bed causing Dina to swear then try to pacify a now distraught George. I try not to laugh.

"Where did it go?"

"I don't bloody know. Just look behind the wardrobe and I'll check under here."

As luck would have it, Dina has just tipped up the mattress and I've managed to walk the wardrobe away from the wall when the bedroom door opens. Brenda/Vera, with Natalie behind her, fills the frame.

Brenda/Vera speaks first. "Is that mouse back?"

Dina tries to bury herself inside the divan. "Why'd you say that?"

"Because George told me."

I peek out from around the now tottering wardrobe. "We'll get rid of it."

"Good because if I see it, I really WILL NOT be responsible for either my language or my actions." Then she stalks out, much to my relief.

Natalie eases her way into the room. "You look like you're having fun. Want a hand?"

Dina drops the mattress. "Stuff it. We need to get a trap. Come on, George. Time for a wee-wee and breakfast." She drags him away before he can begin some over-exuberant trampolining on the bed.

Alone in Tim's room, Natalie digs into her shoulder bag. "I brought these, finally. The car adverts you asked for."

"Great. Thanks. You're a bit out of your way, aren't you? You could have let me know and I'd have come to your office."

"I…" She turns away. "Sorry about yesterday, H. I was being silly."

"No, you weren't. I mean, bloody hell, given what Miles did…"

"I wasn't forced, okay? I knew what I was doing."

I take a moment and shut the door. "You knew you were being photographed?"

She closes her eyes. "This is hard, okay?" She forces herself to look at me. "I knew Miles was watching. He likes to watch. After it… we…" She breathes out a stuttering breath. "It was a sort of game, just a blowjob. That's what I thought at the time."

Like that's nothing, I think.

"All I'm saying is I never knew he was taking pictures. I just thought…" She shrugs. "Everyone knew what was going on. I thought so, anyway." Then, "What you said, just before I caught the tube. About helping?" She's now looking at me, her gaze suggesting an urgency. "Did you mean that?"

I nod, speaking slowly. "Yes. Yes I did. I saw the marks, remember? Where he hit you. I know he's a shit. I don't understand how… why you'd want…" I shake my head; this is no time for inarticulacy, Harry. "The fact is Sven thought you should be rid of him and I do too. So yes, if you want me to help get rid of him, then I will. No, I don't currently know how but I'm pretty sure if we can crack Sven's puzzles we have a chance."

She smiles and steps in close. I hold up a hand. "Hang on."

She grins. "Don't worry. Miles isn't watching."

I can feel my ears heating up. Shit.

She darts in close and pecks me on the cheek. "All right, what can I do to help?"

"Let's go and get a cup of tea and have a look at these." I tap the envelope with the adverts.

Everyone seems to be in the kitchen. Dina looks up from a messy George who is loving being the centre of attention. "Dad is taking me to see Jim. George is coming too."

"What about the shingles?"

"I'll take my chances and it'll look like I care."

"Of course you care. Everyone knows that."

Dina's expression defies me to carry on so I change tack. "I think I need to go to see Frank. I'll cadge a lift."

"Frank?" Natalie looks at me over her tea.

Dina doesn't wait for me to answer. "Not a good idea, H. Dad'll want to know why you're skipping a day's work."

"I can always say—"

"I'll take you. I've got a car."

We both look at Natalie. I say, "You sure?"

"I said I'd help."

I can feel Dina staring at me, so I look anywhere but at her. "Okay, great. I'll need to leave a message to say I'm sick but then we can go."

"I'll call in from a service station. My office is pretty good about it."

I wish, I think.

Dina nods. "Maybe we can work out a way for me to grab a lift back. Would that work if I have to come back with George too?"

Natalie nods. "If you're happy to squeeze in the back of the Porsche. It's pretty much just a shelf. He'll be okay, but it will be a tight fit for you."

"That's fine. How about I get dropped at New Milton station about four and you pick us up?"

"Okay. You may need to hang about a bit."

"If we're not there and it's gone four, we'll be in the park at the swings."

"Great."

"Now who is Frank?"

"I'll tell you later." I tap the still unlooked at adverts. "Natalie has brought the adverts. We can look at them on the way home, maybe?"

She nods. "If you get time before don't let me stop you. Why not take all the photos, anyway?"

"Good idea."

After we say our goodbyes, Natalie and I head downstairs. "Is it Miles' Porsche? Sven's car?"

She nods and dangles some keys.

"I thought he never went anywhere without it?"

"Yes, well… sometimes he prefers the train."

"Really? He prefers a grubby train to his flashy car?"

She unlocks the car. "He doesn't really but when he goes north he takes a train. I think he knows he might have a drink. Or something."

"Is that Leeds?"

She stares at me over the roof of the car. "I suppose. That's what he says, but who knows? Shall we get a move on? And who is this Frank character?"

"Frank Smedley. He's my one hope to crack Sven's puzzles. After that, we might need to see some other people and I should really go and visit Mum in the hospital, even if it means Dad asking silly questions."

"Of course."

The traffic to the motorway is light. We don't speak until we drive up the slip road and she accelerates in moments up to 80. The engine growls with appreciation as she moves over to the fast lane. "You think I'm disgusting, don't you?"

"No. No, I don't. Why would I—?"

"Because I give blowjobs to strangers. Well, near strangers."

"I don't know what to think about that. It… I can't imagine why anyone—"

"That's what I mean."

"Can we forget it? He's a shit and I... I care about you. A lot." I look across at her. "You've friends – Penny, Sven, me. Any one of us would have helped. And none of us would judge you."

"He terrifies me, Harry. Even if the sex was good."

I let out a deep breath. "Fine. The only way to stop him is to get Sven's money and then retrieve the negatives. All of them. Then you can move on."

"He won't let me go. And please don't say you'll make him. You don't know what he's like. You wouldn't stand a chance."

"Let's see, okay? First we need the money."

She is crying but nodding at the same time. "So who is this Frank person?" she says when she's back in control.

"Neat change of subject." We are still doing north of 80 as she takes one hand from the steering wheel and scrubs her eyes with the sleeve of her now free arm. As she does so she swerves the car into the outside lane, back inside and then outside again. As a blue and then silver saloon flashes past I do well not to squeal. It's probably better if I don't look. "He worked for Sven's Dad. He pawned stuff and laundered his money. I think he knows more about where Sven may have hidden what he raised from selling the businesses. I also think there's some connection with Izzy Grimsdale, but I may be barking up the wrong tree there."

"What makes you think that? I don't think Sven ever mentioned a Frank."

I'm silent while we pass on the inside of a wide lorry, praying it holds its course.

"I understand if you don't trust me."

"No, it's... shit, slow down please. I'm not cut out for this slaloming."

"Don't you like women drivers?"

"I don't like reckless... Christ!"

"What?"

"There wasn't a gap."

"Obviously there was or we wouldn't be moving quite so smoothly. You were saying about Frank?"

She does slow down. A little. For now we probably won't take off. "I'm pretty sure Sven converted the proceeds into diamonds."

She looks across at me. "Diamonds?"

We skitter past a Peugeot; as we do so I see the driver glare across at me. I think I may have seen my first zombie. I manage to hiss, "Keep your eyes on the fucking road or I'm not saying another thing."

She makes a pffing noise like a slow puncture but nods and stares forward.

"It is a bit of a guess, but they are easier to hide than most other valuable things. As we know, he died before he could sort out who got what – he had to pay off several people I believe. The trouble is I'm no nearer to knowing if that guess is right, or indeed finding them if I am, than I was at the start."

She shakes her head. "Diamonds? Bloody hell. That's just like him, though, isn't it?"

"It's my best guess at the moment. It looks like one of the last businesses he was trying to sort out was the gambling club, probably the estate agency too. My guess is Miles owed Mr Andersen money and Sven tried to get it back, but Miles used you to stop Sven forcing him to sell."

I hold my breath as she overtakes three BMWs by accelerating to 95. It's a smooth manoeuvre and because it complies with most of the Highway Code – not the speed, obviously – I manage to bite my tongue. After a slight pause I say, "It's also complicated by the fact Mr Andersen took the business from Charlie Jepson in the first place. He wants it back and McNoble wants to stop him."

She touches my leg. "Thank you for trusting me with this."

"Don't make me regret it, for both our sakes."

"I wouldn't. You believe that, don't you?"

"Yes. Yes, I do."

She moves her hand up my thigh and palpates it slightly.

"Natalie, please…" Her hand brushes my fly, which is of course bulging a bit, and then goes back to the wheel. She's smiling as she looks ahead. *Bugger.* "Yesterday, I could easily have taken you up on your offer. In the Park. You know I've wanted to for years. But we can't, Natalie. It wouldn't be fair on either of us and it might not be very sensible. Maybe when— shittttt!"

She spins us across all three lanes and into Fleet Services, slowing abruptly and crawling to park away from the service block. Having switched off the engine, she spins in her seat and looks at me. "We need to fuck."

"What?" I look around in terror. There are cars everywhere. Maybe the fir trees off to the left offer a bit of cover but…

"Not here, moron." She's laughing. "But we both want to and if we don't this will go on and on. Won't it? We need to know."

"Know what?"

She begins to speak and then shrugs. We sit in silence, the engine ticking as it cools, the occasional raised voice floating in through the closed windows. After a few minutes, she pulls on the door handle. "I'm going to the ladies."

I grip the seats. Is that an invitation? Does she expect me...? I pull my seat belt across my lap and strap myself in, like this will keep me safe.

Five minutes later she's back, pulling out onto the motorway at a sensible speed. She doesn't mention what just happened. After a couple of miles she fiddles with the radio and we let Radio 1 surround us with pappy pop music. It's just gone one when we pull into the car park at Sunnysites nursing home. Natalie decides to go for a walk – the home is a couple of hundred yards from the sea. Mr Stammer and Frank are in the sunroom when I'm shown in.

"Mr Spittle. Lovely to see you again. To what do we owe the pleasure?"

Frank keeps his eye on the picture window, but I can tell he's listening.

"Business, I'm afraid. I need to ask Frank a question or two."

"Fire away. We're ready."

I take a deep breath. "Does he...? Frank, do you know Lady Isabella Grimsdale?"

Before Mr Stammer can speak Frank says, "Certainly. Mr Andersen introduced her. They were close once, many years ago." Frank nods and looks briefly at me. "Slippery bitch if you ask me."

It takes Mr Stammer a few seconds to regain his composure. He stands quickly blocking my view of Frank. "Mr Smedley, are you...?"

He stops, all the air knocked out by one sharp jab from a walking stick. "Stammer, go and get us all tea. Now."

Mr Stammer looks around anxiously and then leaves hurriedly. Alone I say, "The list? Diamonds?"

"First, what's with the Grimsdale bird?"

"Did Sven deal with her? Over the diamonds? Or with you?"

"Nah. She and the old man had an affair, sort of repeat fling. Ask Lewis. He'll know."

"The diamonds?"

"Sven told me you'd work out what he needed from you. I told him you'd need help. That list is my best guess, from memory, what he bought with the cash he raised. You found them yet?"

"No."

Frank looks out towards the gardens. "I told him you were stupid and you'd never work it out. That's why I did the list – I thought you might welcome a little..." he rolls his dentures in his mouth, "...hint." He glares at me then, although it could be a smile; with his false teeth now sticking out sideways I could have misconstrued his expression.

I feel anger bubbling away as his sneering tone continues. "He had faith in me and I'm not going to let him down."

"Christ. Listen to you. Have you involved that sister of yours? She's the only one in your family with the brains for this."

I nod.

"Then maybe you've got a chance. Now fuck off while I get some sleep."

"Do you have any ideas—?"

"Nah. I didn't ask and I'd have stopped him telling me. Ask Lewis. He knows most things. He'll help if you say we've spoken." He closes his eyes. "Now fuck off, will you? I'm knackered." As I turn to go he says, "Stammer will help if you need it. The Grate boys, too. They all owe Sven."

Chapter Sixty

In Which Harry Raises His Voice

When Natalie and I enter the reception of Mr Lewis' office I receive a smile most unlike the sort of reception Gloria would give someone my age appearing at Clifford, Risely & Co. Country manners, I suppose. More of a surprise is how we are shown straight through to his office, as if we are expected. Mr Lewis shakes my hand and almost kisses Natalie's.

As tea is served and we are settled around his desk he leans back, steeples his fingers under his chin and says, "Well, Harry. What brings you here? Have you and your colleague decided you want me to act on Sven's estate?" It might be a twinkle or it could be a glint in his eye; whatever it is, it is very disconcerting. I try to ignore a creeping feeling of worry.

"We've been to see Frank. He told us—"

"I heard he spoke to you."

"I suppose Mr Stammer called. Frank suggested you might know something about the way in which Sven invested the proceeds from dismantling his Father's businesses."

"What did Frank say?"

"Diamonds?"

"Diamonds? Yes, that sounds like Sven. Not that I know, of course. He did all that himself. I wasn't involved."

"Do you know anything about a Lady Isabella Grimsdale? Frank said she knew Sven and his Father?"

"Izzy? Gosh, yes. She has a house over Walhampton way. Sir Penshaw, her brother, was at school with Robin Andersen. The Prep."

"You as well?"

He nods, acknowledging the truth. "Not that I was in their circle, you understand, a farm boy like me."

"So Isabella knew Mr Andersen?"

His smile is thin and maybe a little wistful. "They had something going at one point. When Robin was in his last year. They both liked the fast lifestyle: wine, dancing, sports cars, gambling – but her Father didn't approve and you didn't argue with Sir Archibald Penshaw. They came from different classes. Robin's Father was a Swedish naval captain posted here in 1915. Self-made, you understand. I haven't seen her recently. Not since Robin's funeral."

That gets my attention. "Mr Andersen's funeral? She was there?"

"Yes. Not for long, but she came to the service."

"Did Sven ever talk about her? I wondered if she had any business links with his Father or him."

He purses his lips and then shakes his head. "I don't know of any. Can I ask why you are interested?"

"It's just something I heard."

I'm framing my next question why Natalie pipes up, "Did Mr Andersen own any cars?"

"Cars? Yes. He had quite a collection." Mr Lewis looks annoyed at the change of tack, but covers it quickly. "Sven thought all cars were a waste of money. We were instructed to sell them quickly after probate was granted."

"Did he garage them all at his house?"

"I believe so. The stables were converted years ago for that very purpose."

"Do you have a list of what he had and what Sven sold?"

By way of a reply, he picks up a phone and explains to the person at the other end in a terse voice what he wants.

While we wait for his secretary I ask, "Has the house been sold yet? What about Sven's bungalow? Who owns that?"

"We don't know."

"Sorry?"

Mr Lewis holds up a hand. "I apologise Harry, you being an almost solicitor. The title is vested in a corporate entity called Andersen Ventures, but unlike the English company with that name, which was controlled by Robin and then Sven, we have no idea who controls this one. It seems the entity is registered in Vanuatu and we have yet to hear back with the details of who controls it and so on. That goes for both the main house and the bungalow Sven used. It is a reasonable assumption that the amanuensis is a member of the Andersen clan, but until we can identify who…" He shrugs.

"You didn't act when he bought it?"

"Since I don't know who owns it, I think you can work out I didn't act. And before you ask, yes I do hold the land certificate and it is not charged at all."

"There's no agent registered?"

364

"Yes, there is. Sven at the bungalow, but when he found out it was clear he was a surprised as anyone." He smiles widely. "I'm sorry I can't help you more."

Just then his secretary knocks and enters. She hands him a sheet of paper that he glances at briefly before passing across to me. I ignore it.

I say, "Do you have keys to the main house?"

"I do, but I really don't see why—"

"Mr Lewis. I'm young and probably very naïve, but I know one thing. You know a lot more about Andersen's affairs than you are saying. I also know you are holding back the proceeds from the sale of my aunt's garage when you have no justification—"

"Hang on, young man—" He has stood and so do I, conscious that Natalie is staring at me.

"No, you hang on. Either Stephen McNoble or Charlie Jepson has told you not to release the money and you do what they say, like you do for all the other crooks. It may be you've covered your tracks; I expect you have. But do you want the Law Society or the police taking a detailed interest? So lend me the keys, let my parents have their money and I will do my best to keep you where you are now. Sitting very pretty."

I'm shaking when I finish shouting and I desperately need a pee.

He takes a moment and then opens a desk drawer. "Here. You can have an hour and then return them. I will not be releasing that money, which is the subject of a genuine and ongoing dispute." He can't look at me as he says this and it occurs to me he's actually scared, "And I know I have done nothing illegal or unethical."

I take the keys. "We'll be as quick as we can, but we've another appointment first."

Outside she squeezes my arm. "Where did *that* come from? The new decisive Harry Spittle?"

"I don't know. No, that's not true. That man has been patronizing me for years, making me feel small and stupid. I think I've had enough."

"You look like you might shatter if you don't relax a little."

"I'm glad you asked about the cars."

"I just remembered the adverts. Do you think they are for the cars his Father owned?"

"No idea. We can check later. Meantime, let's go and have a look round chez Andersen."

"You said we had another appointment?"

"Ah, yes. And I imagine it will have what I need most right now."
"Which is…?"
"A loo."

Chapter Sixty-One

Where Harry Visits Hospital and an Old Haunt and Sees Some Boxes

Sitting with Mr Lewis, I was hit by a thought. Mum is in the hospital half a mile away, her panic attack having hit her for six and left her needing a few days under observation. And while I'd prefer that Dad didn't know I'd come down this way the same day as he is driving home, I have to see how she is. The receptionist kindly checks and afternoon visiting time starts at two so Natalie and I head over, with me hoping Dad won't already be there.

Mum is asleep when we arrive and alone. Natalie and I sit by her bed talking in low voices. I'm wondering if we should wake her or leave when Ravi and Mrs Ohja appear, smiling. It's like they knew I was here. Do they have a spy? Or are they psychic as I've long suspected? They have no compunction and wake Mum up. She's embarrassed to see me but is clearly exhausted. I manage to say a few meaningless things and confirm George and Dina are well before Mrs Ohja eases us out.

As we leave the building and head to the car park, Ravi says, "Are you staying?" I must look shifty because he adds, "If it helps you could stay at the hotel. We have a lovely room for you both."

I can't help glance across at Natalie, the 'we must fuck' of earlier repeating in my brain on a loop. She shakes her head. "We have to get back, Ravi, but thanks."

I think I'm relieved.

He spreads his hands wide. "Next time maybe?"

She smiles broadly. "Definitely, we'd love that."

I'm watching his expression, keeping my gaze away from Natalie when I see his eyes widen and he hurries past me. Natalie has just unlocked the Porsche. "I saw that beauty when we arrived. Is it yours?"

"My husband's."

That's probably the easiest explanation, although it occurs to me for the first time that actually the car is probably mine according to Sven's Will.

He nods, apparently unaware or unconcerned what that means about the appropriateness of the room he has offered us. "Do you think I could sit in the driver's seat?"

He is like a boy with a new toy. He talks all the time, describing in ridiculous detail all the dials and performance statistics. Mrs Ohja shakes her head and goes and waits by their scabby Ford Escort. I'm barely paying attention when he leans over to the passenger side and opens the glovebox. "This is cool. What's that?" Because of the angle he's having to lean to reach in, and he's peering at something. As he reaches forward a voice pulls him from the car.

"Ravi, come on! We'll be late." Mrs Ohja is performing a very creditable double teapot, reminding me of Penny.

Ravi knows better than to hang around. As he eases himself out of the driver's seat he grins at Natalie. "If you are around the hotel let me know. I'd love to take her for a spin."

"Ravi. Now!"

I shut the compartment and click on my seatbelt. When they've driven away, I say, "Let's go and look at a garage, shall we?"

Natalie looks bored. "Do you think there'll be anything? I mean, wouldn't someone else have found whatever it is we're looking for?"

"The diamonds."

"Do you really think there are any left? I mean, why would he go to so much trouble and then not give them to you? Or put them in a bank or vault or something?"

"I don't know. He did everything for a reason, didn't he? Nothing left to chance and everything for a reason." I stare at the hospital. Poor Mum. "I mean, this car is mine, isn't it? If it was Sven's then it comes to me under his Will." A thought occurs. "He even left me a set of keys. He wanted me to have it."

She's shaking her head. "You'll have a job prizing this away from Miles. He loves it. I don't think he's actually thought about ownership now that Sven's dead. Anyway, you can't drive can you?"

"Nope, never learnt. I suppose I'll have to. Anyway I suspect we're barking up the wrong tree. Frank must have thought it was diamonds but there's no reason why it had to be. And there's no reason why they would be in the garage, other than those adverts."

"You haven't looked at them yet, have you? Which way?"

"Left after the pub and then right by the water tower on the sharp left-hand bend." I pull the envelope she brought this morning towards me and open it.

"Is it far?"

"A mile." I flick through them. They all have a word in the space Sven left blank. I need to make a note of them. "Hang on."

"What?" She swings the car left after the Monkey Puzzle pub, banging me against the door. I ignore the pain and scrabble for the briefcase with the photocopies of the paintings. "Yes, bugger it."

"What?" We spin right in a spray of gravel and shoot up the hill past the water tower.

"Next right and it's…"

I was going to say 'it's an unmade road' but that becomes evident as we hit the loose surface and fishtail rather dramatically, peppering the adjacent farm gate in a hail of stone shrapnel. Natalie doesn't take her foot off the peddle. "Third gate along. Please slow down."

Somehow we arrive at the gate in one piece. She pulls on the handbrake and turns to face me. "What?"

"Look. In the car advert there's a driver and no passenger. In Sven's painting there's a passenger. Me. See what I'm doing in the picture?"

She peers at it. "Yoga? You look like you're trying to lick the dashboard."

I'm already scrabbling at the glove compartment, twisting to look in it. "I'm trying to get something… Yes! There's something here." I pick at something with my nails. An envelope that has been taped to the top of the inside of the glove compartment comes loose. "He knew I couldn't drive but he gave me a key. He wanted me to find this." On the front of the envelope he has written two letters: 'HS.' "Bloody lucky Miles never found this," I say.

"I doubt he ever looked in there." Natalie's eyes are enormous. "Is that the diamonds?" she squeaks.

I give it a squeeze. "Not unless they're flat."

To get into the Andersen property, I have to hop out and open the gate. It's easier than on our last visit. "Go left. I want to get the originals of these paintings. We can have a look then and try the garage afterwards."

The bungalow shows evidence of the police visit. Carpets have been taken up and badly laid back down. We head for the kitchen and sit at the table where I open the envelope. It's another picture on a piece of card that at first looks unfinished. Only one person has been finished fully, the others are just outlines. "I'll lay a small fortune this is the missing number seven."

"Number seven?"

"I'll show you in a minute. Do you think this is meant to be Miles?"

"Yes, for sure. Is that you? The third along?"

"I think the outlines are the other six people. Number four isn't any more obvious, is she?"

"Is Miles meant to get a share?"

"I hope not but it's looking that way. Though…"

"Yes?"

"There are none of those symbols along the top. The ones Marita mentioned from that game."

"What did they represent?"

"We – Dina and me – think they are how many diamonds everyone gets. Still a bit of a guess though."

"That's Marita on the left, isn't it?"

"Yes. Then Monica Jepson."

Natalie is leaning over my shoulder. "He's set it in the club. Although it's not really like that."

A thought comes to me. "Has Marita been to the club?"

"Yes, she…" She stops herself and moves away. After a moment, she turns. "She asked me not to tell you. You won't let on, will you?"

"Why does it matter?"

"I don't know."

"Yes, you do. She's pretending not to know anything about what went on, about any of this, isn't she? But she's fully aware of this stupid game. Were you, too?"

"No. I'd tell you, Harry. And I don't think… no, I'm sure she doesn't know any details. Like the diamonds. If they're real, anyway."

We go back to staring at the picture. I jump as she jabs a finger at it. "Look. On that table."

It's a card table with a light green baize. On it is a hand of cards, all diamonds. "I guess that's pretty clear then."

"Are you sure Marita doesn't know anything?"

"Of course. She's not like that. Let's see what's on the back."

I want to press, but she's already flipped the card over. In Sven's spidery writing he's written,

Remember: however hard you try you'll never be squeaky clean. And if you feel alone, there are a great many people who will help you, post haste.

"What's that mean?"

"I suppose he's saying the money will always be tainted. Or maybe the recipients of it will be."

Natalie runs her finger round the word 'squeaky.' "Typical of Sven to say 'squeaky clean.' He had a way of talking that was, I don't know…"

"Old fashioned?"

"Yes, but something more. Idiosyncratic." She smiles at some memory.

I will always think of it as pretentious, but different folks and different strokes. Squeaking makes me think of that bloody mouse. I make a mental note to get a trap. "It has to mean something, though. He's never simple in his clues, is he? Post haste? Like I'm not going fast enough?"

"Is that what it means? I thought it was something to do with being prompt." Natalie is looking at the picture again. "Do you think he meant 'squeal' rather than squeak? You know, like telling on someone? Grassing? Telling tales?"

"He's not prone to making mistakes, is he? And you don't say 'squeally clean' do you? Let's keep all the options open, shall we?"

"What about the help? Do you think he means us? Penny and Marita and me? When he talks about a great many…"

"Shit. The Grate brothers."

"Who?"

"Bunch of brutes. I'll tell you later. First we need a phone."

"There was one by the front door. It may still be connected."

It is. Soon enough I've spoken to Mr Stammer and we have an address. Before heading for Pennington, we check the rest of the bungalow. Natalie is fascinated by the attic with the original drawings. She doesn't say a word until she reaches the end where there's the mark on the wall. I hold up the painting we've just found. It fits the pencil mark perfectly. "I was pretty sure it was number seven. Miles."

"Why was it taken down?"

"No idea. You'd have to ask Sven. He removed it."

"How do you know it was him?"

"We have a photo of the room. You've seen it. This drawing had already been taken down when the photo was taken, but whoever took it drew round it to show it had been there once. It's the same with the photos of the individual drawings. No number seven. It doesn't make sense for anyone else to take the photos other than him. And anyway, he stuck number seven in the Porsche. My initials were on that

371

envelope. I don't know why he wanted them separated. Maybe Miles is an afterthought." I'm pleased with my faultless logic but she just takes a moment to look at the drawings.

"Okay, let's grab the originals and have a look at the main house."

While I unhook the portraits she goes to the car adverts. "I wonder what the missing words mean. Have you looked yet?"

I haven't. "I'll have a look on the way to the Grates." There's something niggling at me.

"Why do you look like you need a poo?"

"I'm thinking."

"Nice." She smiles at me and after a beat I smile back. The sun shines in creating a square of yellow warmth in the middle of the carpet. "Harry…"

We stand maybe six feet apart. My mind fills with images: summer 1976, her on the swing that still stands in the garden just below us, giving me a drug-fuelled blowjob; that same summer, the little sun trap where I caused her to expose herself in front of all the hotel staff; May this year, the understairs cupboard where I accidentally felt her left breast; last Sunday, the kiss opposite Izzy Grimsdale's flat; and earlier today, the declaration in the car park at Fleet Services. All I need to do is step forward and take her in my arms. No one will disturb us. We can take however long we want. I breathe out slowly. "Come on, we need to get these keys back to Lewis soon. Main house, then garage, then adverts."

"Okay." Something goes out of the atmosphere. I'm pretty sure that was my last chance; I will never make love to the woman I've fancied since I first met her. Oh well.

We spend a while checking the house but it's dusty and rather damp smelling which makes us hurry. The garage were once stables and all the internal walls have been removed making a long open space with a mechanic's pit at one end. The whole thing is empty, devoid of equipment, save for a pile of wooden boxes in the middle of the floor.

Natalie crosses the empty space swiftly and turns the top one over, then screams and drops it. It has a glass front which shatters on contact with the concrete floor. "I hate moths. Who's going to keep a box full of them? It's sick," she says.

When I reach her, she's more angry than upset. The broken box contains a selection of British butterflies. When I look at the rest of the boxes, they are filled with a variety of insects – butterflies, moths, beetles, hornets, all pinned and set on thin strips of cork.

"When I came here, I mean the first time, back when we worked at Hemingways, when Sven's Dad wanted me to tell help him… never mind. That's when Robin Andersen told me he collected butterflies." I shudder at the memory of Robin Andersen catching a Duke of Burgundy fritillary and crushing it in his fingers. It was his less than subtle warning what he'd do to me if I didn't behave. That was the day I realised Sven hated his Father and he was actually on my side.

I hold up a box, admiring the beauty of the insects within. "It's an impressive collection. I wonder why they're here, discarded?"

"Well, if I was Mrs Andersen I wouldn't want them in the house. Talk about creepy."

"But she left over two years ago, before the old man died. And there would have been the cars here then. They weren't sold until after he died." It's so obvious I almost don't say it, "Sven put them here. For me."

"Why?"

"As is so often the case with Sven-bloody-Andersen, only fuck knows."

She rubs her arms and looks sullen. As we walk to the car, she says, "So where next?"

"Time to introduce you to some human boulders."

Chapter Sixty-Two

In Which Natalie and Harry Make a House Call

The Grate brothers live in a small terraced house on the main Milton Road as you leave Pennington village and head for Downton. It's a rather unimpressive piece of sixties infill but the front garden is full of colour and there are lace curtains at the windows. The only evidence that the occupants are not your usual nuclear family are the range of enormous black boots that line the porch; those and the shotgun propped by the umbrella stand.

"Who are these people, Harry?"

She follows half a pace behind as I approach the front door. When I read Sven's clue I was sure he meant the Grates but now my confidence deserts me. What to do? Knock or run?

"Old employees of the Andersen empire who Sven saw right, as they say. They may look dangerous and I certainly wouldn't want to argue with them, but they genuinely loved Sven and are on our side."

I'm brought out of my dilemma when I realise she's sobbing. Her eyes are red. "I really think I loved him, you know. I was so stupid. He tried to stop me getting tangled up with Miles. Why didn't I listen?"

I feel rather exposed standing in the middle of the Grate's front path while Natalie has an emotional breakdown. I pat her arm and make ineffective shushing noises.

"I have to get away from him, Harry. I'll go mad if I stay. That… that photo with your colleague. It was awful."

"He knew what he was doing."

She looks away. "Miles spiked his drink. It removes inhibitions. Same with that woman, Janet. Isabelle."

"Isabella."

"She's not the sort of person who'd indulge in a threesome, is she?"

I wonder whether that's right, not that it really matters. "I think the man, the one with Lady Isabella, is Sean Latterly who happens – happened – to be her brother's gay lover. I suspect if that image got to her brother then it would have torn them apart. That's why Miles could control her."

"Oh God."

"It's the only thing that makes sense. Isabella is, at least by reputation, quite the party girl. I think a photo showing her getting involved in a threesome at a gambling club with another beautiful woman and a young man isn't something that would cause her much, if any, embarrassment. However, if it turned out that the man in the threesome was her brother's homosexual partner, well…"

Natalie whistles. "The slimeball. Poor thing, being set up like that."

"Hmm, I wouldn't feel too sorry for her. She's the one who'd happily see Penny in prison for murder. Indeed, it's possible that Sir Pen's death and this blackmail are connected in some way and she wants Penny to take the fall for it."

"Oh my goodness. Really? You'll have to stop this."

I look at her, widening my eyes. "Didn't you tell me that I have to be careful of Miles and now you want me to 'sort out' a powerful and well-connected woman?"

Natalie doesn't appreciate my admittedly feeble attempt to lighten the moment but it does make me more determined to speak to the Grates. "I will try, okay? What we need are the pictures and the negatives. At the moment, she thinks she's in control and can pressure me into doing what she wants, but if we can get hold of those photos then we may be able to get her to change her tune about Penny. Anyway, that's partly why we're here. These people may be able to help."

"That's still blackmail, even if you do it."

I just about manage not to shake her. "Of course it bloody is. But you want me to keep Penny out of jail, don't you?"

"Not that way."

"Natalie, I… oh, hello." I turn around as I hear the front door open. Greg Grate, wearing an apron and ridiculously fluffy slippers, is standing in the doorway.

"I've been watching you for a while Mr Spittle, wondering if you were planning on ringing the bell. Perhaps you'd like to come in; our neighbours can be a little bit twitchy… as in curtain twitchy."

We're shown into a small room at the back of the house. Grant is seated behind a plain desk weighed down with papers, while two of his enormous brothers stand sentinel by each shoulder. To say it's crowded would be a gross understatement.

When he sees me, Grant stands and reaches across the desk, offering a meaty paw. "'arry? Good to see you. To what do we howe the pleasure? Hand who's the little woman?" He offers Natalie a hand.

As she takes it he bows his head. "Charmed. Hany friend of 'arry's is a friend hof hours. Right boys?"

The rumbling that I last heard at the wake fills the room. I am sure I can feel the vibrations through the floor.

"So what's the reason for the call 'arry? Need hour hassitance with sumfink?"

He indicates a seat for me. The monster to his left sweeps another chair with an enormous white handkerchief and presents it to Natalie, smiling with what looks like one canine tooth in an otherwise empty maw.

"You were Mr Handersen's, er, Andersen's accountant? Isn't that so?"

"Possibly a flattering 'omonym, halthough Hi did regard the books has my responsibility."

"So, when Sven sold the businesses…"

"We like to say 'liquidated,' don't we boys?"

The rumbling is deeper and more pronounced this time.

"A little reminder – hour Proustian moment."

"Sorry?"

"Hi halways thought HÀ la recherche du temps perdu a trifle hunderstated, hat least when happlied to raw criminality."

I am stunned. This time Grant laughs alone. I'm aware his brothers look as bemused as I feel.

"'arry, don't be deceived by the haccent, the dialect. Heducation hisn't the preserve hof the well-spoken young gentleman such has yourself. Yes? So, what haspect hare you looking hat? 'e ad pretty much finished the…" he grins, "let's say winding hup, shall we?"

"Miles Tupps and his gambling club."

Grant nods, looking thoughtful. "Yes, well, that's hin 'and."

"Is it? How?"

"Master Sven transferred the debt to a third party hon the hunderstanding the business will cease to function by the hend hof the year. Hat the time hof 'is huntimely demise, 'e 'eld no hinterest hin hit."

"McNoble?"

"No. Mr McNoble did not hacquire the controlling hinterest. Hi'd really rather not say. Hi think hit might complicate what you hare trying to do."

"But I need to know…"

Grant holds up a hand. "What hexactly hare you hafter, 'arry?"

His eyes are close set and staring at them makes me feel seasick, like my eyes are trying to cross unsuccessfully. "Leverage. Against Miles."

Grant pulls a 'not sure I can help you' face. "He knows hit's hending. Though…" He indicates for his left-hand brother to lean in and he whispers something. Said brother takes a huge stride to a filing cabinet and returns with a thin beige folder. Grant flicks through it carefully. As he does so he says, "Mr Robin was particular that we kept detailed records hof hall 'is matters. Has a result… yes, there we hare." He hands me a large sheet of what looks like graph paper with a sort of family tree on it. "These hare the companies hin which Mr Tupps 'olds stakes hand through which 'e runs various concerns – money laundering via Luxembourg hand Guernsey, himports hof 'eavily hincumbered goods – tobacco, halcohol, precious stones – so has to havoid the, erm, burdens hof the state, shall we say – bars that provide a range hof hintoxicants, that sort hof thing. What you see there his the hidentity hof the companies, who his involved with them hand 'ow they hare funded. We will let you 'ave a copy. What Mr Tupps will heasily hunderstand, hif you show 'im this, his we can show exactly 'ow these businesses link back to 'im and, well, the Hinland Revenue has well has the police would be mighty hinterested. Not that Hi would welcome such disclosure. Such third parties make a habit hof hasking hother, more hawkward questions."

Natalie has shuffled forward as Grant explains.

He smiles at her. "You're 'is wife, hain't you Natalie? Master Sven hexplained. 'e was worried habout you. 'e… well, let me say that the hoffer hof 'elp we hextended to 'arry 'ere, halso hextends to you should you need hit. Though," a sort of cloud crosses his face, "were you to try hand huse what Hi've told 'arry hagainst him, Hi think you'll find we will remain hon 'is side hin hany contretemps, hundurstood?"

She nods rather frantically.

He smiles again and it's like the sun has come out. "Shall we take tea? The back garden his lovely hat this time hof year. My bruvver Grew has a way with pansies." In other circumstances that would sound rather worrying.

Natalie asks for the lavatory.

As she walks off I say, "One other thing. I know Miles has something going on, some business in Leeds. No idea what it is but

Natalie always avoids the subject. Could you maybe have a look into what it might be?"

"Hof course, 'arry."

Wednesday, 29th July 1981

Chapter Sixty-Three

In Which Harry Eats Cake

It's the day of the Royal wedding. For the last week I've been rather frustrated by all the shenanigans over this non-event. Dina and George have returned to the flat – Jim has 'complications' and Dina had no choice but to come back with the boy. Zenda and Brenda/Vera are delighted, even if the rest of us could do without his unbelievably constant energy. He has certainly been enjoying all the preparations. Since I can't seem to get any time alone with Dina I haven't been able to update her properly. There's so much I want to share and get her thoughts on. She promises me that we will go through everything after work tomorrow as Brenda/Vera and Zenda have promised to take George out for a treat – a trip to the seaside – and won't be back until late.

As light relief, and to try to get into the spirit of the occasion, yesterday evening I cycled the route that the happy couple will take, enjoying the light-hearted banter as I practiced a Queen Mum wave to the crowds who are already massing behind barriers. I was almost tempted to grab a sleeping bag and join them.

Almost. Actually, not at all. Back at home Zenda and Mr Jones took delivery of a new TV to ensure they can see 'all the splendour and pomp in full colour' and we've been invited to join them. Zenda has promised treats – "I always bake for a wedding" – which is partly why I've decided to stay at home. Dobbin was having none of Brenda/Vera's enthusiasm to go and join the masses – "I'll get cramp and a cold arse just for 30 seconds of manic flag waving and a glimpse of a gold-plated carriage." His girlfriend, not the most obvious candidate as an ardent royalist chided him for being such a dullard – 'unpatriotic' Brenda/Vera called him – but I suspect the reason has more to do with a fear Brenda/Vera may have 'State Occasion' on her list of love-making settings and he fears accusations of treason if caught humping in the sight of a newly married Prince.

Both Jackie and Jan are on duty, which means it's the seven of us who settle down in Mr Jones' sitting room, trying – tactfully – to accept Zenda's sweet cakes rather than Mr Jones homage to everything Welsh – charcoal and daffodil shortbread with leek icing.

It is just gone 2:00 pm and the commentators are discussing a rather bizarre interview Spike Milligan has given about the Prince who is a well-known Goon Show fan. George has fallen asleep in Zenda's lap and his small snores mimic Mr Jones. The doorbell rings and it's Penny. "I thought I'd find you here. Mind if I join you?"

Dina and Brenda/Vera are thrilled to see her, offering her some of Mr Jones shortbread and squealing with delight when Penny manages to swallow without gagging. Finally, after we all pretend to be members of the wedding party for George who, curiously, wants to be Lady Di and march around the sitting room, Penny says she has to go. I see her to the door. When we are on our own she grips me tight and I wonder if she's crying, although she's clear-eyed when she lets me go. "Thanks Harry. For all you're doing. I don't deserve you, you know."

"How's things? With the police?"

She wiggles a hand to indicate it's still uncertain. "The lawyer tries to be optimistic, but they are still asking loads of questions, often just repeating what they've said before. I just want it over, you know?"

After she's gone and the front door is shut, I remain in the hall staring at the little spyhole. If I could see the future, would it have Penny in it? Or Jackie? Or Natalie?

I'm knocked out of my reverie by George, followed by Zenda, off to make sandwiches. "I'll give you a hand." It's good not to have to worry about reality, just for a few hours while we pretend a Royal wedding is really a modern fairytale. I hope, for their sakes, it is.

Thursday, 30th July 1981

Chapter Sixty-Four

In Which Brenda/Vera Proves Her Relative Worth

It's a bugger having to go back to work, but it's only two days to the weekend and everyone seems affected by a lethargy. Jeremy has been off sick for a week and Lucinda seems to know I have something to do with it. Jean has been especially protective of me, though, like she knows to look after me. Because I've not had much to do, I've registered my name with the recruitment agencies mentioned by Karen. They have asked me in for a preliminary interview next Monday.

I haven't heard from Natalie since we came back from Hampshire, and while Grant's offer of protection was extended to her, I worry what Miles might have said if he knew she'd been away and used the Porsche. I don't know if it's connected, but McNoble has been oddly and worryingly absent. Ditto his Father. I'm horribly suspicious.

When I enter the flat, there is a fab smell from the kitchen. Dina is mashing potatoes.

"What have you cooked? Is there enough for me?"

She smiles over her shoulder. "Zenda's left us a stew. They said they hope to be back by eight so grab the plates and we can spread out in the sitting room."

"Can I watch the cricket highlights?"

"Do you know the score?"

"Yes."

"So you know there are no highlights if you support England. Come on, Dobbin rang to ask if Vera was around and as she isn't, he's out with the boys. I'm not sure he can cope with her, can he?"

"Could anyone?"

"Yeah, well, I think my love life is coming to a grinding standstill. What about you? You snuck off with Penny yesterday. Is that back on?"

"Not so far as I know."

"Jackie?"

"I think I give off this smell that says I like the sex but will always feel guilty. I'm pretty sure she's keeping her distance to see how much I chase her, show how keen I am."

"And are you?"

I scrunch up my face. Dina just nods.

We turn on the TV and let the telly burble away in the background. I keep an eye out for the highlights but I know it will mostly be the Australian bowlers humiliating English batsmen. Again. After the Headingly miracle, I know we will revert to type.

"If we crack this mystery, you can call Jackie."

"She'd not answer."

We lay out everything as we found it in Hampshire using the originals propped around the room and with the photos on the table. Dina stares at number seven. "That's Miles, is it? Be a sod if he gets anything."

I point to the top. "There's no code."

Dina squints at the picture and takes it to the window. "There is. I think it was smudged when he painted it. Look."

There is something, not on the top but along Miles' lapel. "Why'd he put it there?"

"Maybe because of the others in the picture and he wanted to make it clear it's for Miles, not them."

"Yeah, makes sense. Bit of a bugger though."

She nods. "Still no idea about four?" She looks at the outline of number four on the group picture. It doesn't help at all. "Well, on the positive side we have identified six of the seven and Frank says you were right about the diamonds."

"Yeah, although he said he gave me his list because he didn't trust me to work it out for myself." I try hard not to look or sound smug. "I do have an idea about them. I mean, why hasn't Sven mentioned diamonds anywhere yet?"

"Do you mean the car adverts?" She glances at me and then back to the picture she's studying. "Yes, that's pretty obvious." She smirks, well aware it wasn't obvious to me, then taps her pencil on the notepad. "More to the point, we need to understand which diamond type is included in each set of numbers. That brings us to the originals. They are clearer than the photos, aren't they? You can see the colours he's used."

"Hang on. What do you mean 'that's pretty obvious'?"

She ignores me. "With the colours, I think it'll be easy to work out the code – who gets which diamond. For example, according to Sven's code Mum gets a red hen – that's three red diamonds and a white swan – that's seven white diamonds. I suppose they'll each be the same weight and cut. I don't need any more complications." Dina is taking time writing out the code and doing the maths and then comparing it with Frank's list. I try to interrupt again but she shushes me. Finally she looks up. "Go on. What's your theory about the car adverts?"

I pick up one of the adverts – the Audi Quattro. The missing word is 'Original.' I say, "Now we have all the adverts we can see all the missing words." I hold up another one. "Here the word is—"

"'Newest.' You take the first letter of each missing word, insert it into the eighth line of the grid, which is an eight-letter word, and you get 'Diamonds.'"

"You knew? When did you realise? Why didn't you say?"

"A while ago. Probably when we saw Jan's mag."

"You never said." I sound peevish, even to myself. She's still that irritating know-all-16-trumps-20-if-you're-a-girl at heart. What's so annoying though is that Frank's right – I couldn't do this without her and that so pisses me off, even after all these years.

"I didn't know for sure until Natalie got the originals. Stop looking like you've swallowed a wasp. You're the one who worked out we were looking for diamonds; all this is just confirmation."

I stand with my arms tightly folded, still seething.

"Oh H, you are brilliant, you're wonderful, we couldn't do—" she says in a singsong voice.

I jump on her and wrestle her to the sofa where she batters me with a cushion.

"Go and make yourself useful. I need tea and you can make it while I work out the allocation."

She's still sucking her pencil and I'm engrossed in the highlights when the front door opens and closes. Brenda/Vera puts her head round the door. "We're back. Mum is going to bath George and… what's all this?" She walks in and stares at the portraits. "These are good. Who did them?" She looks at me then back. "That's you, isn't it? Who are the others?"

Dina stands next to her. "It's a quiz. We can identify all except this one."

Brenda/Vera peers at number four. "Who did this?" She sounds anxious.

"Sven. The guy who died."

Dina has stopped still; years of living with her tells me she's suspicious about something. "You know who that is, don't you?"

"No. It's…" Brenda/Vera chews her bottom lip.

"You look like you've seen a ghost. Who is it?"

Brenda/Vera looks desperately at me and then back to Dina. "No… really. I just came to let you know we were back. I'll leave you to it." She can't exit the room quickly enough.

Dina is frowning and I know best to wait for her to speak. "What did you say the other day, about her? When Natalie was round here? Something about some relative being at Miles' club?"

"Her step-Father… oh fuck."

"What?"

I grab the painting of number four and peer at it. "It's not a woman. That's a judge's wig and gown. That's her step-Father, Reggie Rother."

Dina takes the picture from me. "Come on."

I follow my sister, admiring the way her mind works. Brenda/Vera's door is shut but Dina just marches in. "It's your step-Father, isn't it?" She holds out the picture so Brenda/Vera can't miss it.

She nods. She runs her nail across the surface of the table, tracing her other hand that rests there. "See this? He has a ring just like that. And there, that looks just like his watch. Did your friend really do this?"

I look at the ring. Rother is always spinning it as he waits to eviscerate someone in court. It's hypnotic, the way he plays with it. It's like an hour glass, spinning, spinning until he stops; that's when he hands down the punishment. Shit, how did I miss all that? I say, "Yes, Sven did it."

She nods, like this satisfies her. "Are you going to tell me why?"

Friday, 31st July 1981

Chapter Sixty-Five

Where Harry Gets into a Posh Car and then Gets Out Again

McNoble is waiting for me as I wheel my bicycle to the gate that leads to the lightwell at the office. "Morning. Any news?" He's cleaning his nails with his penknife. Just like when he turned up at the flat.

I fiddle with the bike lock that Mr Risely has had fitted on the gate. "You usually know before I do. How do you do that?" My mind goes back to Natalie in the car, being pleased I trusted her. Was I mad? Is she McNoble's source?

"I know you've been busy, up and down to Hampshire with your latest tart. Wonder what Miles would say?"

"He's not going to find out, is he?"

"You sure?"

"Pretty sure, yes. Look Stephen, if you were going to screw me or Natalie by telling him something that isn't actually true, you'd have done it already. You know and I know I am the only hope of finding out where the money is so while that's the status quo, you will have to remain patient and schtum."

"Why you little…" He makes a grab, but I'm already through the gate and it's re-padlocked. He laughs and shakes his head. "You need to watch yourself son," he says, but he doesn't sound serious.

I nod. "I'll tell you one thing I've found out for nothing. Sven's got rid of his Father's investment in Miles' club. No, I don't know who to, but it could be your Father."

He shakes his head. "No, I'm sure my old man doesn't have it. Not yet. He and Tupps are planning something, though. Who told you, by the way?"

I think of the pile of display boxes in the garage. "A little butterfly."

"You know what Harry, you'll come a cropper one day. Andersen told me I'd get that business to stop my bloody Father. If he's going to double-cross me then someone is going to pay." He closes the penknife with a snap. "I've got to go before some warden gives me a ticket. Parking around here is a nightmare." He smiles. "Telling them to fuck off doesn't work either." He seems to want a response but I'm trying to remember something, some memory he's triggered and the next thing I'm conscious of is him turning the corner.

What is it, Harry? It's not that bloody knife, the sodding thing. He's stabbed me once; I don't want that again. No, something about parking and...

Ding! *Of course. Of bloody course. Why have I been so blind?*

***

Eight hours later as I carry my bike up the metal stairs to the gate, I'm wary McNoble might be back. My mind is focused on the conversation I will be having in about an hour when I get home. I'm going to enjoy that.

As a result I'm not aware of the car that's pulled in opposite my building until my name is called out. There's a familiar face peering out of the sleek black Mercedes. Mrs Soderberg. She waves me over.

"Hello. What can I do for you?"

"We should drive. Get in please."

Unexpectedly polite. I say nothing until I've locked my bicycle away again and I'm in the passenger seat. I half-expect to find Lady Isabella in the back with her but Mrs S. is on her own. She doesn't set off immediately. "We have heard you know about some unfortunate photographs."

So Jeremy did speak to her.

"If you have them, we want them back. As you will appreciate they're private."

"I've not seen them, only heard about them."

"You'll contact me on this number as soon as you hear anything more." She picks up a plain business card with a telephone number in the middle and nothing else.

"Why does Izzy care? Just her having fun."

"She values her privacy."

"Really? It wouldn't have anything to do with who she's having fun with, then?"

"The Lady Isabella is a client. Your employers would not be best pleased if you lost them her work."

"I qualify in a few months. I will get another job. I doubt you can control everyone in the legal establishment."

She effects what might be a smile. "That risk is yours to take."

389

"No. You need to start thinking about risk. I fully understand reputational risk. This is how it will work. I can get you the photos and the negatives, but there is a price. One, you remove me from the Izzy Ventures where I'm listed as a director immediately. Whatever happens. Two—"

"Please get out, Mr Spittle."

"Two, you will tell the police that Penny was nowhere near Sir Pen when whatever happened to him happened. I saw you driving him, Lady Isabella and Sean from her flat in Portland Place. I don't much care what happens to Sean and Maggie although it would be fair if they were left alone, too. And three, I want to know what business you transacted with Sven Andersen."

"I'm waiting, Mr Spittle."

"Sure. Shame we couldn't have that drive. Looks like a nice car."

As I wheel my bike to the junction another thought occurs to me. A revelation really. How come I've been so stupid? If I've got it wrong then I'll look like a twat but then again what's new there?

Chapter Sixty-Six

In Which Harry Reveals He has a Clever Idea, but then Finds it's Not Really

The kitchen is crowded. Natalie and Marita have turned up and Brenda/Vera and Dobbin are back and joined at the hip. Dina and George have gone to find some fish and chips for everyone.

Dobbin pushes Brenda/Vera off his lap. "Come on Spittoon, let's see what happened to our boys today."

Dina pulls a face. "I watched the last hour. Brearley is bloody useless."

"Did Botham take any wickets?"

"One, I think. He's not going to work miracles again, is he?"

Brenda/Vera is standing next to Dobbin. She's wearing a sober grey woollen suit with mid-length skirt. She'll boil alive if that's her work attire. "My big day tomorrow. What do you think?"

I nod, not sure if I should tell her the office is like a furnace.

"Lucinda says I can work for her to start with."

I put on a large smile. "That's wonderful. You'll soon know all that's going on."

Everyone is nodding, but I note she looks a little unsure.

"Like moving in here. Makes it easy to know what's happening."

That makes everyone stop. "What you on about Spittoon?" Dobbin looks at me suspiciously.

"I had something of a revelation today. Something was bugging me and I've just worked out what it was." I start making some tea.

Dobbin speaks first. "You're talking bollocks, Spittoon. Any chance you can use words of one syllable for me?"

"Life is full of the oddest of coincidences but some seem to stretch credibility too far," I say.

Dobbin tilts his head on one side. "Nope. Still bollocks."

"How did you first hear about the Twats?"

"I don't know. Some chap at work, I think. Tufty Stimpson. He knew I liked punk. He had a spare couple of tickets."

"I know you. You like punk but not enough to drag yourself to a seedy pub in the back of beyond. What did he say made them special?"

Dobbin looks confused and not a little annoyed. "I don't know, do I?"

"What's Tufty's Christian name?"

"Roger. Spittoon, what is this all about?"

"If I ask Zenda would she know Roger, Brenda?" I'm looking at Brenda/Vera who's doing her best not to look at me. I go back to looking at Dobbin. "So, how did Roger sell the Twats to you? Free tickets? A lead singer who gets her tits out? Something to whet your appetite and off you go, dragging me along. And then there's that fight, we're channelled into a room where she leaps on you and before we know it, you're wrapped round each other because she's apparently fallen for your natural charms and you come back here for the longest night of sweaty sex you've ever had." I pause. "How many times has that happened before?"

"What the fuck are you implying?" Dobbin's on his feet, eyebrows knitted.

"I'm not implying anything." What I am doing is regretting saying this in front of Dobbin. I didn't need to do that, but now I'm out there I'm not sure how to row back.

Brenda/Vera saves me. She takes Dobbins' hand and pulls him to her. "It's okay Gary. Harry's spot on. Roger is my cousin. Second cousin, actually. I thought he might get the tickets to you or Harry."

Dobbins' face is now a mess: pain, confusion, anger, upset, incomprehension. Poor sod.

I say, "Let's leave this. It'll keep. Let's go and see the cricket."

Dobbin reacts to my voice by moving in really close, a nasty glint in his eyes. "No, go on. Say what you were going to say."

I take a deep breath. "Brenda's family have close links with Monica Jepson, and through her Stephen McNoble and his Dad. And McNoble seems to be one step ahead of me, always knowing what's going on. I couldn't understand how he did that, but then Vera saw him here, outside and, I don't know, tried to chase him away. I couldn't understand why. That's when I find out from Zenda that they're related – Brenda wasn't about to tell me – which was an odd coincidence. Too odd, really and, well, if you turn it round and realise Brenda engineered us all meeting, it begins to make sense. I'm slow-witted and it took a while to see the links for what they were." I look at Brenda/Vera. "Is that right?"

She nods and looks away.

Dobbin glances from her to me and back. Something is fighting in his expression, some urge to hit someone if only his brain could work out who. "Look Spittle, I think you're right out of order. I think—"

"It's okay Gary. He's right. Pretty much." Brenda/Vera looks at me. "I've wanted to say, really. It's Claude, sorry – Stephen. He knew all about the club and what my step-Dad owed and he needed to know what you planned to do. If he'd wanted to he could have put pressure on the sod and said it was Mum's fault, not using enough of her influence to get my uncle to release some of the trust. He's violent and we needed to leave. Claude said he'd help, but only if we helped him. I think Mum confided in Monica who may have said something, too. Mum was terrified. You can't imagine what my step-Father would do. Stephen told me that he'd keep quiet if I told him everything I could find out about Sven, Marita and you and this Will and everything. It's been awful."

I can believe it. "Are Stephen and Monica close? I didn't think they were."

"I don't know but they both hate his Father – her husband – and I think it may be one of those 'misery makes strange bedfellows' situations. I'm only restarting my articles because I can do it at your firm, Harry. Otherwise I'd be focused on my music. I'll tell them I'm not going in if you want, although I would like to finish them somewhere."

I nod. "No, if Lucinda likes you then don't let me stop you." That seems to help, at least with Brenda/Vera. "Just don't tell Stephen I know, okay? It might work to keep him onside for now, but in ignorance."

Dina hasn't spoken since I started. "Like a double agent, H?" She's grinning. I think she might actually be impressed. I'm not looking at Brenda/Vera so it's a surprise when she hugs me. "I'm really sorry, Harry. I haven't done any harm, have I?"

"Not really, no." As I look over her head, pressed into my chest, I see Dobbin watching us, utterly forlorn. "But I think you need to explain to Dobbin rather than me."

She lets me go and goes straight to him. "Please don't look like that. It's not what you're thinking."

"Why isn't it? You didn't want me, did you? It was just a trick. I'm a thingy. A stooge. A wooden horse."

"You think I could screw you as often as we have without me wanting to?"

"How do I know? You told me early on you had the best fake orgasm ever."

She slips onto his lap, although he does not look as if he's enjoying it. In the end, as I'm finishing making the tea, she stands and pulls him with her towards their bedroom.

Marita has been quiet throughout. "She's a spy? Geez. Poor thing." She takes her mug and cradles it. There's a long silence that she eventually breaks. "Natalie says you've made progress."

I mimic her pose. "I think Brenda isn't the only one holding back, is she?"

Marita colours and looks down. "Why do you say that?"

I pull out the drawing we found in the glove compartment. "Natalie and I saw this yesterday. These people are the beneficiaries of the diamonds. They were at the gambling club; Natalie told me she'd seen you there but you didn't want her to say anything to me, did you? You knew all about it, about Sven plans, but you didn't say when we met."

"I didn't know, not really." She looks at me, expressionless. "No, that isn't entirely true. He knew he was likely to die at any time and he had to find someone to finish things off for him. Genuinely, he didn't think I could do it – and he was right, I don't have the guts – but he thought of you, trusted that you'd see it through as long as he could persuade you to take the job on. He misled you, I know – we all did, but you understand why, don't you? It was a compliment, really. He knew you'd not do it for him. He understood your mind-set Harry, and I let him deceive you."

"A compliment? Great. I think I'd prefer it if people were rude. We all know I'm sucked in, don't we? What were the plans with Miles and this club?"

"He just wanted to close it down, but he knew his Father had screwed Charlie Jepson over it and felt the value should go to him. Sure, he understood he was a crook, but it was our Father and his businesses he wanted to clean up. He didn't judge others."

"Why didn't he just close it down?"

She reaches out and presses Natalie's hand, causing her to look up. "He loved you, Natalie. Closing it would backfire on you. I don't think he really knew what to do. Not really. In his funny way he wanted to make sure you would be okay."

Natalie nods. "He told me he wanted to close it, get me away and just shut it. Miles would have gone ballistic and I told him I wasn't the running sort. Hiding away from everything I knew? No, I told him that wouldn't work. By the end, I think accepting Mr Jepson and Miles should have it to run if he let me go was probably his best plan. Sven wasn't as hard as he made out. He meant well, but he knew he'd not have the stomach for a fight with Miles. He once said he could make Miles disappear but we both knew that wouldn't happen. Too like his Father, really."

The two women are smiling at each other, which frankly seems like a bit of a luxury. "Stephen would never buy that. Giving his Father a toehold back in the business? He said Sven was intent on shutting out his Father and giving him – Stephen – control."

Marita's voice sounds cracked. "Yes, Stephen was always a complication."

Something passes between the two women. Natalie takes her hand and says, "That last night at the club, the night he died, it all came to a head. There were so many furious arguments. It probably brought on his heart problem, pushed him over the edge. They were all demanding he sort things out, make a decision, and he collapsed. Stephen took him. He was really upset and said he'd take him to hospital. I don't know why he didn't."

Marita nods her confirmation. "We all panicked. That's why I disappeared. I was sure they'd be after me, to give them what they wanted. That was before we all learned about you and the Will. I think everyone is waiting to see if you can find out what's happened and come to some sort of conclusion. I'm sorry, Harry, but he told me the less you knew at the start, the better, because that way you would stay safe while you worked out what was going on. He was worried you'd try to be some sort of knight in shining armour before you were ready and get out of your depth."

"He was right on that last point. Did Natalie tell you we heard he transferred his interest – well, your Father's – in the club to some third party?"

"Yes, she did. We've been racking our brains to try to work out who."

"I think, ladies, it's time I told you everything we know and vice versa. We need to pool our resources to get out of this," I say.

Natalie offers a ghost of a smile. "You think we can?"

I smile back but all that means is 'fuck alone knows.'

Saturday, 1st August 1981

Chapter Sixty-Seven

In Which George Grizzles and Harry Makes a Demand

I've been putting off Jackie for a while, but we spoke today. Mr Jones gave me a message with a look that suggested he was becoming rather tired of acting as my secretary. Fortunately, Dobbin's new job means the phone has been reconnected and I left a message, which she returned. It didn't please Dobbin much.

"Can't you answer your own calls?"

"What time—"

"Fuck knows but it's too early for people who have proper jobs. Tell her to ring at a civilised time, okay?"

"Who…?"

Dobbin's already on his way to the bathroom. "She's waiting."

My alarm is showing seven and then something blurry. I toy with ignoring whoever it is but somehow find the strength to shuffle to the phone. I'm wondering who it is when I pick up the handset. "Hello?"

"Harry?"

Shit: Jackie. "Oh, hi."

"Are you ignoring me?"

"No, I—"

"We should speak. Tonight, okay? I need to go. Yours at seven. Will you be home?"

"Yeah. Yes, sure." Will Penny be here? She keeps popping in. I can't think straight. "Seven. We can maybe see Bren… Vera. The Twats have a gig in the Elephant."

"Elephant? Come here then. We can get a drink at the Frog. Maybe eight? Gotta go. Shift starts soon."

Click.

I stare at the handset. The click seems very loud. Final. It's left my ears buzzing. It takes a moment to realise it's not my ears but some small distressed creature that's in Dina's room. The mouse?

As I approach it becomes clear it's George, who's grizzling and Dina is making soothing sounds. When I knock and stick my head round the door, she's leaning over him. I can make out a tear-stained and flushed little face.

"He not well?"

She nods.

"I'll make tea. Any idea what it is?"

A headshake shake. "These are the times when I really want Mum." Her voice suggests she doesn't really.

"Well, a Mum perhaps." With the kettle on, and knowing I probably shouldn't, I head downstairs. Zenda and Mr Jones are sitting in the lounge, having tea in their dressing gowns, while the little room is bathed in sunshine. His whole flat is full of indoor plants and Zenda looks like she's being swallowed by an enormous fern. I've hardly begun to explain to Zenda and she's on her feet and heading upstairs. Inside 10 minutes she has George on her lap in the sitting room while watching something on BBC2, probably the Open University, and Dina is snoring in her bed.

I'm sipping tea when the doorbell goes. Assuming it's probably Mr Jones I bounce to it but to my surprise it's Jeremy. He looks both sheepish and rather desperate. "I spoke to Mrs Soderberg. She said she'd seen you."

"Yes?"

"She's outside. She wants to see both of us. Now."

"That's ridiculous."

He looks even more frantic that when I opened the door. "She called at home," he hisses. "Dale was really suspicious. I can't have her calling again. Please. We need to come in."

"No way." I glance over my shoulder.

"She's insistent!"

"What did she say?"

"She wants to talk to both of us."

"And?" He doesn't answer. "What about?"

"She didn't say."

"Nothing?"

"Nothing."

"You've driven from Wembley and she said nothing at all?"

"Exactly, other than she needs to sit down with us."

"We can go to the office." I can't believe he's a partner and I'm the lowest of the lowest. He's utterly indecisive.

"No, Lucinda's there this morning. Her daughter has a ballet exam at the Wigmore Hall so she came in early. She said she would be escaping and catch up on some paperwork. Harry, please. We need to come in."

I think of Dobbin and Brenda/Vera and a sick George all competing for attention. "I'll come down. We'll do this in the car."

"No, she—"

"Five minutes." I close the door, wondering if shutting out my principal is a sackable offence.

Downstairs Mrs Soderberg, with Jeremy already in the back seat, are waiting. "We can't do this here. We need an office, a table at least."

"Well, you're not coming in. Let's go to the office if we must."

"No." This from both Jeremy and Mrs Soderberg.

"Your flat? Your house? Lady Isabella's?"

More head shaking. "This is ridic... Hang on, I've got an idea. Give me a minute."

I'm back in four. "Right. Head for Wapping via the A13."

"Where are we going?" She sounds suspicious.

"A friend's flat. I've just made sure it's empty. We have it until 9:30."

"Whose is it?"

"Doesn't matter. If you want private it's the best I can do."

As soon as we are settled in Sven's flat, Mrs Soderberg opens a briefcase and pushes some papers at me. "If you sign where I've marked you will cease to be involved in any of Lady Isabella's companies. And this is an indemnity for you from her, against any liabilities you may have incurred while a director. It also undertakes to have the company wound up in the next three months. The business venture with Mr Latterly will not now be proceeding." She proffers what passes for what I assume is a smile in her circle of the undead. "Subject to you meeting your part of the agreement, naturally."

I read, like the dutiful lawyer I am, and it looks okay but I'd love Lucinda to confirm I'm not missing something crucial. With only a slight hesitation I sign as requested.

She slips the papers back in her briefcase with an alacrity that is frankly worrying, like they are so precious she doesn't want to risk losing them. "That was your precondition, I believe. These will be countersigned and dated and submitted to the relevant authorities assuming you can you get hold of the pictures and the negatives. You can, can't you?"

"Yes, yes I can." Woah, where did that confidence come from, Harry?

She nods like she believes me, then takes out a cigarette and a holder, rather like the sort of thing you see in an old back and white movie. I watch, fascinated. Part of me wants to tell her she can't smoke here and part of me is engrossed in the process. I suppose it gives her some thinking time. "I need proof."

"Proof?"

"That you can deliver on your…" she sort of sneers, "promise."

"The pictures were taken by Miles Tupps or on his behalf. You know that?"

She nods slowly. "The demand doesn't say, but it was at his club so we assumed he must be involved."

I know I should explain I know what they are, that I have details of how Tupps runs his businesses, his seedy empire and when I have them I intend on turning the tables on him. But when I try to speak, my voice betrays my nerves. And then my stomach turns over and I need an urgent comfort break in case the anticipated fart becomes something more substantial. When I return, I say, "Give me a few days and you'll have them."

"Lady Isabella is being interviewed by the police – again – on Wednesday about her brother's last few days. She will be confirming, as will Ms. Cloud, that he was a reluctant participant in a sex game instigated by Mr Latterly and which was deliberately devised to lead to his death, but made to look like an accident. Your friend will be implicated in that deception." She holds her lighter close to the cigarette, but seems to think better of it. "If we have the images before then her evidence will be somewhat less unequivocal."

Jeremy, who up to this point is watching open-mouthed, jumps up. "I can't listen to this. That's blackmail." He turns to me. "And you're talking about something similar, I imagine, to get those pictures. I'm going."

Mrs Soderberg puts a hand on his arm. I expect him to shake it off, but he just studies it before subsiding back into his chair. "Well, Mr Spittle? Do we understand each other?"

I'm shaking but an image of Penny looking terrified comes to me. "I need Lady Isabella to sign a declaration about her knowledge of drug use at the club and Tupps' involvement. Ideally she will also confirm the blackmail attempt too."

"Don't be ludic—"

400

"Mrs Soderberg, those pictures are more than embarrassing. They will destroy her reputation and may even make the police suspect her involvement in her brother's death."

Jeremy's eyes go big and round. "What are you talking about?"

I keep my eyes on the impassive factotum. "She understands. Don't you? There's no evidence against Penny. Not really, and all Lady Isabella will be doing is muddying already murky waters. If I then give the police – and the press – copies of the pictures, well, it's not Penny who will be the one worrying."

She puts her cigarette and holder on the table. "Lady Isabella is a woman of strong opinions, exquisite taste and a number of disappointing flaws, one of which is she believes in her own publicity. If I can be honest, Mr Spittle, my sense is the police do not believe they have anything like enough evidence to prosecute your friend and succeed. And I would hesitate to say the pictures, since you seem to know what they show, would be anything more than a nine-day wonder. However," and here she rubs her face, revealing a tiredness that is quite sobering, "let us not put those suppositions to the test, shall we? Let us remove these blocks in a sunlit future for us all. Get me those pictures."

"I really think this has gone far enough." Jeremy is trying to re-establish himself with a role in this grubby little affair.

Mrs Soderberg turns on him with a look of utter distain. "Mr Panther, you of all people know what you have to lose. There is an awful lot of, shall we say, compromising paperwork courtesy of Mr Martindale. So," she opens her bag and slips the tobacco paraphernalia into it, unsmoked, "it behoves all of us to try to remove the, erm, blot of the Grimsdale escutcheon at the same time as we untangle the affairs of Clifford, Risely & Co. and its partners from Lady Isabella's sorry past. If we can do that we can all look forward to, well, maybe calmer waters and a few less storms."

Jeremy looks at her with a desperate hope. "You'll get rid of all that?"

She tssks. "Mr Panther, it is Mr Spittle who you should plead with. Although he seems slightly more keen to help his friend than his employer." She smiles. "I will say, however, that if we can clear this up and no one connects Lady Isabella to those pictures, then she will ensure you are both released from any involvement with her ladyship's companies and your firm will be benefit from the usual indemnities and held harmless against," she takes a moment before adding, "anything unfortunate occurring."

She waits but neither of us speak. "I think we are done. Mr Spittle." She offers me a hand, grasping mine with a grip of if not iron then very hard plastic. "We never had this conversation. Best of luck in your endeavours."

Around 10 minutes later they have both left. The spreadsheet of how Miles' businesses fit together is neatly tucked away under my mattress at home. He'll be back on Sunday night. I have until then to decide what I'm going to do. Just threatening him with the police and the fraud squad and the Inland Revenue may not have the desired impact. At least unless I can also convince him I'm serious about reporting him. If only I knew where the diamonds were so I could also offer to pay him off as well as finding out who has all the paperwork that shows who has legal ownership of Miles' club. My life is a series of 'if onlys.' Bum.

Marita returns at 9:30 as agreed. She stirs me from my reverie and suggests a pub lunch on the river. As we are leaving the postman is sticking letters into the boxes. "I'd better check to see if there's any post." The box has a small lock but the first key I use doesn't fit.

"Problem?"

I hold up the key. "Did he have a safety deposit box, maybe?"

"No idea. He hated banks so I doubt it."

"Oh well, just a thought. Hang on." I fiddle with the second small key. "Here we are." Inside there are a few pieces of junk mail, a letter from the landlord wondering if Sven wants to renew the lease and a postcard from Natalie, from when she was in Venice recently. I stuff them in my pocket, wondering why she sent the card.

Chapter Sixty-Eight

Where Another Face from the Past Appears with a Gift for Harry

When I get back, determined to blob in front of the telly and watch England's overdue fight back against the Aussies, George has gone all floppy and Zenda is worried that it may be chickenpox. Dina wants me to ring Jackie, but she'll be working. I tell her it's pointless. "You're useless," she says, merely reinforcing how I feel. I put my trousers in to soak having picked up an unfortunate stain somewhere and lay down with a sleepy George on my lap. Poor little fellow is pale with red dots on his cheeks like a clown's face paint. While his boisterous, uncontained energy is overwhelming at times I prefer that to this passivity. It's dreadful, staring at his little chest rising and falling and hoping it doesn't stop while I'm holding him. In the background, Alderman is charging in and it looks certain England are slipping to defeat. Such a disappointment after the heroics of Headingly. I look at George again. Who'd be a parent? Exhausting and terrifying in equal measure. Much like the rest of my life right now in fact.

I'm feeling rather sorry for myself when there's a knock at the door. I can hear Zenda answer it and then some female voices laughing. Shortly after there's a knock at the sitting room door. Zenda's head appears. "Oh, you are there. I've someone who wants to say hello."

Appearing behind her is Monica Jepson. Back in the long hot summer of 1976, I met Monica at Hemingways where I was first introduced to Penny, Natalie and Sven. She had been married to Charlie Jepson for a couple of years by then and was hating every minute of it. He hit her with a golf club, or so she said and I wanted to try to protect her. One evening she came onto me in her room. I doubt anything would have happened. I was still an utterly inadequate virgin then and I ran a mile. Later I watched her sunbathe naked in a private field while the pervy hotel gardener polished Percy with the help of a tub of Nivea that I'd laced with cactus spines. I can still hear Cyril's howls and his curses but mostly I remember Monica, without a stitch on, staring at the hedge where we were hidden. To me back then, she was the epitome of a sexy woman.

She hasn't changed. She wafts into the room as I hurriedly stand and lay George on the sofa. One perfectly outlined eyebrow rises a fraction. "Yours?"

"My sister's."

She looks at the little lad with a moue of distaste – how I recognise that gesture. "Charming. Now come and give me a proper kiss. You are quite the hunk these days, aren't you?"

Knowing Zenda is watching is somewhat intimidating, well at least for me. Not Monica who kisses me, open mouthed, butterflying her tongue across mine. She stands back, holding me by the shoulders. "You need to do something about your complexion and your hair is a mess." Then she smiles. "But if you'd like to make love that would be lovely."

"Same old Monica." This from Zenda, who is laughing and we both join in. Monica shrugs off her denim jacket and sits down next to George. It's clear she is still reluctant to invest in underwear.

"I hear he has chickenpox, poor darling. You're immune, are you?"

"That's what I'm told although knowing how incompetent my parents can be, I expect I'll find out."

"You don't want to muck about, Harry. Catch it as an adult and it can make you impotent."

"Goodness Monica, do you always talk to Harry like this?"

"He brings it out in me."

"I'll make tea and give you a chance to catch up." Zenda winks in my direction. "I'll knock, just in case…"

Monica nods and strokes George under his chin. I assume we will fill the time with aimless chitchat, but as soon as the sitting room door is closed, Monica snatches up her bag, pulling out a folder. "Here. Take this. Don't look now, just stick it under the cushion or something. My telephone number is on the front. When you've read it, call me. Call me tonight after seven. Charlie will be out."

"What is it?"

"What you need, my lovely boy. Just what you need."

Moments later, Zenda reappears to find Monica quizzing me about my plans for a career in law and my flatmates and what I think of Brenda/Vera as my work colleague. For my part, I'm struggling to sit comfortably, still in equal parts intimidated and aroused in her presence.

Monica sips her tea and then puts the cup down. "How are things, Zenda? Reggie hasn't worked out where you're staying, I guess."

"Not yet although I think Claude knows."

I suddenly remember creepy Pac-a-Mac man. "God, I should have said. I think this man who's working for Mr Jepson followed you the last time you came to the office. I was worried he might tell Jep—your husband and he'd tell Master Rother."

Monica looks up. "Weasely chap, works for some outfit called Impressions?'

"That's it. How'd—?"

Monica smiles sourly. "When Charlie went inside, he gave me control of our finances. And some businesses that weren't very legitimate. Stephen, or Claude as Charlie insists on calling him, ran some of the more active operations. One was the investigation business, Impressions. Charlie took back control when he was paroled but, well, Albert has a certain loyalty to me, you see. So he doesn't do anything without clearing it with me first. He was acting on my behalf. That's how I found out where Zenda was, and that you and Charlie had met. And why I'm here now."

Zenda nods. "I thought maybe Bren or Claude had said? I didn't tell you Monica because I didn't want to put you in a difficult position. But I'm glad you came. Do you think Claude – sorry, Stephen – will cause problems?"

Monica picks up her tea. "That depends on Harry and how he sorts out Sven's estate and the gambling club. Now, tell me about your parents. Has your Mother got over her infatuation with my husband yet?"

I explain about sale of the garage business and how Mr Lewis is withholding the proceeds. Monica looks annoyed more than concerned although whether that's with Mum or Charlie I can't work out. When I've finished telling them about Mum in hospital with her anxiety and heart worries, Zenda looks upset but Monica merely tuts. "She is a ridiculous woman, your Mother. I will see if I can do something. I'll ring Lewis and have a word, but you may be right, he may have a reason not to release the cash, which will be beyond me. It will work out though. I think so, anyway."

Chapter Sixty-Nine

In Which Harry Uses the Telephone

The flat is empty. George is downstairs with Zenda. Dina is out with Jan. And Dobbin has gone to see Brenda/Vera before her set, expecting me to be along later. That's easier said than done. Since Dina, the last to leave, went at six, I've read through the folder Monica left. I now know who has control of Miles's club – Monica – and read through copies of the title deeds to club premises, the charges in Sven's favour that are over all the club's assets, stock and goodwill and a shareholders' agreement between him and Miles that gives Miles control of it and the estate agency. Monica holds transfer documents for all of Sven's interests that have been signed by Sven and dated. The only thing missing is the person to whom they are to be transferred. It is pretty clear that whoever fills in their name can claim Sven transferred everything before he died and they merely need to register it all post mortem.

I watch the clock make its stately progress up to seven o'clock and the designated time to make the phone call. I need to be getting off to meet Jackie. At just past the hour I dial Monica. "It's Harry."

"Have you read the papers?"

"Yes."

"You know Sven wanted the club closed down?"

"I know, but—"

"Hush and let me finish. He didn't know if you'd be able to sort things out. The reason I have these papers is because he wasn't sure if you'd be able to do it. He thought your relationship with Natalie might complicate things."

I wonder what he meant. We don't have a relationship. Not really.

"Well?"

"I want her safe. She wants out of her marriage. That's all I want to achieve. Her safety."

"Same as him. He also knows about my sister-in-law's problems with her husband. He said I could use these papers in any way I thought might help her."

"Why didn't you tell me all this straight after he died?"

"Marita told me to keep quiet. She's been keeping me informed. She told me today to tell you. It seems you need to have some more leverage with Miles? Have you sorted out where he's put the money?"

Suddenly I'm suspicious. Whose side is she on?

"Not really, but I'm making progress."

"Come on, Harry. You need to do better than that."

"Monica, a month ago I knew nothing about this club and Sven's affairs and Charlie's and Stephen's and Miles' interests and hopes and plans. It's driving me nuts—"

"Stop feeling sorry for yourself. Where have you got to?"

"I... how do I know I can trust you?"

"You don't. You didn't before, but back then you had good reason to be suspicious. But if I was going to screw you and everyone, I would have done a deal with Miles on my own, wouldn't I? Or Reggie or Charlie or, God forbid, Stephen. They all want a piece of this."

I mull that over for a moment. "Yes, that makes sense. Okay, I know how he has hidden the money that he's realised from selling his Father's businesses. I know where he wants it to go. But I have yet to find it. I will though. Meanwhile, I have several people who really really want to get incriminating information that Miles holds, which a combination of these ownership papers and some other information about Miles' business history may make possible."

"How would you plan on achieving that?"

"Bargain with him?"

There's a long pause. "You mean barter the ownership for some perceived benefits? Give Miles back control?"

"I suppose..."

"No, Harry. The one person who isn't getting control is Miles Tupps. He's a nasty piece of work and Sven did not want him even stronger than he already is. Do you think Natalie will come out of things well if Miles is empowered?"

She's right. Saving Penny and Jeremy and possibly Izzy by giving Miles the club will only make Natalie's position more difficult.

"Harry, are you there?"

"Yes. Okay. I see that. Let me think. There may be a way. One thing, you've been to the club?"

"Often."

"Okay, let me ask you a few questions." I look at my watch. "Tomorrow. I need to go out now. What time suits?"

407

"I'll call you. Give me your number. And you need to get a move on and sort this out. I can't wait forever."

"That's okay. If I don't sort it out soon I think I might just self-immolate with anxiety anyway."

Chapter Seventy

In Which Harry Goes to a Gig and is Kissed

Brenda/Vera is irrepressible. Certainly irreplaceable. And Groin is possessed, rather like Wilco Johnson of Dr Feelgood in his energy and verve. I really enjoy the Twats set, with four new songs dealing with, variously, the hell of commuting, why we no longer appreciate self-sacrifice, money as the root of all masturbation and a paean of praise for atheists. Maybe by taking her world a little bit more seriously, Brenda/Vera is allowing her songs to mature into something with legs – as to which, tonight's expose wasn't Brenda/Vera's chest but her fanny as she started the second half without the ripped trousers from the first part of her set. If there are any doubters in the audience, unsure if she favours underwear, those doubts are comprehensively assuaged during one particularly athletic jeté. I wonder when she'll realise she no longer needs to be an exhibitionist to garner an audience and can leave it to her songs. And a second thought tumbles after the first – was this lack of interest in discretion something she picked up from Monica?

At no stage does Dobbin leave the bar. Since Twats' concerts always end with a stage invasion I leave as Brenda/Vera calls for an encore and join him. He's less morose than usual and less morose than I imagined he'd be after recent revelations. "You okay mate? You know, about Vera's reasons for what she did?"

"I suppose. You know, she's a really nice person; she tries to be hard-faced and shocking and all this panto but it's such a pretence. I think the first real emotion she has shown was her terror of our resident mouse."

"Oh bugger. I promised to get a trap. Another item for my lengthy list."

He stops, staring at his nearly empty pint. "What about you? I've not asked but you're always with Di and those weird paintings. Vera said it's getting pretty heavy. You okay?"

I'm touched and it's good to know I have a friend who is supportive.

"I mean as I'm useless in a crisis and if things are bad, maybe you'd better make sure Penny's still talking to you. She always has your back, right?"

Great. Jackie hasn't yet appeared and it's nearly nine and now he's laying it on thick about Penny. Although he's right – Penny has been the most supportive friend I've probably ever had. Mostly. Tomorrow she'll back at work as a barmaid and hoping to get some acting gigs while worrying about the police investigation. I don't even know where she's staying now the Maggie thing has fallen apart. Christ, I'm plotting sexual exploits with Jackie while Penny—

"Hi boys. Why the long faces?"

Jackie walks over and puts an arm around both of us. "My favourite two men." She looks fabulous, strings of glitter tinsel twisted into her hair. "Vera told you about the foursome we've been planning?"

Dobbin's eyes nearly pop. "What? Us and you two?"

"Course. Only you two have to start things off and then we will have a little girl-on-girl action."

Dobbin looks at me and me at him. In a synchronicity that rarely is evident in our friendship we shake our heads together. "Nope. Not happening."

At that point, Brenda/Vera appears clutching a high ball glass full of something green and snotty. Happily, she has put on her trousers. "What's up guys?"

Jackie gives her a big hug. "Sorry I missed your first set. How'd it go?"

"Okay. I'm fed up getting groped though. How was work?"

"Yeah. Same as you. More geriatrics coping a feel. My bum is bruised rotten. Hopefully lover boy will rub in some arnica."

Brenda/Vera looks at me. "About Stephen… you know I really am sorry. Okay?"

"Sure. Don't worry about it."

"Good, cos Mum gave me some money for a curry. If we stick to veggie and papadums it should stretch to four. You up for it after my next set?"

It's brilliant, the four of us. We sit in the sitting room until gone two talking in low voices. I don't know if Dina's back but I doubt it. I hope George is okay with Zenda and Mr Jones. Jackie and I go to bed and make love until the wee hours as dawn is breaking. We shower and then go and hunt out a tea van she knows near Lambeth Bridge that serves the late-night shifts at Tommy's. The Thames moves slowly as I lean on the embankment wall and she chats to some friends. I wish I could stay here, watching time slip by, but tomorrow is upon me and I've decided I don't like tomorrows.

It's when we are walking back to the flat that Jackie says apropos of nothing, "I'm thinking of moving."

"Out of the nursing home?" My head spins. Maybe she should move in. That would end my endless speculation about me and Penny once and for all.

"Back home. Leicester. I'm fed up here. The pay's shit wherever I'm based and I'm not getting any really chances of working in the areas I want to."

"Oh."

She stops and holds my face. "It's not going to stop us." She kisses me, but there's a taste of a goodbye in there somewhere.

Sunday, 2nd August 1981

Chapter Seventy-One

Where Harry Opens His Mouth and Things Fall Apart

"H? You up?" Dina's face peers round my door.

"Eh? What time is it?"

"Nearly 10."

"Oh Christ." Four hours sleep. Marvellous. Jackie is lying against the wall, all of her except her bum and left leg covered by a sheet, dead to the world.

"I'll make tea. Kitchen, five minutes." The head disappears.

I kiss the bottom and am rewarded with a small groan. The temptation to do more with it is very strong but I pull on some tracksuit bottoms and head to the kitchen via the toilet.

I push open the door and freeze. Natalie and Penny are sitting at the table nursing mugs of tea. "Morning. How were the Twats? Dina said you went to their gig?"

"Loud but good." I'm praying Jackie stays put.

Natalie looks around at all of us. "We thought we'd go on a trip. I rang but you were spark out of it. Dina says she wants to go to Hampshire so we thought we'd make a day of it."

"Er, we'd not fit in the Porsche."

"It's in the garage, being serviced or something. They lent us a Range Rover."

"I think I'll stay here, thanks. Grab some sleep. I need to do some laundry too."

"Christ, H. Don't talk bollocks. I need to take George back. Jim's Mum says she'll look after him. I can't keep imposing on Zenda. And these two," she waves at Penny and Natalie, "want to help with the clues. With four of us we're sure to crack it."

What is Dina playing at? She knows Jackie is a few feet away, starkers. And I can't get the image of Jackie sumptuous arse out of my head, even with Penny staring at me. Something stirs in the back of my mind. Just before we fell asleep after our dawn walk, I'm sure I had this revelation and I'm positive I said something. Maybe she'll remember it. "I… look, give me a few minutes." I need to talk to Jackie.

Dina is all smiles. "We'll be ready for you."

The cow. Back in the bedroom, Jackie is sitting on the edge of the bed, dressed like she was last night. Before I can explain she says, "I heard that. What clues?"

I rub my eyes. "It's nothing." I want to scream. "I've been given this really hard puzzle by the friend who died recently. I told you he left me in charge of his estate. I need to sort out the clues he left. Didn't I say?" Oh yes, Harry. Well done. Make it sound like her fault.

"You never mentioned clues to me." She sounds hurt. Understandably. "Was that Penny? Is she helping?"

Oh shit. "He was a mutual friend. They all knew him. They knew how he thought. It's not that I asked her specially. Not like that at all."

She pulls on a red pixie boot. "Not like what? Not that I'm useless? Or stupid? Or you don't think I have a brain, just a nice arse?"

"No. Yes. I mean your arse is very nice, but—"

"Do you know you call out her name in your sleep?"

"What?"

She looks down. "After we've made love, you say her name. Not every time but… last night, I went to have a pee. When I got back the sheet had slipped. You had a stiffy and I thought…" She stops looking at me. "I thought you'd like it if I gave you a blowjob in your sleep, but when I took hold you called out her name." She looks devastated.

I should be able to say something but there's nothing I can think of. She shakes her head. "I'm not going to embarrass you by walking out in front of them so get dressed and go and sort out your clues or whatever they are. I'll go when I'm sure you've all gone."

"No, we need—"

"Don't." She stands and straightens her skirt. "Go. We both need to think about what it all means."

Chapter Seventy-Two

Where Harry Gets Up Close and Personal with a Mouse Trap

God, what an awkward journey. At least Penny sits in the front with Natalie driving and me in the back with Dina and George sleeping (mostly) between us. Dina does her best to lighten the atmosphere, but with Natalie concentrating on the road and not able to look at the pictures and Penny clearly as uncomfortable as me, it has the feeling of the first day at a new school about it. I'm also annoyed that I never asked Jackie if I said anything else last night, not that I could after her revelation. I know there's something else that's important if only I can free it from wherever it lurks.

Inevitably we make no real progress with the clues and when we drop off Dina at Jim's Mum's, Dina says she'll stay and get a lift over later while we head for my house to see Mum and Dad.

When we arrive, there are three cars on the hardstanding out front; my parents less than reliable Austin Maestro and two German ones. Voices, loud cheery voices, increase in volume as we wander round the back. There, a group of six tall blond bronzed men sit in a circle drinking what looks like Dad's incredibly unpalatable oak leaf wine and grinning stupidly. Dad sits between two of the tallest, each sporting minute denim shorts and hairless torsos.

"Harry? That you? Dina didn't say you were coming. And Penny, too! Your Mum will be pleased." He walks forward, glancing nervously back at the guests who are watching us with what appears to be indifference or maybe bland amusement.

Behind me I hear Natalie say, "Bloody hell Pen, cop that lot. Is this what heaven looks like?" Followed by a delightful sound – Penny laughing.

"I think, my silly woman, they are going to be more interested in Harry than you or me." This elicits a giggle from Natalie.

"Who are the guests, Dad?"

"Germans. On a walking break. They were going to stay at the hotel, but there was a scene with the receptionist."

"Magda? She's the last person to make a scene." Well, not the sort of scene I imagine Dad is thinking about.

"I don't know, Harry lad, but Ravi felt he needed to separate them before a conflict ensued. He suggested they stay here and they're very welcome."

I try to visualise Magda getting upset. She doesn't have the emotional range. I have a major soft spot for her and in other circumstances I'd want to find out more. Dad is still talking.

"They are all good friends and they are happy to share." He leans forward. "They're big lads, of course and squeezing into the single beds can't be easy; they do make a lot of noise, creaks and groans and what have you, but they're nice and polite and," he straightens up rather, "they say my wine is as good as their Riesling."

"Where's Mum? Is she well?"

"Better but no, not really well. She's in the gazebo, soaking up the sunshine. Go and see if you can persuade her to join us for tea. Pritti is in the kitchen cooking some roti – our European friends are new to Indian cuisine and are enjoying it immensely. Now Penny and... sorry, I've forgotten...?"

"Natalie."

"Of course, dear. I recognise you but my memory for names is awful these days. Come and join us. This is Jens and Hans and Peter and... oh just call them the lads, they don't seem to mind."

Mum is dozing. I shake her gently and she brightens up. "Harry, dear. Lovely to see you. What brings you here?"

"Natalie – you remember her?"

"Not really, dear."

"Penny's best friend."

"Oh yes. How is Penny?"

"She's here. We thought we'd have a day out in the country and they said they wanted to drive down here. They're talking to your new guests."

Mum pulls a face. "Your Father is so naïve. He has no idea these 'lads' are a queer convention. Will not hear of it."

"Does it matter?"

"Of course it doesn't. But if he ignores what's in front of him, when someone makes a stupid joke in the pub he can pretend he doesn't know and laugh along. It's cowardice."

Gosh. Mum the tolerant one. Whatever next. "I'm glad you're out of hospital."

Mum sinks back in her cushions. "Who is the real coward, eh? You heard about the sale money? That crook Lewis is sitting on it because Charlie has claimed it's mostly his. Which it is, but Petunia and Arthur don't need to know that, do they?"

"Do they know?"

She sinks further. "Yes. Well, your Father does. I had to tell him. To be honest he's been very good about it. You know what he said? He said 'Veronica, I think Harry will sort it out.' Apparently, you were going to talk to that crook of a lawyer. Now," she reaches out to squeeze my hand, "I don't expect you to do anything of the sort, but it has helped your Dad and for that I'm grateful."

"I'm working on it, Mum."

She shakes her head. "It's fine darling, really. I don't need to be mollycoddled. No need to tell fibs to protect me." She lets out a long, tired breath. "Maybe I'll try to sleep now. Don't go before saying goodbye, will you?"

Part of me wants to tell her I mean it, but, actually, right now I'm happy for at least one person not to expect miracles from me. "Mum, do we still have those mouse traps? We've one in the flat and I don't really want to buy new if I don't have to."

"Yes. In the garage somewhere I think. Your Father was playing around in there the other day. Something about getting his old moth collection out; he may have seen them."

The oiled and coquettish Gay Germans are gearing up for some sort of singsong and I just knew it won't be much fun for me. I corner Dad who is sneaking off to his shed. He nods when he hears what I want and we divert to the garage.

While I dig rummage around where he points, from behind a collection of flower pots he picks up a butterfly net and gives it a swish. "Going to the Natural History Museum reminded me how much fun collecting is, Harry, my partner in crime." He gives his belly a pat. "It would get me out a bit too. I could do with the exercise."

"Why have you kept so many…?" I pull at a cardboard box that is half-hidden by a terracotta mountain. "Is this what you meant?"

"Hmm? No, the other shelf."

"Oh for heaven's sake." I move to the other side of a pillar, cursing my Father's useless directions. "Did you ask that chap about the death's-head hawk moths?"

"Hmm? What?" He's picked up a glass bottle and sniffs it. "Crikey! Now that's some killing jar."

417

"You said you'd met a chap who'd found a death's-head caterpillar. You wanted to hear it squeak." Another box emerges from behind a pyramid of jam-jars.

"Yes, that's the one. Careful you don't break any or your Mum will kill you. They're for her jam."

"If that's their purpose I'd be doing humanity a favour if I destroyed them. Grrr." I give the box a heave; it's pretty stuck.

"I did have a word. Colin? Chris? What was his name? He says he'll keep me posted. He's a bit of a fanatic. There!" He darts past me as I'm about to free the box and from further down the shelf emerges with two rusty old traps that he drops on the work bench. "There's oil on the window ledge. Might be worth checking if they still spring."

"Thanks Dad. I'll just put this lot back first, shall I?"

He's back by the collecting bag from which he took his old killing jar, pulling out some stained pill boxes with clear lids in which the caught butterflies and moths could be kept if they were not to be killed immediately. "I gave him the box your friend gave me. He was so excited."

Icy trickles run down my neck. A memory of a conversation comes back to me. "Box? What box?"

He looks up and smiles. "You mentioned it in the museum or I might have forgotten about it. And anyway, your Mother never wanted me to keep it, given where it came from. I mean—"

"Sven? His Dad's moths?"

"That's it." He must see my expression. "Was that wrong?"

"Oh for…" With my mind spinning in manic windmills I must let go of the previously recalcitrant mouse trap since it decides to snap shut across my fingers. I've done many things in my 26 years but up to this point I have avoided swearing in front of my Father. So, when I bellow, "FUCKING NORAH! GETTING THE FUCKING THING OFF ME!!" his reaction is not immediately to help, but to say, "Now Harry, there is really no need for that kind of language."

The pain is almost as excruciating as the time when Rascal, our old cat, tried to circumcise me. Dad prizes the trap free but my fingers are already turning a worrying shade of purple. "I'll get your Mother."

As he leaves I manage to growl between clenched teeth. "I need his address. Colin or Chris." Tears are forming on my lashes. "Please, Dad."

After that it's a bit of a whirl. One of the Germans – Jens, I think – is a doctor and he recommends an x-ray. In no time, Natalie, Penny and I head for Lymington Hospital. As we wait to be seen, I explain what Dad told me.

"These moths are the only ones that make a noise. A squeak. Sven told me about being 'squeaky clean.' He leaves all of his Father's moth collection in the garage where the cars were, except he gave one part – the box with the death's-head hawk moths in it – to Dad as a gesture of apology for all his family had done. It has to be one of the clues. They'll be something in that box."

Natalie claps. "We'll check when we get back."

I try not to look too depressed. "The silly sod has given it away to this chap he met in the local pub. He doesn't even know the man's name but I asked him to find his address. Not sure it registered. Apparently it all followed me mentioning the box the other day so in a way it's my fault it's gone."

Penny, who has been listening carefully, bursts out laughing. "Your life is like a modern Sisyphus, isn't it? Two steps forward and one back."

I smile back at her. "I'm glad you find it funny."

"I'll be charged with murder next week if that cow has her way. That's really funny," she says.

"And I'll have been quartered and used as motorway bridge reinforcement by her husband." I point at Natalie with my good hand, "before that."

That increases the laughter.

Natalie looks from one of us to the other. "You're both sick. I have to sleep with that psycho and pretend I enjoy his tiny little dick being waved in my face."

By the time the doctor comes to find us we can barely breathe for laughing.

"Well, you can't be in too much pain, Mr Spittle. Shall I just check the joint?"

That, it is fair to say, ends the entertainment for the afternoon.

Chapter Seventy-Three

In Which Harry and Penny Visit an Old Friend and Harry Learns a Hard Truth

The thumb is just bruised, or so the torturer in a white coat informs me. He even shows me the x-ray, but it makes about as much sense as one of Sven's clues. When we get back, Mum and Mrs Ohja start fussing over me. Dad is in his shed so while I'm dispatched to the living room to watch the cricket in the hope of a clatter of Australian wickets, Penny heads off to find him. Border and Yallop seem intent on ruining my Sunday by building a winning partnership when Mrs Ojha comes in with a glass of homemade lemonade. She hands me a slip of paper. "Your Father said to give you this."

It's an address. No name. "Thanks. Will there be time for me to make a quick visit before lunch?"

"I thought you wanted to watch the cricket?"

Yallop ducks a Willis bouncer serenely. "I think I'll give it a miss, thanks. I'll go and find the others."

"You have about an hour. My Father was a spin bowler, back in the forties. He should have played for India."

"Really?"

"Leg spin and googly. He disguised it really well but they didn't give him many chances. The wrong caste, you see. It's why he went to Uganda."

"Why didn't I know this?"

She pats me on the cheek. I do well not to growl. "I'll tell you about it sometime. You run along now."

Run along. Pat my cheek. How old does she think I am? Grinding my teeth I head off in search of Natalie and Penny. Penny is just coming back from the shed, a grin growing on her face. "Your father's yoga is coming along. Though…" She snorts, "He needs to get some looser trousers. He said Pritti has the address."

I wave the paper like a younger, spottier version of Neville Chamberlain. "All we need are wheels. We have an hour."

420

Natalie emerges from the kitchen. "I thought I'd pop over and check on Magda. I didn't like the way they said she was upset. She's so tough, whatever it was must have hurt."

"Oh." I fight my disappointment. "We've the address for the moth man. Can you drop me on your way?"

"Can't we do both?"

"Mrs Ohja says lunch is an hour so probably not."

Natalie and Penny exchange a look. Natalie says, "Okay. Why don't you go with Harry, Pen? It might be useful to have someone as a distraction if you're planning on theft. I'll let Magda know; she'll understand."

"No, you go…" I stop. Natalie's expression speaks volumes and, in the moment, having some moral support is actually rather welcome. "Okay, sure. Good idea."

Natalie does a little skip, which is so incongruous that Penny and I laugh. "Can you hitch back?"

The address is near Ramsey Lodge, halfway between my parents' house and Lymington. After we've climbed out and looked up at the thatched cottage with a front door, which is ringed with pink, strongly scented roses, Penny squeezes my arm. "Did Pritti tell you who this mystery moth collector is?"

She's studying the house so I can only see her profile. "No? Do I know them?"

"Come on. This will be a treat."

The small front garden is bursting with colour and fragrance. "He knows his stuff, doesn't he?" Penny bends to sniff a tall thin blue-topped plant and grins up at me. "Well?"

"Well what?" Something is nagging at me, making me nauseous.

For her part Penny can't stop grinning. "Come on. Let's see if he's in."

Before I can press her further, she gives the door knocker a hard rap. Through the small glass window in the top half I can see a figure approach. The owner is large and round and…

"Cyril?"

"Youse? Boiy, what you wanna?"

Penny whispers next to my ear, "Who knew, eh?" and quickly moves past me to reach up and peck him on the flabby cheek. "Hello. Remember me? Penny."

Cyril is momentarily nonplussed to see her. He was fascinated by her 'titties' when we all worked at Hemingways back in the mid-seventies. Cyril Larrard – no wonder his surname rang a bell – was a gardener of huge distinction and also the pervy creep who spied on any women who might be sunbathing in the small 'rooms' he had created with laurel hedges. It was his nob that became perforated with cactus spines as I sought to stop him. He was paid off, if I remember right, by Ravi after he took over the hotel. As for his impaled penis…

He's laughing. "Youse a nerve coming thisa place. What you wanna?"

Penny can obviously see I'm dumbstruck because she takes Cyril's arm. "How are you? Are you still gardening? This place looks fabulous."

He nods with that oh-so-familiar nod. "Ar. Comes and lookie. Bootifool."

He's either forgotten I'm here or chooses to ignore me, because he turns on his heels and heads for the back of his cottage. Penny whispers to me, "See if you can find the box while I flatter his ego."

"Keep away from his hands."

"Don't I remember? Coming Cyril!"

I give them a moment and then dart into the front room. It's really gloomy, the small square windows not giving much light even without all the foliage that's growing over his cottage. A cursory glance at the sitting room reveals no moths. I scoot up the stairs. There are two small rooms between which has been squashed a bathroom. Lying on the bed in the room to the left is a glass-fronted wooden box full of death's-head hawk moths. Bingo!

They are stunning and beautifully set, but I can't spend time admiring their makings. I flip the box over and check the backing; it's covered in brown paper that I rip off. Underneath is a cardboard insert, which I gently prize away.

Downstairs I hear voices returning. Penny is keeping up a stream of chatter while Cyril is articulating his customary range of grunts and mixed consonants. I'm pretty sure Penny has raised her voice, probably to help me hear their approach, but the walls in this place are so thick that I can't make out what she's saying. Inside the cardboard backing there is a folded sheet. It's a picture on one side and some writing on the other in Sven's spidery hand, but it's impossible to make out in the gloom and anyway I don't have the luxury of studying it right now. Quickly I stuff it inside my shirt and carefully feel inside the box. No diamonds, no suggestion of any diamonds. Damn, and I was so sure.

I can't do anything about the backing paper but I manage to re-insert the cardboard and replace the box pretty much where I found it. Downstairs I hear Penny say, "Tea would be lovely. In here?" A door opens. Sounds like the little living room. Time to join mine host.

I make it to the landing when I realise Cyril is at the bottom of the stairs and about to come up. Shit. I really can't make any sort of coherent decision at moments like this but my mind goes immediately to the bath surrounded by a plastic shower curtain covered in blue dolphins. If I hide there… decision made I turn around and slip into the little room.

Cyril's journey up the stairs is clearly a struggle. Each plodding step is accompanied by an explosion of air. Inevitably and predictably he chooses to come into the bathroom. I can just about make out his silhouette as he approaches the toilet bowl. With a lot of groaning and grunting he looks in silhouette like he's taking a pee.

That's when my foot slips and sends the wire tray that holds all his bath paraphernalia flying. In moments the curtain is ripped back and there he is facing me.

I begin to say, "Cyril, I can explain."

"What's yousa doing there, you little shit? Youse…" He peters to a halt as he registers where I'm staring. Very deliberately he pushes what is left of his penis inside his fly. The extent of the repercussions from my adulteration of his hand cream is plain. His nob is now a rather shriveled raw-ended little stump.

"Happy is you, boiy?" He stuffs it back inside his trousers. There is a mix of anger and sorrow in his confused expression. "Whys don't youse booger orf?"

I accept his advice with as much speed as I can muster. Downstairs I pause to call Penny to join me. Once outside we begin walking towards the main road at a fair clip. Penny has a small posy of flowers in her hands and is smiling. "He seems pretty content, you know. Funny old boy. Seems to have landed on his feet, though. He has this market garden – you get to it from a gate at the end of his garden – and he's supplying several places with veg, including Hemingways. Did you find what you wanted?"

I can't really explain to her and really don't want to. I feel awful. I can see that at the time doing what I did seemed like a justifiable thing, but did my punishment really fit the crime? What gave me the right to decide on both his guilt and what was to happen to him? I head for the road without a word – the plan is to hitch a lift home.

Penny catches up with me. "Are you okay? You look really upset."

"Did you know he's had his penis amputated because of me? Because of what I did?"

She nods. "Yes, Sven told me ages ago. We thought you'd feel awful if you knew; that's why we didn't tell you. Did he tell you?"

I can't tell her I've seen it. "Well, you're right. I do feel awful."

"Don't. He deserved it. He's said as much himself. Hemingway wasn't going to stop him perving all the time and someone had to – you had the courage to do something about it."

I stop abruptly and turn and face Penny. "I didn't understand Pen, not really. It didn't make me right, just because others hadn't stood up to him. It makes me a vigilante." I increase my speed and then stop and turn. "If I'm to live with myself, I have to be better than that, play by the rules. I'm not the sort of person who can be some sort of moral judge. I can't make really important decisions. Christ, I'm going to be an officer of the Court when I'm admitted as a solicitor and that terrifies me."

We walk on for a bit with our thumbs held out to hitch a ride. Then she says, "The fact you feel horrid, that you feel guilt does you credit, but sometimes we have choices. Like Sven and his Father's businesses. He could have disowned everything. Walked away and had nothing to do with it. Then there would have been chaos and violence and God knows what else. He's had to deal with some dreadful people and sometimes that's means the lesser of two very big evils. But the bigger the man the greater the willingness to act and not run. At least to me. You do that, Harry. You hate it, but you don't hide from it. That's…"

She's stopped walking. I only realise when I'm a few feet ahead, which makes me stop and turn.

"… and that's why I love you."

Shit. Why did she have to say that? I'm about to say something when she races past me.

"Quick, he's stopping."

I walk slowly after her as she holds open the rear door of a stopped car, making sure the driver doesn't change his mind. Honestly, I'd prefer to walk but she's not giving me that option.

Chapter Seventy-Four

Where Harry Has His Suspicions Confirmed and Misses Out Again

When we get back there's a message from Natalie. She's spending the afternoon with Magda and will pick us up at five to drive back to London. I'm really not in the mood to look at Sven's sketches what with my mind pretty much in bits following Penny's declaration. I am unable to think, let alone think straight, so I sit under an old apple tree until lunch after which I move around the garden to hide, but Penny finds me.

"I'm tired. Can—?"

"Harry, I know I'm rubbish. I know you're with Jackie now. I shouldn't have said that. It wasn't fair. I'm sorry. I… can we just look at whatever it is you've found? I really do want to help."

Her expression is so familiar from those many occasions when we've argued that I can tell the storm has abated. I want to believe it, want to feel something more than a memory.

"He really did trust you, you know? I realise that's hard to believe but he understood you better than the rest of us. Natalie asked him, oh maybe last November, why he didn't tell you what he thought about you, and he said you'd not believe him and it would only make things worse. And you'd never liked him, not really – you couldn't be friends, he said – so it was better you didn't know."

I nod, happy to stop thinking about her declaration and my feelings about it. "He was probably right. If he'd come out and asked me directly to sort this bloody mess I'd have run a mile." As I'm talking I pull out the sheet and smooth it out on the bench between us, picture side up.

"It's a block of flats." Penry states the bleeding obvious.

"It's the block in Wapping where Sven's place is. Natalie's too." My turn to be say what doesn't need saying.

"And Miles." Another utterly unnecessary statement.

"Yes." When did she get so irritating?

"What's that mean, do you suppose?" Written on the top, in Sven's hand, is:

Hurry, before you're too late.

"And who's that?"

Standing with his back to the door to the block is a man who looks like he's waiting to be let in.

"I've no idea. It's not Miles or Stephen or me. God knows."

Penny turns the sheet over. "Why does he write so small?" She squints hard. "I'll read it out."

"I hope it doesn't make my brain hurt. I could really do with something that makes stuff clearer."

In fact it's not complicated, for once.

Dear Harold

Well done on getting this far. I assume you've found the treasure and by now know the recipients. I thought you might welcome an explanation of what I want you to do when you distribute the assets to each of the seven people; I'm not naming names because you know who's who by now. You will have seen, after the treasure has been valued, that it is kosher – in so far as any of the gem dealers in Hatton Garden are kosher – and dated within the last three months prior to my Will so good for probate. I want you to declare and pay all you should by way of tax. Lewis may have some explaining to do about my Father's estate because he didn't want to include any of the business interests when the estate accounts were done but, well, he can talk his way out of that. I'm sure he will.

So, here we go.

Number 1: this one gets everything that is left after you sort out what's below. She will deal with her share as she and I agreed before my death.

Number 2: this is difficult; my Father took unfair advantage of one particular man, who, despite his own unethical business dealings, is entitled to recompense. You may think I should give this money to number 1 but I am only judgmental so far as my own family is concerned. As giving this man all he is entitled to will cause problems I'm leaving it all to that woman to decide what happens to it. I believe her strong enough to deal with any unpleasantness.

Number 3: you – your share is primarily to pay the taxes and duties and other expenses on my death and the rest is for you to do with as you want.

Number 4: He loaned money for the club but he also owes the club money; since it is to be closed this will repay his loan. I know he probably owes the club for his gambling debts, but someone else can worry about that.

Number 5: this is guilt money, Harry, but for my parents this woman would not be struggling and would not have to sell her family business – Lewis will acquire it on behalf of a nominee, which is me, and he will transfer it back at no cost six months after my death or on you giving him a code word – think of someone we both worked with at Hemingways, his nickname was a vegetable – whichever is the earlier; the remaining money is to expand her existing business as she sees fit and provide working capital going forward for all her family's interests

Number 6: guilt money again, Harry – this man has been my one and only true friend over many years and I promised him help to set up a business marketing clothing and other branded gear to young visitors to the New Forest – all I ask is he comes up with a viable plan and the money is his, no strings; otherwise I fear he might smoke himself to death.

Number 7: by now you will know of my concerns for Natalie; I have tried and failed to establish an exit strategy for her but this money is for you to try to establish something. The best I can suggest is you speak to my family accountant. I've discussed some ideas with him and his counsel is always wise and decisive. There is another gentleman who you know and whose views are coloured by some long-term antipathies. You may use his services but be careful. He can be volatile.

That said, if you explain what has happened fully to that gentleman I think you will find him understanding. I hope so. At heart, I think he has good intentions.

Penny sits back, her gaze fixed on the door almost as if she's checking to see if someone is about to come looking for us. "I get some of that, Harry. Does it make sense to you?"

The hairs on my neck have risen. "Yes. Yes, it does. A lot. I wish I'd had it earlier."

"Who is he talking about?"

I sigh. "Number one is Marita. Charlie Jepson is two but Monica gets his share. Three is me and four is Vera's step-Dad. My Mum is next then Christian and last is Miles, well the club and the estate agency but mostly how to decouple Natalie from Miles."

"I know you've mentioned Mr Lewis the lawyer but do you know this accountant? Is he any good?"

"Oh yes. Rock solid."

"You don't look very happy. Is everything going to be okay?"

I really have no answer to that. Without the diamonds who knows what will happen?

Then she kills me. "I thought you'd be happy, what with us winning."

"Winning?" Icy fingers run up and down my spine. Not again.

"Yes, Botham destroyed them. Five wickets for nothing. It's all over the radio. Are you pleased?"

She wants me to smile, to make it all better, but that's twice in succession I've been sure we are going to be stuffed only for a rabbit to be pulled out of a hat.

I try to do what she wants and smile, but all I feel is a sense that Ian-bloody-Botham has used up the whole nation's luck quotient and my hopes of getting out of Sven's mess in one piece are as good as gone.

And I'm still none the wiser when it comes to what to do about the bloody club and Miles.

Chapter Seventy-Five

And so Harry is Asked to Choose

We crawl into the flat at 10:00. It's dark and quiet. I place a trap in the hall with nothing on it. Of course we have no food in the flat; why would we?

Penny makes tea and we sit and talk through Sven's letter. After half an hour Dobbin appears. He's awfully sunburnt. "What happened to you?"

He accepts the tea and sits down. "After the gig, I thought she'd changed but yesterday she was up and determined we went to Kent."

"Kent?"

"Specifically Folkstone. Dungeness power station had an open day. Of course, shagging next to a nuclear reactor was too good an opportunity to miss. And while we were about it, we also ticked off 'bird sanctuary,' 'drainage ditch' 'Martello tower' and 'shingle beach.' I was so knackered by then I fell asleep on the pebbles and woke up looking like this. Oh, Jackie rang. There's a note on your bed." He looks at Penny. "Assuming you're still interested." He sounds terse.

I don't look at Penny as I fetch the note. Easy enough to understand: "Call me."

I creep past the kitchen to our newly restored phone and dial her number. Of course, she answers on the first ring. "Hi."

"Hi. How was the day out? You sort out your clues?"

"We made a bit of progress."

"Good. Look Harry, about last night."

"It was great."

"Was it? Really? I mean the sex is always good" – that's good to know – "but that's not the be all and end all, is it? I've been thinking about this and you're with the wrong woman when you're with me."

"Jackie, I didn't know I would call out her name."

"It's not the first time. You call out a lot, especially after sex. And it's often her. You're always mentioning her. And you don't trust me with these clues and—"

"I explained that's because—"

"Hear me out. I know you like me, maybe more than that, but it's the same with her. You're not over her or her you from what I hear.

429

I'm serious about moving. The opportunities are good too and I know you'll not come with me. I wouldn't expect you to. But I'm not a filler. Either you break up properly and we can talk about us or I move on."

"Oh."

"She's there, isn't she?"

"I... er..."

"Exactly. You trust her to help you. Not me."

"That's not fair."

"Isn't it?"

There's a silence. A thought occurs to me. "Did I call out? Last night? Apart from Penny?"

"Last night? I... you mentioned needing to catch the post. You were pretty—"

"The post." My heart rate leaps to something unhealthy. "You sure?"

"Harry, what the fuck does the postman matter?"

"Anything else? About diamonds, maybe?"

"Oh, fuck you." She slams down the phone.

I've probably ruined another relationship yet I can't help smiling. A light has just gone on in the foggy Spittle brain and it feels good.

When I return to the kitchen, Penny has washed up and is leaning against the sink. She says, "I'd better be going."

"Where?"

"I'm staying in the flat."

"Bit late to disturb Marita. Stay here."

"I suppose as Dina isn't here..."

"With me."

"Are you sure? I mean, what about Jackie?"

"Yes. Well, I may have just 'bollocked' that, to coin a Dobbin expression, like I usually do."

"Only if you don't mind."

Do I? Mind that is. Frankly, just now I don't give a ferret's nadgers.

We get into bed and I'm pretty intent on not having sex and so we spoon for a while. Then my nob, which has always had its own agenda brushes her bum and she grinds and I pull away and she thinks I want her to turn round and, well, that ends with us kissing and things happen. As in... Oh never mind; just take it from me that I'm officially a slimy two-timing sleazeball, but at least if I call out a name the chances are I'll not upset anyone. And for the first time in a while sleep comes quite easily.

Monday, 3rd August 1981

Chapter Seventy-Six

In Which Harry Meets Teddy and Thinks about the Future

I'm getting good at excuses for not going to the office. My interview with the recruitment agency is at 9:30 somewhere in Holborn; I throw caution to the four winds and catch the bus then the tube. My AZ street map is about 15 years out of date and someone has torn out five pages, but somehow I navigate my way to the front door by 9:25. I thought I'd be nervous but after the weekend I've had and the belief I now know where the diamonds may be, naïve though that probably is, the idea of an interview that could define if not my life then at least the next few years is truly rather unexciting.

The receptionist for Peebles and Toss is the double of Gloria as far as hair, make up and dress sense is concerned, but whereas Gloria's approach to a new face is to assume some cunning trickery, Bonny lives up to her name. She virtually quivers with excitement. "Miss Teddy is sooooo excited to see you Mr Spittle. Take a seat; she won't be a mo. Coffee?"

I'm sipping what is actually an extraordinarily nice coffee when John Thomas emerges from a room to my left. For someone who is congenitally morose he is almost chipper. Seeing me dampens his spirits somewhat but he rallies quickly. "Hello Harry. I didn't know you were the competition? That's me buggered then."

Before I can respond Bonny intervenes. "Noooo Mr Thomas, I think Miss Teddy has a different destination in mind for you. You two friends? How lovely. I think lawyers are soooo lovely."

John leaves, clearly convinced that I have ruined his career chances.

"Harry. I'm Teddy."

Teddy, or Edwina as her business card tells me, Moffat is short, dumpy and unbelievably full of energy. In the space of a 30-minute interview, after each question I answer she either makes a call or bellows for the beaming Bonny to make her a coffee or get her something. She has provisionally agreed to set me up with four interviews in property departments in four prestigious city law firms, although she confides that she thinks "Newe Waters is your sort of firm." Everyone has heard of Newe Waters, a legal outfit to the great and the good and with a number of major corporations on its client list. "They don't pay as well as some of the more, shall we say, upstart outfits but it's decent."

What is the etiquette here? Do I feign indifference, like money is secondary to working for a quality name, or do I do what she clearly knows I'm desperate to do which is to ask how much? In such circumstances, I tend to favour the strong silent type, a look often ruined, or so I've been told, because my jaw tends to droop and I dribble a teeny bit.

"Salary is £7000 per annum currently although by the time you join that will be reviewed. And there will be the usual allowances. After three years there's a car available and 25 days annual leave." She makes it sound like it's rather poor show but she is well aware that's nearly double what I'm currently on. "I'll call with some dates. Is it okay to ring you at work?"

"Sure." Is it? Why am I being so daring?

Hell, I float as I leave the room with her final offer ringing in my ears. "Bonny will call you and arrange a practice interview before you meet the partners. We want you as well prepared as possible, don't we?"

Chapter Seventy-Seven

In Which Harry Goes to Lunch

Reality bites when I reach my desk. There's a note saying Miles has called. Before I've had a chance to wash away the sweat of cycling Brenda/Vera bursts in. McNoble has been badgering her about what I've found out. It seems Monica might have let slip she's seen me and he's awfully suspicious, threatening to tell Reggie where she and her Mother are if she doesn't get chapter and verse from me, pronto.

"It's okay."

She's really distraught.

"Tell him I've made a breakthrough."

"Harry, is that wise?"

"Tell him I'm meeting Miles at his flat at 7:00 pm. Maybe he could meet us both there?"

She sounds really troubled by this idea. "Harry, you can't."

"Honestly, I'll be fine. I'll have protection."

"What do you mean?"

"It's in hand. Now I have to make some calls."

The protection – in my head I'm hoping I can get one of the Grate brothers to join me – promotes the first call. To Grant. Before I can explain my request, he jumps in. "'arry, Hi've 'ad a bit hof news. About hour friend Mr Tupps."

I listen carefully and can't help grinning. The other calls are just as encouraging. When I get through to Miles' office, I'm almost bursting but I only reach a secretary who promises to pass on my message. I probably should insist on him confirming but something tells me he will be there.

I carry on with my calls. I'm beginning to enjoy this phone thing and I tick off Zenda, Natalie, Monica and then McNoble, who doesn't answer. I turn to the humdrum nature of my current workload. Within minutes it turns my mood from encouraged to bored.

At just before 1:00 Jeremy appears looking like a wreck – the bags under his eyes are so dark and pronounced that at first I think he's been beaten up – but he then startles me by offering to take me for lunch. That's a first. I assume it's to quiz me about progress with the

435

pictures, but he surprises me further by offering me a job on qualification. "Lucinda and I have been talking. We'd like you to stay with us. I know times are tough out there, but you deserve a break. I'm sure knowing you have a job will be a relief, yes?"

The contrast with Teddy's breezy confidence that 'we'll place you, no sweat' is remarkable. All I can do is stare at him. He actually believes what he is saying. He has no more idea how many jobs there are just now than I had a week or so ago.

"Of course," he adds, "the work will remain the same – mostly what I need from you. I doubt we will take on a new clerk; you will do that work alongside Brenda until she qualifies next year."

He's waiting for me to bite his hand off.

"How much will you pay?"

"Sorry?" It is a pleasure to see him floored by my question.

"What will you pay me? What will my salary be?"

"I… we… do you accept?"

"I need to know what you will pay me. And what other benefits there are."

"Surely being employed should be your prime motivator?"

"Yes, of course but I'd still like to know."

"I think we might run to £4500." He smiles like that's splendid news, which yesterday it would have been, "and we can increase your luncheon vouchers to 30p a day. Although," his face falls slightly, "15p will bear tax."

I smile. "Thank you for the offer. Can I think about it?"

He looks completely flummoxed that I've not accepted immediately.

"Er, of course. Tomorrow?"

"Friday week would be better."

"Right. Okay."

How I don't tell him where to stick his poxy job, I don't know. What has come over me? Do I like the new confident me? I'm not sure I do.

At 5:00 I leave the office. Without my bike, I catch two buses and then walk to the Wapping flat. I'm nervous as I let myself through the front door. I stand, like the man in Sven's drawing who I couldn't identify yesterday but who I now realise is the postman. He was waiting to be buzzed in as I imagine he is every day.

'Hurry,' Sven wrote. 'Post-haste.' Post. Bloody obvious really.

I pull out the four keys Jan Kruis gave me oh so long ago. Four keys and two that are almost the same, but only one opened Sven's mail box.

The letter boxes for the flats are grey tins like the safety deposit boxes in banks. That's what I thought the spare key might be for. Each box has a slot in the front, where the number of the flat or the name of the tenant is written on a piece of card. There are 10 flats. Sven's flat has the number while Miles' name and the flat number are on his. I check Sven's box again; just more junk, this one from the *Reader's Digest* offering glorious wealth if the addressee completes a form. Yeah, sure.

Why didn't I make the obvious connection? Two keys that look like they might be the same. Two keys that work on similar locks. Nervously I cast along the ranks of the other boxes and there it is. While there are 10 flats, there are 12 boxes. Probably because they make them in rows of four. On the front of the bottom far left box someone has written on a card and slipped it in the front slot: 'HS.' It's the same as was on the envelope in the Porsche. It's in Sven's spidery hand.

Taking the one key Jan gave me weeks ago that I thought was a spare or unimportant, I open the box. Inside is a padded envelope. My heart can barely stay put. Checking that Miles or indeed anyone else hasn't appeared I untuck the flap and reach inside. Immediately my fingertips touch little stones through a polythene bag. Yep, this is it. Gingerly I slip the envelope back inside its home and lock the box. Time to get ready to talk to Miles.

Chapter Seventy-Eight

In Which Harry Spills the Beans and Means It

Miles arrives back promptly at 6:00. So okay, I sort of lied to Brenda/Vera. I was pretty sure that even if I failed to speak to McNoble she would and he'd arrive at 7:00. I wait in the pub opposite, drinking a beer and watching the front door. Around 15 minutes later, Monica and Zenda arrive, Monica sweeping into the lounge bar with ridiculous confidence and Zenda scurrying in like a wartime spy. I'm gratified to see how surprised both of them are. "Hi! Drink?"

Monica recovers first. "What's going on Harry? You said you'd sorted out Sven's affairs and needed to explain. Why here? And what's Zenda got to do with it?"

"All will become apparent." I check my watch even though I'm fully aware of the time. "Come on. We have an appointment."

Neither asks any more but follow me across the road. I press the bell.

"Yeah?" Miles is his usual welcoming and charming self when I speak to him over the intercom.

"It's Harry. And a couple of friends."

"Come up." He buzzes us in.

The front door is open and Miles is in a ridiculous red kimono. He has very skinny ankles. "These your bodyguards, are they? Or some sort of peace offering? You've been fucking me around for too long; just give me the cash I'm owed, plus the paperwork to free the club and you can all fuck off."

"Yes, I'd love some tea. Thanks."

"Listen, you little shit—"

Yep, okay, I am terrified at this point but Monica, having lived with Charlie Jepson for years, is made of stronger stuff. She pushes past both of us and shrugs off her jacket. "Don't be childish, Miles. I know you know who I am. This is my sister, Reggie Rother's wife. Just put the kettle on and let Harry explain. He's in charge."

"Him? He couldn't organise a piss—"

"No, you're right I couldn't. Look down there."

Miles comes to the window. Grant Grate and his brothers have lined up on the pavement. Grant was eager that all his brothers came along. "They're keen to 'elp, 'arry." They are all wearing their black suits. They must look terrifying to the casual observer, but I can see that Grew, the shortest of the bunch, is barely able to contain his laughter.

"They're my people now. So, let's have tea and a chat."

His face is a picture and without Monica's calming presence I'd be a wreck. He looks like he's desperate to threaten me, but isn't sure how without it sounding pathetic.

I pull out a copy of Sven's final picture with all the beneficiaries included – Miles is in the centre – and lay it on the table. "Sven knew he was going to die. He worried that he wouldn't be able to complete what he planned, which is why he asked me to do it for him. I know you know what he wanted, Miles. To shut the club down and let Natalie have a divorce."

"Yeah, well, that ain't happening."

"You see, I think it will."

"This is fucking—"

"Miles, sit down." Monica is half out of her seat.

I ignore them and go to the window, giving Grant a wave. "I'll let him in, shall I? He might help sort this out." I signal to him and he walks across the road to the door.

Grant is the epitome of an accountant without the lumps of meat that are his siblings either side. He nods as I make the introductions and sits at the head of the table. Having smiled all around – it's pleasing that everyone just watches him – he puts his briefcase in front of him and pulls out a fat file. When he has it open on the table he nods at me.

"Okay," I say, "Grant is a man of detail. In distributing the estate, Sven's biggest worry was you Miles. You and Natalie and especially your club. Currently Monica here controls it—"

"You? You bitch, where is it? Where are the deeds?"

Grant pats the file. "Hall 'ere Mr Tupps."

Miles sags like a leaky balloon. "Right. Good. So I get it, do I?"

"He gave it to Monica because he knew his Father had acquired it unethically from Charlie Jepson and he felt, rightly, that it should go back to him," I say.

"Jepson hasn't any claim to it. I've built it up. It's mine."

"But Sven also understood how difficult it would be for Stephen McNoble if his Father took it back. The only solution was to close it."

"Well that ain't fucking happening either, lawyer boy."

"I understand your frustration Miles, I really do. From what I've heard you've put a lot of effort into making it pay. Illegal gambling, drugs, setting up blackmail—"

"I will fucking brain you."

Grant stands and goes to the window, waving as I did. Miles watches him, a satisfying glint of terror in his eyes. Shortly Graham appears at the door. After a word from Grant he goes and stands behind Miles. Nothing is said but the implication is clear. I glance around. Monica nods, seemingly vaguely impressed but Zenda looks ashen; she is clearly horrified at the threat of violence.

"Grant has witness statements about all these activities, implicating you. He has detailed records of how you channel the proceeds, how the cash is laundered. Several agencies – Inland Revenue, Customs and Excise, the Police – will be interested in what Grant's folder contains."

Miles' eyes narrow and he shakes his head. "Your pet gorillas keep you safe for now, but they won't always be by your side and when they ain't…" He smacks a fist into the palm of his other hand, making Zenda jump.

"I told you Miles, Sven had a very ethical and indeed non-judgmental approach. He wouldn't want you to feel aggrieved. So he made you an, shall we say, informal beneficiary of his estate. You will receive a reasonable value for the club in the shape of uncut diamonds, its goodwill fix—"

He's up out of his seat, fists clenched, face beetroot. "That's boll—"

Graham's fist comes down hard on his head and Miles drops back into his seat like a puppet whose strings have just been cut.

I cough, not at all comfortably. I take a peek at Zenda. Her eyes are squeezed tightly shut. "Fixtures and fittings and effects."

Miles shakes his head, then rubs his cranium. "What am I meant to do with that?"

I smile and nod at Grant. He slips a single sheet from the folder. It's an official-looking form with green print. He slides it to me and I slide it to Miles. He glances at it and mimics Zenda.

"Your wife in Leeds would probably like to see more of you. Josephine, yes? As would your son. Anthony isn't it? And Ruby? Your little girl. She's what now? Two? With this money you can set up home there, can't you?" I turn to Monica. "I will take over the club and have it shut down. I've no idea what will happen to the site but the staff will be brought into the same trust fund as supports the Grate family, as long as they cease pursuing any criminality. Grant here will administer it."

She nods. "What about Charlie?"

"I will come to that later." I turn back to Miles. "You grievously used Natalie in the blackmail, as well as generally. You will divorce her immediately. If you do and if you give her a generous settlement – which I will fund from Sven's money – I will say nothing of the bigamy. It's not only criminal but would no doubt severely damage your Leeds relationship that, according to Grant's enquiries, turns out to be oddly stable. In return I want all the prints and negatives and any other evidence of the blackmail pictures. One of Grant's brothers will go with you after this and collect all items connected with that part of your sorry game. If at any stage I hear whispers of you trying to reactivate the blackmail we will turn the evidence we've mentioned over to the authorities."

Miles has slumped back in his chair. As I've paused for breath, he leans forward. I assume he's going to have another go at me but he says, "Sven didn't have your balls, you know. He'd not have done that." He rubs his face so hard the rippling looks very painful. "She knows, you know?"

"Sorry?"

"Natalie knows about Jo. And the kids."

"She does?"

He wobbles his hand. "Well, suspects something. She ain't stupid... did she say anything? No, she wouldn't, would she?"

"She didn't, no."

He nods, a small smile on his face. "Yeah, it doesn't look good, does it? Knowing she's just a kept woman, yeah. Not good for the ego. How'd you find out?"

I shrug. "Natalie said you went to the north a lot. Leeds. You disappeared off without your beloved Porsche. There was a train ticket in your coat pocket. You wouldn't catch a train out of choice unless you didn't want someone to know about the Porsche. It's a status symbol for you – you can keep it if you want, by the way – so it made me wonder what dragged you to Leeds, almost incognito. It didn't take Grant's boys long to find out. I think that had Sven known, he'd have done what I've done."

441

Miles shakes his head. "Nah. Takes a clear head and balls to pull that off. Okay, if the price is fair then we have a deal." He rubs his head again, then leans right forward and offers me his hand. After a pause I take it.

The grip is limp. "Is it true?" He asks, almost in a whisper.

"What?"

"You killed his Dad? Sven's?"

I can feel Zenda stiffen.

"Not exactly. I was the indirect cause."

"Good enough for me. Mind you, you'd have got on well with him. He had your ruthless streak." He glances back at Graham. "Do I go with this one and get the stuff?"

"Please."

There's a long silence when they've gone. Monica breaks it. "Well, well. Are you really the same callow youth from Hemingways?"

"The same terrified little boy, yes."

I smile and turn to Zenda. "I'm—"

Her expression has turned purple. She is furious. "How dare you make me sit through that? How dare you?"

"I'm sorry. I hadn't realised it would turn out to be quite so... stressful."

"Why am I here? Why on Earth—?"

"Reggie."

She stops and her brow furrows.

"Monica too. As I've mentioned, Sven felt Charlie should be recompensed for what his Father extracted under, um, false pretences. That said, we know Stephen won't be happy. It's the same with Master Rother. Sven wanted you, Monica, to have Charlie's share and for you to decide what – if anything – Charlie received. While Sven directed me to give back to your husband what he was owed, I've decided you should have it Zenda. There's no documentation, nothing contractual so Rother cannot make any sort of claim to it and if it came out what it was for, he can kiss goodbye to his legal career. I also want to ask Monica if she will arrange for Impressions – they are a detective agency – to help you pull together whatever is necessary for a divorce. And finally I wanted you to meet Grant and his siblings. They are all perfectly respectable businessmen, Zenda, really, but they used to inhabit a very different world. They understand how first impressions can help clarify some stubborn people's thinking. You may not want to use their services. I hope you never feel the need to, but they are prepared to represent you in any reasonable capacity against your husband to ensure you don't have to stay hidden as you are now. And that obviously extends to Brenda." I suck in a breath. "That's why you're here and why you had to go through that. I'm sorry."

The silence this time is extended. I'm exhausted. The two women look shell-shocked. Grant reads the file, apparently in his own little bubble.

The doorbell rings – it's 7:00 pm. McNoble is on time. "Monica. It's your stepson. Can you buzz him in please? I think we might need to run through some of that with him."

When McNoble enters, he's clearly surprised to see all of us despite trying to hide it, especially Grant. "I've found the money and I know what Sven wanted. Miles has accepted my proposal, which was the most difficult one." I smile at him. "I know you pressurised Brenda to spy for you. That ends now, okay?"

His stare is what's described in pulp fiction as 'gimlet-eyed.' Coldly psychotic also covers it. "What about my Father?"

"Sven felt he was entitled to a fair price for what his Father had taken from him. He also knew he wouldn't use it wisely and that you would be upset and he valued your help and friendship."

That gets me a curt nod.

"So Monica will receive it all and she will decide what happens to it. I will not tell him the basis on which she is receiving it. That is for her – and you – to decide."

Monica and Stephen look at each other. Then McNoble nods. "Fine. As long as my scumbag Father doesn't get back into the business. And Tupps agrees? What about the club?"

"It closes. Miles will be compensated. I believe he intends to set up a new venture in the north."

McNoble smiles rather sourly. "With that bint of his? Yeah, makes sense. I bet he'll try to involve the old sod though. Well, let's see what happens, shall we?"

I spread my hands. "So you knew about Josephine? Why didn't—"

"Tell Natalie? I did. Told Sven too. They didn't want to believe me. Well, she didn't and he had other things to think about. They're grownups. Their choice."

"As soon as the money is shared out I'm having nothing more to do with any of this. You, your Father. Monica, you can all go and do your own thing. I don't want to see you anymore. Okay? And I want you to leave Brenda and Zenda alone." I wait. He says nothing. This is one part I was worried about. "He didn't leave anything to you."

McNoble frowns. "Why would he?"

I was convinced he wanted the money for himself and would kick up a fuss, but he grins. "Sven was clear he could trust you and you'd have the balls to see it through. Me, I thought you'd cave but, well, turns out he was right." He reaches over and offers me his hand. "Good on you, Harry. If you change your mind about not wanting me about and if I can help, you let me know."

"Miles will divorce her as soon as possible. She might need someone to help her through it."

"Don't you—?"

I pull a face. "It's complicated." I can't really believe I'm trusting him but Dina felt that was probably okay so it's good enough for me.

"Sure." After another moment he looks ready to leave, standing but still unsure. He glances at the others and takes a deep breath. "The night he died… he was ill, worse than I realised. He wanted to see you. Desperate I'd guess you'd call it and I was bringing him to your flat when he died." He rubs his face. "I panicked. I couldn't get him back to his flat; Miles or Natalie might have been there, or Marita and if I turned up with him dead they'd… well, they'd have thought it was me. And I couldn't take him to you or the police without some awkward questions about what he'd been doing. Or that's the way I reasoned at the time. So I dumped him in the river. I've no idea why he ended up by Wandsworth Bridge. The tide I suppose. I didn't think it would be you who'd the police would focus on. I know you'll probably never believe that but it's the truth." He doesn't wait for an answer and leaves.

I turn to Zenda. "Do you believe him?"

She shakes her head and then smiles. "But you do, don't you?" She hugs her arms around herself. Monica leans across and holds her.

"We'll get through this, Zenda. Really."

She smiles a thin uncertain smile. "Yes, I suppose so. Harry," she holds my gaze; it's really rather uncomfortable, "I wish I'd heard none of that but I think I understand why I had to. You are going to be quite something. Although you may well end up in prison."

Monica leans closer towards Zenda. "I'll sort out Charlie. Don't worry about that."

There's not much more to say. I manage to extract a promise from Monica to speak to Mr Lewis if I need help releasing the garage proceeds but I'm rather hoping Sven has indeed left everything for me subject to a code word – 'beetroot.' Time enough to find out later.

After the two women have gone, Grant and I pack up. We agree to meet tomorrow night with Miles to make sure everything is signed and the blackmail pictures are all with me and ready to hand to the victims. "What hif there hare hothers?"

I rub my face. "I'll worry about that tomorrow. Thanks for everything."

Grant bows.

"Can you wait downstairs? I need you to look after one more thing. I'll be five minutes."

I'm exhausted. I go down one flight to Sven's flat and knock on the door. Marita, Penny and Natalie are there, anxiously awaiting news. Marita points at the windows. "I saw the Grate boys. What's been happening?"

I want to tell them everything but my mind is a whirr. "Come on." We join Grant in the entrance hall. I dig out the key.

"I talk in my sleep." I look at Penny, who nods in recognition. "Apparently I've been going on and on about the postman." I bend and open the spare post box with my initials on it. "Sven left me this spare post box." I pull out the envelope and hand it to Marita. "Your brother's hard work."

She rummages inside, pulls out the first package of diamonds and squeals. There's an immediate hubbub of chatter. Finally I manage to prize them away and hand them to Grant for safe-keeping. Marita offers to make us a drink but I need to sleep even though it's barely 8:30.

Penny understands. "I'll get you home."

We grab a cab. As we filter into slow-moving traffic I pull a letter from my pocket.

"What's that?"

"It was in the post-box." I hold it up. It's addressed to me. Inside is a short letter and another key.

Harold

Looks like you've sorted things out if you've got this far. Thank you. I'd like to owe you, but since I don't believe in any sort of afterlife you'll have to accept what I'm giving you now.

First, I know you are already wondering how to refuse the gift I've given you in the list of seven. That's not a gift, it's for expenses. If anything is left it won't be much. The key represents the gift. When you find it, maybe you will toy with giving it to Marita to add to her funds. Don't. I know your sister will have helped you. She has a son and I heard she wants to go to university but doesn't know how she'll cope. Set up a trust for her. Or Natalie, if she divorces she may not get much. Use some for her.

Second, if you close the club and Monica gives it to you – she said she might – do something with the site. I don't care what. Maybe use some of the cash I'm giving you to redevelop it. You may even want to live there and raise little Spittles. Or give it away yourself. There may be others you'd like to help.

Third, the key is to a safe deposit box with Chambers Bank on Fleet Street. They have your signature for box 714. In it are the documents controlling Andersen Ventures. Through them you can decide what happens to my parents' house and bungalow. They are bearer shares; whoever holds them is the owner. Mr Lewis holds the land certificate and can do the conveyancing if you wish. Personally, I always thought it would make a splendid B&B and the woods and forest rides are chock-full of butterflies; your Dad would approve.

Thank you

Yours

Sven Andersen

Penny is watching me when I stop reading. "You okay?"

Her eyes are still that soft brown that always made me melt. I pull her into a kiss that could go on forever if it wasn't for the taxi driver coughing like he's got emphysema.

As I climb out I say, "I need to get some sleep. I'm going to be very busy over the next few days."

Penny grins. "I can help."

I hold her back. "Sleep. I mean it."

She looks disappointed but seems to understand.

I'm not entirely sure I do.

Friday, 7th August 1981

Chapter Seventy-Nine

In Which Harry Ties Up Loose Ends and Reprises a Little Bit of History

My parents' house has never felt as crazy or as energised as it does tonight. I've spent the best part of two hours trying to explain all that has happened. Since last Monday I have handed Jeremy and Izzy the photos and the negatives and had an assurance from Izzy that all charges against Penny and Sean will be dropped. Unbeknownst to her, I've kept back one set. We agreed she would talk to the police. If she does I will burn it; if not then I will try my hand at blackmail. After all, everyone seems to think I'm some sort of crime lord. I really worry that I might be enjoying it too much.

Teddy has told me today that I will be receiving an offer from Newe Waters and two others who have already interviewed me. On the strength of that I have told Lucinda I will be moving on. Initially she looked disappointed, but then acknowledged I would do better if I did move. She shared with me that she is pregnant and may resign her partnership, making me promise to keep that last thought quiet. In truth that would be a far more devastating piece of news for Clifford, Risely & Co. than me leaving.

Monica rang to say Charlie is livid and blames me. She tells me that he said that one day he will really screw me over. Maybe I should be worried but with the benefit of the loyalty of the Grate brothers, Monica herself and apparently McNoble, I feel reasonably well protected. Still that is a dark cloud on the horizon.

Miles has signed several documents proffered by Grant Grate. He's told Natalie he wants to be with Josephine and has agreed to a divorce. I explained the subterfuge to Lucinda who initially felt we shouldn't be party to it, given the marriage to Natalie is a sham, but it didn't take long to persuade her to go with the idea they are really divorcing for Natalie and Miles' other family's best interests. Still, she isn't happy. She's more content with the news about Zenda and Master Rother. I sat in while she called Rother's lawyer. After a lot of initial bluster, the offer of some real money to settle quickly saw things to a conclusion that looks like it will satisfy everyone.

Before telling my parents my news, I went to see Mr Lewis. I showed him the bearer shares for the house and bungalow and the documents for the club premises in Bermondsey – he claimed to know nothing about it. It was already shut and Monica signed everything over to me. I asked the old crook to act for me, dealing with the transfers but also masterminding a development. He positively beamed. "And what about the Andersen residence, Harry?"

You have to admire his cheek. "Not sure yet, Mr Lewis. I've a couple of ideas. I'm pretty sure we will want you to do the legal work when we know what's involved. While I'm here, can we also have a word about setting up a trust for my sister?"

We had a little verbal dance about the garage, but when I told him about Sven and the password he slumped somewhat and pulled out some papers. He doesn't like me to have the upper hand, that's the main problem.

Frank was next. He didn't speak until I asked if he could point me in the direction of someone who could sell the diamonds I and my parents have been left. If I give Mum real diamonds I can't be held responsible for which of her organs will implode first. At that he held out a crooked claw of a hand, reminiscent of Terry, the head waiter at Hemingways, whenever a tip was in the offing. I told him I'd get Grant to talk to him and he nodded before falling asleep.

Here I am back at home, the centre of attention. I've explained to Mum about Sven's money and how he wants her to be able to live her dream of a really successful B&B. I've handed Petunia and Norman the memorandum from Mr Lewis explaining how they will get the garage business back free of debt and with working capital. Uncle Norman was miffed that the property and business are all to be in my aunt's sole name. When I explained about that she very nearly hugged me, but we managed to avoid that social faux pas.

It takes about 30 minutes before there's a lull in the chatter. "I've an idea I'd like to float, if that's okay?"

Dad looks stunned from all he's heard. "Maybe tomorrow, Harry my son. All this... well, it's a lot to take in."

"No need to comment or react, but I'll explain my thinking and you can come back to it later if you like. One of the bequests that Sven made concerned his parents' old house over near Ramley. It's massive – 10 bedrooms, four bathrooms, garaging for six cars and a separate two-bedroomed chalet bungalow in the grounds. It's mine to deal with."

I let that sink in. Mum ogles me. Dina won't look up. Aunt and uncle look perplexed like they know the individual words I've used but not in the order I've said them.

Penny and Natalie do well to merely watch. They already know about this.

"As I can hardly be expected to use this place, I thought maybe I'd sell it and do something with the money. But he's also given me some capital too. That's going into a trust for George." I look at Dina. "You and Jim too. And before you say anything it was Sven's idea. He knew you'd help me and he knew you wanted to go to uni and be a good Mum. This will help. In fact, he made me think we should keep the bungalow for you and George and Jim, if that's how it works out."

She is speechless. It is a truly beautiful moment; I wish it would never end.

"But the main house. Dad, Mum – that's where you need to set up your B&B. Convert the garages into self-catering holiday lets. B&B the main house. The possibilities are endless."

There's noise and confusion and excited talking across each other. Then Mum claps her hands. "Why don't we go and see it for ourselves? There's still daylight. Do you have the keys?"

I do. I offer them across. "Go on, Natalie and Dina know the layout."

"Aren't you coming?"

I smile and look down before looking up. "Penny and I need a chat. You go and we'll have a glass of something when you get back. Go on, all of you."

Penny doesn't leave her seat, looking sober as she waits for them to depart. I'm steeling myself when Mum's head reappears round the door. "I was always going to repay you, you know?"

"Sorry?"

"The money I borrowed from you and Dina. The money Nanty left…"

I stop her with a vigorous nod. "I always knew you would Mum. When you could."

She narrows her eyes and then becomes all business-like. "Well, quite. You two have a nice time. We won't be that long."

When she's gone and the house is quiet. Penny watches me carefully. "Will we?"

"Will we what?"

"Have a nice time?"

450

I put my finger to my lips and take her hand, pulling her towards the back of the house. As we exit the backdoor I stop her and put my hand on the hem of her T-shirt quickly lifting it up over her head.

"Harry?" She's confused but also smiling.

I point at the old swing. "Remember what happened there?"

She's grinning now. "A horse fly bit you on the nob?"

I wince. "Technically that was in the bedroom." I've taken off my shirt and am hopping out of my trousers while she undoes her bra and pulls at the jeans. In moments we are both naked and not a little breathless, kissing hard. I pull back and grin. "When Mum said, 'Are you coming' just now I did wonder if she knew what I had in mind."

Penny pushes in close to me, grinding at my erection like it needs encouragement. "Hey, don't break him."

"Kiss him better?"

I push her back so I'm on top. And then I stand, knowing she's about to ask what I'm doing. Five years ago in something of a mad rush Penny and I made love for the first time on that swing. It was awkward and messy and glorious. The crazy, wobbly nature of that first coupling rather anticipated our relationship over the following years. This time I use my T shirt to tie off the swing to ensure it is stable and then climb back. I'm determined that, for once we will make slow, leisurely and infinitely wonderful love, although given how things usually pan out that is more a case of hope trying to beat experience but losing on away goals.

Briefly I wonder if this is how it will be going forward. Is this what it is like to be an adult? I force myself to start counting backwards from 1000 in French, pretty much the only thing I've mastered that postpones lift off, when another thought occurs to me. I haven't told everyone of Sven's plans – there's one more beneficiary who I need to speak to. That bloody old hippy he promised to fund. The old sod who knew the colour of Penny's nipples before me.

To try to forestall the inevitable moment I begin to pull back, but Penny is clearly not keen on any delay, grabs my retreating buttocks and gasps, "Fuck, no you don't."

"Christian," I manage through gritted teeth.

Her eyes widen, as she grabs me harder and I give in, slipping inside with a moan.

She sniggers, "Now I know why it's called the missionary position. Oh, yes. Christ!"

When we flop apart some minutes later, I can feel her eyes on me. "You know I'm an atheist, don't you?"

I roll over and gently fondle her nearest nipple. "Frankly I don't care what you eat." She frowns, not understanding my feeble humour. "Come again?"

I kiss her other nipple. I can see her smile as she stares at the blue sky; to give myself time to allow for the return of some penile fortitude, I ease myself between her thighs. Her hands grab the back of my head as she digs in her nails. I'd like to utter a protest of sorts but her actions make it abundantly plain that the use of my tongue as a tool for speech is not her top priority.

I think, *No, life's not going to be smooth. It might occasionally be painful and it's probably going to be hell at times. And I'll probably have to accept that Penny will want, if not the last word, then to stop me having my say. But if that means I don't have to think very hard while making her smile, that's fine by me.*

Printed in Great Britain
by Amazon

22652702R00260